the *Light* in me

*Drifters,
Book Thirteen*

SUSAN RODGERS

Edited by Colleen McKie of Savvy Fox Author Services
Cover design by Alanna Munro. All rights reserved.
Book design and formatting by Valerie Bellamy, Dog-ear Book Design.

ISBN: 978-1-987966-15-2

Thank you, Kathy Gillis, for your manuscript review.
Your thoughts are appreciated more than you know…

Contents

$\mathcal{L}$a Casa was buzzing.

Sunday dinner was always the perfect time to bring Charles and Dee's extended made-up Vancouver family together, and this evening was worth celebrating because Jacob, fresh off a whirlwind round of tour dates in Europe and Asia, was back in Vancouver, his bouncy ponytailed dancer girl by his side. The couple was expected within the hour.

The longer the Sawyer kids waited for Jacob to make his entrance through the pretty Spanish villa's curved mahogany door, the faster their hearts started beating, and the louder they hollered.

Josh had no choice. He had to take control.

He dove in.

Sauntering up the first floor hallway from the playroom with a crinkly blue stethoscope draped around his neck and a fake plastic bandage wrapped around his wrist, Josh called out to his giggling youngest child. "Dylan, you're the only one left! Daddy already found Momma and David. You better come out or I'm going to eat all the cookies Emily-Grace and Carlotta baked. I'm not gonna leave any for you!"

Running up behind him, David swatted his father's backside, his long-ish little boy blond hair swinging. "That's not allowed. You're not allowed to say you're going to eat the cookies just to get him to come out of his hiding place. That's cheating."

Turning, Josh grabbed David around the waist and flipped him over his shoulder. The little boy protested vociferously. David couldn't help letting a wild yelp escape as he twisted and tried to tickle his daddy's side. Grinning happily, hoping to catch a glimpse of Dylan's wild black curls and exultant robust pink cheeks, Josh wandered into the kitchen and peered around the large island. He winked at Jessie as he passed—she was seated at her usual spot at the end of the island, near the wide entrance to the sophisticated kitchen.

Rolling her eyes, she bent an elbow and leaned her head on that hand, crossed her legs, and playfully tweaked David's yowling lips as Josh passed by. Once she had her son's attention she raised her free hand a little higher, accented the movement with a gentle warning in her eyes, and placed two fingers at her lips. "Sshh, sweetheart," she admonished, "Grammie and Grampie will kick us out before dinner if you keep that howling up much longer." Jessie shared a wry smile with Deirdre when her eyes met the older woman's delighted gaze across the island.

Dee was helping Emily-Grace ice a cake they baked for Jacob and Kayla's homecoming. Her eyes lit up. "The children's voices are music to my ears," she said to Jessie with sincere glee. "The louder the better. Grampie might pretend to protest, but don't take him seriously. He's already counting the money that set of lungs is going to make him some day."

Jessie's smile flipped over. "Oh no, he's not. Or at least he better not be. No more Sawyers are going into the entertainment business. Ever."

Emily-Grace fired her mother a withering glare. Jessie's shoulders visibly shrank. The little girl suspended her spatula over the cake and sang out loudly, "Dylan's in the pantry, Daddy. Over here. You walked right by him!" She might have added, "Duh, you dope," but she'd already tried that once and been soundly reprimanded and sent to her room for the comment so, wisely, she mouthed that extra bit under her breath instead.

"Oh, honey," Deirdre sighed as Carlotta, bent over the sink washing dishes, sent the suddenly forlorn Jessie a regretful look. "That's not very nice."

Emily-Grace's small shoulders drew themselves up proudly. "You can hear Dylan laughing, Grammie! Daddy just ignored him. And that's not fair."

"Not much about life is fair," Jessie muttered as Josh came back around and deposited the wriggling David into his mother's lap. Josh's bewildered expression at his daughter's continuous attempts to wound him broke Jessie's heart anew. With one hand she tried to snuggle her son close, but he squirmed off her lap and ran to free his younger brother from his hiding place. Jessie extended her second hand to Josh, grasped his fingers in hers, and silently shook her head in warning.

Lately, many of the couple's discussions had revolved around Emily-Grace's belligerent moods and outright contempt toward the entire Sawyer family, Kayla not included. Zach and his clan were not on the child's hit list either, when Josh and Kayla's oldest sibling and his sprouting family were in the city. It seemed the remainder of the family's discussions were focused on the other dark aura that engulfed them—the one Josh and Jessie were about to be updated on down the hall in the small boardroom behind Charles' study, which was the other reason they were spending a good chunk of their Sunday afternoon at La Casa.

Jessie yawned. The day was wearing her down. Earlier, church and the kids' swimming lessons were exhausting. Constantly refereeing children's fights would be a heck of a lot less taxing if one weren't also always trying to protect one's husband from an eight-year-old's angry snipes.

Josh lifted Jessie's fingers and brushed his lips over them. A small upward curve of his lips raised her spirits a little, and she followed his gaze toward the pantry door and rotated around in Dee's high Italian leather chair. David had Dylan by the hand. Neither of the boys seemed to care a hoot that their sister had given Dylan away. Hollering with unrestrained joy, both rushed their father and leapt into his welcoming arms. Jessie groaned and cringed at the pain this must be causing Josh's patched up shoulder and seemingly constantly aching leg (although he never complained, but she caught him sneaking the occasional anti-inflammatory). To Josh's credit, he laughed and swung both boys up and around, then gave Dylan a knuckled head rub before he moved his fingers to tickle David's belly.

Emily-Grace dropped the spatula she was using to ice the cake. It clattered to the surface of the island and settled there as she seethed. "Can you puh-leeze take yourself and those two monsters back to the playroom? I can't concentrate!" A quick swipe with the back of her hand, and sweaty wisps of hair were swept back on her forehead, punctuating the demand. With the exception of Dylan's muffled laughter as he ducked his face into his daddy's chest, the room fell silent.

"Okay," Josh told his daughter quietly. "We'll go and let you work." He paused. "That's an awful nice cake you're making for Auntie Kayla, Emily-Grace."

Jessie closed her eyes. *Stop trying so hard, Josh. Please. She'll only—*

"It's *mainly* for Jacob." Emily-Grace's bitter response was laced with arsenic.

"Oh. Okay. Well, he'll love it, I'm sure." Hesitating, Josh glanced toward the rows of cookies cooling down on wire racks at the far end of the island. In his right arm, David sat silently watching yet another showdown between his father and older sister. Dylan tried to tickle his father but even his actions were subdued, restrained.

Watching, Jessie sent Josh a telepathic message. *No, don't,* she begged. But he did.

Josh asked for a cookie.

"Just one," he said to Emily-Grace. "You make such good chocolate chip cookies. They're still all warm and melty, just the way I like them."

"*You* are not allowed to have any of my cookies. Jacob learned me how to make them. They're for him." The way Emily-Grace accented the *you* was dirty and mean, as if she'd pulled the word up out of a gutter and spat it at her father.

Speechless, Josh shriveled helplessly under her glare.

Jessie broke the awkward standoff by reaching for Dylan. "Give me one of those ragamuffins before you hurt yourself, Josh." With Dylan in her arms, wriggling and protesting, forcing his head around to send forlorn looks of longing at his daddy, Jessie slipped off her chair and moved down the island to the racks of cookies. She aimed a reproachful stare in the direction of her oldest child and handed cookies to Josh and David, then went back and grabbed another for Dylan.

Josh tried to give his back. He set it on the island. "I don't need this," he muttered, unable to meet anyone's eyes. "My trainer will have a field day if he finds out I'm sneaking cookies."

"Dez can take a long hike off a short pier. Eat the damn cookie." Jessie shifted Dylan in her arms and shot Emily-Grace a look that clearly said *You're pushing your limits. I dare you to keep going.*

Summoning up some strength, Josh extended a finger and slowly pushed the cookie toward his roiling daughter. She was coiled to strike. "You want to throw this at me, Emily-Grace?" he challenged, almost inaudibly. "You think that would help matters any?"

Next to Emily-Grace, Deirdre sounded a low *tut-tut*, but she averted her eyes from Josh and Jessie and picked up the icing spatula. Grasping her granddaughter's hand, she wrapped the child's delicate fingers around the handle. "Finish with the icing, dear," she ordered gently. "Jacob and Kayla will be here any minute."

Jessie ignored her attempt at defusing the tension. "Josh, who's the parent here, huh?" she reminded him with authority. "Because I'm thinking it sure as hell ain't the little girl in the gauzy pink princess dress."

Josh's eyes were locked into his daughter's. The two may as well have been in an old west standoff, pistols loaded and hammers cocked. Neither budged, but Emily-Grace's pretty Jessie-eyes narrowed to slits, and morphed into a deeper, piercing blue.

Josh waited.

"Oh, for Heaven's sake." Jessie glared at each of them in turn, and moved to leave the room.

After less than three steps, she stopped abruptly.

Expressionless, Matt was leaning on one side of the wide entrance, watching the family sort out its dirty laundry in front of him.

Tossing her curls, embarrassed, Jessie once again played mediator and tried to change the tone of this latest heartrending daddy-daughter conflict. Staring into Matt's calm, wise eyes, she threw out a comment Emily-Grace was meant to hear. "Honey, finish icing that cake and package up your cookies. Matt's here, and you know him. He doesn't put up with us girls and our hissy fits. He'll have you up those stairs doing timeout in the nursery before you can throw that rogue cookie at your father."

Behind Jessie, Josh groaned. "Jesus."

Jessie swallowed, and closed her eyes.

Letting his now hard gaze drift from Jessie to her daughter, Matt stepped into the kitchen. "Emily-Grace." That was all he needed to say. His tone was final, a well placed bullet. Emily-Grace sighed and went back to work.

Gritting his teeth, Josh flipped around and focused on him. "This is not your problem, Matt."

"The hell it isn't," Jessie bit off, peeking up at Josh from beneath moist eyelashes. "It's all on him, Josh. Everything's on him. Or haven't you noticed?"

"For fuck's sake, Jessie."

"Swear jar, Josh." But Jessie's eyes were damp, not dark and angry. The flecks in them were light and wet, like lit candles floating aimlessly on a dreamy moonlit pond.

Biting his bottom lip, Josh held his wife's gaze as Matt, in his usual tailored linen shirt and expensive jeans, brushed by them and picked up the rogue cookie. Turning around on the heel of a spit-shined leather desert boot, he pushed it into Josh's hand. "Charles and I are ready for the two of you. Now would be a good time."

Jessie sucked in a pent-up breath. "You wouldn't eat that cookie if it was the last one on earth, would you, Josh?" Swiping it from his fingers, she tried to be playful about it but the words had come out stilted, and somehow, just wrong. Matt's powerful aura was in the air between them; he'd left behind that faint tang of aftershave and male huskiness that brought Jessie instantly back to a sensuous night she would never forget, to a friend she counted on when her world spun, as it often did, out of control. The calculated clicks of Matt's boots were fading down the hallway as Josh's eyes narrowed at his wife.

Dee carefully skirted the island and took David from Josh's arms. "Emily-Grace, finish that cake," she insisted, as Carlotta nudged Dylan away from Jessie. "You both know Charles and Matt," she said to Jessie and Josh. "Less patience between the two of them than a couple of gnats in heat."

"Daddy, pway again. Hide and seek!" In Carlotta's arms, Dylan reached for Josh, who softened and bent to kiss his three-year-old son's forehead.

"I'll just have a quick visit with Grampie, then we'll play again." Josh thrust the chocolate chip cookie into Dylan's small fingers. "Have another cookie, Dylan. Get sugar-wired for Jacob, okay buddy?" A diabolical grin spread across his cheeks.

Grumbling, Jessie took Josh's fingers in hers, and led him out into the hallway. "You're my biggest kid, you know that, right Josh?"

A low chuckle was his answer.

"She wanted you to eat the damn cookie. She just wanted you to work for it, that's all. Emily-Grace is always testing you. She wants you to fail."

"She's not alone." Josh glanced up the hallway to see Matt watching them. He slowed, indignantly dragging his cowboy boots.

A reassuring squeeze from his wife's fingers got Josh's attention. Looking sideways at Jessie, he relaxed slightly when her eyes melted into his.

"She's your daughter, Josh. She'll come back to you when she's ready."

"Will she." It wasn't a question, and it was loaded with Josh and Jessie's shared past, their present, and just maybe…their future. They both knew it, as surely as they were both aware of what Matt and Charles were about to tell them. They were all, for the sake of sanity, just going through the motions.

"Into the breach," Jessie whispered without losing her husband's scared, loving gaze. "I love you, Josh."

She said it within range of Matt's hearing. In her peripheral vision, Jessie saw Matt straighten, saw his pride take a beating equal to the one the two of them had just given Josh in the kitchen.

Next to her, Josh stood taller too. "I love you back," he murmured softly, looking away from his wife. His liquid chocolate eyes were fixed on Matt's somber lighter ones as they passed, and they telegraphed a vicious, haughty victory.

Not a great way to start a meeting with a man in charge of his life. Not a great way to secure the man's undying commitment and faithful duty.

And not a great way to bolster the confidence of his wife when she, Jessie Wheeler-Sawyer, so desperately needed everything to just be okay.

Chapter Two

Ulysses and Big Dan had the day off to spend with their gals, Sam had driven up to Squamish to go elite mountain biking on the nearest, most challenging trails, and Alin was back in Calgary, attending her younger brother Patin's wedding. With only Matt around to represent Keating security, it struck Jessie funny that Charles decided their small group should meet in the formal Keating boardroom instead of in one of La Casa's more personal areas—the media room, for instance, or even in the sitting area of the music room, for that matter.

The glass board table was shiny clean, wiped over earlier by Carlotta with diligence and care, as if by taking away the dust the maid was hoping she could also remove any negative associations haunting the Keating-Sawyer clan. Absently, as Jessie sank into a comfy leather office chair, she wiped a finger across the see-through table surface. The oil in her skin left a tiny smudge, which instantly jumpstarted her heart and tossed worry into the already tense room.

A quick look to Matt as he dropped heavily into a seat kitty corner across from her didn't ease her fears at all. The man's handsome face was white, taut, his jaw line firm and unyielding, his eyes not gentle and sweet the way she liked them best. He was watching her with steady eyes. A cool gray wind swept over those eyes, leaving in its wake a turmoil and a swirling pain Matt couldn't hide. They were a foamy sea, the eyes with thin-lined corners that Jessie once brushed her lips across, on a fateful spring day not so long ago, when Matt was temporarily hers and she was his.

"What?" she asked, sliding her hand off the table, dropping it out of Matt's sight, and grabbing Josh's hand, to her right.

Josh gripped her fingers tightly and nestled their hands, together, on his thigh. Jessie started playing with a small frayed hole in his faded jeans. Josh pulled her fingers away from it so she wouldn't make the tear bigger. As he did so, he realized that she wasn't even aware of her nervous pick-pick-picking at the hole, so intent was Jessie on what Matt wasn't saying.

Still standing, working fretfully at the silk knot on a ubiquitous cranberry tie, Charles avoided everyone's eyes but he cleared his throat and started the meeting before the tension escalated beyond the point of recovery.

Inhaling deeply, Jessie looked at him and waited.

Matt glanced over at Josh. Unable to resist the tiny pang of regret and apprehension that sideswiped his heart, he almost wished he could be on that side of the table with the two of them, in the middle even, where he could hold Jessie's hand and give Josh a manly clap on the shoulder. *I'm in the middle anyway,* he caught himself thinking. *But I'm on their side.*

Charles' gruffer than normal voice brought Matt back to the unpleasant task at hand.

"All right," the Keating patriarch was saying, finally clueing in that he was still standing. A last nervous pull at his tie, and he eased down into the chair at the head of the small table. Forcing his gaze upward, he almost lost his voice entirely when he caught the trepidation stalking Jessie like a shadow. Her attempt to stay calm was tracking across her pale cheeks like bear prints in the snow, leaving uneasy pink dots and pursing her lips into determined, thin lines.

Fearful, Charles dug down for some stoic resolve, then he plunged them deeper into this latest darkness.

"You already know that the note placed on your car, Jessie," he nodded at her, "was left by a teenager in a dark hoodie. Your security cameras picked him up but he was quick, and for the most part he knew where the cameras were, so he managed to avoid giving us any identifying features to work with. Hundreds of kids in Vancouver wear hoodies. He had gloves on at the time. We didn't get a single fingerprint. The kid timed it so he ran into your driveway when Dan was doing an exterior round of the house."

"Go on," Jessie whispered, waiting for the inevitable searing fire to gut her belly at what she instinctively knew was coming.

"Cast, crew and especially all background actors and tech dailies were screened. There is still nothing concrete to suggest that what happened to Josh on *Sacred Peace* was anything other than sheer bad luck."

"He was pushed over the bank into the river, Charles." At Jessie's side, Josh squeezed her fingers tight enough for them to hurt. A warning. *Stay calm.*

"We've long since agreed on that, Jessie." Charles, too, was cautioning her. His tone was even and controlled, his eyes focused and watchful. "But there is no indication that the river incident was anything other than a snap decision to send an Oscar winning actor for an icy swim. It may have been a simple bet with friends. A nasty prank, yes, but there's no obvious connection to the notes we received." He paused, and then added, "All we have is conjecture."

"And the fire?"

Matt and Josh remained quiet. It may as well have just been Jessie and Charles in the small space.

"The investigation into the fire that decimated your barn remains open. Up to now we had nothing concrete. But a few days ago the security guard who admitted to letting the young men on your property to set the fire finally broke entirely. He gave up some clues to the guys who paid him. The police tracked them down. Those men have proven to be the key to a new door. To a few new doors."

"Gabrielle's blog and the press that followed must have also opened some doors, Charles." Jessie was stalling. A new door…one encased in fire and brimstone, apparently, if Charles' and Matt's stony expressions were any indication.

"A lot of dead ends, Jessie. At least at this point. The people who came forward were likely just hoping to connect to you and Josh. Perhaps they hoped what they had to say might prove useful, or maybe they were just throwing out ideas, hoping to garner some attention."

"But the guys who set the fire…" Jessie gulped. "Why don't I have a good feeling about this?" Letting go of Josh's hand, she leaned apprehensively on her forearms and buried a desperate hope in Charles' concerned eyes. "Charles, things have settled down. Since we got that note on the SUV after moving back to Vancouver we have not had any trouble. Josh hasn't had any trouble. Everything's been just fine. Maybe it's all over. Maybe the person—or people—threatening Josh have given up. They've had their fun." Satisfied with the only conclusion Jessie felt she could handle, she sat back with a low *humph* and faced Charles with an air of quiet determination.

Next to her, Josh exhaled slowly and stared at the patterned rug on the floor.

Charles couldn't bring himself to go any further. Despairing, he met Matt's trusted eyes and silently begged for help.

Matt gave him a slight nod of acknowledgement and took the reins. Leaning forward, he reached across the table and took Jessie's hand. Her fingers were clammy, nervous; these fingers that brought such beautiful music into a world that always seemed to be in desperate need of healing. Matt studied them, turned them over, caressed them, avoiding the urge to lift them to his lips and press them against his cheek. Finally, he let his gaze drift upward and he spoke.

"Jessie," he started, with a careful but earnest cadence. "The men were paid to start the barn fire. They had no personal interest in causing you or Josh harm. If our source can be believed, then the gas cans left behind your bedroom, too, were only meant to scare you."

She harrumphed loudly. "So the people who set the fire may or may not have been Jacob Ryan fans who were mad at me for leaving him, is what you're saying. Do you know who these people are? Have you talked to them? Have you talked to the person who paid them?"

"Jacob's fan base has dwindled since, well…" Matt sighed. "Florida. There are fewer of those old hate notes about you and Josh populating the net these days." Jessie bit her lip. Josh turned his head toward the wall. When Matt spoke again, his words were uttered cautiously, as if he was afraid of saying the wrong thing, of saying a combination of words that would send Jessie over the proverbial edge. "We have reason to believe the person responsible for paying the two people who destroyed the barn really doesn't give a damn about Jacob, Jessie. We think he may have just used your relationship with Jacob to throw us off the real path."

"What? Why?"

Josh's rusty voice floated on the air. "Because he—or she," he grimaced, as the remembrance of Nadia's sensuous body and her diabolical plan twisted his gut in two, "has another motive. Quit talking in circles, Matt. Just fucking spit it out, will you?"

"You don't think it's over, then." Jessie held tightly to Matt's hand. She couldn't bring herself to look away from those beautiful, gentle, trusted, loving eyes, despite the anxious aura she easily read inside them. Matt, too, had not looked away.

Josh shuffled nervously. Charles locked his gaze on the conjoined fingers as Matt brought Josh and Jessie to their knees.

"The fire starters were hired by someone who, not all that long ago, was an inmate at Brody River Penitentiary, Jessie."

"Brody River…oh." The room swam. A sudden attack of nausea forced Jessie to grip the edge of the table with her left hand. Still, she held tightly to Matt's fingers with her right hand. "That's where…that's where Morgan was moved to. Brody River's near Edmonton. North of…north of Calgary."

"About eight hours north of Calgary, Jessie."

Josh stilled. Even hearing Morgan's name was enough to completely derail him. What the man and his wife did to him…to his family…already…

"He almost destroyed us." Jessie said it as Josh thought it. "He's still…he's still trying? You think Morgan caused all this latest shit? Why? Why, Matt?"

Matt's eyes flicked over to Josh. Charles was watching him now, too. Jessie seemed to have forgotten that her husband was even in the room. She didn't seem to clue in until Josh pushed back his chair and stood.

"No!" Jessie cried as Josh headed for the door. "You sit until we know what we're dealing with here." She grabbed the arms of his chair and shoved it toward him. It rolled, and came to an uncertain stop a few feet away from him.

"Ha!" Josh tossed indignantly back at her. "Who are you trying to kid, Jessie? Morgan. You heard Matt. We know what we're dealing with. It's too fucking bad, but we know now. Don't we?" Grabbing the door handle, he yanked the door open and left the room.

As her husband's footsteps faded off down the hallway, his boots heavy with the weight of his fear, Jessie laid an arm on the table, rested her cheek on it, and moaned. "It was Nadia's vicious game, Matt. It was never really Morgan's. What he did, he did for love. Of her," she added, in case there was any confusion in that regard.

At the head of the table, Charles exhaled and said his piece. "Jessie, we have yet to talk to Morgan, to see whether he may have cajoled some old cellmate or 'friend' of his into doing his bidding. It's not easy getting inside Brody. My lawyer's on it."

Soundly cutting him off before he had a chance to say more, Jessie spat out, "What, your millions won't buy you a free pass into the bowels of insanity, Charles?"

"I won't dignify that with a response, Jessie." Charles lowered his voice. He anchored both hands on the table for leverage and stood. "But only because I know what's fueling that mean-spirited lack of respect you have for the abundance God has graced us with."

"Well, you know what they say about God, Charles."

"Be careful, honey," he warned, but stood statue-still to see what she would fire at him. Emily-Grace's knack for throwing pointed spears was come by honestly, thanks to her mother.

Forlorn, Jessie lifted her head up from her arm. "God giveth, and God taketh away. Just ask Morgan. Why should it be us who are blessed, as you say, Charles? What did we do to earn enough money to never have to worry about bills and rent and where our next meal is coming from? Why are we blessed with three amazing kids, yet Morgan and Nadia lost their only child?"

"What did we do to earn this constant fear, honey? Maybe that's what you should be asking."

"The fear comes from the money, Charles. From the fame and the celebrity and the abundance, as you call it. A yin and a yang kind of thing. Everything evens out in the end, doesn't it?"

"I won't deny that we have our share of troubles, Jessie."

She countered hotly. "So don't deny where our troubles come from. Money."

"If you want to step away, step away. Go. Take your husband and your children and go. Hide somewhere."

"Wh-what? Fuck, Charles. You must really be scared if you're ready to let us go." *To let me go,* she thought as a new wave of sickness slipped up from her belly and choked her.

"I am. I'm scared, honey. Morgan has already proven what he is capable of. And although we have no solid proof yet, it would seem it may be him who is behind this latest threat."

"Does Dee know about this?" The thought of it was almost worse than knowing herself. Deirdre had already lost so much…Jessie had brought so much worry to the woman she loved like a mother.

A slow shake of his head preceded Charles' answer. "No. I'll tell her tonight after she's had a perfect day with her family."

"Or maybe don't, Charles. Let's see what Morgan has to say first."

"Let's see? Meaning we?"

"Yes." Her voice was a whisper, and Jessie stood to punctuate the point. Leaning toward Charles, one palm flat on the table now, one set of fingers still entwined in Matt's, she said, "He'll talk to me. Maybe I can convince Morgan to lay off. To leave us alone. To leave my husband alone."

"No." Rising, Matt finally let go of Jessie's hand so he could swing around the end of the table. Taking Jessie's shoulders in his, he turned her to face him and placed a warm palm on her cheek. "You won't be seeing Morgan, Jessie. You don't need to look into the eyes of the man who caused you so much pain."

"It wasn't all pain," she managed softly, placing her hand over his on her cheek.

A tiny smile lifted the dark countenance sinking Matt today. "Dylan," he stated quietly, with an unspoken assurance that told her he understood she was also referring to the blissful, sensuous time he and Jessie had shared together last spring. That glorious time was really cemented in New York the night Matt took a bullet meant for Jessie. As tragic and terrifying as that night was, it had in all respects elevated their connection to a whole new, much deeper, level.

She said it anyway. "And you," she murmured, letting herself rise above the clouds for one sweet moment to see a rainbow.

"Ahem." Clearing his throat, Charles strode up behind his superstar and touched her back.

Sighing, Jessie forced her gaze away from Matt and turned to her pseudo father who, now, was putting his producer hat on. Matt twined his fingers back in Jessie's and let their hands drop to their sides as Charles spoke.

"Jessie, we'll stick to the original plan and keep you and Josh home in Vancouver as much as possible until we get a grip on this new—uh, old—threat. The kids can continue at West Point Grey but, apart from the occasional necessary public appearance, like the Grammys, we've agreed that you and Josh need to remain in an environment we feel we can control. So that means…"

"No films in the foreseeable future. I'm okay with that, Charles. But Josh wants to do the new Marc Jouet film before *Sacred Peace* starts up. I assume your 'keeping a low profile shtick' doesn't mean forcing him off your own series." The last bit was spoken with distaste.

"Josh wants to do *Sacred Peace*, Jessie. Thank God. Because we know that environment. It's manageable for all of us."

"Thank God is right. Jesus, Charles, you and Charlie are a helluva pair. You want to pull Josh off a film with a script and a director that already have Oscar buzz, yet because everyone loves Josh on *Sacred Peace*—which is making you money hand over fist—you're thrilled to keep him on your own roster. You make me sick."

"Enough." The anger in Charles' harsh directive stunted Jessie's desire to counter. Shuffling her feet, she bowed her head so she couldn't see the hurt in his eyes. "On *Sacred Peace* we at least have a chance at managing Josh's safety. Having him close by in a familiar setting where we have at least some control is far better than trying to herd lions in the wilderness. We're doing the best we can here, Jessie." With a final hard stare at Matt, Charles stormed from the room on harried, clipped footsteps.

The door closed behind him with a soft and unexpected *shufttt*. A loud jarring bang would have seemed more suited to the man's incensed departure.

Jessie turned back to Matt. He was regarding her now with carefully concealed concern tinged with deep love and understanding.

"Sweetheart," he asked quietly as she looked up at him, her eyes damp. "Do you trust me?"

"Do you?" she asked pointedly. "Do you trust yourself, Matt?" She answered for him. "Not entirely. Do you. You still second guess yourself."

He didn't answer.

"Some things are, and always will be, in God's hands, Matt."

"Good sermon at church this morning, was it Jessie?" A hint of a smile tinted with sarcasm fueled the half joke.

"Some are better than others," she responded darkly.

"C'mere," he said, and pulled her warm, quivering body close. The simple feel of the familiar arms around his neck were enough to send Matt deeper into despair. *I can't do it,* he told himself. *I can't keep her husband safe. I cannot guarantee her happiness.* Closing his eyes, Matt breathed her in—the lavender scented hair, the faint hint of coffee on Jessie's breath from an earlier mocha, and something else...

Fear.

Jessie shrank into his embrace and buried her face in his neck. "Oh, Matt," she breathed. "I would, you know. Go, I mean. I would take Josh and the kids and just run away again, if I could..." She moaned.

"If you could what?" The question was murmured in Jessie's ear. Matt's voice alone, that husky, much loved, familiar trusted voice, made Jessie's knees weaken.

"If I could leave you. If I could be away from you." A depleted chuckle lightened the ache of that simple truth. Jessie peeked up at Matt, and was sorry to see that his eyes were misty and sad. Poking him in the ribs, she laughed a little louder. "Don't go getting all arrogant on me. Or sad and mushy. I can't leave the others, either. You're just first in line, that's all."

A shuffle in the hallway alerted them to the fact that they were being watched.

Josh. He'd come back to fetch Jessie and steal away to hold her, like... like Matt was doing now.

Matt eased his girl away from his body. "Sweetheart," he said again, "go be with your husband. And promise me you won't go all rogue on me again and try to see Morgan. I'm expressly taking steps to ensure you won't get in to Brody."

"I need to see him, Matt. I need to find the *old* Morgan, to convince him to leave us alone."

Matt shook his head. He was adamant. "You don't need to bring up all those terrible memories, Jessie. You don't need to look into those dead eyes."

"Ah. But maybe he needs to look into mine, Matt. You ever think of that?"

Speechless, he let her drift out of his arms.

Before Jessie left the room, she leaned toward Matt and brushed her lips across his close-shaved cheek. "I love you," she told him.

He let his eyes close over, and swallowed back the pain of worry and loss that seemed to have once again escalated with the knowledge that Morgan may have had something to do with the nefarious acts dogging the Sawyers.

In the hallway, Josh was leaning against the wall, his back to it, one knee bent and the foot raised. His hands were buried in his front jeans pockets. He caught Matt's eye as Jessie moved between Matt and himself, as she opened the transparent glass door that divided them. It didn't seem to be enough, that door. As far as Josh was concerned, it should have been a brick wall.

He fixed his gaze on his wife as Matt finally forced his feet to move and left the boardroom via an interior door leading to Charles' study.

"Jacob and Kayla are here," Josh managed to say as Jessie stopped and stood in front of him.

She tipped one ankle over and shoved trembling fingers into her back pockets. "Okay." Sighing, Jessie forced her scattered emotions back into her hurting belly. *Be strong for Josh*—that was her endless goal these days, it seemed. *Thank God for Matt. ThankfuckingGodforMatt.* "Somewhere over the rainbow," she added, tilting her head at Josh in that adorable way he loved. "Someday we'll have peace, Josh. You and me. Someday."

"That what you told Matt just now?"

"N-nope. No, babe. I told him I love him."

"Ah. Nice. So glad you have a backup in case we go sour again."

"Matt's not a backup, Josh."

"Mmm. I forgot. Thanks for reminding me that he's actually the here and now."

"He has our lives in his hands, Josh. All of our lives."

"You sure about that, Jess?"

"Jesus, Josh," she gasped. "That's a helluva thing to say!"

"Look, I take it back, okay? But there are days when I get tired of all your ex-lovers nipping at our heels. Especially the ones responsible for our safety, Jessie. For my safety."

"Are we gonna talk about Morgan? Or do you just want to keep attacking me yourself?" The eyes were swimming now, regardless of Jessie's noble intentions to be strong for her husband.

"I don't want to talk about that bastard. Ever." Josh fixed a sorrowful gaze on his pretty wife.

She deflated, her shoulders sinking. "Okay. Fine. Probably not much point, anyway. The only thing that's changed is that our fear now has a name. Again. A familiar one, for that matter."

Propelling his body away from the wall, Josh slipped an arm around Jessie's waist. "Let's go see my baby sister. I need to be sure your musical soul mate treated her right on the tour."

"Josh? Let's go down to Seattle to see Zach and Hilary soon, okay? Or… invite them up here, maybe. And let's take a trip to Peterborough to see Sara, and another to P.E.I. Soon, okay?"

"Maybe just before *Sacred Peace* starts up. The new film is only a few weeks from going to camera, and I want you to myself before things get crazy again."

"Uhh…"

"What?" Josh stopped and studied her.

Jessie shrugged. "Later. Not now. Let's go see the lovers."

"I'm doing the film, Jessie." Josh wasn't moving.

With a groan, she melted into his side. There seemed to only be one thing left to say, but since she'd also just said it to Matt, Jessie knew it had already lost some steam. "I love you," she breathed anyway into the safe and cherished hollow of her husband's neck and shoulder.

Josh stiffened, but pressed his lips to her hair, to her neck. His breath was warm on his wife's skin. As he kissed that coveted, cherished place just behind the top of her ear, his expression softened into a tenderness Jessie couldn't see, but easily felt.

"I love you back, little one," he acknowledged with a patient grace that said he understood the Matt thing too, then he gave Jessie a heartfelt squeeze, and led her down the hall toward laughing children and the sweet love of family.

Chapter Three

Jacob stood shyly behind Kayla just inside the entrance to the kitchen as his bouncy fiancée approached Josh and Jessie for hugs. In Jacob's arms was Dylan, trying hard to keep his eyes open, but losing the battle. The child's curly-haired head was comfortably ensconced in the safe curve between Jacob's neck and shoulder; the small arms were lazily wrapped around his biological father's body. Still, Jacob got a hug from Jessie too, and a quick handshake from Josh.

Emily-Grace, in her princess dress, was clinging to Kayla's hand, but she was not communicating the same love and devotion Kayla telegraphed. Instead, she was combative and angry, but silent. She faced her parents with a determined alliance that clearly read *I am with Jacob and Kayla.*

Josh passed them and dropped into Jessie's favorite high leather chair at the kitchen island. He used a foot to propel it around to face the new arrivals at La Casa. Half sitting on him, Jessie leaned back against his chest. Josh wrapped a strong arm around his wife's belly, drawing her to him, protecting her—and himself, it seemed—from the world, from anything that might still hurt, including a confused and angry young daughter.

Standing on a low stool across from them on the other side of the island was David, putting the finishing touches on Emily-Grace's 'welcome home' cake—little silver balls and colorful pastel pink and blue candles. Carlotta was fussing at the stove, and Deirdre was behind David, ensuring he didn't fall off the stool. Down the hall in Charles' study, Matt and Charles were drowning their worries in a bottle of scotch.

"We have something to ask you guys," Kayla said shyly in the kitchen.

Jacob nervously nosed his way closer to end up just behind her, as if somehow Kayla could protect him from any negativity that might come his way from Josh in the next few minutes. The guy sure seemed down and out at the moment, enough so that Jacob had almost told Kayla to keep their request on the down low for now, to ask at a better time. But the thing with Josh was, you never quite knew when that better time might be. Also, Charlie and Steve were expected soon with their busy families. Time alone with Jessie and Josh was already counting down.

Kayla swung around and regarded Jacob. *You ready for this?* she asked with a look.

He scratched an ear and stepped out from behind her lithe dancer's body just as Dylan finally gave up the battle and drifted off to sleep in his arms. Jacob's heart swelled, and tripled in size when he glanced up to see Jessie smiling wistfully—a little sadly, but with genuine love and affection—at him. He wanted to grin widely back, but there was that question of a rather morose Josh nearby, hanging onto Jessie for dear life, as if he was still terrified of losing her. Occasionally closing his eyes and burying his face in her hair, for that matter, which seemed curious…

Jacob narrowed his eyes. His brows shot up in a curious question mark. Jessie chewed on a nail and sent Jacob a hard look that clearly meant *Later.* Shrugging, he nodded while Kayla posed her question.

"We've had some shaky times, the four of us," Kayla said, "but…well… in the interest of having all of the people we love together at our wedding, we wanted the two of you to know that we've set a date we think works for everyone. We want you guys there."

Kayla's eyes were all sparkles and glitter. She was glowing, effervescent even, in a pale butter-yellow swing coat with black leggings underneath. Her hair, as usual of late, was all blonde instead of colored in funky shades the way she used to wear it. Now, she ran her long fingers over the sleek pony she'd styled it into today. One finger touched a diamond studded hairclip— Jacob had given it to her, almost as a tease because she wore her hair in simple ponytails so often.

Before Jessie could speak, wide-eyed and happy for the two of them, Kayla thrust a palm up between them. "There's more." Once more she looked at

Jacob, hoping to strengthen her spirit with his energy in case this plan of theirs backfired. "Um, well…" She, too, frowned at Josh's downcast demeanor. Before she continued, Kayla touched Josh's arm and called him back to them. He seemed to be off in Never Neverland. "Um, Josh? This is kind of important, bro."

Blinking rapidly twice, Josh looked up. "What?" He sought out Jacob's curious stare, and landed on Dylan in the guy's arms, pink-cheeked and snoring lightly. To everyone's dismay, Josh sank lower in the high chair. He almost buried himself behind Jessie, and solemnly regarded Kayla from between the big curls Jessie'd styled into her hair that morning.

Kayla ran a forgotten finger over and over her diamond hair clip and continued, her confused gaze darting from Josh to Jessie and back again. "March second," she told them. "The day I am going to marry this amazing man. It's a Friday," she added almost unnecessarily. "We couldn't book a Saturday on such short notice."

Jessie lightly touched Kayla's arm. "That's wonderful, Kayla," she said in a low, caring voice. "We'll be there. If you really want us to be, I mean," she backpedaled, recalling the fiasco over Talia and Jacob's wedding.

"Of course we do." This was from Jacob, spoken from under Dylan's soft curls. The simple statement, from between his lips, healed a lot of old hurts. He hugged his son tight and wondered again why Josh and Jessie both seemed so downcast and afraid.

"Um, so, we more than want the two of you there," Kayla tossed in, trying for a light and playful vibe. "Actually, we would like both of you to stand for us. Like…maid of honor kind of thing," her smile widened as Jessie immediately brightened. "And," she added to Josh, "like, usher kind of thing. Um, John Paul's the best man but Zach has agreed to be in the wedding party too, and Hilary, of course. And, um, Sophie and Steve and Jane and Charlie."

"Katrine and Charlene are flying in," Jacob elaborated. "But…" He looked back at Josh, who was totally clued in now and staring at him in a sort of confused wonder, "Kayla wants you by her side, Sawyer. So the way this is all working out, it kinda puts you at my side."

"Uhhh…." was all Josh could manage. He cocked his head at his baby sister and tightened his hold on his wife.

Jessie's body was shaking. She was laughing, releasing the anxiety that was constantly stalking them, and replacing it with joy. Reaching her right hand up behind her, she rubbed a palm over Josh's rough cheek, and followed the movement with a turn of her head so she could plant a happy kiss on his lips. "Babe, it's perfect. It's really perfect." While Josh searched Kayla's twinkling, hopeful eyes, Jessie threw her arms out to the room and hollered, "He says yes! We both say yes!" Bounding out of her husband's tight hold, she grabbed Kayla and swung her around. "We're honored, Kayla. Really. Truly, we're honored."

"It's not a lot of time," Kayla started, taking hold of Jessie's elbows. "I mean, to get dresses sorted and stuff, but we wanted to do this before *Sacred Peace* gets crazy. Josh will have to fly home from the new film he's signing onto…" Her voice drifted off as Jessie sobered and casually steered Kayla off to Deirdre's formal front room for a more serious girl chat.

As they were leaving the kitchen, Jessie turned around for a quick glance at Josh and Jacob. The two men were watching each other carefully, neither sure what to say. With a tiny grin, Jessie wrapped an arm around Kayla's shoulders and left the boys to it.

Jacob shifted Dylan in his arms. "He's getting heavy," he said to Josh.

Rotating around on the high chair, Josh shoved the chair on his left side around and gestured for Jacob to sit. Hesitant, in a kind of stilted silence, Jacob accepted the gesture as it was meant. Adjusting Dylan against his body, he made himself comfortable.

Josh leaned both elbows on the kitchen island and pawed thoughtfully at the Sunday scruff on his cheeks. He focused on David across from him. Every few minutes, the little boy rubbed icing he got on the tips of his fingers onto a green and white striped oversized chef's apron that almost completely covered his small frame. Underneath the apron, the sleeves of David's checked shirt were rolled up. Dee's careful hand was lightly guiding David as he dropped the silver balls on the cake. Deirdre was smiling; when she looked up at Josh and Jacob and let her eyes pause at the sleeping child in Jacob's arms, she seemed inordinately pleased at the way things were working out for all of them.

Jacob waded in and tackled the issue at hand. "Look, Josh, this isn't just for Kayla's sake. Like it or not, I don't have a lot of friends. I kinda need you to help me out here. Otherwise I look bad." He attempted a grin.

"We're not friends, Jacob. We won't ever be friends."

Surprised, David and his grandmother both stopped their delicate work. "Josh, honey." Deirdre angled her head toward David.

"I'm sorry, buddy," Josh said to his oldest son. "It's complicated. You'll understand when you're older. Unfortunately."

David, like his sister, thanks to circumstances beyond his control, had aged quickly over the course of his young life. He sent his father a wise, restrained smile and said simply, "It's okay, Daddy. You act like you are friends."

Even Josh allowed a faint smile at that as Dee relaxed and spooned minuscule colored candies into David's small, upturned palm.

Jacob chuckled. "He's right, Josh. Somewhere along the way you've started being pretty decent to me. You oughtta be. You're the one who got our girl. Who gets to keep her. Who gets to rock Dylan to sleep, most nights."

Glancing sideways at him, Josh considered what to say. In the end he went with, "Don't tell me my sister's the second best thing, Ryan. Or you'll be out that door faster than you can swing a cat."

"Daddy!" Wise David was not a fan of swinging cats around.

Josh laughed casually and leaned forward to tousle his son's surfer locks.

"Kayla's an amazing woman, Josh. I know it's taken you some time to get used to us being together, but we're blissfully happy. I would never compare her to Jessie. They're very different people, with a similar love for music."

Josh grunted and watched David drop the tiny candy balls on the top of the cake. The little boy was slow and careful in his movements, very precisely planning where each should go. Dylan would be the opposite. If he were awake and taking a turn, Josh knew the decorations would be randomly tossed everywhere. On the floor too, no doubt, to be squished underfoot, the way it felt Josh's temporary respite into happiness was being crushed once again.

"Josh, look," Jacob tried. "You and me, we have a lot in common." He held up two fingers, then allowed all five, thumb included, to pop up and fan out. "We love two women who we would protect with our lives, if need be. We're crazy about a certain three kids. And we'll both insanely love the next few that are coming along. We better, because we'll be sharing them around, I'm sure."

Really? How sure? Josh thought as the name Morgan slid across his brain and sickened him with its power to destroy. A thought struck him. His eyes darted over to Jacob. "You and Kayla…uhhh?"

Across from him, Deirdre's ears perked up.

Jacob's face bloomed an instant red. Beet red. "Umm…"

A happy scream from the front room confirmed it. Jessie's yell had Matt and Charles running into the hallway. After gleefully hop-skipping into the kitchen, Jessie wrapped her arms around Jacob and Dylan. To everyone's half-assed annoyance—because Dylan was never a happy camper when woken abruptly from a nap—she swooped up the son she shared with two men.

"Jacob and Kayla are having a baby!" she cried, hugging Dylan to her chest and laughing as she tried to soothe him. "This is the best news ever!"

Arms and ankles crossed, swiping at tears, Kayla leaned against the wall at the entrance to the kitchen.

Tentatively, Josh swung around on his leather chair and faced her. She moved forward when he opened his arms to her. "My baby sister's having a baby. With this doofus. I might just have to stand in your wedding after all. Someone's gotta be sure he treats his family right."

"He always has," Jessie cut in, eyes alight as she took in the happy people in front of her. Bending forward, she one-arm hugged Jacob and kissed him lightly on the lips. "He's a good man. And a great daddy."

As if on cue, Dylan let out a pissed off whine and kicked a booted heel into his mother's thigh.

"Ouch! Nice one, Dylan." Jessie held her shared son back out to Jacob who, with one raised eyebrow, grasped the three year old under the armpits. "Here," Jessie sulked with a glint in her eye. "Parenting. In good times and in bad." A dark shadow crossed her face as she said it. Jacob stashed away a mental note to make a private enquiry about the cryptic comment later. Maybe Josh had gotten another nasty, threatening note…

A swoosh of cool, crisp winter air suddenly swept down the hallway beyond the kitchen. La Casa's elegant mahogany door had swung open. Courtesy of the January chill, Charlie's welcome voice was carried into the warmth of the cozy home. "Do I smell freshly baked chocolate chip cookies?"

Wandering in as if he owned the place, he clapped Matt on the shoulder as he passed, and made a questioning gesture about handing him his baby son, Lucas. To Jessie's delight, Matt graciously took the little guy and cuddled him. Sleepy, Lucas wiped his eyes and settled in the strong, comfy arms. Stella ran in with some new electronic game to show Emily-Grace. Jane strolled in just behind her daughter with a platter of veggies and dip for the kids, which Carlotta took from her and opened up on the kitchen island.

A good old Keating-Sawyer celebration was just the thing to dispel bad times and dark thoughts, even if only for a short time. Steve, Sophie, Caleb and Cole were along within the next few minutes, which did wonders to brighten Josh up. Shyly ducking his head, Josh had no choice but to endure a lot of good-natured teasing the second his buddies discovered he'd be donning a tux to stand in Jacob's wedding.

Happy guffaws and roars filled the kitchen.

Charles wandered up to Matt.

Standing on the perimeter of the joyful group, Matt was taking everyone in, soaking up the bliss while it lasted. Occasionally he resorted to scanning the dusky corners of the room; these were the times when the heavy emotion and power of the unknown threatened to disarm him. Matt's eyes always landed back at Jessie who, again—as often as she could, actually—was casually half sitting on and half leaning into Josh's welcoming arms.

"She'll be okay," Charles assured his good friend, with a confidence he couldn't quite manage to feel. "She's made it this far."

"She won't be. She won't be okay." Matt handed a now wiggling Lucas over to Deirdre, who wandered out of earshot before either he or Charles spoke again. "If something happens to Josh…" He shook his head.

"We know who we're dealing with now, Matt. We're one step closer."

"We don't. Not really, Charles. Morgan can't do anything more from the inside than place orders. We don't have a clue who we are dealing with. Or if it's even that manipulative bastard."

"It's a helluva coincidence if it isn't."

The men grew silent, partly because both of them caught Jessie's eye. She had been watching them as they talked, taking note of the serious bent to their heads and their cautious, lowered voices. Now, Jessie boosted herself fully upright away from Josh, and she stepped through the happy throng of bodies and made her way to Matt and Charles. Taking a hand from each man, holding the fingers she loved so dearly, she smiled sadly.

Hopefully.

"Thank you for trying," she whispered. "Thank you for caring. And, for now, thank you for letting go of the hurts that haunt us. Now is a time for celebration. Now is a time to be happy. For however long it lasts."

A chill swept up Matt's spine and raised the hairs on his arms. Jessie saw alarm pass over him, and she swallowed fearfully, but pushed the dread away. "Sweet Matt," she managed, letting go of Charles' hand and wrapping both arms around Matt's toned shoulders. "Stop trying to save the world. It can't be done, baby. We can only do what we can do. Let it go. For tonight just let it go."

Over Jessie's shoulder, Matt looked up to spy Josh's eyes on him. Curious, Charlie and Steve both turned to see what suddenly silenced their friend, but neither Josh nor Matt took notice of them. Josh and Matt were enveloped in the new-old terror that threatened all of them, and that held Jessie, by association, in the center of its diabolical grasp.

Carlotta broke the tension with a loud, "Out, out of my kitchen, if anybody here wants dinner before midnight!"

Jessie touched her fingers to Matt's cheek, bent nose-to-nose to him, and issued a subdued demand. "Go forth and spread light, my friend. Take my husband and children with you. I'm going to help Carlotta and share some precious me-time with my girlfriends. And smile, please. It's one day at a time in the Sawyer camp again. Which means it's one second at a time for me and Josh and everyone around us. And this second, honey, is soaked with happiness."

Dropping her arms away from him, her smile grew wider. Jessie started to back away. Throwing her arms out wide, her eyes glistened with forced happiness. "Oh, look! So's this one! This second's a glorious one too! And this one! Oh, and this one, too!"

Matt was actually lightening up when he heaved himself away from the door frame and left the kitchen. He was chuckling, even, as he shook his head and scooped up Steve's youngest and headed off to the playroom. Josh wandered alongside him.

"Your wife's a little bit nuts, Josh," Matt said as they moseyed down the hall.

"Thank God for that." Josh grinned. "Sometimes the only sane way to see the world is through her wild and crazy eyes."

In the kitchen, Jessie flipped around and offered Sophie, Jane and Kayla a wide smile. "Okay, so who in this room is not breastfeeding or pregnant? Because…I've got wine!"

Laughter followed her to Deirdre's fancy temperature controlled wine fridge, and successfully—if only temporarily—tossed out the shadow of darkness haunting La Casa once again.

Chapter Four

The first thing Morgan noticed when he strode into the gym was the smell. Dirty sweat socks and disinfectant. Familiar. Gyms the world over smelled the same. Like the Catholic church, they were alike no matter where in the world you were, no matter whether you were in a middle-of-the-road Goodlife Fitness in downtown Toronto, in a small town gym in Prince Edward Island, or in a yuppie yoga studio in Vancouver's elite Kitsilano neighborhood.

Or in a maximum security prison.

The gym was where the men of Brody River Penitentiary—Brody Pen, to the men—shed their fright, if any of that ill weakness remained deep in their damaged crevices. This was where they regained control. With every black-crystal drop of sweat, when they were in the gym, like snakes in the desert they shed their skins and sought renewal. Here they were reduced to nothingness, to bare elements that gripped and pulled and lifted and hauled, bending at the knees to help their bodies carry the weight and the pain that got them to Brody Pen in the first place; that got them to Alberta's maximum security prison, where the only fight most of the men had left was for dominion of their souls.

Grunting, groaning with the effort, in the gym the men fixed determined gazes on blank walls as they hoisted their stoic prey. With pressed lips and stony stares, their muscles rippled and screamed in crescendos of whipped pleasure; their bodies cried and strained. Each his own man, or the essence of what men were supposed to be—strong, resilient, capable—they pushed their bodies to their limits in the struggle to gain control. To stay physically fit. Some sucked the marrow out of the pleasure. Some worked out so they could outrun themselves.

Morgan's body was as taut and strong as ever. The veins on his biceps ran like tiny rivers down his skin, brittle in appearance as if, with the lightest graze of a split fingernail, they would burst open and crack him apart.

Expose him. His naked truths, his blistered existence, his empty heart.

Now, he made his way to a corner and stood in a wide stance to assure his balance. Hesitating as he reached for a pair of thick battle ropes, Morgan rotated slightly around. He could feel a man's hard gaze on him, and he wanted to see where it was coming from.

Oren Caulfield, whose piercing snake eyes were known to obliterate men with a simple glare, was watching him. Like those old pink and purple candies Morgan and his buddies used to drop on their tongues as kids to feel them crack and sizzle, Caulfield's brutal stare had energy. The kind of energy a man wilted under. The kind of energy that made a man instantly sink to his knees in terror.

Oren Caulfield, corrections officer. Known to the men incarcerated at Brody Pen as Oren C, or sometimes just as C. Even that one letter spoken aloud—whispered, even, beneath wide eyes and from the most hardened of tight lips rippled with jagged scars—had the capacity to snap a man in two.

Grasping the heavy battle ropes, Morgan leaned slightly backward, adjusted his grip, and at the same time centered his stance. Sucking in a breath, he focused on the ropes. They became living things under his fierce grip, undulating and rising and falling as he forced them up and down, his biceps tensing and taking the challenge with grateful, satisfied eagerness. Morgan's heart picked up its pace; focused, concentrating, he tried unsuccessfully to force Caulfield from his mind. Grunting with the effort to keep the battle ropes moving rhythmically and fast, he cursed inwardly as the man's dark nature invaded what, to Morgan, was usually one of the only sacred times he had to himself each day, when he could close his mind against the demons that relentlessly haunted him—Jessie's wide, frightened eyes; Josh's unyielding, judgmental stare; Nadia's half-lidded wet-eyed ill concealed lust for Josh; Teenage Mutant Ninja Turtle figures spread out in a child's coffin, stiff and still, their frozen eyes and grotesque grins guarding the lifeless body of Morgan's five-year-old son, Darin.

Forever five. That's what the child was. That's when he stopped living, before grade school, before hockey and soccer and buddies and a succession of endless Friday night pizzas. Life stopped for Morgan then, too. This, now? Shuttled to and fro like cattle? Pissing and stripping and moaning in his sleep always under the careful scrutiny of staunch-lipped correctional officers? This new existence wasn't living. To Morgan, it wasn't even surviving. It was robotic movements through days devoid of light, devoid of meaningful connection.

Devoid of hope.

Urging his body to its limit as he gravitated through the sweaty weights and bars so he could feel—well, anything—Morgan managed to avoid Caulfield's dark gaze as it followed him from the bench press to a round of squats to the treadmill. But Caulfield was stationed at the gym's entrance, one of three guards in the midsized gym, there to keep the inmates from bashing each other's heads in with weights when short fuses demanded retribution for some detected slight. At some point, Morgan would have to pass by him. He was expected on shift at the prison's furniture factory in an hour.

When he finished his workout, Morgan trained his eyes on the floor and headed for the door. Caulfield grabbed his bicep as he tried to pass.

Halting, Morgan focused on a crack in the tile three feet to his left as, at his right, Caulfield, a man responsible for Morgan's 'rehabilitation,' spoke in his ear, his voice gruff, his tone low, and his breath a weird schoolgirl pepperminty fresh. The man was crunching on a new mint as he spoke. He regularly popped them between his lips the way Caulfield's own long dead chain-smoking father had once lit cigarettes.

"We gave them Christmas," he informed his subject.

Morgan's fists, knuckled at his sides, clutched at empty air.

"That was damn good of us, wouldn't you say? Huh, Mor-gie?"

A low *sssssstttt* was all Caulfield got back from his favorite inmate so he squeezed a little tighter. A thrill shot up the guard's spine when Morgan's muscled bicep went rigid under the viselike grip.

"Mor-gie."

To its recipient, the name was oddly suspended in the stale, sweaty air. It sounded unrealistic, detached. Foreign. Musty.

But Morgan knew that the way Caulfield drew it out, extended it, meant that Morgan ought to give the loathsome man something. He forced his half-vacant eyes up to the guard's steely, penetrating stare. Accustomed to the darkness he knew he would find there, Morgan settled his stance and narrowed his gaze instead of jumping, startled, like he did the first time he allowed himself to meet the man's malevolent eyes. Still, the gray, daunting aura that surrounded Caulfield's essence was as demoralizing and as real as if the man wore a black cloak over his stiff, broad shoulders. As if he carried a grim reaper's scythe.

Morgan shook him off. Caulfield tossed back his head and sneered at Morgan's audacity, giving Morgan a sense of pride and victory at his power over the guy. A power that was seeded by Morgan's fame in the prison, a notoriety he'd earned from his connection to Jessie Wheeler and Josh Sawyer. *Jessie Wheeler-Sawyer,* he reminded himself with a bitterness and regret that overshadowed—only slightly—Morgan's memory of who he used to be, a quiet guy married to a gorgeous woman, the two of them going about their business with the jubilant joy of young parents.

Before.

Nobody else would dare shake Oren C off. Not one other tough, virile, bearded or non-bearded man, not the full-body tattooed biker gang guys. Not even the guy who'd once won the world champion bench press competition would dare shake off the one guard they all feared, the one guy who had the remorseless, psychopathic capacity to put prisoners in solitary in the hole for weeks on end, who could round up a circle of officers willing to deny privileges, to beat an inmate bloody, or to leave a man shaking with fever or cradling an untreated, broken arm or a seeping knife wound.

Caulfield was deeply respected for the warped power he lauded over his charges. Much of it was earned for what he orchestrated—with the help of former inmates—beyond Brody Pen's heavily armed walls.

Morgan sucked up his resilience and called upon his own power—his bizarre fame. He answered Caulfield with a grimace and a rusty, mostly unused voice that landed somewhere between insistence and a need to beg.

"No more," he demanded. "They've had enough."

"Ah. You're wrong there, Mor-gie."

Recoiling at hearing his name drawn out that way, in that appalling, distorted way from this excuse of a man with the narrowing, dark eyes, Morgan took a halting, sideways step.

Caulfield continued, "You know the drill, kid. You know my rep. I am the maestro. I even the score. It's who I am. It's what I do." To solidify his point, Caulfield brought a hand to his chest. He pressed it firmly against the place where Morgan felt the man's heart would be, if the guy actually had a heart. "You're at the top of my list, kid. Fame gets you things, sometimes. Right? You enjoy that big juicy steak last night? Sautéed onions and mushrooms layered so deep overtop you couldn't even see the flesh? Or was it too juicy for you?" He leaned closer. Morgan recoiled as the guard crunched hard on the last bit of his peppermint. "Too…bloody."

The steak, a very rare treat, had been perfect, grilled just the way Morgan liked a good steak, medium rare, with melted butter drizzled overtop. He licked his lips in succulent remembrance.

Caulfield noticed. Guffawing loudly, he attracted the stares of the other men in the small gym, all of whom stared at Morgan with ill concealed distaste mixed with a measure of longing. The guy had spent years with Jessie Wheeler. He stuck his dick inside her and moved around. Heard her moan with pleasure, they figured, as she likely writhed underneath him. They'd all heard Shawna Coupland's televised interview with some famous psychologist. Jessie had not agreed to speak publicly with the famous talk show host about her forced time with her once trusted security, but it seemed everyone else on the planet wanted to, back then, after she was rescued from the dismal depths of the Langley basement.

Morgan, in prison circles, was under Oren C's claws. He got the rare juicy steak. He got protection. He got respect.

Caulfield gave Morgan a light shove. But Morgan's feet were solidly planted. He didn't budge. He was a rock, a well rooted tree stuck to the earth destined to wander alone and lonely like some long dead ghost searching for a place to land. He waited.

"You know the drill, Mor-gie," Caulfield drawled, wiping away a drop of saliva from the corner of his lip as he leaned in, his minty breath hot in Morgan's ear. "An eye for an eye, remember? That was your woman's game? A wife and a child. That's what you lost. That's what Josh Sawyer will lose."

They think this is about Josh, Morgan breathed as he took in his guard's cold, unyielding stare. *Josh, Jessie, Matt, Charles, Charlie, that arrogant bitch Deirdre, all of them. They think it's about Josh.* He couldn't help himself. Morgan curled his shoulders inward. *The Josh shit was just to throw them off the real threat.*

"No," he managed. "Not yet." *Jessie. I can't…the kids. I…can't. Not…yet.*

"They'll be back in Calgary soon." Like drool from a teething baby, the terrifying truth slipped between Caulfield's lips. "In a few months."

"Yes." The feet, the big ones in the Nike cross trainers…*I think they're mine. They're mine, right?*…wouldn't move. Morgan's eyes refocused on his toes. He begged his feet to move, to take one small step, for starters.

Caulfield gave him a harder shove. Morgan stumbled forward. Behind his back, a low voice followed. "Fame, Mor-gie," it said. "You've earned this."

Finally, Morgan summoned up a semblance of courage. Of fight.

He turned. "Retribution? Vengeance?" he whispered, his voice gravelly, uncertain. His big paws remained fisted, grasping at a nothingness he tried vainly to use to rudder him away from this fearful man. From this vengeful excuse for a human being. "Is that what I earned? I don't need it. I don't want it."

"Nah." Caulfield's lips drew themselves tight over perfect white teeth. A big hand straightened the already perfect knot in his tie. "The right to transmit terror." He lifted a foot and leaned his boot back against the cinderblock wall as he settled against it. "That's what fame gets a man. You just get to deliver it. Terrrorrrr."

Morgan's eyes widened in surprise. His lips parted but he couldn't dredge up any more words. Even the few he had spoken, in low tones and colorless nuances, had exhausted him.

Caulfield grinned, but it came out crooked, only one corner of a sadistic lip turning up. The other remained down, giving him the effect of a man confused. But that was his power. He wasn't confused at all. He was just mean. "Ask your old bosses," he told Morgan. "Ask them what fame got them. What it's still getting them." He held up two fingers. "Two months," he said, the psychotic eyes hardening into concrete beneath neatly styled salt and pepper hair. "I know you love her, Mor-gie. But she goes."

"You're wrong," Morgan managed before he turned on his heel and forced his feet away. "I don't love her. I never loved her."

As his footsteps echoed down the brightly lit hallway, Morgan heard one last comment from the man who really ran Brody Pen. From the man who manipulated a lot of nasty happenings outside the daunting walls, and who got respect for doing so. "Then it won't hurt to let her go. Will it, Mor-gie?"

Crumpling in despair, Morgan dipped his chin and hung his head.

Behind him, Oren Caulfield laughed, and dug another peppermint out of his pocket. Popping it in between his lips, he sucked hard on it, and watched Morgan limp away. Part of him wanted to follow him, to rest a hand on his firm bicep as they walked, to chat the way old friends do, to laugh, to soak up the lively benefits of friendship. But there was a metaphorical wall between the corrections officers and the inmates. It was as high, it was as solid, and it was as insurmountable as the walls separating the prison from the real world.

They were in different dimensions, the corrections officers like him, like Caulfield, and those they watched over. Like electric fans on different speeds. They didn't mix, not really.

But there was a way to get inside the hearts of the inmates. To earn their respect, to feel their love, however misaligned it might be.

It was called revenge.

Not for him, for Oren Caulfield, but for them—his charges, his…children.

And it was always, always sweet.

$\mathcal{A}$ few days later, Josh was just pulling Dylan out of the bath and wrapping him in a large blue, fluffy towel when his signature cell phone ring, *Under The Bridge* by the Red Hot Chili Peppers, alerted him to an incoming call. The phone was in Dylan's room—Josh and Jessie had long since learned not to leave their cell phones anywhere near water or swirling toilet bowls any time their youngest child was in the vicinity. One can only try to dry out so many phones in beds of rice before that lesson gets ingrained.

"Jessie, can you grab that for me?" Josh called over his shoulder.

At her quick, "Got it," he smiled at Dylan and rubbed a corner of the towel over the little boy's wet hair. "Someone needs a haircut, huh, Dylan?"

"Daddy too," the little boy said wisely, drawing his tiny fingers through Josh's long layers.

"Deal. We'll go together, once I meet with Marc and the production designer on the new film. So I know what kind of hairstyle they want. Okay, little buddy?"

"Okay, Daddy. Maybe you get curls like me. Momma likes my curls."

Dylan's innocence humbled Josh. "Yeah, sure," he grumbled halfheartedly and silently sent Jacob a few well placed curses. As he picked the child up and snuggled Dylan's tousled head in close to his shoulder, he added, "Momma likes curls, all right." But Josh's words weren't layered in the old hostility, nor were the curse words. Instead they were more of an acceptance that Josh long ago had no choice but to deal with. The little boy in his arms, all love and cuddles now, was Josh's shadow, most days. He grinned. So far everything was turning out quite all right, all things considered, at least as far as Jacob's involvement in their lives went.

Jessie popped her head around the door and they almost ran into each other as Josh moved to go at the same time. "Awww, Momma's baby boy," she gushed. "Look at you, Dylan, all adorable little boy love. What are we gonna read tonight?"

Dylan refused her open arms. He cuddled in tight to his daddy. "Daddy wead me."

"Way to break my heart," she scowled affectionately, and held Josh's cell out to him. "Hilary," she announced, trying to hide the dread in her heart.

Raising his eyebrows, Josh took the phone. "Good," he said. "Hopefully she's got some dates for me. Dylan and I are going for haircuts together before the film."

Jessie looked away.

Josh recoiled. "What? What'd you do that for?"

Exasperated, Jessie reached again for Dylan and took him, protesting, out of his father's arms. "Daddy can take over reading when he gets off the phone. Come on, let's go in David's room and find a book both of you boys will love."

Watching them go, Josh fought a rising alarm. Nervous all of a sudden, he put the phone to his ear and strode into the master bedroom. He was standing at the large sliding door watching the wind whip the Pacific into mini cyclones before he finally said, "Hey, Hilary."

Often these days, his brother Zach's wife consulted Deirdre before she sent serious projects to Josh. For one, Hilary respected Deirdre's wisdom and experience and two, managing Josh's career was directly tied in to managing Jessie's. Both had agents, too, to fine tune deals, in more than one country in fact, but it was Hilary and Dee the two consulted and trusted the most. Hilary, who worked from her Seattle home office, supported Josh's career almost full time these days, although she had a small roster of up-and-comers on her books as well.

"Hey, Hil, how're those youngsters of yours?" Josh continued, feeling that asking about Hilary and Zach's sprouting teens was a safe place to start, given Jessie's ambiguous look a few minutes earlier.

Hilary skipped the formalities. A heavy sigh preceded the new crack she delivered to Josh's already smashed up heart. "Honey, Jouet is rethinking the part. I'm sorry."

Josh went white. "What? What do you mean? He called me himself. It's—it's in the bag, Hil." Outside, the spray on the waves looked like racing horses, their manes and tails stretched via salty droplets long into the wind's grasp. Fierce competitors, it seemed they were trying to outrun each other to the shore, but when the waves crested they merged back into the ocean and disappeared.

Disappeared. Vanished back into the sea.

"Josh, this happens all the time. You know this. He was likely talking to a whole host of actors he was considering."

"Aw, Hil, please don't try to tell me this was Jouet's doing. You and I have been working together for far too long for you to pull that crap on me." Josh scratched his head and sank backward onto the bed. The movement sent Jessie's old armless teddy bear, Tedsy, slipping weirdly down the pillow it was propped up against. Next to it, her stuffed tiger tipped over and landed on its nose. "Can we do something? Look, I'm not putting my life on hold while that fucking Morgan plays his wicked games."

Silence from Seattle telexed to Josh that his instincts were spot on. He was in danger of losing the gig because Charles, likely on behalf of Deirdre—and maybe on behalf of even Jessie herself—was demanding that Hilary take Josh out of the running for the film.

After a moment Hilary tried to nudge her way back into Josh's good graces. "Honey, Marc Jouet has already sent me another script. It's half funded and will be going to camera probably by next January."

"Next January. In a year, Hil. You think I'll still be alive then? You're optimistic."

He could almost hear her crumple. A distant voice—Zach—mumbled something Josh couldn't hear, and then Zach was on the line.

"Little brother, my wife is in tears here. Don't shoot the messenger, okay?"

"Zach, I have no control over what Morgan has planned for me. And I've got news for you, for everyone. For one, the asshole's tentacles are far reaching. He can get me here in Vancouver or in Alberta on *Sacred Peace,* not just on the Jouet film. Two, Jessie and I have learned to live our lives day by day, moment by moment, as much as that sometimes sucks. But it's also taught us to really treasure each other, and our family. It's not all bad."

"It's bad, Josh. Charles Keating called me this morning. He wants you where he can see you. He's got reason to be concerned."

"Oh, fuck him," Josh cursed. "He's not concerned about me. I'm not at the top of his list of people to be *concerned* about." Josh said 'concerned' the second time as if it was something bad he ate and had to spit out. "Hell, Zach, I'm so far down his goddamned list after Jessie and the kids, and Jacob and Charlie, that I'm surprised I'm even on his and Matt's radar. In fact, I think Matt'd be glad to get rid of me. I'd say he'd step right in, but let's face it, he's already there. The only thing he doesn't get these days, at least as far as I know, is regularly fucked. By my wife, I might add!"

"Easy, Josh. And don't go taking this out on Jessie," Zach ordered. "The last thing the two of you need is a rip-roaring fight. Charles cares more than you give him credit for. Everyone does. Don't ask me how, but somehow you've become someone a lot of people care about."

"*Sacred Peace*, that's how." Absently, Josh picked up Jessie's stuffed tiger and set it upright. It did a second nose-dive. Josh left it alone.

"And Shanda Ellis doing the talk show circuit and gushing over how amazing you are. That woman's crazy in love with you. Her words carry a lot of power. The tide is turning, Josh, in your favor. Just give it a little more time so that you're on the planet to enjoy it."

"I want to do this film, Zach. Ultimately it's my decision."

Zach made a frustrated *mphhffftt* sound. "I've got news for you, little brother. You're a married man with three beautiful children. If you care about your marriage, you'll let Jouet cast his second choice, and you'll walk away."

Josh paused. "Zach, is this Jessie's call? Is this her doing?"

"Josh, don't ask me to get in between you and your wife. I won't. But if it puts your mind at ease, my understanding is that it was merely suggested to her that you don't take the film. Knowing how much you want this part, I'm sure I can say it hurts her as much as it hurts you." Zach hesitated. "Ultimately, Josh, that girl wants you in her arms, living and breathing. She doesn't give a rat's ass if you ever work again."

Josh released a frustrated, pent-up sigh. "That's the thing, though, Zach. I don't much feel like I'm living and breathing if I'm not working."

"You are, Josh. *Sacred Peace* has done a lot for you, for how people see you," Zach replied in earnest. "For how the world sees you. I'm not saying you owe Charles, or Charlie and Jon for that matter, or even Shanda. But don't sell *Sacred Peace* short. It's a good project for you to be on right now. It's not stalling your career, is what I mean. You're still moving forward."

"Aw Jesus, Zach! This sucks. It really sucks. I've worked damn hard to get to this level. I deserve this film."

"I know, Josh. So don't blow future opportunities by jumping back into the fire too soon, okay bro?"

"So who gets to play my part, then? Who is Marc going to cast?"

"Forester. He's casting Ryan Forester."

A low groan alerted Zach to Josh's increased desolation at that unwelcome news. "This just gets better and better," Josh decreed. "You and Hil really made my day, big brother."

Ten minutes later, when Jessie padded quietly into the bedroom, Josh was still sitting on the bed, shoulders slumped and cell phone twisting around and around in his tired fingers. Climbing up onto the big bed behind him, Jessie folded her knees on either side of him, leaned her body against his back, and wrapped both arms tightly around his shoulders in the hopes that somehow her energy could soak into him and cheer him up.

It was a futile effort, although Josh laid a hand over one of hers and took Zach's advice, which was not to take his frustration out on his wife.

"The house is shaking," Jessie said. "The wind's really come up tonight."

"Kids asleep?"

At her husband's forlorn voice, Jessie buried her nose in his warm, musky neck. She breathed him in. "Dylan is, although he fought the sandman til he just couldn't anymore, waiting for you. Emily-Grace is reading to David. Something about princesses and unicorns."

"Great," Josh groaned. "I'm going shopping tomorrow for books about motorcycles and trucks."

"Redneck. David knows all about things with big engines. He loves having his sister read to him. He lets her read whatever she wants as long as she spends time with him."

"They're lucky to have each other."

"You bet they are."

"Jess…"

"Mmm?" She snuggled in closer and started planting tiny kisses on Josh's neck, moving his layered hair aside so she could let her lips linger fully on his skin and more fully breathe him in. Tonight he was also communicating a mixture of chili spice and Dylan's bubble bath, which would have made Jessie giggle if the earlier phone call hadn't assaulted Josh's already low spirit.

"Would you hate me for calling Jouet and asking for my part back?"

She stilled and sat back. "Please don't, Josh. Let's not make Matt's job harder than it already is."

"Seriously, Jessie?" Pushing her arms completely away from his body, Josh whipped around and stared at her. "You think I give a sweet fuck about your precious Matt at the moment?"

Pride snaked up Jessie's back. Suddenly her eyes iced over, threatening to let loose the same cool rage that was whipping the Pacific Ocean into a fury outside their window. "I know you do, Josh. You care about Matt because you're a good man who doesn't want to hurt people. Did you see him the other day? Did you take a good look at him? He was barely capable of speech after finding out that Morgan might be engineering this latest shit."

"No, Jessie, I didn't take a good look at Matt, but I'm pretty damn sure you did."

"Hell, yeah! I'm worried about him!"

"Are you." After a long pause in which Josh studied Jessie at length—watched the hard emotions flit across her eyes and disappear under the surface like sinking ships—he turned back to watching the salt-spray horses careen over the waves outside. Momentarily Jessie settled down beside him on the big bed, hung her legs over the side, and took his hand in hers.

"So what if?" she asked softly.

"If I die, you mean. What if I die?"

"Yup. That. What if Morgan wins?"

"Then I die knowing I lived well. That I had what many men never get." A strong arm settled across Jessie's shoulders and nudged her close.

"Yep. You do. You've already got everything, Josh. You have an Oscar. You've got amazing kids. What else do you need?"

"To live. To challenge myself. To be the best actor I can be."

"And what about the best husband and father, huh? Being dead won't get you that. Being away from us working on a film won't get you that."

"This is the thing, Jessie," Josh said. "You've always been willing to let that go, the career stuff. You'd be happy hiding out on your little island and being a wife and mom. Which is amazing, really. I love that about you, that the other stuff doesn't matter. And I love being a husband and a dad. You guys are everything to me. But cutting out my need to have a career and taking away my choices to do films that challenge me, that make me the best actor I can be is like chopping out my heart. And it lets Morgan win. Not to mention Forester." He grimaced darkly, remembering the night he pulled Jessie out of Ryan Forester's bed all those years ago.

"So you'd rather die. I feel kinda sick, Josh."

"I'd rather die knowing I lived, Jessie. You know? That I lived."

Without losing his gaze, Jessie wrapped her fingers around the cellphone Josh was cradling in his left hand. She lifted it up to him. "Do you still have Marc's number?"

"He may not even be able to give it to me now," Josh said quietly. "Forester may have already signed the contract. But if I get it, and I go, I accept the risk. Do you?"

"In good times and in bad," she responded softly. "If it's really what you want, then I do, Josh. But babe…"

"I know," he answered for her. "If I take the job, Arnie's at risk too, since Matt will stay with you."

Slowly, her head turned from side to side. "Nope. Matt won't stay alone with me. He'll go with you, babe."

"Ah." Suddenly Josh got what she was telling him. It chilled him.

Jessie fought this new rising panic and, for the briefest of moments,

Josh was sorry he was pushing so hard for this acting job. But his sorrow was quickly being superseded by a growing excitement that the coveted part could maybe still be his.

He reached out a quaking finger and drew the back of it down his wife's cheek. "I'll watch out for him," he murmured as the solemn blue eyes pleaded silently with him. "The same way he will watch out for me. Okay?"

She swallowed. "I know." Her next words were directed at the floor. Jessie was picturing Matt's wrath upon finding out that Josh was going rogue on him. "Call Marc. If you get a yes from him, I'll tell Charles and Matt myself, tomorrow. You don't need them jumping down your throat."

And you are likely the only person who can handle them, thought Josh, silently thanking his wife for her support, and fighting the guilt that assaulted him when he realized he, in fact, was not supporting her. Not really. Taking this job was, in fact, a direct hit on their marriage.

Leveraging her body upright, Jessie kissed her husband sweetly on the lips and banana'd around the foot of the bed to make her way into the washroom. Inside, she gripped the edge of the vanity and hung her head, watching her teardrops splatter into the basin and merge into a tiny puddle. She could almost hear each drop as it landed, each magnified bigger and bigger, as if releasing her worry from her soul this way also carried tremendous, hulking, silent, screams.

After Josh saw Jessie reach behind her and close the bathroom door, he pulled up Marc Jouet's contact information. He paused only slightly before tapping the green 'call' button. Anxious but hopeful, he was relieved when the respected French Canadian director answered.

When Jessie opened the bathroom door a few minutes later and stood there sawing her toothbrush back and forth across teeth framed by fresh scrubbed pink cheeks, Josh was standing again, his back to her as he stared out at the windswept waves once more. Turning back to the sink, she spit, and faced him again.

"Was it worth it?" she whispered as she contemplated the broad shoulders of the man she loved beyond all others.

Josh turned. His grin was wide and his eyes were flecked with light. "You better fucking believe it," he told her.

"I mean us," she added, and Josh had to bend an ear to her and ask her to say it again. "I…mean…*us*. In case this is it. In case this is the tipping point, the choice that ends everything."

Without answering, Josh tossed his phone onto the bed. It landed oddly by Tedsy's ragged ear. Despite the new euphoria that had cascaded into his heart like fireworks, a seedy disgust at his selfish choice crawled up his legs like spiders.

Jessie jumped back in. "I'm glad, Josh. For you, I mean." She swung back into the washroom and finished merging her tears with the water in the sink as she cleaned the foam off her toothbrush. "Because it sure ain't worth it for me," she wept under her breath. She took her time toweling the moisture off her lips. "Not yet. I want more, universe. I want him forever. I want this man forever."

Gazing at her reflection in the mirror, all sad-eyed and scared, Jessie saw Josh come up behind her and lean against the door frame. Meeting his eyes in the mirror, she threw the hand towel at his reflection, lifted her foot, and kicked the door closed behind her.

He backed away before it hit him, but Josh got the message loud and clear. Still, he couldn't avoid the wide grin creasing his jaw as he left their bedroom whistling a happy tune. Easing into the rocking chair in Dylan's room, he lifted his feet and crossed his ankles on the nearby ottoman, linked his fingers across his belly, and settled in to watch his curly-haired boy sleep.

Chapter Six

"Oh, shit," Jessie said and sat back. "Hmmm." Raising a hand to her chin, she scratched at her bottom lip with a thumbnail. She glanced toward the doorway as a set of clipped footsteps making their way down La Casa's main hallway grew louder. Grabbing a paper bag she'd tossed aside when she reached for Charles' computer mouse earlier, she retrieved a chunk of warm muffin and abstractedly placed it between her lips. After dropping Emily-Grace and David off at school, and pausing to admire the gorgeous view of cargo-ship dotted English Bay behind the sloped hill the school was built on, Jessie had pointed her Lexus toward North Van, pulled up in front of Elysian Coffee's newest café on Burrard Street along the way, and grabbed a cappuccino and a fresh-from-the-oven raspberry ricotta muffin. But she was too stressed to savor the yummy treat, and swallowed the muffin bite without really tasting it.

Now she averted her eyes from the iMac screen in Charles' study, and hunkered deeper in his soft leather chair. She'd settled in to do some research while she waited for Charles and Matt to return from the Keating Building's large gym.

The men were back. The footsteps on the way down the hall were Matt's, Jessie knew, and she peeked up at him now as he filled the doorway and stood there, casually spooning yogurt and fruit out of a cereal bowl. Carlotta had thrust the bowl into his hands when he started to bypass the kitchen after seeing Jessie's Lexus parked crookedly in the curved driveway.

Jessie bent a knee and planted her foot on the edge of the chair. Encircling her knee with her arm and resting her chin on it, she sighed and watched him savor his yogurt. At the same time, she pulled another chunk of muffin out of the bag and poked it between her lips.

After a bit, Matt nodded toward the computer. "Checking out your competition?"

"YouTube?" Jessie conjectured. "Nope." Drawing up her shoulders, she said, "Did you know that Brody River Penitentiary is supposedly built on a Native burial ground?"

Matt's spoon floated in midair. Dropping it into his bowl, he walked behind Charles' large desk and looked over Jessie's shoulder at the blog post she had up on the screen. "Forever cursed," he read. "A place of turmoil." Wandering back around the desk, he dropped into another leather chair in front of it. "It's a prison, Jessie. With or without the burial ground, there's negative energy there."

"Despite everything, Matt, I hate picturing Morgan there. In a place that dark."

"He earned his ticket. Why are you looking at this stuff anyway? Let Charles and me handle the bad stuff."

The way Jessie ran her eyes over him, drifting over Matt's impeccable white shirt, open at the neck, and the dark shadows under his eyes, made Matt sit up straighter.

She told him directly, "You're not handling the bad shit so great, Matt. Your dark circles are running rings around themselves, baby."

Tensing, he waited a minute before he stared down into his yogurt and murmured, "Don't call me that." Letting his eyes float upward to meet her worried frown, he added a gentle, "Please."

Jessie held his gaze and ignored the request. At the same time, she steeled herself against getting up, circling the desk, and climbing into his loving arms for a good solid cry. "Josh took the film," she announced instead. "Marc told him the part is still his if he wants it. They're going to camera the first of February in New Mexico. Mostly shooting six days a week. I hope you have some plaid shorts left over from your party days with Jacob in the Caribbean."

"Damn it," Matt cursed, and unceremoniously dropped his unfinished yogurt on the desk. With the tip of a finger, he shoved the bowl toward the computer monitor, away from the edge. "Do either of you ever give a fuck about what your security thinks is best for you? Ever? No," he answered himself as his blood pressure shot up and blood started pounding in his ears. "No, you just ramble along on your little spoiled asses and leave the suffering to us."

"You don't think we suffer, Matt?" Jessie's voice was dangerously low. Her raised foot fell to the floor and she spun the chair around to more fully face him. She tossed the half-eaten muffin back on the desk, where it lay in its bag in crumpled dejection.

"Don't get me started on who is hurting the worst here," Matt mumbled, unable to look away from the pale blue eyes he adored. "New Mexico, is it? With a midway weekend break as usual, likely. I suppose Josh will fly home to get measured for the second round of Jacob Ryan nuptials."

"Yep. The film wraps before the wedding, and shortly after that Josh will be expected in Calgary for season two of *Sacred Peace*. Which makes me sick just thinking about it, after last year…and now…" Jessie sank lower into her chair. "I'll work with Ulysses and Arnie to sort out our household move. And with Charles too, when he's not up to his eyeballs schooling Charlie on all the funding paperwork."

"I'll stay." Crossing one ankle over the opposite knee, Matt raised his chin and challenged his wary superstar. "Arnie can go work on his tan."

"Sure. You and me can make pizza for the kids and practice being parents in case Morgan gets his grimy hands on my husband. By extension, of course, since Morgan'll be hiring someone entirely unknown to us to do the dirty work. Oh, you and I should probably throw a few practice rolls in the hay in there too, in mine and Josh's bed, if you like, just so you can figure out the bounce of the mattress and how it affects that thrusting motion you do so well."

"Jessie, you're crossing a line. Shut the hell up before you—"

"You might want to check out the echo in our bedroom too, Matt. It's got a different ring from the spare bedroom. There's only so loud you can grunt and moan before you wake up Dylan next door. Light sleeper." She waved an arm distractedly in the air. "Jacob's kid, you know. The sensitive type. Needs to be held when the shaking of our bed disrupts his beauty sleep."

"Jesus Christ, you spoiled bitch. Drop it, your highness, before I—"

That was the last straw, the final proverbial nail in the coffin Jessie had pictured her husband in from the time Matt first told her Morgan might have some association with the attacks on Josh. She couldn't take anymore, no more trying to be strong for Josh, who was going to do his own thing anyway, and no more watching Matt's eyes swim and his heart crumble every time Jessie was in his company. She knew damn well this new twist—Josh taking the film—would spiral them all in new and frightening, stressful directions.

"Oh, fuck, Matt," she moaned, and did what her soul ached for. Jessie stood suddenly, startling Matt, who had meandered off into his own set of worries infused with a new round of planning Josh's security on the film. Jessie zipped around the desk in a few short steps and landed in Matt's arms, sideways on his lap with her pink lips buried in his neck, and both slender arms circled around his tough shoulders.

"Ahh," she sighed when she was there, before puffing up her cheeks on the next inhale and letting the air escape with a grateful *ppuuuhhh*. "Sweet Jesus, Matt, I can't do this without you. I can't do all this worrying and fretting and cursing and swearing at Josh under my breath without you by my side, cursing back at me. I'm so glad you're here."

Matt held her close before gently pushing her away so he could peer into the eyes he was certain would be laced with fatigue and anxiety. "Sweet girl," he started, resorting to an endearment that felt right all of a sudden, "let him go if that's what he wants. Josh is a wild stallion raring for a place to run. Maybe he thinks that by staying busy he can outrun the fear, I don't know. I'll talk to Arnie and Charles and we'll do what we can to keep an eye on him. But Jessie…if you want me to stay here with you and the kids, I'll stay."

"You're hoping I'll say yes."

"Mmm." The hope in his eyes dimmed. "But girl, you know me." His voice dropped. "I'll do whatever you ask."

"Then you'll be packing shorts, Matt. Although just so you know, you're way sexier in jeans."

Her attempt to inject humor worked. Matt tossed back his head and laughed. Drawing her face to him so they were nose to nose, he kissed the lips he dreamed about when perfect memories woke him at three a.m. The kiss was long and tender, Jessie's lips still tasting of the ubiquitous coffee she drank like a drug. In the end, both sighed and pulled away together, but they held hands and let their foreheads touch until Charles' steps down the hall suggested quick, last, sorry looks and painful farewells.

Jessie's final words crushed Matt more than the aching longing he kept, for the most part, buried in his soul. "Keep him safe for me, Matt. Please. I'm begging you." Charles was there before Jessie got the chance to add, "He promised to watch over you, too. For me."

Matt turned his head away when Charles strode in.

He let Jessie give the Keating boss the good news.

Chapter Seven

"And last but not least, don't be texting pictures of snakes. I don't want to know that either of you is close enough to any kind of snake—long, short, round, skinny, lethal, or not—to get a good picture of one. Y'hear?"

"Wussy east coast Canadian girl," Josh teased, but the lighthearted jibe fell flat. Jessie was scowling.

Arms crossed, she was standing at the base of the steps leading up and into the Keating jet, trying with all her might to hold herself together as two of the men she loved most in the world were about to embark on what she felt was a dangerous, unnecessary mission. Her attempt to joke about snakes wasn't fooling Matt or her husband. Both were watching her warily for signs of an imminent breakdown. Thankfully, trying to keep the three Sawyer children from running into the path of the airport crew was enough of a distraction to, if not dispel Jessie's tears entirely, at least pretend they were aimed, in frustration, at the kids.

The air was damp and cool today, what Jessie's grandmother or old P.E.I. George would call soft. A lingering whispery breeze after three days of brittle, hard wind out of the north lightened the ominous parting. Fortunately it helped deplete the Hitchcockian mood that had stalked the Keating-Sawyer camp since the cruel moment Morgan's unwelcome name was once again uttered. A tempestuous, bitter wind would only have raised the bar higher and higher on this already difficult day.

"Dylan! Damn it, Josh, would you grab him before he runs himself underneath one of those god-awful big tires?"

Josh gave Jessie a hard look before he moved to grab Dylan. Normally she wouldn't ask him to go after their wild youngster. Instead, Jessie would grumble but go chasing after Dylan herself. Clearly she needed a few moments alone with Matt who, like Josh, was posed in front of Jessie listening to her lecture on the highs and lows of potential New Mexico hazards ("Don't be stubborn, sunscreen was invented for a purpose") while wholeheartedly avoiding what they were all really nervous about, which was just how far Morgan's tentacles could reach. Worse, the impending separation had been eating at all of them over the past few days, in choice snipes and militant orders barked at each other and at the children who, now, were running circles around the three adults in a gleeful game of tag that burned off some of the kids' own anxieties but which stressed their parents out more.

Instead of lashing out at his son, Josh grabbed him when he ran by, wrapped him up in his big arms, crouched in a squat, and swung him back and forth between his legs as Dylan yelped with unbridled glee. David came running over and tagged Dylan on the arm, but the good-natured youngest Sawyer only laughed and lifted his legs and demanded that his father swing him higher. Emily-Grace stalked over to them and, from what Jessie could see by Josh's tense shoulders and their daughter's angry frown, righteously told all three guys how tag is meant to be played.

Jessie turned back to Matt. "Do you see those kids, Matt?" The words passed through quivering lips.

He raised his chin and studied her—the faintly pink cheeks, the indignant pose, the parted feet that, to Matt, signified a fretful worry, while at the same time telegraphed strength he sometimes wondered if Jessie even knew she had. "I see them," he told her, forcing his hands to remain firmly in the pockets of his leather jacket. Matt was securely burying his own raw trepidation at leaving Jessie and the kids behind, or at least he thought so. The dark sunglasses propped up on his nose were meant to mask the enduring burden Matt carried, that his sensitive eyes always gave away. The smoky lenses were designed to fortify Jessie's faith in him as Josh's protector, but his superstar charge knew her security friend well. Matt wasn't hiding a damn thing.

"Well," Jessie choked, "despite the little princess' constant rage and apparent disappointment in everything her daddy does, she needs the old man. David has to have him around because without his redneck father Emily-Grace will ensure he never learns about engines and car kits, and Dylan needs Josh because, well, he quite simply is lost without his arms around his big strong daddy's neck."

As are you, Matt thought. *My lost little girl, always trying to heal the world while it just breaks you down. You need those strong arms too.* Out loud he said, while raising a hand to salute her to try to ease the dread in Jessie's cloudy eyes, "Sunscreen. Nothing less than 50 SPF." He wrinkled his nose. "Is that still acceptable?"

"I don't know what's acceptable anymore, Matt. Wear sunscreen, don't wear sunscreen. Who the hell knows where cancer really comes from, anyway? For all we know, we smear it on our skin every time we supposedly apply protection."

"Listen." Shooting Josh a sideways look to make sure he was still occupied with refereeing the kids, Matt planted his feet more securely and grasped Jessie's elbows. "The shoot will fly by. Enjoy your time with those kids while you have them to yourself. They're healthy and happy, and soon the move back to Alberta for *Sacred Peace* will throw everyone back into a tailspin."

At her panicked look he shook his head. "No, Jessie. I mean the move itself, how busy you will be. That's what I meant. A new school for the kids, the ranch, a new routine."

"A new barn," she grimaced.

"A bigger one, your obstinate husband says. So he can fit in a stall for a Dylan-sized pony."

"Oh, is that what Josh says?" The worry lines shooting out from the corners of Jessie's eyes deepened noticeably. "Lovely. Just lovely."

"You've got a wedding to help plan, too, girl. Kayla and you will be so into it, with Dee overseeing the whole thing, I hear, that you won't even notice the time flying by. Josh will be home before you know it, underfoot and leaving the toilet seat up just to piss you off."

"Damn him." But the words were soft, the tenderness underneath them sweet and infused with the gentle love Matt knew Jessie reserved for Josh, and only for Josh. "The dork," she added lightly, uncrossing her arms and wrapping them around Matt. "You too," she murmured into his neck. "You'll be home before I know it too, right? Bossing me around and undressing me with those handsome gray eyes of yours."

A heavy sigh right from the toes of Matt's leather boots passed through him. His warm breath escaped in a tender kiss on the ear Josh couldn't see. "I don't undress you with my eyes, Jessie. You promised me we could try to work together in a way that's comfortable for me. Needling me with those kinds of comments are like poking the bear, as they say. You have to stop."

"I can't help it if every time I look at you my heart splinters into a thousand pieces, Matt. I can't help it if I'm as worried about you as I am about Josh." Leaning back, Jessie lifted his sunglasses and lost herself in the dewy hazel-gray eyes peeking back at her. "Honey, don't think I don't know the toll we take on you. I know you're scared, of how you and I feel about each other, about this whole crazy New Mexico shoot, of Morgan's capacity to hurt us. And Matt…I know that what you're scared of the most is of letting me down. Of something happening to…" She swallowed and rallied with a stronger voice that for some reason still came out raspy and unsure, despite Jessie's effort to give it depth. "To Josh. But I want you to know that I release you from that. From sole responsibility for his safety. Because, Matt," she added, placing a finger on his mouth to quell the rising tide of defense she saw coming as he parted his lips to speak, "because I know that none of us are capable of something only God can do. We're all just human, you included. There are so many holes around film shoots that there is no way you can fully protect him. I know that. He knows that."

Bubbles of uncertainty filtered up to the surface of Matt's searching eyes. He wished he could pull the sunglasses back down over them, over the difficult feelings he was unable to hide from this obstinate woman to whom he had devoted a good portion of his adult life. But as it was, the hard emotions floated across and through them like troubled ghosts, their haunting of his soul complete, embedding themselves in his spirit like fishhooks.

"Stop it," Jessie demanded, wiping her thumb across the lips that had once kissed her with a passion and an intimacy that even now made her body sizzle with remembrance. "I can read you, you know. I know what you're thinking, and I don't like it."

Matt settled his gaze on Josh before he responded, his voice gravelly and unsure. Josh was still busy with the kids, intentionally giving Matt and Jessie a few moments to collect their wits and say what needed to be said before the imminent parting. Matt looked back at Jessie and smoothed a loose wisp of hair away from her frightened eyes. "He's a good man," he said with a gentle authority. "The man you chose. He's a good man, Jessie."

"So are you, you dork. Don't do anything stupid, Matt. No more," she gulped, "jumping in front of bullets." But even as the loathsome words escaped her lips, in her heart Jessie knew that not only would Matt do that for Josh if it came down to it, but she would also expect him to.

It was his job.

"Oh, God," she breathed, almost sinking to her knees, knowing as the thought had crossed her face that Matt, too, recognized what was required of him. "Matt…" His name was a whisper on the wind, a prayer on loan from time.

"It's okay," he told her, shoving her hands away from his body, from his soul. "I get it, kid." Holding Jessie's wrists, gripping them tightly, Matt pushed away the agony of not being able to hold her, to soothe her worries, the way he longed to. He trembled at the memory—no, the need—of holding the small, strong arms above her head as she lay on her back on his big bed; of succumbing to Jessie's whining, begging *please please pleases* as she writhed beneath him, naked, her eyes half-lidded with desire and with the desperate ache for him to go inside her; to release her from the need to climax, to clench her body around him. To…set them both free of the constant lust that dogged them from the night when everything changed, in Brussels, when Jessie's game went too far and she stripped in front of him before she got in the shower.

She, too, felt the power of their unremitting attraction, and quivered. "Oh, God," she whispered again, and took a step backward. "Go, Matt," she demanded. "Please. Just go."

He held on, gripping her wrists tighter, his lips thinning as he pushed the tension there and into his jaw, which tightened and tensed as a pulse started in his neck.

The way Matt was looking at Jessie now, with a confused mixture of desire and power, unnerved Josh, who let go of Dylan long enough for the little boy to sprint off down the tarmac. Emily-Grace growled at her father and ran after Dylan. Josh stood and stared at Matt and Jessie; he was incapable of looking away. Jessie's lips moved, but Josh couldn't hear what she said. Still, the hardened, damp sheen in her eyes gave her away.

"Go down to New Mexico and find yourself a whore, Matt," was what she was saying. "Better yet, I'll book one for you. Will that do the trick? Or, I know, maybe there's a female grip on the crew. That worked for Jacob all through *Mystic Nights*. You wouldn't have to pay the crew for sex. Oh! I almost forgot. The way I heard it from Josh on *Freedom Ride*, the girls from hair and makeup are usually keen to go for a roll."

"Jesus, Jessie. You never give up, do you?"

"Put it this way, Matt. You have my blessing to do whatever the hell you want—or need—to do, to make this work." She yanked a wrist out of his grasp. "Hell, find a goddamned fur-lined hole, for all I care, if that's what you need to do to get by. But please, baby, please…don't leave us. Don't leave…me."

But save Josh first. The unspoken statement put a whole new chill on the light morning breeze. *Go fuck whoever I want,* thought Matt, *you won't give a damn, as long as your husband makes it safely home.*

Jessie's voice was small when she spoke again. "You know I love you, Matt. Please tell me you know how I feel about you."

"I know," he said softly, letting go of Jessie's other wrist. "I know how you feel about me."

But what he was telling her was not, in truth, what Jessie wanted to hear. What she needed to hear. And she knew it. She could read Matt as well as she could read her husband, and the verity of his statement cut her to the core. Jessie gasped, and bent over double.

Josh strode darkly over, and glared at Matt as Matt backed away. He grasped Jessie's elbow and steered her more completely away from him, but Jessie watched Matt stomp up the steps to the jet. She didn't take her eyes off of him until he ducked through the doorway, handed his leather messenger bag to Victoria, and disappeared.

"All right," Josh growled as he studied Jessie's flushed cheeks and watery eyes. "What the hell did he say to you? Or better yet, what did you say to him?"

"Oh, Josh," Jessie crumbled. "Just take care of each other, will you? Go rock this film and watch your goddamned back. And his. Please."

"Uh huh." Josh rocked back on a boot heel and swiped a hand over the coarse stubble on his jaw. He softened. "I'll bring him home, little one," he promised. "We'll be back before you know it, safe and sound."

"Okay, then." Jessie took a deep breath and stood a little taller. Behind Josh she could see Dan scooping up Dylan, who had stumbled on the tarmac and, judging by the way he was howling, skinned his knee. Emily-Grace was consoling her baby brother while David watched, appropriately concerned. Jessie's eyes flicked back to Josh as she started to walk toward her crying child in Big Dan's capable arms. "Find him a woman too, will you Josh? Preferably one with a load of tattoos and an insatiable need for sex. And maybe an occasional cigarette habit for those late night post-coital snuggles underneath those big, open, Albuquerque skies. Just do me a favor? When Matt's satisfying himself in some willing woman's bed, stay alone in your own, okay? The bar fridge in your suite will be empty, I asked Hilary to take care of that, and I told your beloved French Canadian director myself that I expect you and him to swap film tales over steaks and virgin Caesars every night after wrap. In the safety of his suite or yours, not out in an open dining room when Matt's off fucking his little honeys."

At that, Jessie swept Dylan up in her arms, buried her face in his curls, and wiped her tears on his T-shirt. It was a quick motion because, as usual, Dylan cried for his daddy and leapt into his arms the moment a very puzzled Josh was at his side. By the time they got Dylan's knee tended and bandaged, thanks to a vigilant Victoria and her on-jet first aid kit, it was time to say goodbye.

Matt did not leave the jet to say a second farewell—a half one was enough on this pliable, soft day when everyone's emotions were as tight as guitar strings waiting to be plucked. But he watched Josh and Jessie say goodbye until he could bear their hushed voices and Jessie's tears no longer.

Before he turned his head away from the window, though, he saw Jessie's eyes pass up to him, over her husband's shoulder; saw her touch her eye, gesture toward her heart, and brush her lips with two fingers before floating them outwards. *I love you.*

She loves me. How and when, in a physical sense, all of a sudden didn't matter. All that mattered in that instant was that, despite Matt's job as Josh's shadow on the New Mexico shoot, there were hard and true feelings between himself and the wife of the man whose life was in his hands. The feelings would never, could never, trump Jessie's love for Josh. Even if Josh were dead, a part of Jessie would just disappear with him.

But she loves me too. Physical needs aside, the knowledge and Jessie's little gesture were chock full of meaning and comfort.

She's right, I can find myself a body to hold, Matt thought as Josh finally leapt up the few stairs and darkened the jet's doorway. *I can find myself a way to deal. We can do this. Like in the Caribbean with Jacob, living on the sailboat, it won't be enough…but it will ease the ache, at least.*

Josh stood at the front of the small jet and eyed Matt carefully. "It's you and me now, buddy," he finally said, as the doors to the jet were closed and, outside, Jessie and the kids walked across the tarmac, ably guided and watched over by Dan. They would lean against the SUV and watch the jet float off into the fluffy clouds of this light breezy, weighty Vancouver morning.

"I guess it is," answered Matt, forcing his eyes on Josh, forcing himself to try to lighten up, to forget the sadness and longing in Jessie's eyes; the worry and the hope that, despite what she said to him, was still there, in her soul. *For me.*

It was a helluva load to bear, trying to protect a man who, when all was said and done, was really just simply, plainly, in the way.

Chapter Eight

"You can't text that picture to Jessie. She'll lose her mind."

Josh was laughing so hard that he had to circle around a few times to regain control before he could speak. "She'll be mad for a minute," he hooted. "My girl gets over shit quickly. Hold still," he demanded, his sides shaking. "Don't be moving, Matt. You don't want to startle the thing."

"Startle the thing?" Matt was losing it in a completely opposite way. "You're startling the thing. It's already doing that defensive, protective rearing thing the wrangler told us about. Josh, get back. You're too damn close."

One of the older guys on the local crew, a bearded salt and pepper haired prop master, was calmly leaning back against the ass end of his dusty pickup, watching the two Canadians angle for positions near—or away from, in Matt's case—a five and a half foot long bull snake the crew'd haphazardly discovered when they were setting up, in long grass, a large twenty by twenty silk meant to soften the light for filming.

"It's not venomous," the guy told Matt. "No reason to be concerned." To the prop master, an indigenous man known to the cast and crew as Joe Kid, Matt was far too GQ to be on this shoot in the first place. The guy looked like he'd never seen a snake in his life. Joe Kid would have been much more impressed by Matt if he actually believed the rumors that the guy'd once taken a bullet to the shoulder in order to save Jessie Wheeler-Sawyer.

Now Josh—that guy deserved respect. The actor was probably a little too close to the snake, but taking a pic to send to his wife meant sneaking in just a foot or two closer to get a clear, focused shot. Eyeing Matt, though, Joe discerned real concern. He recrossed his ankles and nodded at Josh. "You might wanna step back," he suggested in a blasé kind of way. "If you're a little less threatening, you'll get a good picture of a non-moving snake and not give your security here a coronary."

"Might not kill you, but those things still bite, Josh." Matt had a moment when he wondered whether protecting Josh from huge motherfucking bull snakes was in his contract. The big snake read his mind. It coiled its thick, reddish-brown blotched yellow body up a little tighter and focused its beady eyes on Matt with an 'I dare you' stare. Matt inadvertently took another step backward.

"What I'm gonna do," Josh grinned as his eyes literally shone, "is text Jessie that I was watching over you, for a change. Look here." He spun around and grabbed a shot of Matt nervously eyeballing the snake. "No more Matt the hero. Matt's actually afraid of stuff. Who knew."

The mischievous, playful light in Josh's expression suddenly dropped away like melting ice. Matt didn't have to know what Josh was thinking. It was obvious. They were all afraid of stuff. It was nice to have briefly forgotten...

Watching, Joe Kid wondered what had come over the actor and his security.

Shortly, one of the show's producers wandered up and cornered Matt just as an A.D. called Josh to set. Ferne MacAvoy hitched up her olive green Columbia hiking pants before she bent over to tie up a stray lace on a leather boot. As Josh jogged over to the shooting set and met up with Marc, the director, she asked Matt how his actor was doing.

"Fine," was Matt's brief response. *Happiest I've seen him in a while,* he intoned to himself as he watched Josh and Marc exchange greetings.

"To the production, he's an enigma," Ferne said honestly. "We all expected a dark, brooding mystery man who keeps to himself. This guy," she waved at Josh, "is having a great time out here under the big sun. I have to tell you, Matt, Marc had to fight me and the other producers in order to get him. One of the producers on *The Wyatt Boys* warned me to stay the hell away from casting Josh."

"Josh is happiest when he's working, Ferne." Matt took a sideways peek at the powerful producer at his side. Ferne was lovely—all apple-cheeked and dimpled, and the way her blonde hair was tucked into the black ball cap she wore to protect herself from the desert sun was absolutely adorable. As a successful film producer, there was no doubt she was tough as nails— but Matt hardly cared. Eyeing her now, he wondered if she had a partner…

Beyond Ferne, the snake sensed freedom from curious onlookers as the crew settled into their work in the field beyond. The big creature also sensed heat in the asphalt, and slowly started to slither away toward the center of the narrow road past the hood of Joe Kid's truck. Idly, Joe watched it go but he stayed tuned into the conversation Matt and Ferne were cautiously skating around.

"He must miss his wife and kids."

"They're in touch. He's about to text her a picture of that snake, though. That'll no doubt put him on her bad side for a couple of days."

Ferne did a double take. "The famous Jessie Wheeler's scared of snakes? That actually surprises me. Didn't she live in Charleston for a while? Snakes are common in the south."

Matt jumped on that. After all, defending Jessie was his forte. "Jessie's not scared of much, Ferne. I doubt she's actually afraid of snakes. But that doesn't mean she wants them in her direct company or too close to her husband."

"She's very protective of him." The pronouncement came without judgment or any kind of edge. Ferne seemed like a reasonable, straight thinking woman, as far as Matt could tell. "I've heard that about the two of them. I read about all the trouble they've had. I guess they need to give each other shelter from the storm, as they say."

"Unfortunately." Matt wasn't really willing to get into the ins and outs of the threats that seemed to be constantly dogging the Sawyers. Stretching, he arched his back so he could peek behind Ferne and the truck to see where the bull snake had gotten to. He could just make out its slow moving back end as it sluggishly glided across the road. Visibly, Matt relaxed.

"You scared of snakes, Matt?" Ferne raised her eyebrows and crossed her arms. A sweet, almost shy blush arced across the tops of her dimpled cheeks as she wondered what else she ought to find out about the attractive man at her side.

"Should I be?"

"There are forty some types of snakes in New Mexico," Ferne offered helpfully. "Less than a dozen are venomous. And even those don't generally bite unless they're cornered. Besides," she explained with a wry twist of a lip, "we've got snake bite kits on the production. As long as we treat you in the first five minutes, you'll survive. Maybe," she added with a lighthearted laugh.

On set, Josh was casually standing with his back to Matt, both thumbs hooked in his front jeans pockets, and one booted ankle turned over sideways. A few crew were gathered around him, all smiling, laughing, joking, all cheerful and happy. Marc tapped him on the elbow and Josh had a good chuckle at something he said.

"It's good to see him relaxed like this." Matt didn't even realize he'd spoken aloud until Joe, who had just been beckoned to set, wandered up behind him.

"A lot of the vibe on set comes from the actors," Joe said as he strolled by. "Josh Sawyer's one of the good guys. He's well liked here. This is a good film to be working on." Joe continued on through the knee-high grass until he met up with the rest of the crew. He whistled as he walked, but Matt noticed that he swished a long snake-hunting stick along before him as he moved.

Matt pointed nonchalantly at him. "Joe Kid's a good fella. He didn't blink an eye at that snake. I thought he might grab a rifle and shoot him or something. The snake, I mean," he muttered almost incoherently, catching his breath and wondering what he himself might have done had the props man actually hauled out a rifle earlier, in such close proximity to Josh. Working in the States was a whole other ball game to working in Canada. Guns, almost visibly nonexistent in Canada, were far too prevalent down here.

"Bull snakes sometimes get mistaken for rattlers, and they are often, I'm sad to say, destroyed," Ferne clarified. "It's a tragedy, Matt. A snake like that one is virtually harmless. People sometimes get the wrong idea."

"Kinda like they do about other people, I suppose."

"Some people are simply hard to read." Taking a chance, Ferne turned her body toward Matt and laid a graceful hand on his arm. Shivering at the solid muscle she found underneath, she lit up. "Hey, your actor's got eyes on him here, Matt." She pointed out several assorted black-uniformed security that were watching the perimeter of the set. Lowering her voice, she almost purred. "Why don't you and I head back into the air conditioned comfort of our hotel and have a drink?"

Thrown, Matt took a closer, longer look at the producer. Even in her outdoor hiking clothes, worn for the comfort of a long day on a film set, she really was quite attractive. He glanced at Josh—who was vibrating, he was so jubilantly keyed up—and took a second scan around at the security team the production had kindly co-hired with Charles Keating to help keep an eye on their actor. Something in Matt's hard body stirred and he couldn't help but think how nice it would be to have a lady to 'play' with during this shoot. *Heck, I sure as hell ain't gettin' any in Vancouver,* he thought. *And she's obviously willing.*

A slow smile erased a bit of the earlier tension over the snake. "How much longer do you think Josh will be today?" he asked.

"You can't leave him, huh?" She was one of Hollywood's top producers, but Ferne stuck out a lip and pouted.

Jessie swept into Matt's mind and out again when he spied a very feminine fuchsia bra strap peeking out from underneath Ferne's scoop necked T-shirt. *Is that lace? I see lace.* Silently, he groaned. "Nope. I really can't. I made a promise. But this is Josh's last scene today, right?"

"He may want to stay out here and watch the rest of the shooting."

"He won't have a choice. Josh has gotten used to room service." Matt's smile grew large again as the anticipation of a night in this pleasant woman's company edged toward possibility.

"Room service. Why do I like the sound of that?" Hooking an arm around Matt's elbow, Ferne nudged her toned, curvy body closer.

"Here's to getting this scene in as quickly as possible."

"Go, Josh, go. He know his lines?"

"Hell, yeah. The guy's a pro."

"Thank God for Josh."

Inwardly, Matt had a good roar. "Yeah," he said with a growing eagerness for the shooting to get underway, "thank God for Josh."

On set, Josh and Joe Kid had a good laugh about something, before Josh followed Marc to his first position at the top of the scene. When he got there, Josh looked over at Matt to see where he had settled to watch the filming. Nobody was more surprised than him to see Ferne MacAvoy's slender arm tucked around Matt's elbow, and a wide smile creasing Matt's face.

Well, well, Josh thought with a grin, *looks like good old Matt might be hooking up. He might just start enjoying this shoot after all.* Under his breath he added audibly, "Which means that so will I, although Jessie might not be as equally thrilled."

Josh had to wait a minute for lighting tweaks before the rehearsal for camera would be called. Slipping his cellphone out of his back pocket to hand it to an A.D. to give to Matt—he'd forgotten to leave it with him, and his character in the film didn't have a cellphone on him at the moment— he paused before handing it over, and opened his text messaging instead. Tossing a roguish grin toward Matt, who was watching him, Josh poked at the phone, and sent the photo of the snake catapulting through space and time to land on Jessie's iPhone.

He handed the cell off to the A.D., who hustled it over to Matt for safe-keeping during the filming.

Both guys were fairly certain they heard Jessie scream all the way from Vancouver a few seconds later. But it was Matt who intercepted the reply on Josh's phone.

"What'd she say?" Josh hollered happily to Matt. They still weren't shooting. Looked like it would be a long scene.

"One word. Hissssssssterical." Matt's laughter was infectious. "Lots of s's." After tilting the phone sideways to show Ferne, who sent Josh a good-on-ya thumbs-up, he held it up toward Josh, snapped a pic, and started typing back a reply.

"Uh, no you don't," Josh called from twenty feet away, suddenly panicked. "Give me back that phone. I don't trust you."

The First A.D. gave him a nasty look that translated to *cool it, church voices on set,* before calling out, "First positions, everybody!"

"Shit." Throwing Matt a playful dirty look, Josh settled into position and sent a happy grin tumbling off in Joe Kid's direction. "I might have to move to New Mexico," he declared, and pointed a thumb toward the phone in Matt's hand. "My wife's gonna divorce me for sending her the picture of the snake."

"She's never seen a snake before?" Joe was blown away. He'd lived with snakes his entire life. Hell, they used to follow him to school when he was a kid.

"She's seen plenty," Josh told him, as he eyed the camera operator to see if he was ready behind the lens. "Just most of them had two feet and a heartbeat. And they were a helluva lot more dangerous than that old bull snake on the road."

"Ah." Joe was finally starting to understand the dynamic that seemed to take both Josh's and Matt's moods up hills and down valleys. "Maybe you ought to keep the snake pics to yourself. Maybe she's the kind of lady don't need the reminder."

Never thought of it that way, Josh thought, as he mumbled a humble, quiet, "Thanks," in Joe's direction.

Watching, Matt tapped *send* on the phone, but what he sent to Jessie wasn't some off-the-cuff retort designed to get Josh in trouble. Instead, when she got the message, Jessie would know instantly that Matt was holding onto Josh's phone while he was shooting, and thus had control of Josh's texts. What Matt sent was a snapshot of a happy, beaming man at the top of his game thrilled to be working on a film that already had Oscar buzz, under the big open skies of the rugged, warm New Mexican landscape.

Matt tucked the cell away just as the director called, "Action!"

Late that afternoon, Josh relaxed in his suite for a few good hours of script studying, television and room service, while Matt got rather raunchily serviced in his.

Somewhere that night near the day's exterior shooting set, a young man mistook Josh's brave, unthreatening, regal bull snake for a rattlesnake, and shot it dead.

Chapter Nine

"Arnie is supposed to come," Charles said in frustration to Jessie a few weeks later, after he stormed down the hallway at La Casa and ushered her into his study. "Arnie's got the harder crust. Matt's too damned soft for this trip." The harsh way he set his jaw and avoided Jessie's surprised stare gave far more away than his actual words did.

Frowning, Jessie ducked aside when Charles reached to the door behind her and gave it a hard push. It didn't close—Matt intercepted it, his dress shoes clicking on the floor, demanding and terse, even as he walked into the heartbeat of Charles' existence at La Casa—the study where Charles spent most of his time working, despite his advancing age, an age when he should be slowing down instead of speeding up.

Matt slammed the door. Spinning around to look at him behind her, Jessie glared. She too was, at least for the moment, on Charles' side.

When did I become so damned protective of Matt, she wondered. *When did I lose my faith in his ability to do his job with a detached perspective?* She didn't have to answer her own question. Brussels sprang to mind at the same moment her eyes dampened and softened. Jessie turned back to Charles, but it was Matt's voice that filled the room, and his steady grip on her elbow that guided her toward the leather sofa lining the west wall. She tossed him off but didn't look at him.

"I don't want to sit!" she cried, spinning back around to face both men. They waited, but Charles' face was blooming red, and the corners of Matt's lips were turned down. To Jessie, Charles seemed about as ready to burst as a blood red overripe cherry tomato. Matt just looked ready to cry.

Raising her hands, Jessie forced both palms gently downward, as if some invisible energy were there to push on. "Look," she said in a voice she hoped both men would interpret as matter-of-fact and calm, despite the inferno raging in her belly, "it's a good thing the kids—well, two of them, anyway—" she grimaced, remembering Emily-Grace's insistence on having a sleepover at Stella's tonight, "are so excited to see their father, because they've got him preoccupied. I don't want Josh knowing about this. Okay? He doesn't need to know where at least two of the Keating heathens will be spending a good chunk of their Saturday."

"He's stronger than you think, Jessie," Charles ascertained, striding toward the sofa Jessie refused to sit on, and dropping heavily down onto one of its wide arms.

"None of you are as damned strong as you make yourselves out to be," Jessie interjected sharply, finally letting her troubled gaze rest on Matt, who visibly deflated under her careful scrutiny. "Especially Josh."

Nobody spoke. The only sound in the room came from under the door leading to the main hallway, and it was the exact opposite of the crackling tension in Charles' hallowed interior chamber. From the other side, distant laughter was heard, the sound of children in ecstasy, being tickled, hugged, and cherished by a father they hadn't seen for almost three weeks.

They'd been outside, all of them, in the back of the pretty Spanish villa, sliding down the gardener's lane on new sleds Sam bought for the kids at some big box store. The kids had been wound up tight waiting for their father to arrive home from his shoot on a mid-production weekend break, and outside under the early evening stars seemed like the only reasonable place to wait—the only place capable of containing their effusive youthful vitality. When Josh and Matt arrived, not dressed for the weather, but happy to be outside just the same, both of the young Sawyer boys were injected with even more energy, as if the sun itself had hovered above them and filled them with its vital source.

Sam had been outside with the family, as surely a member of the Sawyer and Keating clans now as Matt and Dan. With him was Alin, but they were both distracted since googly eyes were floating back and forth between the two, and Jessie was fairly certain she was the only one who'd noticed. She'd have to think on that later, though, as to whether it was something to be concerned about, or something to celebrate. For now she had Matt and Charles to worry about—they had both been outside for a little while, one moping and sulking, and the other standing next to an empty Sakura tree with his shoulders back and his stance rigid. When Matt finally opened the back door to La Casa and glared at Charles to come inside, Jessie had begged off the fun of slipping and sliding down the small, narrow slope with her much missed husband and two of their children. She did it by citing a pee break—too much coffee, she said—and went inside to find two of the men responsible for her family's safety fiercely firing angry words back and forth.

"What the hell?" she had said to the men, at first surprised and controlled, and then again, with a fierce intensity that matched the building tension in her body. Throwing herself between them before fists started flying, Jessie cried, "Jesus, Matt! He's had a goddamned heart attack! Relax!"

The subject of their brawl was, as Charles admitted between gritted teeth when he ushered her to the study, Arnie.

"Why not Ulysses?" Jessie asked now in the office after Charles told her he was flying to Brody River Penitentiary in the morning. "Take Ulysses. His corner of the sandbox is neutral." Her heart was pounding. Morgan… they were going to see Morgan. Part of her wanted to stow away in the jet with them, or at least be a fly on the wall at Brody Pen, but the other part of her decided she'd already spent way too much time away from her husband on account of Morgan. Months, in fact, and that didn't even include the long days spent locked in the Langley basement.

Matt…the way he was looking at her now, with those gentle eyes and hurt gaze, the way he kept swallowing and looking away and then back again… the fact was, Jessie would do anything to protect him.

And he knew it.

He raised a finger now and cocked his head as he faced her. "No," he demanded. There was no need to explain what the 'no' referenced. All three of them were well aware that because of Jessie's position as Charles' sort of daughter and, really, his superstar, she had a lot of power. If she insisted on Matt staying behind, he would stay. But he didn't want to. Matt needed to see Morgan. He needed to look the guy in the eye and read his thoughts. He needed to know whether Morgan was once again playing a vicious game that threatened Jessie's husband. Matt needed some clarity so he would know which direction to go, where to look, how to organize and supervise security for the vulnerable Sawyer family. What he didn't need was to be left out of what he felt was likely one of the most important conversations—if they could even get Morgan to speak—he would have all year.

So far on the New Mexico shoot not a thing was out of the ordinary. In terms of security, the production was as cooperative as it could be, and the man Matt escorted home to Jessie this evening was the happiest Matt had seen him in a very long time. Josh thrived on work, on taking on characters that weren't himself, on burying himself in fictional lives that only had the capacity to hurt him on a fractional level, as if he himself lived in one dimension, and the characters he played lived in other, more distant worlds. The sounds coming from the kitchen now, where the clan was starting to gather for some of Carlotta's homemade, thick marshmallow topped hot chocolate, was proof. Teasing and joyful, Josh's voice rose above the rest.

It saddened Matt to see tears threatening Jessie's eyes now. She didn't deserve this, to know this trip was happening tomorrow. What she deserved was an untainted weekend with a confident, safe, contented husband.

Charles' voice brought Matt back to the issue at hand. "Ulysses has been with Deirdre for too long, Jessie."

"I get it," she retorted, tossing her curls for effect and absently unzipping her black North Face jacket with one quick motion at the same time. "Arnie's tough as nails. He's my Downtown Eastside guy, the guy who knows where the guns are when he needs 'em." Both Matt and Charles blanched at the callous reminder of a difficult past they all preferred to forget. Jessie went on, pointing to Matt as she spoke, but eyeballing Charles' stiff jaw and clenched teeth. "And Matt's the guy who left the R.C.M.P. because he couldn't handle what he was forced to see. Meaning the awful things people do to each other."

Steaming, Matt was about to erupt again, and go up one side of Jessie and down the other, when Jessie bit her lip, ducked her head, and peered up at him from underneath long eyelashes now damp with worry. Charles, too, recognized the depth of pain buried deeply in those hurting eyes, and so he stepped between them. His voice was calmer when he spoke this time.

"I asked Arnie to come, Jessie, because Matt is too close to you. I've seen this guy at the gym," he tried to joke, pointing to Matt as he explained, "and I saw him just now with his fists raised outside in my hallway. I don't need to put him and Morgan in the same space together. I don't think there's a correctional officer in Canada capable of keeping Matt from doing to that boy what I wish I was capable of doing."

The sobering thought settled Matt to a point where he no longer saw red, where he thought he might be able to reason with Charles. Jessie was watching him now, her face quietly composed and the tears that threatened buried underneath layers of a past that had somehow given her a strength and will that eclipsed any weakness or sorrow.

"He's still the same old Morgan," she said simply, almost bringing the two men to their knees. But neither was completely surprised. As much as their former security had hurt and tried to destroy Jessie and her family, she pretty much instantly forgave him. "He's the one who lost everything," she reminded them, and corrected herself by adding, with a small wave, "every-one, I mean. He did what he did because he loved Nadia. He did it for her. You guys are going on a wild goose chase. Morgan is not capable of hurting Josh and I anymore. He never was, on his own. You'll see. You'll come back with nothing, with no answers." Part of her reasoning was said simply to calm Matt down, to make him realize that the trip to Alberta might not be all they expected it could be. To convince him to stay home, where he'd be safe from sad old memories and the potential to be hurt yet again.

Matt was thinking of the bull snake from the New Mexico shoot. Harmless. But it sure didn't look harmless. Even now, he shivered at the memory of coming across that big snake, and how close Josh got to the thing. Could Morgan be harmless? He very much doubted it.

"You're not coming, Jessie." Charles spoke with the caution he'd learned to use with Jessie over the years, when she was in this kind of mood—dangerously quiet, as if she had an alternate plan. As if she knew she would win.

"Nope," she said, hunching up her shoulders with conviction, and surprising both Charles and Matt. "I know that. I'm staying here with my family. And I'm going to sleep next to my husband with my face buried in his neck and with his hand in mine."

Matt stopped breathing and focused on the base of a lamp in the murky shadows of a semi-dark corner.

Jessie kicked him lightly in the shin. "Hey. You. Handsome."

He forced himself to look back at her.

"You've been with Josh 24-7 over the last few weeks," she said. "Take the weekend off. Let tough old Arnie go. Don't get yourself worked up for no reason."

"How can you be sure Morgan's not to blame for what's been happening to Josh?" Matt asked her. "You think everybody's redeemable, Jessie. You ought to know by now that some people just aren't."

"Oh yeah they are," she said softly. "Maybe not in this lifetime. But they'll get there."

Charles harrumphed. "If only your faith alone could save the world, Jessie. But it can't. Honey," he said a tad more gently when he saw her shoulders sag, "we can't deny that there's a Brody Pen link to what's been happening to Josh. We need to check it out. Whether or not Morgan has anything to do with it might, as you say, be completely irrelevant. At the very least, he's had some time to consider his part in what he and Nadia did. Time to think can send a man one of two ways—either deeper down a dark path, or toward some kind of remorse and regret. If your instincts about him are right, and he's not involved, then maybe he knows who is and he's ready to talk."

"All right," Jessie said quietly, and considered how to respond. In the end she acquiesced, turned a corner in her thoughts, and went with, "Then take Matt, if he really wants to go. Charles…" Jessie took his hand and gave it a tender squeeze. "Not that Arnie couldn't get the truth out of Morgan if he wanted to. In fact I'm sure he could, without too much trouble. But I think maybe Matt is the more intuitive of the two. Arnie has the street smarts, but Matt's had the training to look deeper into Morgan's eyes. And…" She sucked on a lip and pondered her next thought. When she spoke, Jessie let go of Charles' hand and took Matt's. Still sulking, he tried to pull it away, but she moved closer to him and held on tighter, and used her free hand to turn his face toward her. "You're right that Matt's the soft one. It's his heart that Morgan will respond to. Not Arnie's."

"Why?" Charles asked, absolutely certain that he did not want his good friend exposed to a man who might still have a dreadful power over all of them.

"Because," Jessie answered with a sad smile, "this man knows love."

"Arnie's got a lady," Charles argued with a knowing, nervous snap of his tie.

"Ah," Jessie sighed, still gazing into Matt's eyes.

He, too, was lost in her again. Almost three weeks away, guarding her husband, no less, and with a new woman to warm his bed, and Matt was as hopelessly lost in Jessie's aura now as he ever was. His stomach tightened and he swallowed again.

Reaching out a finger, Jessie touched his lips and then let her hand fall away. Her eyes stayed locked in his, but their color changed; they morphed from an intense, searching blue to a soft crystalline, almost liquid hue. "But this man knows heartache," she said. "He understands Morgan in a way that I hope Arnie never will."

And with that, Jessie brought the room to silence. Nobody moved—or hardly even breathed—until a hard knock at the door cued them back to the reality that Josh was home, and happy for a change; that the small boys were rosy-cheeked and wired; that everyone was healthy and robust; and that most of the made-up Keating-Sawyer clan was present and accounted for. There was a peace in knowing that Emily-Grace was happy too, under the care of Charlie and Jane, likely having a late evening snack at the moment, safe and snug inside Charlie's luxurious home in nearby Burnaby.

Josh stuck his head in the doorway. "Jessie?" he asked simply. He saw Jessie let go of Matt's fingers, and wondered about the tiny frown on her lips, but knew her well enough to discern that there was a certain peace in her eyes. Something was up, but Matt had been with Josh for the last few weeks and, despite all, Josh and Matt were still good friends. *Besides,* Josh told himself, *I'm deliriously happy. The shoot's incredible, and I'm exhausted, but my boys are here, safe and sound, and I'm getting laid by my beautiful wife tonight. Matt's not. Matt's new woman is in New Mexico.* He pushed any niggling jealousy aside and grinned at Jessie, whose eyes lit up the second she allowed herself to take him in as he stood in the doorway—all glowing sexy goodness of him, as he extended a hand, took her fingers in his, and pulled her toward him.

"I can't promise there will be any cookies and hot chocolate left if you don't come now, Jessie," he teased.

The tips of Jessie's ears crimsoned immediately. Lifting his arm, she squiggled underneath its welcoming warmth. "I'm *so* not responding to that particular wording," she said, trying to force a giggle so Josh wouldn't read anything too dark into why she was in Charles' office with two very anxious men. "At least not now," she whispered in his ear as they wandered down the hallway. "Later, though. For sure."

"Can't wait," Josh laughed. "It's been too damned long."

"And who decided to go away to shoot a movie? Huh?" A pointy finger in his ribs got an *ouch* from Josh, but he lit up and twisted Jessie's finger around behind her back. She yelped with unrestrained—but partly edged—glee, that the buoyant Josh was too happy to recognize as not entirely authentic.

Moving into the office doorway, Matt gripped the edge of the door and watched them go.

A hand clapped him on the shoulder. "She has a point, I suppose." Charles sighed, the earlier anger completely drained from his tired voice. "As much as I hate to admit it. Do you think you can keep your cool, Matt? In front of Morgan?"

"You're going to let me go with you? To Brody?" Matt turned around and leaned his back against the wall. Jessie and Josh disappeared from sight, but before Matt took his eyes off Jessie he saw her throw him a final concerned over-the-shoulder peek before she swung into the kitchen underneath Josh's arm.

"You'll probably mutiny if I don't," Charles grumbled. Striding over to the desk, he opened a drawer and took out a bottle of his favorite aged scotch. "You didn't answer my question." Pouring two fingers in each of two heavy crystal glasses, he handed one to Matt, and took a healthy sip out of the other.

Shrugging, Matt sipped too before he responded. "Depends on what Morgan has to say."

"She's right, you know." Carrying his glass, Charles started to move through the doorway, past Matt. "We may not learn a damn thing that'll help us."

"Maybe not," Matt agreed. He started to walk next to Charles, toward the sound of laughter and joy. He let his empty hand rest loosely on his boss' shoulder. Both of them were still wearing their outside jackets, and Charles' was dripping wet from an earlier snowball fight with his grandchildren. Matt didn't care. The water on Charles' coat was well earned. "Let me rephrase that," he stated carefully. "Maybe I hope not."

"You really have gone soft," Charles muttered. "You don't want Morgan to be behind this. Jessie has way too much influence over you."

"Thank God for that." With a wry grin, Matt looked sideways just in time to catch Charles' face lightening noticeably.

The older man chuckled. "Yes," he agreed warmly. "Thank God for that."

They wandered into the kitchen where David stood on his tiptoes and grabbed two freshly baked cookies. He thrust one into Matt's hand, and one into his grandfather's. "There," he announced proudly. "Now everybody's happy."

Dylan was now in Josh's arms. A wide yawn almost cracked the small child's jaw in two, and he laid his small face against his father's shoulder. Jessie leaned back against the kitchen island and ran her fingers through her son's hair. Glancing up, she met Matt's eyes but this time her smile was definitely forced. Matt took two steps backward, shifted his weight to one leg, and bit into his cookie.

Jessie looked away, let her hand fall down Dylan's neck and back to where Josh's strong arm was wrapped around his son, and slid into a high leather chair as she let her head fall sideways onto Josh's shoulder.

Charles' wet ski jacket dripped a final few drops onto the floor. Standing alone near the kitchen's perimeter, Matt listened to the family's happy hoots and hollers, but he could no more look at them than he could find it in his heart to let Arnie, instead of him, accompany Charles to Brody Pen. The next time Jessie turned around to look at him, she found only empty air. In Matt's place was only the soft, muted light that had backlit him from the hallway when he first stood alone; in Jessie's heart was the gray, lonely solitude he left behind.

Chapter Ten

"Twenty bucks a week. You're in the big time now, Morgan."

Brody River Pen's official prisoner uniform was jeans and blue shirts, meant to save Corrections Canada a few significant dollars and instill some psychological security and sense of comfort in its inmates. Needless to say, the privilege of wearing jeans didn't extend to belts.

Morgan gave the droopy butt of his jeans a pull. The movement was meant to loosen his boxers underneath as he stood up from the lunch table, but it backfired. Caulfield was standing over him. The guard interpreted the quick upward motion as the usually silent Morgan's way of telling him to fuck off.

Lifting a foot, Oren C gave his prisoner a hard shove. Everyone in the lunchroom startled when Morgan's big body crashed into a table and his tray went spinning sideways over the floor. The more nervous inmates—mostly the fish, as the newbies were known—jumped up. The seasoned vets, watched by uniformed corrections officers who barely blinked at the sound, sullenly went back to their refried beans and tacos.

Morgan avoided falling to the ground. In his mind, he was still a strongly rooted tree incapable of being pushed over by the likes of this power hungry Caulfield guy. He was a model prisoner, a positive example for the politicians who wanted results from the warden's promise to institute new rehabilitation programs that urged calm into the prison curriculum. On Tuesday mornings, Morgan did guided meditations with other inmates; on Thursdays, he practiced yoga in the common room. These earned privileges, along with his time in the gym, gave him more freedom than the standard ninety minutes a day outside his cell that being incarcerated at Brody usually earned its inmates (time that only included showers every second day, outdoor yard time, and phone calls—the latter of which was of no interest to Morgan, since there was nobody in his life he cared enough about to call). Granted by virtue of good behavior since his move to Brody Pen, the highly supervised rehab privileges were extras beyond Morgan's part-time furniture building work detail.

Without the chance to move around, Morgan would have lost his mind. Yoga, which in his pre-Brody civilian life only interested him because of how perfectly it toned his wife's butt, now rooted him. He imagined telling Jessie he now did yoga. She'd raise a finger to her lips in that questioning way Morgan knew well, and probably stand back on one leg and crook her lip up in a half-smile. In the old days, that is. In the pre-Nadia/Josh days. To Jessie, Morgan knew he was the antithesis of the kind of man who did yoga, or meditated. He was into lifting weights, not downward dogs; hell, he'd run until his iTunes playlist ran out if he could. But now? Now he could stand in tree pose for an hour without wavering, one big foot on the opposite thigh, knee pointed out to the side, arms framing his head, hands pointing upward. Eyes closed. Yoga was no longer something to ridicule. Now it was a necessary tool to salvage what little respect for life Morgan had left.

In the complicated Brody Pen subculture, Morgan was deemed dangerous by virtue of his silence. It was generally the quiet guys who broke, who finally lost all control and went on the deadly rampages that snapped bones like twigs, that had the guards reach for tear gas or tasers. Yet it was the stillness and the quiet that Morgan revered; it was the hushed tones of the yoga and meditation room that brought calm to his heart and peace to his mind. It was in the quiet that he switched the world off, when he connected to some inner source that brought healing.

Morgan's silence wasn't the boiling over kind. It was the saving kind.

Even if he was a talker, he knew better now than to focus his gaze on Brody's notorious 'fixer' and tell him what he thought of being pushed around. Instead, he let Caulfield's low, venomous voice go in one ear and out the other.

Caulfield touched a hand to the black ball cap he wore on easy days like today and tweaked the brim. "What'd you make when you worked for Jessie, huh, Mor-gie? She pay you more than minimum wage? It's the rich folks that are the cheapest, am I right? They're the cheapest sons a bitches on the planet, even though they got more hundred dollar bills stuck up their tight asses on a Tuesday than normal folks like you and me will ever see in our lifetimes."

Pushing past him, Morgan cringed in the heat of the man's nefarious glare. Caulfield's arm shot out and he gave Morgan's left wrist a vicious rap from the solid wood baton he carried on his belt. Yelping, Morgan grabbed his wrist and shrank away from the guard who, in all his glory, was a good foot shorter than Morgan.

"Where do you think you're goin,' asswipe?" The question was delivered with a sneer that made Caulfield's nose flatten against his pasty face.

Damn, Morgan seethed inwardly as he pressed his damaged wrist into his chest. Bench pressing would hurt like hell for the next few days. Pushups would be positively tortuous. Downward dogs would downright suck.

"This way, you stupid ass. No wussy chair building for you today."

Surprised, Morgan looked up and caught the man's steely eye. One thing about Brody Pen—the place ran on routine. Even the little bit of grass in the yard knew to turn green when it was time, and not a minute before. Nothing happened out of schedule, ever. But if it did…well…

Morgan forgot about his wrist. Something about the way C was looking at him was unnerving. A peculiar energy snaked up his legs and landed in his stomach. "Where am I going?" he asked, so quietly that Caulfield guffawed loudly in response as he roughly cuffed Morgan's wrists together (which hurt the sore wrist like hell) and motioned for him to walk.

"Candy ass," the guard retorted. "Wouldn't you like to know." A snicker and a single command followed the phrase. "Walk."

Fifteen minutes later, intimidated by the clanging of metal doors as they opened and shut, and unnerved by the guns recessed high into walls as he passed, Morgan was led into a small private room utilized by inmates who had select private visitors, like lawyers, or detectives, usually. And there, waiting for him, were two men from Morgan's past whom he figured he would never again eyeball in this lifetime.

Part of him wanted to turn tail and run.

But the other part of him—the one that remembered the good days on tour with Jessie—ached to stay in their company forever.

After cuffing Morgan to the lone table in the space, Caulfield took up a post against an interior wall, next to a young corrections officer who had led Morgan's visitors to the interview room. The warden, a large man who still, at age sixty, fit the linebacker build of his much younger pro football days, was there too; he nodded at Caulfield before looking at Morgan, narrowing his eyes, and giving him a hard look that said much more than the quiet greeting of, "Gentlemen," which was meant to encompass Caulfield as well as the inmate in his care.

Morgan was too stunned to respond. Straightening, a rush of air stirred his senses further when the warden moved. He decided the prison boss was only present because of Charles' and Matt's distinguished company.

There was a high, open window in the small space. *I can hear dogs barking,* Morgan thought oddly as he stared down at the sterile, institutional table. *I can hear the K9 dogs, and somewhere out there are leaves in a tree, rustling in the breeze.* He cricked his neck to the side. A far off echo of chirping birds brought another world to mind, an old world where Sunday afternoons meant hanging out with his young son in a Toronto park—where the laughter of children was almost taken for granted. The cherished memory gutted him; it curdled his stomach into one big, decaying lump. Before he mustered up enough courage to look up, Morgan closed his eyes and prayed for an end to the turmoil mercilessly turning his insides to mush.

Matt was standing in the west corner of the room.

Matt.

Three quarters facing Morgan, almost side-on to him, the man's pose seemed to suggest that he was ready for action—*running,* Morgan wondered? Or maybe the tense shoulders and the hands at his hips—which brushed back his navy three quarter length cashmere coat so that it flared out like it was in the way, as if it was some extraneous piece of the man—were meant to draw Morgan's eyes to Matt's freedom and wealth. To laud the man's power over him.

If so, it didn't work. All Morgan thought Matt's stance really did was prove that Morgan's old boss from those last few months with the Keatings had a layer to hide behind, if he needed it.

Matt wasn't looking at Morgan. His head was slightly turned toward him, but he was fixated on some random part of the wall, at a bare spot near the corner. His stare was so intense that Morgan felt compelled to look around. He found only a long forgotten cobweb dangling from the low ceiling like a ghost.

Charles was staring at Morgan, however. The Keating patriarch's gaze was so determined, so absorbed in studying Morgan that once Morgan got up the nerve to focus his attention away from Matt and on to Charles, he lurched, startled, in his seat. Charles was as forcefully present as Matt, but Charles' eyes were fixed and angry. Behind them was a layer of desperation and confusion that Morgan could only interpret as befitting a parent in danger of losing a child. He knew that look well. It was the same way he studied the doctor all those years ago, when life was ebbing out of Darin and when Nadia was alive and by his side.

Morgan looked away, back to the cobwebbed corner where Matt's resentment hung like death.

Matt shifted and forced himself to take in the man who had brought them all to their knees.

It was a few minutes before anyone spoke. It was Caulfield who finally broke the silence; he did it with a rusty clearing of his throat. The abrasive sound moved Charles to action. On shaking legs, he yanked out a chair that sat unobtrusively before the plain table where Morgan was seated, and eased his tired body down into it with a solemn, heavy sorrow.

Morgan blinked but didn't move. Matt's mind raced back to the night before, when he and Charles almost came to blows over today's meeting. When Jessie clued in to what Saturday's short trip to Alberta might possibly unearth.

Studying Morgan now, Matt knew he was right about insisting on accompanying Charles to Brody. Arnie was street smart and street tough, and he damn well cared for Jessie and her family as much as anyone, but Matt agreed with Jessie on one point he wished he didn't—there was a common verisimilitude to grief, to loss. It was written all over Morgan's fatigued face. Morgan's eyes were once again locked on the table's surface, but Matt knew what he would spy inside if he could see into them. He would see despair, ten thousand times worse than the anguish that haunted Matt—that Matt was reminded of when he looked into Jessie's eyes last night. Morgan's despair was permanent, buried in a child's white coffin and in the final gunshot that killed his wife. Matt's was mitigated by his continued involvement with Jessie's family. That was, at the very least, enough to keep a man hanging on.

Another muted guttural sound from behind Morgan…Matt looked up to see, aimed at him, the steady gaze of the beady-eyed correctional officer who accompanied Morgan to the small room. Bristling, Matt shuddered when goose bumps—truth bumps, Emily-Grace called them—danced up his arms and legs and made the hair on his head stand on end more than it did even after he spiked it with gel in the mornings. *Geez,* he thought. *Not much wonder Morgan's staring at the table. This is a helluva dark place.* Jessie's online research about the prison being forever cursed because it was built on an ancient burial ground crossed his mind.

Taking his hands off his hips, Matt finally faced Morgan fully. *Enough drama,* he lectured himself. *Let's do this thing.*

He took a step toward Morgan and asked his first question.

Chapter Eleven

At home in Vancouver, Jessie and Jane were entertaining the kids in the UBC house while Josh and Charlie tackled a dryer repair in the downstairs laundry room.

"Keeps us humble," Jessie had explained to Charlie when Josh asked him to go downstairs and have a look at the machine, which was humming a lot more loudly than it should. She didn't have to add that the real reason Josh liked to fix things in the Sawyer household himself was because they were nervous about inviting strangers into their home. They'd learned that the hard way, back in the Deuce McCall days. Now, with the threats that started on *Sacred Peace* last season, there was no question. When things broke down in the Sawyer home, one of the trusted close-knit team Googled the repair, or Josh (and Jessie on occasion, at least as helper and sometimes as the main fixer) did it himself.

Jane handed a small plate to her daughter. On it was two colorfully iced cupcakes, lovingly decorated by Emily-Grace and Stella. "Hold it steady," Jane advised. Stella gripped the plate on both sides and started marching toward the stairs leading down. "Be careful not to trip, Stel."

Stella stopped and looked behind her. Precocious and domineering, she griped at Emily-Grace. "Hurry up, slowpoke! I want Daddy to see our cupcakes sooner rather than later."

A small set of Jessie-eyes peeked from behind darkening blonde bangs up at her mother. Emily-Grace reached out her hands and accepted two tall glasses of water from Jessie, who said, "Daddy will be very grateful, honey. He's always thirsty."

"I wasn't making those for Daddy, Momma. I don't want Stella to be giving those cupcakes to Daddy. I was making them for us." With a stealthy, haughty glance at her best friend, Emily-Grace added, "Stella has no right to take over and just do what she wants."

Bending at the waist, Jessie touched her daughter's cheek. "Emily-Grace, Stella is a guest in our home. Her father is helping Daddy fix our dryer. She wants to do something nice for him."

Jane was close enough to hear. She winced. In an exaggerated flurry of impatience, Stella huffed, tossed her long, dark hair and stormed over to the stairs.

Emily-Grace frowned. "Well, I would too if Charlie was my daddy. But he's not."

Don't you dare add 'but he should be,' Jessie fumed inwardly. Out loud she said, "Your father is working hard too, Emily-Grace."

Stella's high voice rang through the house. "EG! Now!"

Embarrassed, Jane touched Jessie's hand. "Sorry," she smiled, and followed it up with a firm, "Stella! Take it easy. Emily-Grace is right behind you." Her kind green eyes met Emily-Grace's defiant pale blues. Without speaking, she tilted her head toward her own daughter.

Emily-Grace had to maintain some semblance of dignity in front of this woman she revered, the woman who was smart enough to hitch herself to the side of a man worth admiring. A low, indistinguishable murmur accompanied her slow steps toward the stairs. Stella was already halfway down. Emily-Grace's small figure, in a pink tutu that matched Stella's purple one in style and form, tiptoed quietly down behind her.

"She spends far too much time with Charles and Dee," Jessie bit off as her daughter's messy ponytail disappeared from view. "My own daughter is a card carrying member of the powerful Keating mafia."

"She'll come around," Jane ascertained lightly, swooping her finger into the bowl of icing and sticking it between her lips. "Umm, cream cheese icing. Love it." She reached for a bowl so they could start cleaning up the afternoon's baking mess. "Emily-Grace just needs more time with Josh, that's all. It's got to be tough with those two adorable boy ruffians always after Josh's attention. She simply can't find her way in."

Jessie humphed, yawned, and grabbed a cupcake. Taking a generous bite, she grumbled at the same time as she chewed. "She's scared." The pronouncement came out as garbled as Jessie's brain felt. A lack of sleep from an almost all night playtime with Josh didn't help although, she told herself with a secret inside giggle, she'd be happy to stay tired forever if it meant she and her much missed hubby could duplicate nights like last night.

With a sigh, Jane flipped on the tap and started filling the sink.

In the laundry room, Josh was on his knees behind the malfunctioning dryer when Stella walked in, her plate of cupcakes held high like a trophy. Josh knew better than to be effusive and praising like Charlie. He simply smiled at Stella and gratefully accepted a cupcake.

"Thank you, sweetheart," he said with genuine affection for Charlie's busy daughter. Peeling off the cupcake wrapper, he dropped it on the plate. Emily-Grace's eyes were on him, he could tell without looking at her. Frustrated, Josh wondered what he could do that wouldn't piss her off. Should he reach for the glass of water he discerned was meant for him, or should he wait until she offered it to him? He decided on the latter, and kept his eyes trained on the cupcake in his hands so he wouldn't have to face the humiliation of also spying Charlie's eyes on him.

Stella being Stella, she immediately took control of the situation. Grabbing a glass out of Emily-Grace's hand, she handed it to her father, then she pointed at Josh. "Give that one to your daddy," she demanded, as if Emily-Grace was a little slow on the uptake. Stella preened when her own father's arm, with a cupcake suspended from the fingers, wrapped itself around her waist.

"Thanks, Stel." Charlie was glowing, but his gut knotted at why Josh was having trouble earning his daughter's trust and freely given love. Charlie couldn't meet his friend's eye any more than Josh could meet his. Shitty memories were just easier to bear alone and in silence.

"Hard on the knees," Josh muttered. Unbending his body so he could stand straight and tall, he turned away from the three people crowding the small room, and wished to hell he could shrink into the drain in the oversized laundry sink and disappear.

Watching Charlie hug Stella, Emily-Grace was at a loss. Easily, she could feel her father's angst. It waylaid her the same way she knew it crippled her mother. But there was an invisible wall between Emily-Grace and her daddy. The thing about that wall, though, was that in her eight-year-old wisdom she knew it was up to her to scale it. It was just hard to figure out how...

Josh's reappearance in the home after his three weeks away had added a layer of joy to the house that, although always filled with love of late, was often as troubled as today's looming gray skies. Everybody was happy today, despite the undercurrent of quiet worry Emily-Grace spied in the way her mother's lips were pressed together, and in the way she overlooked some of the more mischievous things the boys got up to that morning, like taking a toilet paper roll and using it to wrap Emily-Grace's dollhouse—'just for fun,' David said, because he liked going inside and peeking out of the window from between the gauzy strips of tissue. Dylan was a willing participant in the morning hijinks, but even if their momma had raised her voice, Emily-Grace knew she would have been doing it with a smile, because for some reason everything Dylan did amused their mother.

So. The wall. It hurt Emily-Grace to see her father turn away from her like that. He was finished his cupcake now and was licking his fingers. He used a wrist to turn on the tap of the laundry sink, and she watched him hold the gooey fingers underneath the water. When her daddy finally turned the tap off, he turned back around and wiped his hands on his jeans. The wall seemed a little smaller when Emily-Grace looked into her father's eyes and saw a lingering sadness there. She stepped toward him and held out the glass, surprising even herself when she whispered, "I love you, Daddy."

At first Josh was too stunned to respond. He was even more confused now. Smile, or cry with relief and gratitude? Choosing the joy that filled his heart just by virtue of being in a safe circle of family and friends for the weekend—a circle that included his wife and children—he extended a hand and took the glass of water from his often distant daughter. "Thank you, sweetheart," he said, his voice gravelly but firm.

He took a chance. Crouching, he took a sip of the water and waited, but kept his eyes locked on his daughter's face. She was still feeling uncertain, he could tell by the nervous way she was studying him, with the occasional glance toward Charlie and Stella tossed in for good measure. She'd said she loved him, and although it was in some ways an obvious one-upmanship of Stella and Charlie's obvious bond, Josh took it to heart. Rare, this was, to hear that phrase from this child who'd grown old long before her time. Rare, it was, to feel the raw emotion almost strangle the room with its power.

Emily-Grace made her decision. Wringing her fingers together in that anxious way she'd learned to do from the time she was three, when she was locked in a Langley basement with her mother and baby brother, she tiptoed toward her father and wrapped her arms around his neck.

Josh set down the glass of water and pulled her close. Rising, he lifted her up with him and turned away from Charlie and Stella the same way he had turned away from everyone the night he got Emily-Grace back in the Calgary hospital all those years ago. "I love you back," he murmured into her hair. "So much, pretty girl," he said, his lips tickled by the messy pony-tail, his cheeks flush with the sweet delight of being loved by this often lost and lonely child, by the daughter he feared would abandon him altogether by the time she hit her difficult teen years.

Behind them, Stella sank back in Charlie's arms and watched her best friend tighten her hold around her father's neck. Charlie saw Emily-Grace bury her nose in the strong curve of Josh's shoulder. And he saw her exhale— a long, low exhale that may or may not have been accompanied by moist eyes and trembling lips. The sight of them together should have been normal; it should have been accepted and glossed over. But it wasn't—this father and this daughter had paid far too dear a price for this kind of difficult love. What Charlie and Stella were witnessing was a coveted and special moment. It was humbling.

"Come on, Stella," Charlie urged softly, unable to take his eyes off his good friend as Josh held his daughter safely close to his body. "Let's take a break and go see what kind of trouble your baby brother has gotten into."

For once, Stella didn't speak. She just took her father's hand and walked out of the room beside him.

Upstairs, Jane and Jessie had the dishes under control when Charlie and Stella appeared. Charlie's expression was soft and tender. The smile he gave Jessie was genuine. Tilting her head quizzically in his direction, she stopped drying the bowl in her hands. Charlie didn't have time to explain, though. Lucas was at his feet whining to be picked up, Jessie's phone was bleeping at her, and Dylan was tugging at Charlie's shirt, calling, "Chawlie! Chawlie!"

"Chaos," Charlie grinned at his wife and Jessie in turn. "Sweet chaos. Just the way I like it."

Jessie held up her phone. "It's gonna get a little crazier," she told him. "Jacob and Kayla are on their way over with their designer. Looks like it's time to get measured for the big wedding. What do you say we order us some takeout?"

By the time Josh and Emily-Grace emerged from the lower level of the boxy home, the others had decided on ramen for the adults and sushi for the kids. Pizza was on its way too, since Jacob wasn't partial to either of the other two choices. Jessie was texting him to drop by Elysian to grab coffee for all of them when Josh walked into the kitchen carrying his eight-year-old daughter.

The phone fell to Jessie's side.

"I'm not going to say she's too old to be carried," she whispered to Jane.

"Don't you dare," Jane chided her. She flipped around and leaned back against the counter. The two of them watched as Josh set Emily-Grace down and settled his butt into a seat at the kitchen island to help Charlie navigate the three small boys.

"It's loud in here." Taking a glass from Jane, Jessie wiped it with careless abandon. "But ask me if I care." The boys were screaming. Charlie was trying to shush them, but Josh was just laughing. Jessie leaned into Jane's side and laid her head on her good friend's shoulder. "Something's working, Jane," she admitted. "Something about Josh being on that shoot is making him very, very happy. I don't think I've seen him glowing like this for a very long time."

"Soak it up, honey," Jane replied. She didn't add 'just in case,' but both women thought it at the same time, and when their eyes met over the next passed glass for Jessie to dry, both sets were unable to disguise alarm.

We've just gotten used to it, Jessie thought. *We've gotten so used to the bad stuff that it's hard to enjoy the good.*

Frowning, Jane squeezed Jessie's elbow. "No," she said firmly. "Tonight is about safety and friends and being happy, Jessie. Tonight is not for worrying about what's coming down the pipes next. Wipe that panic off your face before your husband sees it."

Josh had already spotted his wife's furrowed forehead. He watched her bite her bottom lip before she looked back over at him. Something was at play today, and he didn't know what. He was as intuitive as Emily-Grace when it came to reading Jessie. Sam and Alin were around, sitting in the front room entertaining Stella and Emily-Grace now, but Matt was nowhere in sight. Was that it? Was Jessie missing Matt? He regarded her with a curious concern.

Outside in the driveway, Kayla, always the chauffeur since Jacob didn't do a lot of driving, screeched to a halt and leaned on the horn three times. The girls screamed in delight, and Jessie couldn't help but smile at the blissful way Josh looked over at his daughter when she leapt up to go meet Jacob.

That's a change, Jessie mused with a wry grin. *See, Wheeler? It's all good now. It's all good.* Pivoting back around to the sink, she took the last glass from Jane, and wiped it clean.

Chapter Twelve

"Cocky bastard," Matt muttered, striding next to Charles toward the stairs leading up into the Keating jet.

"Did you think so?" Charles asked him. "I thought he was the same as always. Mostly quiet and unresponsive."

"I didn't mean Morgan." They'd reached the steps. Matt stood to one side and waved his boss forward. He jogged up behind Charles and handed his leather messenger bag to a cautiously smiling Victoria. Charles took a seat at the back of the jet and put his feet up on an ottoman. Settling across from him, Matt stretched out, yawned, leaned back, and closed his eyes.

Charles gave him an inquisitive look. "Are you referring to the guard?" Before Matt answered, Charles spoke to Victoria, who was making her way toward the men after storing Matt's bag for the flight. "Scotch," he told her. "I think I can speak for both of us. Today is definitely a scotch day."

"Corrections officer," Matt reprimanded him. "Guard sounds too World War Two. Somebody, in their great wisdom, figured nobody would rehabilitate if they were surrounded by guards." From his reclining position, he raised his fingers as quote marks to emphasize the word 'guards.'

"Nor would they rehabilitate while wearing uniforms, either, apparently." Charles' voice was brisk, impatient. He wanted to get to the crux of the matter. Who the hell cared what modern day prisoners wore, anyway? He just wanted—needed—to know what a certain inmate was thinking. "I appreciate you keeping your cool, Matt," he added carefully.

Matt's eyes blinked open. His fingers were linked across his stomach. His only response was a low, "Whatever." He looked away.

"So what about the corrections officer?" Charles inquired. "Guard. It's a helluva lot easier to say guard, Matt."

"Federal government," Matt mumbled. "With them, it doesn't matter what's easiest. You haven't figured that out by now?"

Ignoring him, Charles bit off, "So what about the guard? What about him bothered you?"

Wriggling against the back of the small sofa so he could scratch an itchy spot on his back, Matt replied, "Oh, I don't know. Just a vibe, I guess. There was something mean and commanding in his eyes, that's all. And those damn peppermints! He made a point of crunching at the oddest times. Intentional, if you asked me."

"He was just trying to get our attention."

"To show that he was in control, you mean. To show off his power. I'd almost feel sorry for Morgan, if…well, if."

"Jesus. Not me. I'll never feel sorry for him. I'm sorry for what I missed about him. That's all I'm sorry for."

They were silent for a moment as they pondered their time at Brody Pen. Something about being back on the jet, with Victoria taking care of their creature comforts and their butts securely aligned on soft leather cushions made both men deeply grateful, as if they'd escaped a fate and a darkness they didn't quite have the capacity to understand. This jet, this metal tube, was a cocoon, a place to be coddled and cherished. A place where a man could exhale.

"What will we tell Jessie?"

Matt shrugged. "What can we tell her? The truth?" He shook his head. "I don't know, Charles."

Charles pinched his shirt collar between a thumb and forefinger and traced the edge three times before he spoke. The words he chose were aimed up the narrow aisle, but meant for Matt. "What do you think the truth was, Matt?" Victoria was getting their drinks ready with as much sleek professional silence as she could muster, but still, the odd clink of crystal reached Charles' ears. It was comforting, that sound, and he wondered how the hell men in prison functioned with no freedom, no creature comforts like good, stiff drinks after a hard day, and virtually no privacy. After a two second pause, Charles looked back at his good friend. "What did you read in Morgan's body language?"

Matt shifted in his seat and emitted a slow *pfffttt* as he thought about how to answer that. By the way Charles was nervously fingering his collar, it was obvious he was at a loss as to how to interpret the meeting. Morgan's response wasn't a surprise to either man—they expected a certain dead silence from the guy. The losses Morgan suffered in his lifetime were enough to mute a man's vocal cords and tie a chain around his heart. But the thing about Morgan, from what they understood, was that he had never been a big talker anyway. Social and fun at one time, they'd been told, yes, but likely the quietest guy in the bar. Now? You had to read the guy through his body language. They should have talked to the corrections officer standing behind Morgan, that's who they should have spoken to. They might have gotten something out of him—not the young guy who kept blinking nervously at the older man, no, not him. The one whose presence gave Matt the willies. The creepy one chain smoking peppermints. That guy.

The guard's domineering presence sent Matt's thoughts careening down another road.

"This is the thing about federal pens you need to understand," he explained judiciously, catching Charles' eye and holding it. It seemed Charles was ready to listen. In the car on the way back to the jet, the man was lost in his own dreary worries. As much as Jessie brought joy into the Keatings' lives, her presence had also, over time, been a hard lesson for Charles, in that his power was relegated to business. When it came to controlling the outside forces that hurt the people he loved, he was virtually helpless.

Matt waited until Victoria delivered their drinks and lowered herself into a seat at the front of the jet before speaking again. "You have to look at the prison this way," he told Charles. "It's a subculture. And within its walls are multiple other subcultures divided by race, which are sometimes divided by gangs, divided by strengths and weaknesses, divided by the crimes that got the guys in there, divided by the kind of power the guys had on the outside, and divided by inmates versus staff. Divided even by outside forces, as we're learning the hard way."

Sitting up straighter, Matt sliced a knife-edged hand down in front of his chest. "Like this," he explained. He repeated the gesture a few times over. "Divided and divided and divided. Prisons are all about territory and control. Turf. Who controls what turf. The guys have very little choices left to them. They take control over their circumstances by taking control over each other. Guys on the outside are puppeteers. And guys on the inside are puppeteers. Unless we're a part of that," he took a sip of his scotch, "community, if you want to call it that, then the best we can do is guess who is pulling the punches."

"Alton might have more to say on the matter if we push him."

"The warden? He was as close-lipped as Morgan." Leaning forward, resting his forearms on his thighs so his drink bobbled over the carpeted floor, Matt added, "The staff is also divided. That young guy was trembling when the older fellow brought Morgan into the room." Lifting his drink, Matt pointed it toward Charles. "Alton has to be careful what he tells people like us. Outsiders."

"Especially us, I suppose." Charles kept a tight grip on his heavy glass.

Shrugging, Matt sat back again. He was as distressed as Charles at the futility of their meeting. "A man like Alton knows not to trust people. He has to protect his turf as much as anyone. That place is a powder keg waiting for a match. Always. Every second of every day."

"There are female guards in there. I can't imagine how protected they feel."

"There's some theory about men staying more calm when women are around. Like they'll behave better if a female guard escorts them here or there. Something leftover from the cave man days about protecting women."

Scoffing, Charles said plainly, "Protecting women. Maybe we should have brought Jessie in after all. She might have gotten something out of Morgan."

"Like hell," Matt bit off. "I wouldn't put her within five feet of that Caulfield guy. Something's not right about him. Besides," he said, "we did get something out of Morgan. We got a bite."

"At the end."

"Yup." Matt and Charles stared at each other across the narrow divide that separated them. Neither was glowing with satisfaction; instead both were sinking into a sort of fractious despair. They wanted to feel happy, productive, that the visit to Brody could be considered a success, given what Morgan said at the end of their meeting, but a niggling worry had descended over both the instant Morgan left the room. Something about what he said just wasn't sitting right, and the men intuitively knew it but somehow it seemed that voicing it was the wrong thing to do. Voicing it would give energy to the unspoken words. Voicing it would make what was unsaid, real.

A somber gloom passed between them. Just as Victoria stepped forward to ask Charles and Matt to fasten their seatbelts for takeoff, Charles put their worry into words anyway. Maybe, just maybe, Matt didn't get the same weird vibe from Morgan that he did. "He said that Josh is safe. He said he won't be harmed."

When Morgan said that, neither Matt nor Charles noticed that, behind him, Caulfield sniggered. The men's eyes were locked on Morgan. Throughout the entire meeting, Morgan focused his eyes on the table surface and only answered their questions in a monosyllabic tone.

Fine.

Good.

Uh...

Morgan didn't meet their eyes until he was released from the table and stood to go. He asked a question. "Is she, uh," he licked his lips as if the nervous action would help him find enough moisture to form words, "is she okay?"

Matt was speechless.

Charles fumed. "What the hell do you think, Morgan? She's trying to put the pieces back together. Their whole lives, they'll be trying to put the goddamn pieces back together."

Morgan just nodded, and looked at the young guard in the corner. Everyone called the kid Red, for the close-trimmed red hair that topped his crown, and for the slight peach fuzz that the guy was always rubbing. In Morgan's experience, Red was a nice enough fellow. If anything, he was a pawn for guys like Caulfield. Red was the kind of guy who should be ushering school kids across quiet neighborhood crosswalks. In Morgan's opinion, he didn't belong in a den of iniquity like Brody Pen. The place would just ruin him, if it hadn't already.

Without realizing they were both thinking the same thing at the same time, Matt had followed Morgan's eyes and silently agreed, but he looked back quickly when Morgan gave them that last tidbit—the comment about Josh.

"What?" Matt had asked quietly, tilting his head to one side as if his ear would dislodge anything that kept him from hearing properly. He asked again, "What?" There was desperation in Morgan's eyes when he locked his intense gaze in Matt's. It was like he was imploring Matt to understand something that he wasn't saying.

I can't breathe, Matt thought at the time. *Tell me we're good here. Tell me we're all good.* For some inexplicable reason, a vision of the New Mexican bull snake had catapulted into Matt's brain. Threatening in appearance, but harmless overall. He shook it away.

Over the duration of the entire meeting, which lasted twenty minutes, Morgan had barely looked at Charles or Matt. At the end, though, he couldn't bring himself to look away. Matt was a cherished, highly respected man in the Keating camp. For a while, when they actually crossed paths, Morgan hated the guy. But the thing about hate was that it could be eradicated, or at least mitigated, by commonality. And in this case, the common bond was Jessie. In this case, she had suffered enough. *Don't let anything happen to her,* Morgan was begging, his back to Oren C, but it was a silent, telepathic communication brought to light only by the deep need in the way Morgan stared at Matt, in a silent petition for the safety of her and her children.

By omission. By the simple weight of words.

Josh…is safe. Josh…won't be harmed.

Matt wanted to ask more, he had so much more to say, to wonder about, but his head was whirling. He was standing, facing Morgan—facing the man who'd damaged the Sawyer family so badly. He seriously considered grabbing him around the throat and choking the truth out of him, but he knew it would do no good. Matt doubted the older guard would even interfere. He'd probably just sneer and pop a new peppermint between those surly lips. The redheaded kid would likely just cower in the corner.

Silent giants like Morgan could not be coerced to speak if they weren't moved to do so. Silent giants might tower over others, but in places like Brody where they spent their days in solitary suffering, they were still preyed upon by relentless pity and self-loathing.

On the jet now, Matt sighed heavily and finished his drink. The warmth of the liquor soothed his throat but did nothing to ease this newer darkness that was taking over his body in bits and pieces, threatening to strangle his heart.

The worst terrors were the unknown ones. The worst terrors were the stalking kind, the kind that snuck up and pounced unannounced.

Throwing a furtive glance in Charles' direction as the jet breezed up into the sky and pointed its nose west, Matt noticed that the older man hadn't taken a single sip of his scotch. He thought about saying something, so the glass wouldn't slip sideways and embarrass Charles, but there was something about his boss' expression and sunken shoulders that Matt didn't want to disturb. It would be like waking him up in the middle of a bad dream. Best to let Charles ponder what it was he needed to reconcile, before they landed in Vancouver and had to look Josh—and Jessie—in the eyes, and tell the truth about what Morgan said to them, and consider lying about what he left out.

Chapter Thirteen

"He asked about her, at least."

Leaning against the Audi, Charles and Matt were facing Arnie. Parked side by side at the far end of La Casa's pretty curved driveway, the three men were feeling each other out to see what could be safely shared, and what should remain unsaid.

It was Charles who had spoken to Arnie, who was standing in front of them back-dropped by the truck he bought a few months earlier, a white Toyota Tundra. Jessie had told him it suited him to a T since to her, and to many others, he was known as a Downtown Eastside angel. Both of Arnie's strong hands were stuffed in the pockets of the canvas bomber jacket he wore over his sturdy frame. His legs—muscular thighs tense against the fabric of the faded gray jeans he wore against the cool day—were apart, giving him a triangular stance that made him look like he was stabilizing himself on the ground in preparation for bad news.

Arnie was used to bad news. He fixed a hard stare on Matt, who had yet to speak. "Word on the street is that Caulfield was with Morgan today."

"Jesus," Charles exclaimed, laying a hand on the Audi's hood to steady himself. "You've gotten a communication from that place? Already?"

Arnie just looked at him, his stare as penetrating as Morgan's, but far less sinister. Arnie almost always just looked serious. The only person capable of making him smile, most times, was Jessie. And now...sometimes, at least... her children could coax an occasional half grin, too.

Charles grumbled, and curved his spine so he could droop over and stare at the ground. Arnie was a man of the streets. Of course he had connections inside Brody Pen. That part of Arnie just wasn't usually something they talked about.

Now, though, Matt took Arnie's declaration as a sign that he wanted to talk. He dove in. "What do you know, Arnie?" he barked. "What about this Caulfield guy? Is he prison mafia?"

"He's his own mafia. He gets first pick of the fresh meat when they land. Attaches himself to any guy who'll give him street cred, who can raise the respect he gets from others. He steers clear of the mob mentality and he does his own thing."

Matt didn't want to ask. But he had to. "And what's that? His 'own thing.'"

Arnie paused but didn't waver from Matt's commanding stare. "He's a fixer."

"A…fixer." Charles looked about ready to pass out. "What's he fix? Toilets?"

"He's an equalizer, Charles. An avenger. For inmates."

"Let's go inside," Matt directed, ignoring Charles' defeated attempt at a jest. Arnie's too-calm pronouncement had hurled Matt's heart into racing mode. "It's cold enough to freeze the balls off a snowman." Taking Charles' elbow in his hand, he led him toward La Casa's arched mahogany door. Arnie flanked Charles on the other side, and he and Matt exchanged concerned glances behind their boss' back. Charles shook Matt off, raised his chin, and led the way.

La Casa echoed in quiet welcome as their heels clipped down the polished hall. Not even Carlotta was home. Deirdre had responded to an earlier text from Jessie; with Ulysses at the wheel, both women had crossed the Lions Gate Bridge and headed to the Sawyer home to supervise the dress and suit fittings for Jacob and Kayla's wedding. Relieved that he'd have some time to process the trip to Brody before the discomfort of his wife's inquisition, Charles led Arnie and Matt to the media room near the back of the house.

Matt poured the scotch this time. By the time he handed Arnie a crystal tumbler, the boxer was telling Charles that Oren Caulfield's appearance beside Morgan meant that Morgan was somewhat protected at Brody.

There were men at Brody who'd been locked up for over thirty years. "They live by an unwritten code," Arnie explained. "Part of it is a breakdown of power. Caulfield, or Oren C as he's sometimes known, is tied into that power. It encompasses the entire penitentiary, but it also extends far beyond the thirty foot razor wire topped fences."

"How long have you known this?" Matt was asking a question Charles was mulling around but was afraid to ask…mostly because he didn't really want to know the answer.

Arnie held his gaze for a long time, long enough to make Charles nervous and Matt almost crumble. "Since it became clear there was a connection to Brody."

"So why didn't you…?" A wave of nausea passed over Matt. He knew damn well why, but he needed to hear Arnie say it. Charles, too, needed to hear Arnie say it.

The man was a brick wall. As much as he had become an integral part of the Keating-Sawyer security team, Arnie was still a product of the tough Downtown Eastside. He had his secrets, and as long as he continued to protect Jessie and her family as best he could then Matt, Charles and Ulysses did not ask any questions. Arnie was dependable and capable. But nobody had forgotten that he was also the man who swifted Jessie away when she needed a break from the pain, who found guns for her when she asked for them. However…he was also the man who protected her when Caryn and Eric threw her away. He was a conundrum, an intimidating, strong man whose eyes Jessie loved for their gentle light, but whose heart had walls of stone that helped him separate emotion from business.

Arnie's voice was dangerously low. What he said back to Matt was, "You were already doing what you could. We all were. Nobody needed the distraction—the kind of pain—that comes with knowing Morgan enlisted a man as powerful as Caulfield to do his dirty work."

"You said Caulfield was a fixer. An equalizer. And Morgan told us Josh is safe…" Charles was whispering. He dropped carefully onto the black leather couch where Jessie and Jacob sat when they first—so shyly—played music together for him.

"That's right," Arnie said, his eyes shifting over to Charles and his stone wall of a heart leaking. He wished to hell he could protect this man who was so good, so kind, to Jessie. Charles was one of the first few men in Jessie's life who proved to her that the male species could be good and kind.

"Jesus Christ." Bending over his knees, Charles set his scotch down on the rug.

Matt knelt before him. "We don't know anything, Charles. This is all speculation."

"He's in prison, yet he can still hurt her." The truth was unbelievable. Charles looked up. The dampness in his eyes—a rare thing—was more terrifying than concern for whether or not his troubled heart might attack him again. It was humbling and disconcerting to see a man of Charles' power and wealth be brought to his knees this way, by the fear of potentially losing someone he loved dearly, whom it was his responsibility to protect.

"Matt...Arnie...maybe...look at it this way...maybe this was what trying to hurt Josh was all about. Just to scare Jessie, to worry her." There was hope in the eyes now, just a bit, but it was there, lifting Charles' shoulders and lending him the innocence of a six-year-old boy. "Maybe it's over. Maybe that's what Morgan was trying to tell us. If it were Jessie he wanted to kill, he would've made damn sure she died when he had the chance. The fire...the smoke was a damn beacon...she was meant to be rescued."

Bullshit. And even if that were true, Nadia wasn't dead then, Matt was thinking. *If Morgan wants to even the score...* Angling his head around to peer at Arnie in the dim half-light, it sickened him to see, on the man's usually unreadable chiseled features, that there was more to the fear than Charles, as yet, understood. But Matt got the picture loud and clear. He stood.

To Charles, he issued a firm directive. "Rest."

To Arnie, he communicated a vicious message that he voiced loud and clear in the media room later, after Charles was finally convinced to go upstairs for a nap.

Matt did it by grabbing Arnie by the scruff of his neck. "Tell me what the hell you know, Arnie. I have a short memory, and I'm tired as hell of lies and untruths. I've had enough of those from Jessie over the years. I don't need them from you!"

Searching Matt's half-crazed eyes, Arnie raised his hands and tried to back away. "Matt, we have the same goal here. If I knew of anything else we could be doing differently, you'd have already heard it from me."

"That's not what I asked." The growl in Matt's throat was foreign to him, but when it came to Jessie and the kids, he often found himself a stranger to his own body, to his own mind.

"What I know about Caulfield is that he is a lone ranger at the top of the tower. He attaches himself to a guy, does the guy favors. Rights wrongs, or what the guy he's doing the favor for sees as wrongs."

"Like a fucking warped Robin Hood from hell."

"Let go of me, Matt. Now."

The demand left no room for debate. Trembling, Matt forcibly unfisted the knuckles he'd clenched around Arnie's jacket.

Rubbing his neck, Arnie sent Matt a look of utter anger, but it wasn't really directed at Matt. It came from years of dealing with guys like Caulfield, unreasonable men with screwed-up agendas designed to serve their own sense of self-esteem and worth in the eyes of others. "The only way to mitigate this, that I can see, is to convince Morgan to call him off. To call off Caulfield."

"You didn't see Morgan's eyes today," Matt retorted. Sparks flew as he stormed around the room. "Jesus, Arnie, for a second I thought I saw compassion there. A flicker in those mostly dead eyes…understanding. A guarantee, when he said Josh would not be harmed. But then…the silence… the things he wasn't saying…and again, those fucking mostly dead eyes… do you think he's after Jessie again? Or…or one of the kids? Is that what he was trying to tell me?"

Arnie stood tall and faced Matt, a man he respected above all others. A man he knew Jessie loved with such a soul strong passion and reverence that she was never quite herself when he wasn't nearby. "Matt," he said, with the respect and solemnity the hard truth deserved, "my man at Brody told me Caulfield makes things even. If a man loses his wife, he arranges to kill the wife of the man who killed his woman. If a guy loses a brother, he has a brother killed. He never gets his own hands dirty."

"So if Caulfield was with Morgan today, there's an alliance there, an allegiance."

"And Caulfield's just waiting for instruction."

"Morgan won't hurt Jessie. He won't let anyone hurt her." Thinking out loud, Matt added with a trace of hope he really didn't feel, "Jessie and Josh didn't kill Morgan's son. Cancer did. He won't touch the kids."

Leaning against the bar at the back of the room, Arnie pondered that. "Look, I'm staying in touch with my guy up at Brody. If I hear anything, you and I will talk again."

Considering that, Matt asked pointedly, "Is your guy a corrections officer or an inmate?"

"Does it matter?"

Slumping, Matt sank down onto the couch. "I don't suppose it does. Not really."

"Look, Matt. Our job is to keep everyone calm. Fanning the flames will only ramp things up and scare the hell out of everyone again."

"I don't think we can scare Jessie any more than she's already scared, Arnie."

"I would normally say that I agree because I saw her survive the streets, Matt. She's tough. But back then she was only looking out for herself. You saw what happened when Josh was threatened by McCall. You see how afraid she is for him now."

Once again, what wasn't being said sickened Matt. "Jesus," he breathed. The breath hurt. His whole body was shaking now. *Shock,* he thought as a new numbness overtook him. *The children.* He looked up at Arnie. "Morgan won't hurt the kids," he rasped. "He won't."

"That's right," Arnie said, circling around and refilling his tumbler with Charles' expensive scotch. "And that's because we won't let him."

"I think the real problem here, Arnie," Matt said as he rose and wearily walked toward Arnie for a refill, "is that the enemy who can touch us is really unknown. And the target is even less certain." He refused to say targets, because…well, just because.

"You need to reframe your thinking, Matt," Arnie said blankly. He raised a glass. "You're too focused on the problem, not the solution. We know the root of it. And so that's where we need to go."

"I won't send Jessie in to Brody to see Morgan. That's not happening. I don't see what good it would do, anyway."

"She'd be real. That's what good it would do. One good look in those soft blue eyes and Morgan—and Caulfield—will back off. That's why Morgan wasn't able to finish the job in Montreal."

"Jesus, Arnie! He set a house on fire while she was tied to a bed! The man is capable of murder! He fired point blank on the woman he loved! And he won't even be doing this, someone else will. He's separated by so many damn degrees—"

"Will you listen to your goddamn self, Matt? If Jessie goes to see Morgan, he might back off. She can promise to stay in touch, whatever, anything to soothe his messed up brain. She's all about forgiveness, we know that about her."

"No! No, Arnie. We'll find another way. We'll watch them, all of them."

"And that's worked so damn well in the past, Matt. It's like," Arnie waved an arm uselessly in the air, "it's like sending butterflies to war!"

"Is that what you think? You think the kind of security I—we—provide is a goddamned joke, Arnie? Fucking butterflies? Why the hell are you here? You think I'm so damned incompetent that you need your stupid ass on the team to correct my mistakes, is that it? You fucking asshole."

Arnie strode menacingly by Matt and headed for the hallway. "I refuse to fight with you, Matt. You're out of your mind with fear." At the hall, he spun back around and pointed a finger at his friend, at least as much a friend as Arnie let anyone become. "You can't see past your heart to see straight here, buddy. You need to step back."

"You can't see *into* your heart. You put her in front of Morgan again and you'll dredge up sinister memories she was finally starting to see her way past. And you damn well should have told us about Caulfield. You don't keep those kinds of secrets, Arnie. Not on my watch."

"We've got one chance here, Matt. Morgan's calling the shots. So it's only Morgan who can end it, once and for all, and he sure as hell wasn't interested in bargaining with you."

"Don't you dare go behind my back, Arnie. You and Jessie. Just don't. You don't know her the way I do."

"Is this a fucking pissing match? Is that what this is? About who knows her the best? Jesus, Matt. Grow a set of balls. I'll see ya." With that, Arnie stormed down the hallway and out of the house. He slammed the door so hard behind him that the house shook.

Striding up the hallway behind him, Matt rifled a hand through his spiked hair. He was still shaking; the strong scotch didn't do a damn thing to ease the tremors. Resting his fingers on the handle of the front door, he leaned to one side so he could peer out of the side window. It was easy to see clearly right through to the driveway—Deirdre's prized English roses were asleep this time of year. Deflating, he wheeled his dog-tired body around and was about to head into the kitchen to put on a pot of tea when he spied a movement at the top of the stairs. Charles was sitting on the top step. Judging by the look of terror on his face, he'd heard every anxious, worried word of Matt and Arnie's tense standoff.

"I wouldn't take it back," Charles said. "If I had it to do over again, I would still choose to bring her home. I wouldn't leave that girl alone on the streets. She's a fighter, Matt, but her heart is too damn soft. Like yours." Rising, clutching the banister for help, he added, "Soft hearts are great in peacetime, but in a war I'd just as soon have myself a damn rock."

Matt had to swallow past the sticks suddenly choking his throat.

So.

"What are you saying?" he asked. "You want her to go to Brody, Charles?"

"Not on your life. But Matt—this is Arnie's world. Disturbed men like Caulfield and Morgan—they're his domain. Not yours. I think you proved that the day you walked out on the R.C.M.P."

Matt's mouth opened and closed. Speechless, he faltered at the bottom of the stairs.

"Arnie's right, Matt," Charles said as he wheeled slowly around. "You're too close. Back away."

Hunkering up his body, Matt fought to protect his wounded pride. "You want me to back away? Fine. I'll see you when I get back from the shoot with Josh, Charles. I'm taking tomorrow off."

Striding out into the cool, gray day, he closed La Casa's big door gently behind him. Framed by the arched mahogany behind him, he let his eyes close over, and bowed his head in prayer. It seemed, now, that this new battle was best left to the hands of God.

Chapter Fourteen

Matt was missed at Sunday dinner the next evening. And that was only part of the odd dynamic floating over Deirdre's expansive dining room table. The extra leafs were in to accommodate everyone. Festive and in love, Jacob and Kayla were at the table, glowing over their upcoming nuptials. Charlie, Jane and the kids were alongside, clearly as happy as ever, deep in prep work now for the move back to Alberta for *Sacred Peace's* second season. And Steve and Sophie, in the city for a brief time, were invited to dinner with their boys Caleb and Cole in tow. The reunion would have been sweet if all seemed well at La Casa, but as it was, Arnie was in Matt's place, Ulysses was watching a pale Charles carefully, Dan was sticking close by the kids in the playroom, and Alin and Sam were both—mysteriously, Jessie mused with a knowing smile—off for the day.

"Josh?" Jessie grasped her husband's elbows. They were in the music studio at the back of the house. After dessert, Jessie had followed him to the washroom, waited in the hallway, taken his hand, and drawn him into the studio. "Do you mind if I take off? I'll meet you back home in a bit."

The hairs on the back of Josh's neck stood up. He was well aware that Jessie hadn't heard from Matt all day.

During dinner, Jessie had been unable to sit still. Matt's conspicuous absence made the long day unbearable, and neither Charles nor Arnie had said a word about the previous day's Alberta jaunt.

"I just need to see him," Jessie whispered, staring into the liquid chocolate of Josh's soulful eyes and aching at the tender worry she saw there. "I need to know if he's okay."

"I'm leaving tomorrow, Jessie. At five o'clock in the morning. As far as I know, Matt will be with me." Josh's words were kind, not accusing, but Jessie got the message loud and clear.

"I know, babe," she said softly. "We're getting there. Your shoot, I mean. The film. I can see the light at the end of the tunnel."

"That doesn't mean I don't want to be with you tonight, Jess."

"It's not what you think, Josh. I want to be with you right now, but I can't… I can't focus. Matt will be straight with me."

"Why do you think he isn't here?" Josh asked. His lips were turned down at the corners.

Jessie reached up and flipped her favorite strand of his hair behind his ear. She kept her fingers there, and ran them fondly through the chestnut layers. "I think he's not here because he knows I can read him. He's still worried."

"Wrong."

"Hmmm?" Jessie's loving motion stopped. Her long fingers floated in midair before falling slowly, featherlike, back to Josh's elbow.

"Well, maybe that's a part of it," Josh admitted carefully. "But overall, Jessie? Arnie told me they had a fight. Matt legitimately took the day off after leaving bruises on Arnie's neck." He lifted a hand and pantomimed, on his own shirt and neck, Matt's angry hold on Arnie, as described by Arnie earlier in the day. "Hell, the guy deserves a break. Matt needs a life beyond us, little one."

"And that works so well for him, the big galoot." Crossing both arms over her chest, Jessie frowned and paced in a circle. Stopping a few feet away from Josh, she turned back to him with sorrow lining her compassionate eyes. The overhead lights were dim; they flickered lightly in the ice blue depths as if they believed some kind of rescue was possible in what seemed like a never-ending storm. "I just need to see him. You guys can't go away again without me saying goodbye. Okay?"

Something untoward and definitely unwelcome fluttered in Josh's stomach, but he knew his wife. She'd do whatever the hell she wanted. This attempt at asking his permission was just a formality, meant to help him feel like his opinion mattered. Josh knew damn well it didn't, not really, although maybe it eased her conscience a little to at least let him feel like she would listen to him, he supposed. When all was said and done, though, he trusted her, even with Matt. *Especially* with Matt. Jessie loved the guy unconditionally, with a fervor and deep trust that scared Josh, but at the same time, Matt deserved that kind of singular devotion from her. The man had given up his life to serve Jessie.

As far as Jessie was concerned, she wanted—needed—to know what had transpired in Alberta. Matt would be truthful. Charles seemed incapable of talking about what the men learned yesterday. Usually when the kids were around, if there was something important to discuss, he'd call the adults into his study. Tonight, though, there were just hard looks and lingering worry.

Jessie slipped out through the side door so she wouldn't have to explain to anyone else where she was going. Josh's truck keys were dangling from her fingers—she left the silver Lexus for him, since it accommodated the kids' car seats better than the truck. Watching her go, Josh fought off a squeamish worry. His throat was raw, but Jessie'd kissed him softly with the same tender love she gifted him with right from day one—now so much more deeply layered and tantalizing, blessed from years of loss, separateness, and shared grief over the times they were apart.

Standing by the door, watching Jessie disappear around the corner, her curls bouncing lightly in a cool midwinter rain, Josh jumped when Jacob called out behind him, "Where's she going? I thought we were going to play some tunes tonight. We were supposed to lay some ground for that fundraiser in Seattle we foolishly agreed to, since it's just a few days before I tie the knot with your sister."

"She's on a mission. Saving the world as always," Josh answered pensively. "One person at a time."

"Ah. Jessie's being Jessie." Jacob shoved his hands in his jeans pockets. "She okay? She was pretty quiet tonight."

Chuckling warily, Josh thoughtfully flipped around and treated Jacob to one raised eyebrow. "You didn't notice the big black cloud haunting La Casa this evening, Jacob?"

"Nah, getting laid regularly does that to a guy. I'm marrying an amazing woman in a few short weeks. Dark clouds are below my radar at the moment."

That pleased Josh. A wide grin lit up his somber brown eyes. "Kayla is radiant, Jacob. I can't say I'm not happy for her."

"You're just glad I'm off your ass, Sawyer." Jacob sobered as they sauntered quietly down the hallway together, toward the light and happy laughter emanating from the playroom. "Seriously, Josh, what's up, man? Is Jessie okay?"

"She's got a few things on her mind. She'll be all right."

"Did you guys get, um, another note or something? Did something happen? Besides that covert trip to Morgan in prison, I mean?"

"What?" Josh stopped short. "What covert visit?"

"Uh, Matt and Charles? Oh, shit. Thought you knew about that. Jessie told me."

"I guess that'd explain Jessie's mood today, then," Josh decided grimly. "Lucky you. I wish she'd told me."

"She didn't seem to know much about it," Jacob said. "And with Matt not being around today, I figured no news was good news."

"Not in this case, Ryan. If that's what today's black cloud was all about, then the silence will only serve to terrify us more. That explains a lot." Josh released a pent-up breath. Arnie, down the hall, spotted them and headed in their direction. "She went to see Matt. I guess now I know why."

Jacob didn't have a chance to respond. Arnie was on Josh in seconds flat. "Thought that was you that pulled out of here, Josh. I'd be cursing you except that since you're standing in front of me, but your truck just tore off down the lane, it's got to be your stubborn wife behind the wheel."

Josh pawed at his chin. Arnie seemed pretty wound up. "She's fine, Arnie. She just wants to see Matt before heading home. I can wrangle the kids."

"Josh, neither you nor Jessie should be wandering off on your own until we get a handle on things." Arnie was vibrating. "Call her and tell her to get the hell back here."

"Like hell," Josh said, his tone rising with his blood pressure. "You know my wife, Arnie."

Jacob would have grinned if the undisguised alarm on Arnie's face didn't surprise and somewhat shock him. Some days it seemed everyone knew Jessie either equally or better than Josh knew her himself. Jacob knew that pissed Josh off. It had to be hard on a guy. Jessie was everybody's business.

Fishing keys out of his pocket, Arnie swung around. Without speaking, he marched to the end of the main hallway and yanked open La Casa's big door. The way he saw it, he could at least follow Jessie to Matt's place. He wouldn't need to go in. But the things his incarcerated guy at Brody had told him…nothing concrete, really, all just speculation, but still…he'd already read Dan the riot act, and Sam and Alin were going to get the goods too, so everyone would be on high alert for the next while, watching the entire Sawyer clan closely, not just Josh. Too much focus had been on Josh lately. The balance was off. Jessie should not be running off to her old lover alone. As much as he admired Josh for beating his demons and staying true to Jessie— who was not always easy to stay true to—Arnie was just a little bit sickened at how Josh let her do whatever the hell she wanted.

But, Arnie admitted to himself, *with a wild woman like Jessie, what choice does a man really have?* Really, from those early days on East Hastings when she barely spoke, when she looked at everyone including him with her chin lowered, peering upward and out from hurt, suspicious, lonely eyes, Jessie was a wild card. Add the guitar and music to that, and she was downright affecting. Everyone found her compelling. Even when she busked on the streets, nobody could pass by Jessie Wheeler without feeling somehow called to her, without being captured by her mysterious aura.

Arnie drove over the speed limit. Through the dense dark greenery of Stanley Park, he zoomed toward Matt's condo overlooking the beach beyond the end of the seawall. He caught up to Jessie just as she parked along the street and jogged across the road. She didn't see him. Sitting back, Arnie watched, and messaged Josh at the same time.

Text her. Make sure she gets inside Matt's actual condo okay.

Arnie had been to Matt's place before, to hang out and swap annoyed stories about Jessie's disregard for their protocols. Craning his neck upward, he wasn't surprised to see Matt silhouetted in his window, backlit by a standing lamp, watching Jessie make her way to the main door of his building. Matt would know Arnie's new truck. He would discern the extent of Arnie's renewed concern for Jessie's safety.

～～～

At La Casa, Josh picked up Dylan on his way to the playroom, and sighed when the little boy snuggled into him. "Tired, little buddy?" he asked. In answer, Dylan rubbed his eyes. Next to him, Jacob scooped up David. Steve and Charlie wandered over together just as Jessie texted Josh—*All is well. C u in a bit.*

"S'up?" Steve asked. "Doing the music thing?"

Jacob glanced over at Josh to see if he would answer. When he didn't, Jacob said, "Nope. Jessie took off."

Charlie covered David's ears. "Whatcha do to piss her off this time, Sawyer?" Dylan was already drifting off to sleep.

"Wouldn't you like to know?" was Josh's sullen response.

With a laugh, Charlie tossed in, "Could be anything with that girl."

Steve leaned a shoulder against the wall and absently ran a hand over Dylan's curls. "Something's up," Steve stated. The boys sobered. Josh's pensive gaze was trained on the floor. Charlie's smartass remark had gone unanswered. "You talking, Josh?"

"What?" Josh looked up. Three sets of concerned male eyes were locked on him. It was disconcerting. "I dunno," he said with a shrug. "Something about Matt not being here today. He and Arnie had a fight. You know Jessie, she has to stick her nose in every Tom, Dick, and Harry's lives." There didn't seem to be much point in getting into the trip to Brody yesterday, not here with everyone's families around, and two small boys with big ears snuggled into Josh's and Jacob's arms.

"Everybody's lives, or just Matt's?" Jacob mumbled. "Are you sure you want her going there, Sawyer?"

"Ha," Josh harrumphed. "Seriously, Jacob?"

Nudging David onto his other shoulder, Jacob paused before he said, "Matt's drunk, Josh. And he's not in a good place today. I dropped by his condo this afternoon, while Kayla was meeting with Benjie at the workshop space."

A long look passed between Josh and Jacob; it said legions about what can happen when a guy mixes alcohol with pain. Charlie gave Steve a look. Both avoided Josh's darkening eyes, yet both stiffened in response to the fists he curled around Dylan's back.

"Easy, buddy." Resting a hand on Josh's shoulder, Steve jarred his friend out of a lot of hard memories, many of them coming from staring at Jacob, a guy Josh had to work very hard to have in his company without any kind of lingering malice or shame.

"I trust her," Josh announced quietly, all the while holding Jacob's steady gaze. "And I sure as hell trust Matt. He might be drinking, but a guy with that kind of class knows his boundaries."

Charlie reached for David and lifted him out of Jacob's arms. "Let's go, Jacob," he said, noting the sudden rigidity of Jacob's stance. "This little boy needs his Auntie Kayla's arms around him."

Extending a hand, Josh touched David's head and let his hand linger there before Charlie walked away. The child's long hair strongly resembled his father's at that young age, whereas Dylan's black curls were echoed in Jacob's faltering, receding footsteps.

"Jesus, that guy," Josh muttered to Steve as Charlie and Jacob disappeared into the playroom with David. "He's counting on Matt to fuck up so it'll somehow redeem his own stupidity."

"Matt won't fuck up. Whatever's bugging him, Jessie will get to the bottom of it without being stupid. And Josh," Steve added, glancing down at the small body snuggled against Josh's chest first to be sure Dylan was snoring peacefully before he spoke, "it goes without saying that what you said about Jessie is true. She can also be trusted. What happened with her and Jacob was not her doing. And what happened with her and Matt came from a place of alienation and loneliness. She's okay now, right? You two are good?"

"We are," Josh affirmed. "We're real good, Steve. Seriously. Even me being away on this film is all good. We talk every day. We're happy."

"Then she's fine. Jacob's an ass for bringing up old shit."

"Fucking power tripping. I suppose it's his way of still trying to have control over her." Still, as the guys heaved themselves away from the wall to join the rest of the gang, both knew that Jacob's real intent was simply to voice concern. And in all truth, it likely hurt him to do so, to bring up the 'old shit,' as Steve called Jacob's transgression in Florida after Talia died. Because the thing was, Jacob knew more than anyone how pain could mess a guy up, and Josh sure as hell knew how lethal it could be when it was mixed with alcohol. The bigger question was just what kind of pain was Matt dealing with?

It would be up to Jessie to sort that out. Apart from Charles, she was Matt's best friend. It made sense for her to check in on him. She was the right person to offer comfort if comfort was needed.

At that very moment, Jessie was standing in the hallway on Matt's floor, hammering a fist against his door. The building's concierge had buzzed her up without Matt's consent; not that Matt would have said no to her visit, it was just that when Jessie Wheeler was facing the freckled twenty-something part-time worker, a UBC student who'd just started the job last week, all Jessie had to do was smile and request to be buzzed in. The student was too bashful to even ask who she was there to see.

"Matt!" she was hollering now, "Matt Kelly! Unless you've got some sexy date in there, open up this door and let me in!"

Inside, Matt was listening to Jessie repeat his name. It wasn't a stretch to figure out why she was there. Still, he needed a minute to compose himself, to figure out how to wear some kind of stoic mask so she wouldn't sense his angst. He needed a minute to try to regain his balance. A sleepless night and more than one bottle of Scotch since he got home last evening had left him unbalanced and soft in the brain. It was almost as if he'd stuffed cotton around the insides of his head and stepped off Jacob's sailboat after a two day cruise around the Caribbean. In his hands was a bottle, squared at the edges, its cut glass glinting in the semidarkness and its sweet nectar soaking up the dim light. Because it was a pain in the ass, he'd stopped refilling his glass hours ago.

For some weird, inexplicable reason, Matt's feet started walking toward the door without his brain's permission. Jessie must have sensed he was coming, he figured, because she stopped wailing at him before he even unlocked the thing and shoved it open. She was standing there facing the door, both hands shoved now in the back pockets of tight black jeans. Matt had to swallow at the naked hollow visible at the bottom of her neck—he vaguely remembered pressing his lips to her there, once. The dark, small patterned floral silk blouse she had on right now, open at the neck, covered with an unzipped jacket—the slim tailored tan leather one she wore a lot of days—just begged to be unbuttoned, slowly, one button at a time.

Contrasted with Matt's mostly dark place, in the brightness of the hallway Jessie cut an enticing silhouette. One light was all Matt had on, just a standup lamp tucked into a corner of the open concept living room. Well, that and a tiny light over the stove so he could see the sushi he'd ordered earlier and hadn't bothered to eat.

Jessie's eyes flitted down to the bottle dangling from Matt's right hand. "I see," she said, catching him unawares and grabbing it. Lifting it, tilting it back, she took a few good swallows. "Scotch, is it? Charles' favorite brand. He must be rubbing off on you. If you were emulating Josh, it'd be some random brew, maybe Kokanee or one of the Granville Island ales. I wonder which is the worst to wake up from at 4 a.m."

Pushing past him so abruptly that Matt almost stumbled, Jessie headed right, ducked into the small kitchen area, and tipped the bottle fully upside down. Its amber liquid trickled down the kitchen drain like oil from a blown transmission, defeated and suddenly powerless. With a haughty glare, Jessie tossed her curls and slammed the empty bottle down on the counter. "Jesus, Matt. You're picking my husband up in like, nine hours. You look like you need a good twelve to sober up."

Faltering, he gripped the condo door by its interior edge and shoved it hard, so that it banged shut with a menacing crack.

Swallowing, Jessie jumped, but she placed a hand on her hip and glared at him. "You and Arnie had words. What the hell, Matt? I'd think y'all were maybe fightin' over a woman, but Arnie's long been with Lucie now, so I doubt that's it. I don't think his hardcore street lady's quite your type."

"And what's my type, Jessie?" Matt drawled sleepily. "In your humble opinion."

"The whore type, apparently," she sniped back without a break. "Although it ought not to be."

Softening, Jessie sighed and moved out from behind the kitchen island. Lifting Matt's chin, she was sorry to see the worry and sadness sneaking out from under the usually firm, strong, light eyes. This was a man who would give his life for her without a second to mull it over. "What is it, Matt? Are ya gonna tell me?"

"What?" he mumbled, aching to pull her into his arms where she would stay safe forever. After yesterday, his arms seemed like the only place Jessie would ever, could ever, possibly be sheltered fully and completely from the perils awaiting her in the big, wide world, if both he and Arnie were correct in calculating that Morgan's reign of terror was as powerful as ever.

"What happened yesterday. At Brody. Why you left your fingerprints in Arnie's neck." Jessie dropped her hand and studied the ashy bags under Matt's eyes, and the wilted, mussed-up tips of his usually perfect hair. "Don't take this the wrong way, handsome, but you do realize Arnie could break your neck with one hand, right? Or with a finger or two—with his pinky, likely."

"Hilarious, Jessie." Wavering, Matt frowned at the way she was watching him, as if she was sorting out whether she ought to order him to stay home in Vancouver and not accompany Josh back to his shoot. He raised a hand and held it palm out. It kept dropping, so finally he propped it up at the elbow with his second hand. "Donnn'ttt," he slurred.

"Don't what?" Jessie crossed her arms and rocked back on one boot.

"Don't go see Morgan."

With a gasp, Jessie froze. Taking his arm a moment later, she led him to the low sixties style quilted black couch lining Matt's window, facing out. Above the city, winter stars peeked daintily back at them. Below, on English Bay, warm yellow lights in cargo ship windows hovered pleasurably above the inky black water, the lights proof that there was life aboard—life that included food and music and rowdy card games as the ships awaited their turns to pass under the Lion's Gate Bridge on the north side of Stanley Park so they could unload or pick up cargo somewhere along Burrard Inlet.

Urging her good friend to sit, Jessie said, "That's what you and Arnie were fighting about? Am I to take that to mean you and Charles didn't make any progress with Morgan?"

"We did and we didn't," was Matt's careful response. "I don't want you going there."

Sitting back, Jessie considered his request. "Honey," she said, taking his hand between both of hers, "if Arnie thinks I can help Josh by going to see Morgan, then I—well, maybe I ought to go."

A loud grunt was Matt's gut response. He followed it up with a quick rebuttal that included waving his empty hand toward his body. "You see me, Jessie?" he asked her. "I'm a shining example…of what that dark place…can do to a guy."

Her eyes narrowed. "You're a strong man, Matt. I'm sure you've been in prisons before, back in your R.C.M.P. days. You knew what to expect. There's something you're not telling me."

Matt's voice was thick with drink. He spoke slowly. "Look, Jessie, Arnie and I are polarized opposites. He's a street thug—"

Jumping up, Jessie let Matt's hand fall to the couch. He had to grab the edge to keep from swimming over and landing on the ground. Finding the strength to speak past his fatigue and growing nausea was excruciating.

Jessie whipped around to face him. "Arnie knows a part of me you will never know, Matt. And you ought to know by now that I am more like him than I am like you. He knows I can handle Brody."

"Can you?" Matt asked wearily. "It's a bizarre feeling, Jessie, walking in and having doors clanging shut behind you as you pass. Double doors…you can't get out unless someone who likes you…chooses to push a button. And there's…a dark energy there. Stay the hell away from the place. And don't let Arnie talk you into going."

Forcing himself upright, Matt glanced past Jessie down toward the street. Arnie's new truck glistened under a watery streetlight. From the condo, it looked like one of the kids' dinky cars. In his drunken state, Matt thought about pinching it between his fingers and dropping it into English Bay.

Regarding him critically, Jessie blinked back tears. Without telling her exactly why, Matt was clearly revealing an overall feeling of hopelessness. Why else would he be here wallowing in self-pity while everyone else was hanging out at La Casa talking about wedding plans and new babies and a future that practically jiggled, it seemed so full of promise?

Clueing in to her thoughts, Matt reached over and brushed a strand of loose hair off Jessie's cheek. Trying out an attempt at a smile, he tucked the hair behind her ear. The movement was so like the way Jessie tenderly liked to touch Josh that she closed her eyes and inhaled to a count of six. She opened them when he spoke, but was unable to quell a rising fear.

"Look, Jessie," Matt said softly, both warm palms on her cheeks now, his breath reeking of liquor but in a sweet way that made him vulnerable and real to her, that stirred a desire Jessie always had to try to defeat when she was alone with him. The benevolent eyes were pleading now, pleading that she would listen and that she would understand. "We didn't get shit all from Morgan, okay?" he half lied. "I'm sorry. And yes, Arnie and I disagreed on how to move forward. All of that just made me want to take a day, you know?"

"You gonna be okay, Matt? You're gonna be…umm…" Jessie couldn't finish. It seemed like it would hurt him to remind him that he was still responsible for watching over Josh for the next three weeks.

"I know what you're thinking," he said quietly, stroking her cheek with his thumb. "I'll be fine, sweetheart. It's just one day. I just needed one day."

"Do you have any more liquor here, Matt?" *I can't talk about Morgan right now. I can't talk about what he said or didn't say. Josh…*

The terror was never ending.

"I do," he murmured. "But I'm done with it, Jessie, for today, at least. Okay?" He was still looking at her in that awed, humbled way Matt looked at Jessie when he was gifted alone time with her, when they could be honest and raw and open about how deeply their blood ran in each other's veins.

It was disabling her.

Reaching up, Jessie took Matt's hands in hers. "Let me tuck you in," she whispered, and quickly shook her head in case he misunderstood. "I'll lie down with you for a bit, honey," she said, "but we're not going there. Okay? We'll just lie down. Just for a little while."

At his slow nod, Jessie turned him around and gave him a gentle push toward his small bathroom. "Go brush your teeth," she demanded, forcing a lightness into her tone. "I'll meet you in the bedroom. And don't please ever tell Josh I said that to you just now." With a tiny forced giggle, Jessie pulled her phone out of her coat pocket and texted Josh. After what happened with Jacob, and with Matt—despite what got them there—she wasn't taking any chances. Josh deserved full disclosure, at regular and honest intervals.

Staying with him for a bit. Sobering him up. Text me when u head for home and I'll meet u there

Wandering into Matt's bedroom, Jessie had to poke the remembrance of their intimate time together back down in her heart where it belonged. Tonight she would be a support for her good friend, but tonight their intimacy would stop where, out of respect for Josh, and for Matt too, it needed to.

She was lying on top of the covers when Matt trundled in. Shuffling off his white linen shirt to reveal a white T-shirt underneath, he lay down on his side next to Jessie and frowned when she smiled at him.

"Kept the jeans on. Good man," she teased. "And I like the white T-shirt. Reminds me of someone."

Matt yawned. Gathering him close, Jessie wrapped her arms around him and kissed his forehead. "Sleep well, my friend," she sighed. It was on the tip of her tongue to add, "And take care of my husband," but she fought it off.

A muffled voice reached her ears as Matt settled into a comfortable position with one hand relaxing on Jessie's hip. "He'll be okay," Matt was saying. "Josh will be okay." It was a truth he knew she needed to hear. Matt felt Jessie's body relax as relief washed over her. *I'm being deceitful for not telling her the whole truth,* he thought. But—why worry her?

This moment was the only one that mattered. This moment was the only one that counted. With Jessie's arms comforting him, offering a safe place to land that he could rely on, Matt breathed out the stress of the last few days and drifted off to sleep.

Arnie was still parked outside Matt's building when Jessie headed across the street to Josh's truck an hour later. Sidling over to him, she shot him a look that he knew well. It was a remnant of the Downtown Eastside days—a strength and power of will that helped Jessie survive a lot of almost unbearable years. Now, here, standing in front of his truck window with her hands dug deep into her jacket pockets, she was that homeless waif again, the one that slept on his couch when the nights got too cold to bear, the one that dodged unwanted advances but who climbed into bed in Caryn's studio with a camera on her, when it meant the difference between eating and surviving, and going hungry and giving up the battle altogether.

This woman was one who, when push came to shove, always surprised everyone with her strength.

"I'm going to Brody," she told him. "I don't know when, but I'm going." Swinging around, she marched ahead to Josh's truck and hopped into the driver's seat without waiting for his answer.

Arnie just nodded. "Atta girl," he said, and turned his key in the Tundra's ignition. He tailed her back to the UBC house, walked her to the back door, gave Dan a wave when Jessie went in, and jogged back up the flagstone steps.

Jessie Wheeler was a fighter. There was a soft side to her, sure, but when all was said and done, the girl knew how to fight back…

Good thing, too.

Because she had a hell of a fight ahead of her.

Chapter Fifteen

$\mathcal{B}$efore Josh left the next morning, Jessie found him standing at the doorway of Emily-Grace's bedroom. He looked like he was holding the wall up or, Jessie considered, maybe it was holding him up. Yet, as fatigued as he was in the early morning darkness, there was a lightness to the way he was standing, a lift in his shoulders.

Stealing up behind him, Jessie wrapped both arms snugly around his waist and sighed into his body. Her voice tickled his neck. "Couldn't you just pretend you're not happy about leaving us?"

Josh wheeled around and pulled her close. "I'm not happy to be leaving you," he stated with a tiny smile. "But I'm not gonna lie about how much I love this job."

"Oh, you just want another Oscar. You can't stand being second to your woman." Giggling, Jessie brushed her lips against Josh's freshly shaved cheek and snuggled her nose into that cherished spot behind his ear, under his layered hair, that was just begging to be kissed. "You smell so good," she breathed. "Like soap…lime soap…something green…all fresh and clean." Tilting her face back up to him, she winked. "Come back to bed, big boy." At the same time, she reached for his belt.

Perfectly timed, the bright headlights of a car swept over Emily-Grace's room, a guiding light that split the darkness in two. The little girl's window was cracked open just a mite to let in a touch of winter's dreamlike magic. The car outdoors ground to a halt, and two male voices calling greetings to each other rose over the crisp, cool air.

Josh placed his hand over Jessie's. "Your best buddy has impeccable timing," he said.

"He can wait." They were whispering, since Emily-Grace was sleeping nearby, but Josh still had to shush his wife when Jessie's giggles escalated.

"Don't wake her," he chided. "I don't need her mad at me." Lifting Jessie's fingers to his mouth, Josh brushed his lips across them. "You already kept me awake half the night. You're insatiable. I need the remainder of this shoot just to rest up."

Jessie would have laughed outright but, clearly, there was something else on Josh's mind. The easy bent to his body transformed into a serious tautness. The chocolate eyes became intent and earnest.

"What?" Jessie asked, letting her hands drop inside Josh's leather jacket to rest on his hips.

"Was Matt okay last night? I wanted to ask you when you got home, but," he hesitated, "it didn't seem like the right time. Between the kids' needs, and me leaving today…"

In her bed, Emily-Grace rolled over and moaned in her sleep. Both Josh and Jessie looked over at their daughter. Her butterfly lashes remained closed; blonde hair fanned out over the pillow. She was lost in some obscure dream.

Unsure, Jessie started picking at the zipper on Josh's leather jacket, zipping it up and down and up and down until he covered her fingers and urged her to stop. "Nope. He wasn't," she finally answered him. "Not even remotely, if you want the truth. I guess prisons have some kind of nefarious hold on him."

"Prisons? Or prisoners?"

"Inmates. Certain ones. The term prisoner is apparently no longer widely used. Human rights."

"Hell, they get three square meals a day and a dry place to sleep. They oughtta call them guests."

"I hear they even have pillows." Jessie chafed at her own comment. "Seriously, Josh. We are nobody's judges, remember? Most of those people didn't have a chance the moment they were conceived."

"My beautiful girl," Josh smiled sadly. "Always looking for the good in people."

"What choice do we have, babe? Wallow in anger forever?"

"I'd be more optimistic if we could at least eradicate the fear."

"Oh, Josh. I know, but it's not doing us any good to worry. Right? You know your Bible." She wasn't fooling him, though. Josh read right through his wife's false bravado. She'd looked away from him, moved her glance back down to his belt, and slid her fingers along until she could clutch the buckle and obstinately pick at it.

"Hey," he said, lifting her chin so she had no choice but to look at him. "I'm sorry. I shouldn't have brought that up just before I leave."

"I'll never get enough of you," Jessie murmured. "Won't matter when we pass away, you or me. Age ninety. Or a ripe old hundred. Our time together here will never be enough."

Josh offered comfort the best way he knew how. "We'll always be together, you and I. With our kids, and our friends, even. Every lifetime, little one."

The sea-pearl color was back in Jessie's eyes, dreamy and optimistic. "Josh? Do you ever just wish we could stop time? Like…right here, right now?"

"Last night around 1 a.m. would have been good for me." Josh's grin was genuine, his lips crooked and his eyes alight with the remembrance of a real good night of lovemaking. Something about their imminent parting had injected a vigorous new level of desire and connection. For Jessie, lying next to Matt earlier—holding him as he drifted off into a confused and frightened alcohol infused slumber—had only increased the ache for Josh. Easing her body off Matt's bed and leaving him alone in a darkened, sterile condo only served to remind her to cherish the sacredness of shared love. She'd tiptoed away from Matt after bending over and anointing him with a chaste kiss on an earlobe; he'd stirred, but not awakened.

At home, once the children were settled in their beds, Jessie took her husband to bed and celebrated the gift of physical love. Josh was happy; he was here. They'd been through a lot of separations and hurt over their time as partners; lovemaking was a gift, a sanctified unity, a time to hold each other under the crisp stars of a winter's night, in the safety of their own home, with their deeply loved children asleep nearby.

Now, Jessie leaned in for a kiss but she giggled and moaned instead when Josh slipped his hand between her legs for a last quick tease. The roguish playfulness whizzing across Josh's eyes gave a lift to his soul that Jessie hoped she would witness forevermore in his cherished company. Blushing, remembering their lovemaking, she slipped a hand up underneath his T-shirt. The warmth of his skin underneath her fingers soaked into her body. With an aching moan, she closed her eyes and pressed her forehead to his shoulder. "Last night around one a.m. was pretty good for me, too," she agreed. "I could use me some more of that kinda goodness."

"And the kind you got at one fifteen, and one thirty, and at least three more times before two."

"Liar. You're not that good."

"Ouch," Josh sulked at her spirited, good intentioned comeback.

The mood this morning was like ocean waves—watery hills and valleys with a moving, liquid refuge underneath that mercilessly tossed safe footing out the window. Like a ship about to be tossed onto rocks, Jessie's little slip got picked up by the current and deposited outside the realm of safety. As a result, even the remembrance of making love was suddenly tenuous and uncertain.

Josh knew that Jessie realized her faux pas the instant she spoke, because she immediately groaned and buried her face in his chest. He wrapped his arms tighter around her shoulders and listened to Matt's faraway voice float over the soundless night toward them. There was no way of ever outrunning their tumultuous past. All they could do now was mitigate it and pass through life one day at a time. A safe and harmonious future was the lighthouse they would aim for.

"I have to go," Josh said suddenly. Pushing Jessie away from him, he studied the worried, subdued, watery eyes peering back at him. "I love you." His voice was gruff, his actions hurried. There was never an easy way to let go, to say goodbye. Brushing by her, Josh picked up the duffel bag he'd left earlier outside their bedroom door. "Go back to sleep, Jessie," he called quietly over his shoulder just before he descended the stairs. "The kids'll be up before you know it."

"I've got them trained," Jessie told him, trying to make light of a tough morning. "They know to bring me breakfast in bed. Toast and yogurt. With blueberries sprinkled on the yogurt, and cinnamon on the toast."

"Hard to believe they're old enough already."

"Speaking of which…" Jessie smiled, twisted around, and crossed her arms. She leaned on the wall between Emily-Grace's room and the playroom.

"What?" Josh stopped on the top step, but he was poised to keep moving. He half expected Matt to start blaring the car horn.

"Five, baby," Jessie whispered, a new light crisscrossing her face the same way Matt's car headlights lit up Emily-Grace's room a short time before. "We said we'd have five. Dylan's halfway to four years old…"

"Ha." Josh was beaming wholeheartedly now. "Do what you need to do in terms of birth control. I look forward to trying when I get back. Multiple times a day, if you like."

They shared a moment then, the sweetest of the entire weekend, when an unseen delicate golden-white energy flowed between their bodies, giving both Josh and Jessie a blissful peace in the certainty of wanting more children together.

"Jacob and Kayla's new little one will need a cousin around its own age to play with." Jessie lifted a finger to twist a ringlet in a rogue strand of hair. "I'll start thinking up names."

"Don't you miss working?" Josh asked then, cocking his head to one side, still grinning happily.

Dropping the finger from her hair, Jessie drew up both shoulders. "Nope, Mister Sawyer, I do not. I would never work another day in my life if I could spend my days with you and our babies instead, with all of our friends and loved ones nearby."

"Ah, but wouldn't the world miss out." Josh's voice was soft and melodious, hushed and respectful of what Jessie's music—and acting—had done for so many hurting people in the world.

"They've got YouTube memories." Glowing, Jessie moved toward Josh and treated him to one last, enduring kiss. "I love you so much, Josh. Heed what Matt says, don't get careless, and babe, please, please, please come back to me."

"I will." A final lingering moment, thinking about the promised new baby and who he/she would be, and Josh brushed his lips against Jessie's cheek and jogged down the steps.

You're too excited to be scared, Jessie thought, hugging her belly tightly when she heard the back door quietly close with a decided and final click. After a moment, she turned around and went into the playroom. It was tidy; she always insisted the kids pick up after themselves, but one small toy had been left out. It squeaked when Jessie stepped on it in the hazy darkness. It was a small white lamb, one of Dylan's old teething aids—a lamb that had survived the slaughter, Jessie chuckled, considering Dylan's rambunctious nature. Holding it to her chest, she sidled over to the window and watched Josh greet Matt, and Sam, too, who was on Sawyer house duty overnight. Their voices were low, so she couldn't make out what they were saying, but it was evident Josh didn't waste time on too many social graces. He dumped his duffel into the Audi's trunk before Jessie could blink an eye, and opened the passenger side door without so much as a glance back up to his house.

Matt, on the other hand, seemed like he didn't want to leave. The driveway was well lit; Charles and Matt were strict about always keeping the light bulbs fresh and the security cameras working. It was easy to spy sweet Matt's uncharacteristically unshaven chin as he strode around to the driver's side while Josh got comfortable and buckled up. It was harder to bear his expression when Jessie saw him glance up and see her shadowy form in the playroom window.

Sorrow. It was clinging to him like a ghost. But that wasn't a surprise. What would have surprised Jessie—had she been able to hear what Josh said to Matt when he approached the guys, and which enhanced Matt's despair— was what Matt was thinking.

On his way to the trunk to drop his duffel bag, Josh had said hi to Sam and Matt, shot Matt an understanding look that said *I get why you were drinking,* accented it with, "You okay to drive, Matt?" And added a happy, "She wants another baby. Jessie. We're gonna have to buy a bigger house."

Apart from the stinging jealousy that gutted Matt was a frightening, sinister thought that erupted like a volcano the instant Josh's declaration about the baby struck home. A thick hot lava snaked its way down Matt's throat and seared his heart as he rounded the front of the car and stopped at the driver's side door to look up at Jessie.

No, he begged her, in a troubled, telepathic silence. *No more. No more Sawyers to worry over. No more Sawyers to try to save.*

Josh glowered at Matt when he finally slid into the car. The despairing way Matt was staring hopelessly up at Jessie… "For fuck's sake, Matt," he growled. "I thought we were all good here."

Matt started the car, but crouched over the wheel without putting it into reverse. The nausea was debilitating, and it wasn't all from a weekend of drinking. He half thought of asking Josh to drive. "Us? Good?" he said. Sitting back, he gave Josh a stony, hard look. *Take the emotion out of this,* he warned himself. *This is business. These fucked-up people are just plain business.* "I didn't touch her last night, Josh. But I sure as hell wanted to. Keep your wife on a leash, will you? As close by you as you fucking can when you get back, okay?"

Stunned at the outburst from the usually professional Matt, Josh just stared. Outside, tall, athletic Sam wondered what the hell the holdup was.

Matt didn't blink at Josh. His eyes were ice. "You don't give her that baby. Not now. Maybe not ever."

Erupting, Josh fired back. "You forgot to add 'not as long as I'm working for you.' You fucking bastard, Matt. You couldn't just let me have this?"

"You're leaving her. You're leaving your kids, Josh. We're backing out of this driveway and flying far the hell away from Vancouver so you can shoot a goddamned movie!"

"So I can work! A man needs to work, Matt. What the hell's your goddamn problem?"

"A man needs to be with his family, that's what! You ought to be here watching out for them. That's what!"

A stillness rocked the car with as much power as a frenzied wind. The storm was sudden, and it was fraught with a supreme strength that drained Josh of the hope that he and Jessie could have another child, and could absolutely, without question, keep that child from harm. "What happened on Saturday, Matt?" he asked icily. "What the hell did Morgan say?"

A raspy growl was Matt's answer. Whipping open his door, he leaned over the side and puked onto the asphalt. Immobile, Josh watched him retch for a few seconds before he exhaled painfully and turned to the side. Sam was leaning against his own car; if it weren't for the worry of leaving Matt alone with Jessie, Josh would have asked Sam to come on the trip instead. Beyond Sam he looked up to see Jessie watching them. She was faintly backlit by the hall light; in the playroom window, her expression was unreadable, but her tense poise was easy to comprehend—fear.

"Jesus Christ," Josh said flatly, squeezing his eyes shut, and sinking back against the seat. Matt slammed his door and echoed Josh's position. He, too, closed his eyes while the car idled underneath them, anxious to slip away from this pressure cooker and slink into the darkness like a wounded spirit.

"No more kids. Not right now," Matt finally said. One last look up at Jessie, and he wiped his mouth on the sleeve of his $ 3500 cashmere coat, shot Sam a look of warning, and put the car in gear.

Josh's voice stopped him. "We're not gonna stop living, Matt." Devoid of emotion, drained, Josh was staring straight ahead now. "We're taking what we can get."

"Yeah. Good luck with that, buddy." Stepping on the gas, Matt propelled them backward. "Coffee?" he asked, and didn't say another word apart from what was absolutely necessary until later that day, after Josh shot two scenes that the director called, "Brilliant," and after he sought out Ferne to warm his bed, and a new bottle of scotch to ease his heart.

Chapter Sixteen

Jessie didn't get to Brody right away. It was Charles who had the power to get Jessie and Arnie in, and he was having second thoughts about making that happen while she was home alone with her children. In his mind, Arnie's urging was on one side and Matt's caution was on the other. Torn, Charles just wasn't sure if sending Jessie to see Morgan right away was a good idea. Period. If ever.

David picked up a bug from school, so while Jessie waited in hopeful optimism for a call Charles was hesitating to make, she stayed home to nurse her son. As busy as Jacob and Kayla were between the Downtown Eastside workshops and planning their wedding, the couple picked up the slack with the other two Sawyer children. Dylan was doing pre-school now, and Emily-Grace was rocketing through grade three, but since their schooling would be morphing over to Alberta soon, nobody seemed to care a whole lot about schoolwork the first week Josh was gone, while David was fighting a sore throat and fever.

Dylan and Emily-Grace were in their glory. Already the oldest Sawyer was a skilled dancer and guitarist. Dylan watched and learned, but drums were his thing. They spent their days at the workshops, and their early evenings hanging out with Jacob and Kayla.

Arnie dropped by to see Jessie one evening five days after Josh and Matt's tense departure. Deirdre was at the house with her, in the kitchen drying dinner dishes while Alin washed. Ulysses was outside in the driveway talking to Dan. Arnie didn't wave, he just nodded tersely at the men as he passed by. Inside, he was respectful enough to ask Deirdre if he could talk to Jessie.

Well aware of the trust between the two of them, Dee sent him upstairs to David's room with the warning to step cautiously since David might be asleep.

Arnie found the middle Sawyer child in his mother's worried arms in Dylan's room. Wrapped lightly in a fluffy blue towel after a lukewarm bath Jessie hoped would bring his fever down, David was enjoying the sweet, rare pleasure of having his beloved momma all to himself as she rocked him in the big rocker in his little brother's bedroom.

He was asleep by the time Arnie knocked carefully and entered the room. "Deirdre let me come upstairs," he said to Jessie. "Is that okay with you?"

"Of course, Arnie." Jessie spoke in a subdued tone, her tired voice hoarse with concern for her sick child. "Although you never come up here. What's up?" She gestured for him to sit on Dylan's small bed. Arnie was not a tall man, but he was fit. Out of place on the bed, a childless man himself, he fidgeted and she smiled. "You look good there, honey. Want me to toss you that soft Paw Patrol blanket so you can wrap it around yourself? Josh loves it."

"He would," Arnie grimaced. He looked around the room. It was cozy, postered with small boy things. One of those was a framed photo of Dylan's biological father, on stage with Jessie at the Grammys one year. The two had guitars slung over their shoulders and were facing each other. It was easy to discern their soul level musical connection—love was clear in each other's eyes. Arnie nodded at it. "Josh must love that."

Following his curious stare, Jessie made a quiet *mmpphh* sound and shrugged. "Sometimes Josh doesn't have a choice. Anyways, he doesn't want Dylan to grow up resenting him for keeping him from Jacob. It's not always easy, but there's a reason I worship my man. He is kind and forgiving. And he's one helluva dad to Dylan, regardless. Josh and Jacob both are. To all three kids, actually."

Arnie sat back and leaned against the wall. He searched out Jessie's pale eyes and watched her adjust David in her lap.

"I can take him to his room," she said quietly. "You and I can go down to the media room to talk. I'll ask Dee to come sit with David."

"Is he asleep?" Arnie asked.

"I think so," Jessie replied. "But you look like you've got some serious shit to talk about, Arnie. Asleep or not, I don't want that kind of negative energy anywhere around my son."

"Understood," Arnie agreed with a nod. "I'll meet you downstairs." He stood.

Jessie's voice followed him to the doorway. He stopped, and listened. "So I'm right. It's serious."

Arnie waited. Absently tracing a finger along the door frame, he said, "I'll meet you downstairs, Jessie."

Ten minutes later, leaving an awakened sleepy, whiny child with his grandmother, Jessie lowered her weary body onto the leather couch in the downstairs media room. Arnie was across from her in a big black easy chair. She raised her arms. "What?" she challenged him. "Make my day, Arnie."

"You remember James Vaughn, Jessie? From the old days on East Hastings? Big black guy?"

A chill iced its way up the back of Jessie's neck. She tossed her hair and folded her legs underneath her so she could lean on one elbow, which she rested on the arm of the couch. "I do," she admitted. "But I don't want to. You saved my ass from him. Literally."

"He cut a few girls."

Arnie was as serious as Jessie ever saw him. She shivered. "I'm aware. I know."

"You were not very street smart when you first came to the Downtown Eastside."

"I was hungry," Jessie whispered. "He took me out to dinner."

"By that you mean he bought you a cheeseburger, if I recall."

"Hey. Fatburger makes awesome chocolate milkshakes." The lightness Jessie was trying to inject into her tone wasn't doing a thing to ease the dark mood that washed over her at the mention of James Vaughn. Sighing, Jessie looked down at her fingers. One nail was cracked, and another was jagged at the edge. "I need a fucking manicure," she complained.

"You're damn lucky he didn't cut you bad, Jessie."

A clock was ticking in the far corner. Looking toward it, away from Arnie, Jessie said matter-of-factly, "Who the hell says he didn't?"

Bristling, Arnie scolded her. "You didn't say anything. You were starting to talk a little, by then."

"Sure I did," she said, looking back at the gentle but life-hardened eyes of a man Jessie trusted with her life, then and now. "I said something. Just not in words. I bled all over your fucking car." Tears pricked at her eyes. "You're in my house now, Arnie. You're bringing shit into my home that I don't want to remember. Josh has never even asked where that scar came from, where any of my scars came from. He knows better."

"Has Matt?"

The bitter coldness in Arnie's stare was freaking Jessie out. "None of your fucking business, asshole. Jesus, Arnie!"

He sat up straighter. "Vaughn might not have killed those girls if you'd said something, Jessie," he railed. "But then again he might not be in Brody Pen right now, either, where we need him."

That disclosure jarred Jessie to a new level of attention. "He's in Brody? He's talking to you?"

"You're his connection to glory, girl. He's all about talking to me."

"Ah. My past is so irreverent. It refuses to stay where I fucking put it. What the hell's he got to do with me now, Arnie, besides the gory fact that every con in Brody likely now knows he got to play where many men have played? Some more fun than others, I might add. Like the ones who don't take hunting knives to bed with them." She was still shaking. *Am I coming down with a fever too?* Jessie wondered. *Or maybe it's just the fallout from this latest darkness stalking me.*

"Vaughn is my guy, Jessie. He's my eyes and my ears."

"In Brody? Lovely. What do you have that he needs? Cuz I'm damn sure he wouldn't be reporting to you if you didn't have something he wants."

"You have something he wants."

"What? A signed poster? Damn, Arnie. I'll give him a thousand posters if he can get Morgan to call off his damn wolves. I'll sit here all day tomorrow while my kid whines in pain from his sore throat and I'll sign posters. What's he want me to say? Thanks for the loving? Or should I just come right out there and say 'thanks for not cutting me dead like you did the others?'"

At that, Jessie shoved herself upright and paced the small room a few times. Arnie stood too, and waited until she settled down before he faced her. "He wants a song."

"What?" Aghast, Jessie froze. "He wants a what?"

"He'll keep me in the loop if you write him a song. And say it's for him."

"He killed women." She held up her fingers. "Two. Women. Girls, really. I can't write him a song. You have a helluva lotta nerve even asking me!"

"You want him to be a conduit to Morgan? Vaughn's got power at Brody. His lot helps keeps the general population in check, and he has access to the gym. Morgan's favorite hangout, apparently, when he gets out of his cell. Apart from yoga and meditation."

Scowling, Jessie stared at Arnie. "Morgan and yoga. I hope he and Ghandi are having some good long chats these days. Preferably the peace infusing kind." With a cautious, guarded unease, Jessie slid her fatigued bones back down onto the couch. Leaning forward, she hung her head between her hands. "I'll write your guy a song if that's what we need to do to keep the lines of communication open. We need any hold over Morgan we can get, right Arnie?" A thought struck her. "He won't hurt him though, right?"

Arnie shook his head slowly from side to side. "You blow my mind. Morgan's still got power over you—over your family—and you don't want him hurt."

"Morgan's a shell, Arnie. So's Vaughn, likely. People don't end up on the wrong side of the law for enduring perfect lives. That's why I'll write that song. Maybe it'll inject some kindness into those bones. Arnie…you and I know the Downtown Eastside. We know the people there. Or at least…I used to. I don't so much anymore. The life span there, it's not…well, you know what I'm trying to say. The thing is, though, guys like James Vaughn, they're not so different from you and me. Even with his strong body and that handsome face, he's still got to survive. And you know how it works in a place like that. Survival of the fittest, just like in the jungle. It's no different. And with that kind of bid for survival comes a choice—you turn right, or you turn left. You and I, we turned right. James turned left. Morgan wasn't on the Downtown Eastside, but metaphorically speaking, Nadia was. And when she turned left, she dragged Morgan along with her."

Arnie took that in. After a long-assed minute, he said, "There's no real way to win this thing, Jessie. The only thing I can figure is letting Morgan see your eyes, your heart. Letting him connect with you. Vaughn can only do so much. He'll be a voice for us, mostly."

"I'll sing there. I'll set up and I'll sing. Maybe it'll get us in sooner."

"Yeah, Matt'll be all over that one. Don't get carried away." Striding toward the stairs, Arnie said, "Matt's too close to you. I don't think he needs to know everything, by the way."

"Matt's a part of me, Arnie."

"So's Josh. You tell him what drove Matt to drink on Sunday?"

"I don't even know what really drove Matt around the bend last Sunday. I'm just guessing."

Arnie rested a hand on the banister. "Care to tell me what you guessed?"

Jessie put on the mask she always wore to help keep the tough emotions at bay. She shrugged. "The general negative vibe of the place. Seeing Morgan again. Not really getting any solid answers."

"Go deeper."

"Okay. Fine." Thoughtfully scratching her bottom lip and slipping a nail inside her mouth to absently give it a chew, Jessie said, "All right. Let's add up the pieces. Matt mumbled something in his drunken glory about Josh being okay. Still, the day before, at La Casa, Matt lunged at your throat and then went on a fucking bender. If we bring Charles into the equation, well, he can barely look at me." Inhaling, she added much too calmly than was warranted, "I'm guessing Morgan still wants someone dead. And if Matt's telling the truth about Josh being okay, then I suppose that someone is me. And because you have a contact at Brody who is, by virtue of a mutual connection with me and Morgan, interested in Morgan's diabolical thoughts, you've likely known this all along. Hence you driving like a bat out of hell to follow me to Matt's condo Sunday night. You've probably been secretly tailing me for a while now, huh Arnie?"

Arnie gripped the banister tighter. His knuckles whitened.

Jessie stared him down. "You're lucky Matt didn't go digging around for that pistol of his and shoot you outright. No wonder he chose to hide inside a bottle for most of the weekend. Much preferable to looking me in the eye sober, I suppose."

Arnie swallowed. Suddenly his throat was scratchy and dry, and he was fairly certain it had nothing to do with the bug little David was suffering from. Jessie was spot on, but she hadn't mentioned the children. He wondered if she'd figured that part out, but what she said earlier was right. This discussion had already brought too much darkness into her home, and he was not willing to take her any further down a terrifying road that may or may not already register on her radar.

Sticking a hand in his pocket, he withdrew a small package—it crinkled. It was cylindrical, a plastic wrapped gray something-or-other that made Jessie's eyebrows uplift into a question mark.

"White sage?" she asked with surprise.

"Clear the energy here, Jessie," he demanded. "Every room." He watched the interpretation of that comment drain the blood from her face.

She blinked, shuddered, and nodded. "I will," she promised. "Thanks, Arnie." As he started up the stairs, she called to him in a hollowed out voice he recognized from years earlier. It was soaked with pain back in the day, and saturated with a new dread here today. "Arnie?"

"Yeah, kid?" He rotated around to watch her process what to say.

In the end, Jessie hugged her belly tightly and crumpled so low over and into herself that for a second Arnie thought she might curl right up into a ball and collapse on the floor. She whispered, "I just wish Josh was home."

There was no response to that. Arnie uttered a low *humphh* of agreement and made his way upstairs. As Jessie dropped back down onto the couch, the white sage held reverently in her fingers, she sighed and realized that, during his unexpected visit, her old Downtown Eastside pal had not once smiled.

Chapter Seventeen

By the time Josh was ready to wrap his shoot, the rest of the Sawyer children had battled strep throat, and Jessie and Jacob had played at a Seattle fundraiser. On the jet on the way home from Seattle, Jessie argued with Deirdre over a film role Dee thought she should take, while Jacob and Kayla, coasting toward their big day, snuggled up on the back sofa and fine-tuned their wedding plans.

Josh's shoot ended early in the week. By then Jessie was home frothing at the bit, anxious for her husband to get his ass back to Vancouver so she could hold him, and so he could hold her right back. There was a strength in their twoness that, after the crazy last few weeks, Jessie sorely needed.

He called before the wrap party. In the midst of dinner prep, still tired out from a seemingly endless cycle of all-nighters tending to illness, and the exhausting Seattle show, Jessie sank onto a stool at the kitchen island and hung her head in her hands.

"Hey, babe," she managed wearily. "You and Matt taking care of each other?"

"Yeah, sure, we got each other's backs."

The sarcasm in Josh's tone further deflated Jessie's spirit. "The two of you are a walking Hallmark TV special."

"And whose fault is that?"

"Oh, for God's sake, Josh. Let it go, cowboy. I'm not in the mood. Just grab your Oscar and come home. You better be getting one for this movie because it's been earned, trust me. And I'm not talking about your acting. It oughtta go to me, for those midnight tears that come with sick children. My tears, in case you're wondering. Which you probably aren't."

"The kids are feeling better, right? And FYI, heavy gold statues aren't handed out at wrap parties, Jessie." With a chuckle, Josh switched the phone to his other hand. "But I wish they were. That way I wouldn't have to wait so long for my new one."

"Cocky bastard. Yes, our three beautiful babies are well and energized. Finally. After school, for instance, Emily-Grace and David were bickering over who should get first crack at the piano for practice. Seems Jacob's issued them a challenge, and you know the drill, they gotta please Jacob."

"Great."

Jessie had to sneak in a tiny smile at that. She could almost hear the *grrrr* in Josh's voice. "While his older siblings were arguing," she continued, "Dylan ran between them, jumped up on the bench and hammered out his own version of *Twinkle, Twinkle.* It was quite dramatic. Even the birds in the trees flew away."

"Maybe Dylan should stick to drums."

"I closed the piano lid and banished all three of them to their rooms to read. There may have been tears."

"Yours or theirs?"

"Not answering that."

"Softie." Reclining on his big bed, Josh smiled. "I would have liked to have been there."

"Soon enough you can referee their fights. And dry my tears. Oops, did I admit that?" Jessie giggled. "Where are you now, you big goof?"

"In my suite. Just heading out to the party."

"And Matt is…?"

"Next door. Waiting anxiously. Probably pacing. I would have thought he'd be in as much of a hurry as me to get back to Vancouver except that— are you ready for this? He seems quite attached to his new bedmate down here." Pausing, Josh cocked an ear and listened closely. Jessie said nothing. Josh jumped back in with, "I can tell you're overjoyed."

"I really don't care." The small, thin voice worried Josh. Jessie had more to say. "And I don't appreciate you telling me that like you think it'll hurt me. What part of you could possibly think I don't want Matt to be happy? To find someone?"

Josh grabbed a spare pillow and hugged it to his stomach. "Oookaaayyy," he said in a long exhale. "I'm sorry. That was shitty. I don't want to fight with you."

"No, you just want to soak up all the happiness and joy you can at your stupid party before you have to come back to the reality of noisy little kids and a wife who wears messy ponytails and Lululemons every day. Pardon me for stepping on your sunshine."

In his mind, Josh pictured the stunning glamorous shots of his wife in haute couture at the recent Seattle fundraiser, which were now all over the Internet. "Lululemons," he grinned. "Yeah, I'll try real hard to feel bad about those on your tight butt. Glad to see that the news of Matt's new woman hasn't put you in a bad mood, little one."

"Don't call me that. I'm about to hang up on you, and I don't want to. I don't want to let you go." Realizing what she said, Jessie raised her free hand and squeezed hard at the corners of her eyes. *I'm just PMSing,* she told herself. Truthfully, she'd been an emotional wreck the entire day. Just under three weeks of family sickness; a concert she really hadn't gotten into the vibe of; a bouncing, ecstatic Jacob (like an out of control puppy) at her side in Seattle nuzzling with Kayla—who was along for the fun even though she didn't dance at that show; a song Jessie was writing for this Vaughn guy that sucked the life out of her even though she was trying to find some light in it; and Arnie's serious warning eyes…all were overwhelming her today.

"Just come home," she pleaded into the phone. "Please. Sooner rather than later."

They disconnected with strained apologies from both ends. The next day, Jessie wished to hell she'd put her own dark mood aside and been more patient and understanding with Josh.

Ulysses was at her bedroom door at five a.m. And he, like Arnie of late, was not smiling.

～ ～

Josh was in a low mood when he and Matt pulled their rental vehicle into a parking slot in the hotel's underground parking. Everyone at the party had been drunk except him, and the phone squabble with Jessie had left him disconcerted and annoyed. He just wanted to enjoy this last night with his

132

new friends. Every film's cast and crew bonded after weeks of hard, close-knit work, and some of this gang were folks Josh had worked with before. Goodbyes were always the hardest part of any shoot. And twenty minutes earlier, Josh had said his goodbyes.

Matt was in a pissy mood too. In fact, Matt had been in a super pissy mood the entire last three weeks of the shoot.

Josh, hostile and not super anxious to head back to Vancouver despite the ache to see Jessie and the kids again, which he compartmentalized into a whole other area of his heart, grumped at Matt as they left their vehicle and headed toward the enclosed elevator door in the underground garage. "Are you meeting your woman upstairs, Matt? You gonna get one last good lay in before you start fantasizing about my wife again?"

"Maybe. Got one in today already," Matt sniped back. "While you had your hands all over Elizabeth Cayo this afternoon."

"On camera doesn't count." Elizabeth was Josh's co-star—blonde, agile and happily married. She was no threat to Josh or to Jessie. "Where were you banging Ferne, in my dressing room?"

"Grip truck." Matt almost sneered. He and Ferne hadn't been anywhere near the grip truck, but he got a kick out of Josh's shocked expression. Matt and the producer did have sex while Josh was safely on set shooting, but they were nowhere near the set. This was Matt's second time returning to the hotel today. "You had lots of eyes on you, Josh."

"Yeah, your new local security buds. You're getting a cut in pay for that." Shaking his head, laughing, Josh actually felt a little of the tension recede. He couldn't put his finger on what was really pissing Matt off these last few weeks and, to be honest, he didn't friggin' want to know. Even the calls to Jessie, with the kids sick at home and her fear snaking through the connection, were disturbing and, in his selfish opinion, rained on his parade. Guilt sliced through Josh now at the remembrance. *I should have been more present,* he scolded himself. *Even over the phone, I should have been more supportive.*

Just as Matt was reaching for the handle of the glass door that led into the elevator landing, a sudden and unexpected dark image beside him filled the glass. Whipping around, Matt grabbed for the gun he was wearing on a shoulder strap underneath his linen blazer, but before he could extract it, something hit him hard enough on the side of the head to blacken his vision. As he sank to his knees, he saw Josh half turn toward him, then heard a thud as Josh got shoved, hard, belly-up against the glass. The door didn't shatter, but it shook. Matt saw Josh's cheek get pushed against it, and his arms get bent high up against his back, forcefully folded there so that he winced in pain. He was gasping for breath. The last thing Matt thought of before he passed out was *Jessie's going to kill me.*

Josh was having a hard time breathing, but he was strong enough to shove, backward, the big guy holding him in place. The attacker lost his footing, and Josh spun around, but the second guy, the one who'd knocked Matt out, was ready. He brought his knee up, and dealt Josh a sickening thud to the groin. Josh dropped like a brick. Writhing on the ground, he wildly considered any self-defense moves he knew, but they were useless against these two balaclava clad giants. The guys hoisted him roughly upward, and shoved him back against the glass door.

"What do ya want?" Josh gasped. "You want my money? Take it. Take my wallet." Spread-eagled, his wrists held up and out to the sides, he tried to kick the closest attacker in the balls, but the guy dodged him. The other man whacked him on the side of the head with a fist. The damp, musty garage spun.

"Listen closely, Sawyer," the first guy said. His hot breath stank of stale onions and cheap beer. Josh gagged. "You got a choice to make."

Shit, Josh thought. *This is what I get for being an ass to Jessie and Matt. Fucking mugged on my last night in the city!* Morgan crossed his mind; Season One on *Sacred Peace* crossed his mind, but he pushed them both away. One of the big guys grabbed his chin and squeezed, hard. Josh's balls were on fire. *Matt…where is Matt? Oh, there. That lump, on the ground.* Josh tried to focus on his friend but failed miserably.

"You listening, Sawyer? You ever heard the expression 'an eye for an eye?'" The biggest guy shook Josh until he yelped. That was taken for a yes. "You remember your old pal Morgan, right?"

Oh, Jesus… Josh hit the panic button. *What the fuck? These guys are Morgan's minions?*

"Listen. Morgan wants retribution. What did Morgan lose, Sawyer? Huh? Tell us what Morgan lost."

I'm gonna puke. I'm gonna lose my shit. Josh's knees went weak. He stopped struggling. There was no sound in the stale, concrete hole now, no sound apart from his wheezy breathing and the ominous words spewing forth from this crazy guy's lips. Putrid spittle accompanied them, and startled Josh. A black curtain was falling over his eyes; there were stars in it. For a minute he thought he was outdoors.

The guy sucker punched him. Josh reeled. "Tell us what Morgan lost, Sawyer! Who—tell us who!"

"His—his wife," Josh managed. *Jessie. No more. No more of this. I—we—can't take any more…*

"And?" Another swift punch, this one in the gut, derailed Josh completely. The guys had to hold him up while he groaned. "Who else, Sawyer? Who else did Morgan lose?"

Josh found some fight. Despite the threatening blackness and the spinning nausea, he spat at the guy closest to him. "His kid died of cancer. Cancer. Not…not anything to do with…us…" *God, no. Please God, no.*

"Ask Morgan if that matters to him. He's down two. You're not down any." The meaty fingers shoved Josh's chin up higher, since he was sliding down the glass. "But you still got some power here, Sawyer. Choose!"

"Wh-what?" Incredulous, struggling to follow, Josh blinked rapidly in an attempt to stay conscious. "Ch-choose what?" His teeth started to chatter. Already, his head was pounding. His groin was on fire and his ribs were screaming. No sign of life from Matt…Matt was as still as death.

"Choose! Which kid, you idiot!" The guy leaned closer. His teeth were rotten, his breath, rancid. Josh gagged again and tried to swallow. Blood was filling his mouth, trailing down his chin like baby dribble. It tasted like rusty nails. "Choose which of your three kids!"

Josh's children danced through the flashes of nitroglycerin exploding in his brain as methodically as well placed bullets. Dylan's happy nature. David's quiet smile. Emily-Grace's…bitterness.

The man holding onto him laughed weirdly. "I take that back!" he snarled. "You get to choose between two."

Somewhere in the distance, sirens sounded. Josh wondered if Matt had somehow gotten a hold of his phone and called the police, but he intuitively knew Matt would be up with fists blazing if he could be. Josh heard a groan, drifting up from the cold cement. Matt was down and out, but at least he was alive.

A disembodied slur was making demands Josh couldn't reconcile with the pain in his head, with the fireworks bursting in his eyes. "The youngest one, Dylan, he gets a pass," the thick, raspy voice determined. "He gets a pass because he ain't your kid! Choose, Sawyer. The girl or your boy. Choose."

"N-no," Josh moaned. "No." Emily-Grace slid through his mind. He choked on a vicious, sour taste as it gushed up his throat, mingling with the rusty blood, and tried desperately to push the image of his daughter away.

It only took one split-second thought, one brief knowing, to betray his child. The shocking awareness—like a menacing, distorted photograph—reverberated around Josh's electric, confused brain.

The thugs let go of Josh, and he slid down to the ground, his back against the glass. Closing his eyes, Josh retched. The blood that erupted from his strangled throat spattered over his lap. "Me," he choked. "Me. Instead." It was a feeble attempt to erase the wounded image of Emily-Grace from his mind. Disgusted with himself, with his capacity to so irrevocably fail his only daughter, Josh sank deeper against the unforgiving glass.

"We'll have to run that by the boss," the biggest guy sneered. "But I don't think he'll go for it. Give him a few," Josh heard the guy say.

Three well placed kicks badly cut and bruised Josh's hand and wrist, damaged an already fragile rib, and left a bruise the size of a grapefruit on his thigh. But none of that pain equated to the agony roiling around his gut at this new awareness, the awareness that Morgan's wicked game was, as they suspected, indeed still being played, and likely had been, from that very first day when the chowder was spiked in the *Sacred Peace* lunchroom.

"You got it figured out now?" the bigger guy was saying. Bending down, he leaned into Josh's ear. "Morgan gets retribution. Vengeance. You can't protect your family, Sawyer. Morgan's got an army on his side, and our reach is far."

"Why—not—me?" It hurt to breathe.

"Easy. You can't suffer if you're dead. Just ask Morgan."

Josh heard it echo through his brain again and again. *You can't suffer if you're dead. You can't suffer if you're dead.* It was a theme that filtered through his scattered thoughts again and again over the next many months. It was a theme that settled in his brain like the lifeless, dried up mud of a barren lake.

"You didn't decide, Sawyer," the big guy spat as he backed away. "We gave you a chance but you didn't take it. You didn't grab the brass ring when it was handed to you. Guess ole Morgan will be making the choice for ya. You shoulda spoke up. We might take the wrong kid."

As he faded into a sickened oblivion, Josh considered what Matt had said that early morning a few weeks ago as they sat idling in the Sawyer driveway, about Jessie wanting another baby.

"You knew," he mumbled at the motionless lump lying next to him. As the boots of the two attackers disappeared into the distant cacophony of city traffic, Josh discerned in his cloudy brain that Matt's crappy mood over the past few weeks most likely had to do with keeping a very dark secret. "You stupid bastard. You fucking knew."

Chapter Eighteen

*U*lysses' robust five a.m. rap at the bedroom door scared the shit out of Jessie. Deep in slumber, she was dreaming in black and white of Audrey Hepburn, as if she was the grand actress herself. It was a happy dream set in an innocent time that Jessie wanted to freeze frame and drift deeper into, if just for the chance to sport the pretty smile and wear the adorable dress.

Being jarred out of the pleasant dream was as frightening as what Ulysses had to say.

Leaping out of bed, instantly awake, Jessie threw open the bedroom door before grabbing pajama pants and a tank top. She dressed in front of Ulysses, who shielded his eyes while prefacing his reason for waking her so abruptly by telling her that Josh was fine.

"He and Matt got jumped by a couple of hoodlums after the wrap party," he explained. "They're hurt but not too seriously. We're hoping they'll be home a few hours later than planned, that's all."

Jessie instantly paled. "What? Why? What happened?"

"Let's go down to the kitchen so we don't wake the kids. I'll make you some breakfast." Placing a hand at Jessie's back, Ulysses exerted a little pressure.

With a racing heart, Jessie headed for the stairs. "I don't want breakfast. Are you here alone? Where's Charles?" At the bottom, she turned right and dropped, trembling, onto the couch.

Ulysses sat at the opposite end and told her what he knew. "I stayed here last night as a favor to Sam and Alin so they could both be off at the same time," he said. "I got a call from the Metro Police here in Vancouver. I've already talked to Charles—he and Dee are driving up here as we speak." He noticed Jessie digging her nails into the back of a hand. Grabbing her fingers, he pleaded, "Jessie, settle, please. The guys are okay."

The tall, good-looking black man scanned her for other signs of distress. Jessie never took these things well, and this, well, they didn't really know what it meant yet, or how it would trickle down to all of them in the future. Ulysses voiced his thoughts carefully, ferreting out the information with discretion. The Keating-Sawyer security team had a rule—never tell Jessie more than was absolutely necessary.

"You talk to Matt?"

Ulysses found the query interesting. Jessie hadn't asked whether he'd spoken to Josh. "Not yet," he told her. "Matt was knocked unconscious, Jessie. They were jumped with no warning. He's still at the hospital. They're running him through a scan."

"I see," she fumed. "So this attack is nothing to be concerned about, yet Matt's undergoing tests. And my husband?"

"A badly bruised hand, and ribs, I think. Likely a nasty headache," Ulysses said, shrinking from her. In the past few years, he'd never been the one to deal directly with Jessie's moods and worries—he was usually on Deirdre duty. The Keating matriarch was enough of a handful, but this—knowing what kind of threat possibly lay under this latest attack—added layers to the emotional intensity.

"Ribs," Jessie echoed, stunned. "I need to call Josh. Are you telling me the truth, Ulysses? Are they both okay?" Charles and Dee were on their way up from North Van. Maybe Ulysses was waiting for their support before admitting that things were worse than he was making out. Sitting back, Jessie didn't make a move to fetch her phone, which, in her angst, she'd left upstairs by the bed. Instead, she ran her eyes over Ulysses to try to gauge the extent of his concern. He seemed okay, overall. He was cool as a cucumber, most days. Jessie rarely saw him flustered, and today was no exception. The man was all business.

His phone rang, jolting Jessie's frayed nerves and frightening the heck out of her in the eerie early morning stillness, but she took the fact that he answered the phone in front of her and stayed seated on the couch as good signs. Exhaling, she dug her trembling fingernails back into the skin of her other hand and waited.

When he disconnected five minutes later, all Jessie had mined from Ulysses' conversation was a series of 'I sees' and 'all rights.'

"Tell me," she breathed, the second his eyes met hers again.

"They think it was random. Josh told the police he didn't even think they realized who he was."

"So they just stole their wallets? They were looking for drug money, maybe?" Hopeful, Jessie sat up straight, her spine tall and her chin raised.

Ulysses' hesitation was disconcerting. "No. They didn't take anything. Josh said he fought back and it threw them. They got scared and took off."

"What? You said they knocked Matt out. He'd be easy picking for a wallet!"

"Your husband's a strong man, Jessie. Josh would have put up a fight."

"Oh, Jesus." Dropping her head into her hands, Jessie fought a wave of nausea. "What if this was another one of Morgan's directives?"

"No point in jumping to conclusions. Josh didn't think so. Let's get them home safe and sound and go from there. Come on, Jessie. Let's put the coffee on. Charles will be wanting his morning brew."

As he turned to rise, Ulysses felt a hand on his arm. Looking back at Jessie, he was saddened to see the fear in her eyes, flickering just under the surface like lit firecrackers, spitting and sparking and dancing to the menacing rhythm of this latest attack.

"We were doing okay," she proclaimed in a thin, scared rattle. "We thought maybe it was all going to be okay."

Flipping his hand upside down, Ulysses took Jessie's fingers in hers. "Who's to say it won't be, Jessie? Come on. I'll put the coffee on. Go get your phone and give Josh a call."

Nodding, Jessie did as she was told, but calling Josh was fruitless. He didn't answer.

Despondent, leaning on an elbow at the kitchen island while Ulysses whipped up some breakfast omelettes, she couldn't even joke about his job description including 'cook,' like she would have on any other day. Deirdre and Charles landed, and were immediately put to work. Dee sliced peppers and onions, and even Charles got involved, making toast and pouring orange juice for the women. Carlotta was off today, so the older couple was on their own. Soon the children would be up, and Jessie really hoped she'd hear from Josh—or Matt—before she had to look into any small sets of eyes and worry the kids.

Ulysses' cell rang again at 6:13. This time, he glanced at the call display and moved away from the kitchen to take it. Jessie slid around on her stool and watched him. Charles followed him to the living room. A cool hand with dainty manicured fingernails touched Jessie's fingers and pulled them away from her other hand. The crescents on the back of Jessie's left hand were angry and raw now, after more than an hour of trying to focus her worry anywhere other than in her sore belly.

Charles and Ulysses talked quietly for a moment after the handsome black man poked his cell back into a pocket. Clapping a hand on his shoulder, Charles walked back to the kitchen with him.

"Well, we'll have Matt underfoot for a week or two at La Casa. He's taken a nasty bump to his noggin, but in his words if Sydney Crosby can still hit the ice after, what, seven concussions, he ought to be able to get past one."

"And Josh?" It was Deirdre who asked it. Jessie was numb. There were rumblings coming from upstairs. Emily-Grace would read angst and worry into having her grandparents and Ulysses around this early on a Sunday morning. Even David would clue in that all was not right again. Idly Jessie considered what kinds of lives her children would have as adults after living through childhoods of seemingly constant turmoil and anguish.

Charles faced Jessie instead of Deirdre. "He's sore. But he insists that he put the muggers on the run feeling worse than he is."

"Thank God they didn't have knives," Jessie whispered. "Or guns. They didn't, right?"

"No knives. They were just a couple of low grade thugs looking to make a quick buck."

"Were they. Um-humn." Jessie wasn't buying it. She squeezed Deirdre's fingers until they hurt enough for the older woman to wince and forcibly adjust her grip. "Cameras, Charles? Lights? Matt's anal as heck about that stuff."

"The camera aimed in the general area where they were attacked—by the door to the elevator—was smashed. We're waiting to hear whether Matt was aware or whether it was a new thing. And as muggings like this go, it all happened very quickly."

"Matt's my husband's security. Why wasn't he more aware?"

The tone of Charles' voice changed. "Jessie," he said firmly. "Don't lay this on Matt. It was three o'clock in the morning. The fellas were tired after a long shoot and a late night wrap party. They were jumped very suddenly. Matt didn't have a chance to react."

Jessie didn't respond. A small voice called to her from the base of the stairs, so she pulled her hand away from Deirdre and opened her arms. The first child out of bed today was David.

Rubbing his eyes, he moaned all the way over to his mother, snuggled up into a ball in her lap when she lifted him and sat back at the island, and sobbed with his face pressed into her chest. "I had a bad dweam," he croaked in his sleepy morning voice, ducking his head to hide from the stares of the adults around him.

"Lovely," Jessie sighed to no one in particular, and kissed the top of his head. She laid a hand over his forehead. "Are you feeling okay, honey?" she asked. "You're a little warm. Dee, he's a little warm again, don't you think?"

Checking him for a fever was a good distraction. David was okay, and was soon laughing at Ulysses, who decorated an egg for him with strategically placed slices of cheddar, so it looked like the egg was smiling up at him.

The jet went 'wheels down' at three o'clock. Ulysses, Charles and Jessie were waiting at the runway by two thirty. The last half hour was a long, tedious wait, the kind that seemed to tick on forever.

Nobody, least of all Matt, was happy about his struggle to make it down the few stairs. Victoria hung on to one arm so he wouldn't lose his footing. He was settled in Ulysses' SUV with his head back and his eyes closed before Josh even left the aircraft.

Watching from his window, Josh was wishing Jessie hadn't come to meet the jet, but in his heart he knew she would. She'd been trying to reach him all day, but he couldn't bring himself to take the calls. Nor would it be any easier to look her in the eye in person. When Matt had stepped tentatively onto the asphalt, Josh couldn't look away when Jessie approached and took his elbow from Victoria. Unable to discern what was spoken between them, he'd watched her hand Matt off to Charles and Ulysses, and turn her eyes upward to scan the open doorway of the Keating jet for him. When he didn't appear, Jessie's eyes had drifted sideways toward the small windows.

Josh shrank back into his big leather seat. After a few extended minutes to collect his wits, he gripped the armrest and eased himself upward. He was standing painfully, half crouched, when Jessie's footsteps rattled on the steps at a quick pace.

She ducked into the cabin and faced him in the narrow aisle.

They studied each other before she made any attempt to step closer, to take him in her arms and hold him the way both wanted her to do. It seemed there was an invisible cloud of dark dust that had to be moved out of the way first, before Jessie could approach Josh's personal space.

She started them off. "Was this Morgan's doing?" she asked outright.

"Unlikely," Josh lied. "They were too stupid to be Morgan's minions. They didn't even take our wallets."

"They were smart enough to smash the video camera. It was premeditated. Morgan makes sense. He wouldn't give a shit about your wallets."

"They were high. They probably tried three times before they even managed to break the glass around the camera."

"Josh, I—"

Sharply, he cut her off with an air palm and a harsh demand. "Don't read more into this than what it was. You have to stop going down the darkest road every time something unexpected happens."

"Unexpected? Josh, flat tires are unexpected. Parking garage muggings of A-list actors are usually not random occurrences."

"Did you say that to Matt? I'm sure he's hoping it was pretty random."

Cocking her head, Jessie responded with, "What's that supposed to mean? Ulysses and Charles said Matt didn't see it coming."

"Only because your beloved Matt was distracted. He had one thing on his mind, and one thing only. Dumping me so he could meet his bed buddy in her suite for the rest of the night."

"Oh, so that's how this is going to go. You're tired and mad cuz your fun shoot is over, so you're gonna balance the scales by blaming Matt and hurting me."

"Karma's a bitch, huh?"

"That's low, Josh. You're seriously going back there? Matt and I are old news."

Josh looked away before he rallied and swung them down a safer road. "Face it, Jessie. Matt sometimes does a damn poor job of protecting me. Us. But don't worry, the universe says. I've got your back, Sawyer."

Tears stung Jessie's eyes. She threw her arms out to the sides. "What the hell, Josh?" There was something unreadable in his expression. Layered deeply beneath the angry bullets he was firing ruthlessly at his wife was something Jessie recognized in her husband. Anxiety. A lack of control over his life.

Her suspicion was confirmed later at the UBC house, where Arnie had driven up to take his turn watching over the Sawyer home. In the meantime, Sam and Alin arrived together to share angel duty with the kids, Dan remained off for the day so he could get to his wife's 'around the house honey-do list,' and Ulysses, Charles, and Dee swifted Matt off to La Casa (against his vehement protestations) so they could keep an eye on him.

At home, surly and practically unable to look Jessie in the eye, Josh stopped inside the living room and rubbed his palms again and again on the thighs of his jeans. On the floor below were children's books, a few lone stuffies, a couple of containers of Emily-Grace's miniature dolls and their clothes, and about twenty collectible vintage cars, police cars, ambulances, fire trucks, and other assorted mini-vehicles. Purely by accident, Josh stepped on an ambulance and set off its siren. At the tinny high-pitched squeal, he jumped, and cursed.

His children were everywhere. Their existences was spread out all over the floor, abandoned and discarded like in a post-apocalyptic world.

"Where are the kids?" he managed, his voice a gruff whisper and his eyes still, to Jessie's bewilderment, avoiding her confused stare.

"I can hear them in the playroom," she responded hotly, as if he ought to know that without being told. "They're up there with Alin and Sam."

Josh headed that way, as fast as he could go with his bruised body. He kind of shuffled his way toward the stairs, and used his good arm to haul himself up each step. There was a bandage on the bad hand. Jessie was still eyeing him for damage. Given his understandable irascible mood she didn't want to probe, still she hadn't expected him to be this beat up. And she sure as hell didn't expect him to be so damn pissed at the world and everyone in it.

Looking over at Arnie, she puckered up her cheeks in a sort of confused perplexity, and shook her head in alarm. "I don't get it, Arnie," she said.

"Give him some time to adjust," Arnie suggested. "He's hurting. He can't do much in terms of meds, remember?"

"How could I forget?" Exhausted at the futility of trying to manage Josh's mood at a time when Jessie really just wanted to undress him piece by piece and assess the real damage, she whipped around and headed for the stairs. With Arnie right behind her, she got to the playroom just in time to see Josh's eyes sweep over the messy space and land for a few seconds on each of his children. Before either of the boys could jump him (they'd been warned to be cautious so they wouldn't hurt him), Josh bypassed them, and despite his paining body, landed on his knees next to his daughter. Sweeping her into his arms, his shoulders shook as he clutched her to him.

Emily-Grace was as shocked as the rest of them. She knew better than to try to pull away, but her small, frightened eyes stared past her daddy's heaving shoulders and up at her equally alarmed mother.

Jessie only hesitated for a moment. The floor creaked when she strode across it. Her boots became muffled when they hit the colorful rubber puzzle matting halfway into the room. She landed on her knees behind Josh, touched her baby girl on the cheek—a warning, of sorts, that read 'just let him be,'—and she wrapped her arms carefully around Josh so that Emily-Grace was also encompassed in her embrace. Josh was quaking—not trembling, *quaking*. Reaching up with his bandaged hand, his sore fingers touched his wife's arm. Jessie lifted it carefully and laid her skin against his.

A random mugging, huh? she thought to herself as she laid her cheek against her daughter's soft pink face. *Bullshit. Fucking bullshit.* Josh was falling apart in front of her, and for some reason, Emily-Grace's small body was what set him off.

Behind her, Alin, Sam, and the boys were surprised, silent observers. Arnie straightened, ran uneasy fingers over his stubbled chin, and left the room.

Chapter Nineteen

*S*tonewalled by the reticence of both Matt and Josh to talk, Jessie took it upon herself to corner Arnie. Dropping by his Downtown Eastside digs—Arnie's new condo instead of the cramped apartment she'd visited in earlier years—Jessie pushed for the planned chat with Morgan.

"You need to sit down with Josh and get him to talk," Arnie demanded as he dug out a pack of smokes he kept for emergencies and handed her one. "He cornered me last night and made the same demand. Only for him to get inside Brody. Not you."

A sour taste washed through Jessie's mouth. "Something's messed up, Arnie," she said as he touched a lighter flame to the end of her cigarette. She didn't need to say another word. Arnie was around the Sawyer house last night. Josh wasn't talking, but the way he sat and watched his kids, as if he was memorizing their small faces…

"Did you see Emily-Grace eyeballing her father all evening?" Jessie asked, and took her first puff. The head rush from the rare cigarette immediately made her all spinny and off balance. Inching closer to the edge of the couch, she rested her forearms on her thighs and looked down at her feet. She crossed one set of toes over the other. They were sitting in Arnie's living room. His gal, Lucie, was in the kitchen rustling up some coffee.

Across from her, reclining on a matching chair, Arnie scratched his chest. He yawned. All night duty at the Sawyer residence had meant he wasn't quite ready to face the day when Jessie landed at his door at precisely eleven a.m. But she wasn't the patient sort. Grimacing as he forced himself awake, Arnie had strolled to his condo's intercom and let her in.

"He scared her," Arnie said in response to Jessie's comment about Emily-Grace.

"So much for the two of them ever meeting comfortably somewhere in the middle. Josh tries so hard but then he just messes up with her."

"His fear is seeping into hers." The smoke from Arnie's cigarette curled upward, snakelike and sinister. He sighed. "Look, Jessie, whatever Josh has to say to Morgan, it's urgent. He wants in this week. Only Charles has that kind of power, and I doubt he'll go for it. He shouldn't, in fact. Josh is pissed enough to do some serious harm if he goes barging into Brody with retribution on his mind, if that's even what this is."

"Maybe this thing after the wrap party just scared him. Maybe it had nothing to do with Morgan, but it's become the catalyst to make Josh try to settle things so we can live in peace."

The serious way Arnie looked at her when she said that...Jessie just shifted her position, curled her lip downwards, took a long drag on her cigarette, and wrapped her free arm around her belly. *Live in peace?* "As if," she mumbled aloud, stricken by his tense posture. "You don't even fucking believe it's possible."

Tapping his smoke on the side of the ashtray, Arnie pondered her unplanned appearance at his digs. "I do believe it's possible," he replied. "But I think you and Josh are on two different wavelengths when it comes to attaining a quiet life."

"Meaning?" Jessie pointed her cigarette at him. "Speak, Arnie." She willed him, the quietest of the Keating-Sawyer clan, to speak his mind.

"You would be happy to limit your public life. Josh is still on the way up, and he's power hungry."

"I don't really think that's a fair assessment of Josh, Arnie." Jessie tapped her ashes into the glass ashtray Arnie was using. They settled on the bottom, used up and useless, reduced to a powdery gray waste. The smoke was a bad idea, the way it was making her sick and shaky. Looking through the condo's floor-to-ceiling window down at the people on the street across from Arnie's building, she continued, "It's not the power that he wants. It's the self-esteem. He needs to feel good about himself."

"And being a family man isn't good enough? Why does he need to be some famous actor?"

"Because of me, maybe. I dunno. We joke about stuff like Oscars, but in my heart I don't think he really cares about winning awards. Maybe there's a part of him that doesn't feel deserving of me unless he's also successful." Waving her cigarette in the air, Jessie's eyes grew wide. "Don't get me wrong, Arnie, you know me, I never asked for what I got in the first place. If Josh is insecure, it's his thing. His fame is not connected to anything I've ever expected, said, or done. But he is a brilliant actor—you know that—and us creative types like the challenge of doing better and better at our chosen art."

"And you creative types like the adoration and acknowledgement from your fans. From the world. Josh needs to find peace within himself so he can let that stuff go. That's the key to living without fear, Jessie."

"To Josh it would be giving up on his dreams, Arnie. It would kill him to let it all go, everything he's worked for. Suffered for."

"It might kill him to hang on, Jessie. I think the two of you know that."

"Oh, Jesus, Arnie. You wanna give the knife a more lethal twist? Could you maybe soften the truth a little?" Swallowing bitterly, Jessie took a final deep pull on her cigarette and snuffed it out without looking at the wasteland in the ashtray. "You fucking loser. Saying it out loud just makes it real."

"Ask him what he wants, Jessie. Get him to talk about the possibilities."

"I would, except I know what he will say. He'll say the same thing we've told ourselves since Deuce McCall's reign of terror. Giving into the fear will be like giving up our power. We need to claw our power back."

"Maybe," Arnie suggested as Lucie brought the coffee in, "it wouldn't be a bad thing to give in to the fear. Maybe you should consider taking your kids and just laying low. And maybe then you can take your power back."

"What are you saying, Arnie? Or do I want to know?" Jessie forced a grim smile up at Lucie, who took a good look at her husband before handing a mug to him. "Thanks, Lucie," Jessie said gratefully. "I needed this."

Wrapping his fingers around the handle on his mug, Arnie took a careful sip. "S'good, Luce, thanks."

He touched her wrist tenderly before she wandered back to the kitchen with a subdued, "I'll get you a snack to hold you over until you can eat something more substantial, Arnie." Jessie wrinkled her nose. Lucie seemed a little perturbed that she was there.

Arnie didn't seem to notice. When he spoke again, he was looking at Jessie over the rim of the steaming cuppa. "Vaughn," he said simply. "He's got some power at Brody. He prides himself on his personal connection with you."

"Jesus. Is that what knifing your whore is called these days?"

Arnie blanched. When he looked back, his eyes were accusing, in a concerned kind of way. He skirted around Jessie's insolent remark. "Look. If laying low is not an option, how about this—I think Charles is still considering letting you in to see Morgan. Having Matt down and out right now has given him time to pause and reflect."

"On Matt's general incompetence, you mean."

"On Matt's blind side. That's what I mean. His blindside being—"

"Me."

"Yeah, Jessie. That rainbow vision of you that he carries around with him. The one that suffocates his heart and stuffs cotton around his brain."

"He's only looking out for me, Arnie. He's doing what he thinks is best."

"Regardless, Charles is starting to see the light. He remembers where you came from."

"Oh, yay. Lucky him." Her sarcasm was biting. A glance to Arnie's gal in the nearby kitchen put a soft edge around the sharp rim of Jessie's anxiety. She tried to smile but it came out crooked.

The woman Arnie had fallen in love with was sober and attentive. Jessie had always cowed Lucie, to a point, because of Jessie's connection to and deep faith in Arnie, and vice versa. Now, Lucie sidled back over to them, lifted a tray and offered Jessie an Oreo cookie.

Taking one, Jessie bit off a tiny part of the top wafer. It was fresh, but in her jaded and frightened mindset it tasted like cardboard. She forced herself to swallow it anyway. "Thanks, Lucie," she said.

"You're welcome." With a quiet look to Arnie, Lucie tactfully tiptoed back to the kitchen. If Jessie was in their home, it meant that this conversation required a certain modicum of privacy. She could hear what they were saying, but she distanced herself enough to stay out of her man's way. Still, she cocked an ear and moved with an air of caution so she could more easily eavesdrop.

"Look, what I'm trying to say is that Charles might come through for us,"

Arnie explained. "Not for Josh—no way. He's too volatile, too unpredictable to be let loose in a jungle like Brody. But if Charles doesn't come through, and even if he does and we feel like we've gotten nowhere, we do have one last recourse." A steady light was burning in Arnie's eyes.

Jessie reached for another cigarette. "I can't be party to murder, Arnie," she said in a shallow voice, tasting the horror, swallowing it, and discarding the sweetness of the sugary cookie by placing the remainder down by the ashtray. "If that's what you're suggesting." She couldn't look at her old Downtown Eastside friend. "Deuce…and Nadia…they were enough. We can't even really say that hurting Morgan would be justifiable self-defense. We don't really know that he's to blame for anything that's happened recently." Fingers shaking, she lit the smoke herself as Arnie watched her.

At this point, he wasn't sure if she really understood the extent of this ramped-up danger. But watching Josh reach for his daughter the way he did…and judging by Josh's new and desperate demand to get in to see Morgan, Arnie was certain the attack after the wrap party was not a random occurrence.

It was a warning.

"Tell your husband I'm taking him to an A.A. meeting tonight," he said abruptly. "He needs one. For now, go see Matt. See if you can get anything out of him about what happened the other night. Maybe he'll remember something. Tell Josh I'll pick him up at seven."

"Don't tell him about this. About what you're thinking." Peering up at him, Jessie implored Arnie to listen, to understand. "We don't need Josh going off the rails, and we don't need him involved."

"So…" Arnie set down his mug and focused on Jessie. "You're in? You're okay with this?"

"Using Vaughn as a conduit to Morgan until I can get in, yes. You can tell him I've got his song half written. But not murder. Not violence, Arnie." A wet sheen floated across Jessie's eyes but she blinked it away and sat taller. Shortly, she sighed and stood. "I'm sick of this, of all of it. The anxiety, the worry, the dread, the way my husband is shutting me out again. In the immediate future I am going to celebrate the happy parts of life, one being love, in fact, at Jacob and Kayla's wedding. And the second being gratitude, in the next twenty minutes, actually, when I go hold Matt in my arms and get down on my knees and thank God that he's okay."

Heading for the door, the smoking cigarette still gripped tightly between two fingers, Jessie stopped, retraced her steps and bent over the pack of smokes on the coffee table. Shaking out a half dozen, she frowned at Arnie. "There's one more recourse I believe in," she stated resolutely. "Prayer. Energy goes where energy flows. You'll hear me all the way to North Van, my Downtown Eastside savior. Seems like you've got a direct line. Mind firing up a few prayers of your own?"

With a quiet 'thank you' aimed at the distant but attentive Lucie, Jessie slid through the doorway and headed down the hall.

As the hard click of her boots disappeared, Arnie knit his brow and lit up one of the few remaining cigarettes. "Prayer, is it," he muttered as he touched a flame to the tip of the smoke he poked between his lips. "A direct line, huh?" Fixing a gaze on the outside world, he noticed that the day had grayed and a heavy mist was spotting the large window. Looking through the water droplets made the outdoors distorted and unreal. "I've got a direct line, all right," he added under his breath as he puffed. "Right to Morgan's bastard heart."

Life on the Downtown Eastside may have earned Arnie a savior's reputation, but men who fight and win wars to save souls don't always reveal how they fight them. At the same time, Jessie deserved to call the shots. For now.

As Jessie left his building, Arnie continued to stare at the mist on the window. The day turned to rain, and wept openly against the glass.

~ ~

"You're one hell of a sulky patient." Perched on the edge of Matt's luxe La Casa guest bed, Jessie was trying to feed him Carlotta's homemade cure-all, chicken soup. "You're just a big baby."

"I'm not crippled," he growled, taking the soup bowl and spoon from her. "I can hold a damn spoon."

Studying him, Jessie sat back. Matt was even grumpier than Josh. Frustrated, derailed by the honest conversation with streetwise Arnie, Jessie was losing it.

"Who pissed in your cornflakes on the shoot, Matt?" she asked. "Yours and Josh's both, I mean. The way the two of you are acting now is scaring the shit out of me. Or is it just that you missed out on your last chance to get laid for a while?"

Matt handed her back the soup bowl. Nauseous from the lingering headache, he lay back against his pillow, which Jessie sullenly fluffed and positioned for him. "Her name is Ferne," he grumped. "And I'm not interested in talking to you about my sex life."

"Ferne? Ferne MacAvoy? The producer."

Jessie's surprised, testy tone got Matt's attention. "I suppose you think she outclasses me. Me being one of your lowly minions and all."

"She's beautiful. That's all I meant. Like, an outdoorsy fresh-air kind of beautiful. I suppose she knew which buttons to push, huh? In bed?" The sweet memory of the night Jessie and Matt finally took refuge in each other's arms waylaid both of them at the same time. Matt swallowed and forced himself to look away from the deep hurt in Jessie's eyes. No night, before or since, in his humble opinion, would ever equal the magic of that first cherished coupling with Jessie. Ever, ever, ever. He wrestled with the pillow. He just couldn't quite get comfortable.

"Men," Jessie grumbled, helping him until he swatted her away. The half bitter sentiment got buried in Matt's neck when she unexpectedly leaned forward and sighed into the welcoming warmth of his skin.

Quietly, Matt left the pillow alone, lifted an arm, and wrapped it around her waist.

When Jessie raised her head and repositioned herself on the bed, her eyes were damp, and so were Matt's. "He's distanced himself from me again," she disclosed despondently, trying to change the direction of their conversation with an awkward attempt to remind both of them that she was committed to the man she was married to. "It's like Josh is back on the outside looking in. Unreachable. Arnie's taking him to a meeting tonight, hoping he'll talk, I think."

Matt didn't answer in distinguishable words. He just mumbled something incoherent and stared at his hands, the knuckles of one bruised from the way he landed on the cold cement floor of the Albuquerque hotel's parking garage.

"And how am I supposed to interpret that, exactly?" Jessie's voice was rising. "Do you know what Josh will say if he talks?"

"He's got every right to be angry at me, Jessie," Matt finally said. "And so do you. In fact, I'm pretty damn pissed at myself."

"Don't matter. I really don't give a sweet damn if he's mad at you. I just want to know what those thugs were really up to."

"No good, that's what they were up to. That's all you need to know."

Alarmed, Jessie's voice fell. "You heard something," she whispered.

"Wishful thinking," he muttered. "I didn't hear a damn thing. Except…" Matt closed his eyes and scrunched up his mouth, which Jessie took to meaning the headache was bad, and that she ought to leave so he could rest, but she couldn't force herself to get up and walk out. She was wrong, though. What Matt was recoiling against was not the insistent pounding in his head; instead it was a vivid memory of the attack that struck him numb with hurt every time the visual—and its accompanying sound—rose up to haunt him. "He was crying," he admitted softly to Jessie. "When I came to. I heard him, first. This quiet sobbing…"

"Wh-what?"

"I'm sorry, I know you're already worried, kid."

"I don't know how to respond to that, Matt, except… Josh must have really gotten a scare. He was probably scared for you." In Jessie's heart, this was just another piece of the puzzle. Now the frank discussion with Arnie was coming into focus, making sense. *Leave, disappear, go under the radar. Take Josh and the kids with you.* A little moan snuck out from between her lips. *I'm so sick of running away. I'm so tired of missing people I love.*

"I heard voices, Jessie. As I was coming to." Matt was watching Jessie now. His eyes were red, bloodshot from the injury, fatigue and worry. "I couldn't make out what was said. But something was said."

She nodded in acceptance. "Okay. That explains a lot. Thanks for that, Matt."

"I want to go back to my place." *I need to change the subject*, Matt thought. *I need to erase the angst that's stalking this room, that's taking over our lives once again.* Out loud he said, "Deirdre's driving me up the wall with her incessant fretting."

A wan smile crossed Jessie's pallid cheeks. "Dee wouldn't be Dee if she didn't fret, honey. Why do you have such a hard time letting anyone take care of you?" Without realizing it, Jessie twined her fingers around Matt's. He might be resting and unwell, but to her he was still her pillar of strength.

He took a breath. "Maybe because she's not who I wish was taking care of me."

"Ferne. Gorgeous, beautiful, goddess-like Ferne, huh? I'll bet she knows how to take care of you. Real good care, in fact."

"Go away." Trying to smile, Matt lifted Jessie's fingers and brushed his lips across them. "I'm sorry, Jessie. I'm truly, truly sorry. I saw that the camera was toast…"

"The way I heard it, you didn't have time to blink. Sleep, my dear sweet Matt, and be well enough to come to the wedding, okay? We need to find us some happiness."

"Jessie?"

She was edging off the bed now, about to bend down to give him a tender, chaste, parting kiss. "What?"

"About that baby…you and Josh…"

She stilled. "He told you."

"Rubbed it in, more like." Matt held onto her hand and stroked a thumb across the fingers he loved. "No baby in the immediate future, okay?" he said, almost inaudibly. "Not until things even out again."

Jessie blinked, uncertain. She had already been to see her gynecologist, Dr. Wyatt. As far as she was concerned, all systems were a go. Jessie's body was ready and her spirit was willing. Tilting her head at Matt, she spoke her mind. "I know you're worried, Matt. But let's face it—if we wait for things to settle down, Josh and I may never have the family we've always wanted. We said five. A few more after Dylan, we said, a few more of our own. I want more of his children. I want every part of that man that I can possibly have."

"Not now, Jessie," Matt demanded, almost too quietly for her to hear. He couldn't stop himself from adding, "Just in case."

The color drained from Jessie's face; it left in gasps and shudders. "Bastard." She backed away. "You, out of everyone, ought to be giving me hope, Matt, not feeding me terror. Not much wonder all you've been doing lately is bickering with Arnie and with Josh. Just in case nobody else has the nerve to tell you, you've turned mean. That was heartless."

Uneasy, Matt's tired eyes followed her to the door, which Jessie pulled closed behind her without a backwards glance.

In the hallway outside his room, she stood trembling, fists clenching and unclenching, wondering what the hell the comment she considered nasty was meant to convey. *Just in case? Just in case what? In case I lose Josh?*

The appalling thought was too terrible to bear. Striding away, Jessie resolved to spend more time hanging out with Arnie. Arnie wasn't colored by jealousy and anger. Everybody was right. Matt was too close. He'd gone too soft. He was becoming a bitter man whose judgment and ability to act with clarity was colored by unresolved passion and unrequited love.

In the bedroom, Matt wriggled lower in the bed and wished to hell the damned headache would go away. Maybe then he would be able to retrieve the lost words he'd heard as he was stirring, there on the hard cement floor of the dim garage. Maybe then he'd have some insight into what drove Josh back inside himself, and into the sobs the actor had unleashed to the dark night after the attack.

For now, unable to reconcile what unthinking part of himself had fired such a worrisome parting shot to Jessie a moment ago, he had his own pain to deal with. It slid down his cheeks in salty trails, in harsh wet reminders of what he'd lost, and of what he still stood to lose.

Chapter Twenty

"Hey, dancer girl."

Something fantastical about the early morning light had summoned Kayla to the outdoor terrace this morning, the day she would finally trade in the single life and commit to a lifelong partnership with Jacob. Wrapped in a fluffy white blanket, sitting upright on a seasonal lounger, she was hugging her knees to her chest when Jacob approached behind her.

The city was just coming to life on the streets far below, in beeps and honks and in the occasional odd siren. The vibrancy of the day was echoed in Kayla's spirit, in the way she sat alert and watchful, but in a peaceful sort of way, like a cat watching a butterfly, lost in the mysticism that surrounded such a beautiful winged creature as it flitted about a powdery pink sky at the first light of dawn.

Looking up, she was grateful to see that Jacob was holding two steaming mugs of coffee. Jacob handed her one, and eased his body down next to her.

"Thanks," Kayla smiled, and lifted the heavy pottery mug to her lips. "You've gotten good at the whole cappuccino thing, Jacob."

"Practice makes perfect," he said. "I've got marriage all figured out. I'm working on my skills one at a time, starting with mornings. Wait til you taste that new pizza frittata I mastered while you were at the workshops."

"Pizza that doesn't come from a box? I'm impressed."

"Pizza *frittata*. A breakfast thing." Proud, Jacob sat back with a smirk. "Sounds fancy, doesn't it?"

Kayla tipped her head back and laughed.

Jacob watched her, his smile widening. "Sometimes," he declared, "I still can't believe I am marrying you, Kayla. I'm in awe."

He was, too. Sincerely. What had captivated Kayla about the new morning light was now gracing her blonde hair; the sun's golden pink hue had an energy that almost hummed. It was as if it was infused with fairy dust; Kayla's hair was all aglitter, her apple-bright cheeks were sprinkled too, with a kind of joy that emanated from somewhere deep in her soul.

"You're glowing," Jacob said, admiring the halo effect that, to him, was the universe's approval of their union.

"And why wouldn't I be?" Kayla couldn't take her eyes off Jacob now that he was up early, enjoying the beautiful late winter morning with her. He was still sleepy-eyed and his red plaid flannel western shirt, the one with the pearl snaps he wore yesterday and had picked up off the floor this morning, was fastened unevenly, but she didn't have the heart to tell him. "Mornings like this are a sneak peek into the future," she said. "The cherry blossoms will be out soon. Spring is almost here. Our city's about to be reborn."

"Just the city?"

In answer, Kayla extended a free hand and took Jacob's fingers in hers. They were warm from being wrapped around the hot mug. "What do you think, Jacob?"

In a husky voice, he said, "I feel like I've been completely reborn."

Jacob's shy glance down at her belly was Kayla's cue to move his fingers over her abdomen, over the place where their baby was growing and resting and awaiting its turn to walk the earth.

"Is this for real?" Jacob asked, his cobalt blue eyes as big as saucers, mirrored in the beautiful blue of the sky and of the calm water below. "You and me? A little family?"

"You bet. Want me to pinch you?" Kayla rubbed Jacob's fingers over her belly and smiled when she felt their baby flutter. "She knows you. Right now she's doing arabesques because her beloved daddy is close by."

"She?" Jacob lit up. "Do you think it's a girl? Is that what your intuition says, dancer girl?"

"I think Emily-Grace and Stella are hoping it's a girl. They're feeling outnumbered."

The thought was only slightly sobering. Jacob was beside himself with joy and peace, on this, the day he would marry Kayla Sawyer. Still, Kayla saw the little spark of pain that crossed over his features. He withdrew his fingers but treated her to a small smile as he wrapped the hand back around his mug.

"It's good we're here, Jacob. Living in Vancouver. Dylan's adapted to you. Josh has adapted to you."

"Josh hates my guts."

"If he did, he wouldn't be standing for you today."

"He's standing for you, Kayla. Technically."

"Doesn't matter. He'll be there, and he'll behave. I read him the riot act at rehearsal last night. Jacob…" Fiddling with her mug, Kayla ran a finger around the rim a few times.

"Mmmm?" Jacob leaned back on the lounger and gazed over the pretty sailboats of False Creek the way a king looks out over his kingdom. A peaceful ruddiness was evident in his repose; the increasing stream of traffic rushing here and there in the city around them did nothing to sway Jacob from the comprehension that today was a day to cherish. Today was a miracle.

Kayla fidgeted before she spoke. Her brief silence got Jacob's attention. Refocusing on her, he balanced his mug in his left hand, on one thigh, and extended his right hand to play in the early sunlight ringing and bedazzling her hair.

"It's just…this is our day, you know?" Glancing up at him, Kayla let one corner of her lip ease up into a half smile.

Jacob knew that look. He twisted a ringlet in a strand of her hair and tried not to smile. The careful apprehension on his bride's face…this conversation was about Jessie. "We let each other go, Kayla. She's moved on, remember? Her new shoulder to cry on is older, supposedly wiser, and sporting a nasty enough headache today that you might not even get a dance out of him. Mr. GQ himself has Jessie's back these days."

"He's always had Jessie's back. Matt's given up a lot for her."

"Including his self-respect, at times." Jacob returned his gaze to his kingdom. Somewhere near the docks by Granville Island a solo mariner was putt-putt-putting his sailboat out toward English Bay. Jacob filed away a reminder to take his own boat out to test the winds again soon. It might be cooler up here than in the Caribbean, but the winds were just as rowdy, by times. They had an equal power when it came to banishing a man's demons and making him feel free.

Jessie. Her name and her essence still riled up Jacob's emotions with knife-like thrusts to his gut, but the pain didn't last as long these days, and was usually replaced with a kind of harmless cloudy cotton that settled into his belly with a sigh. "Jessie has that kind of power," Jacob muttered, alluding to the comment about self-respect. "She and your brother deserve each other." Winking, he peeked sideways at Kayla, who he could see was doing that cute, twisty thing with her lips that cued an oncoming rebuttal. Jacob laughed. "Easy, Mrs. Almost Ryan. I'm joking. I'm good. We're good. We've all made our peace, even though at times I feel like Jessie should have never forgiven me for what I did to her. I've got the girl I want; your brother has the damaged goods. Balance has been achieved."

"Oh, honey," Kayla said, watching Jacob process the old pain. "You have to promise me you won't hide those crazy mixed-up feelings from me. I know you love me. I know that you and Jessie have a history that still hurts. I also know that she's crazy happy for you. For us. They're trying for another baby. Did you know that?"

Surprised, Jacob was momentarily rendered mute. "No," he acknowledged. "I can't say I knew that. It's great, Kayla. Really."

"I'm sorry," she whispered. "I shouldn't be talking about Jessie on our wedding day. I just…I wanted you to know that I care enough about you to let you be you, Jacob. You don't have to hide anything from me. Ever. Least of all the thing that hurts the most."

"You really are some special girl, Kayla," Jacob said, in a hushed, humble tone. He couldn't take his eyes off her. "Thank you. I mean that. We both have baggage, you and I. But we're coming at this the right way."

"Starting with you not picking a fight with my brother on our wedding day."

"Our wedding day…"

The sun was rising higher now, blessing the Ryan-Sawyer nuptials with the promise of good tidings for today, and forevermore. If the sunny day was going to be any indication of their union, Jacob and Kayla would grow old together, in love, gifted with abundance. As they sat quietly and watched the goings-on of the awakening city, while sipping on their cooling cappuccinos, they were silently grateful for having found each other, and blissfully indebted to Josh and Jessie for, in their own inimitable way, bringing them together in the first place.

Chapter Twenty-one

The wedding, all things considered, was a small affair. Grateful that Kayla was amenable to keeping it simple, Jacob relaxed and soaked up every blissful moment. It was late in the evening before he finally cornered Jessie and coerced her into a dance. She'd just come downstairs from the hotel suite she and Josh rented for the children so they could keep them close by during the latter part of the post-reception dance. Alin and Sam were on duty, which was a small source of amusement during the dark days leading up to the move back to Alberta for season two of *Sacred Peace.*

After settling her children in their beds before coming back downstairs, Jessie'd given Sam and Alin a playful parting shot. "You promise me you'll watch the kids? You can still make out, just keep an eye on the kids too, okay?" Jessie was all smiles as she walked to the door of the hotel suite behind Josh, who she was quite certain didn't hear the good humored comment. Since the mugging, nothing seemed to register in his mind. It was as if he were locked in some prison of his own making. Desperate to pinpoint exactly what was bugging him, Jessie even stooped so low as to wonder whether he'd fallen in love with someone during the shoot, but Matt put the kibosh on that the instant she voiced it. Somehow, though, that would have seemed a more viable option than the frightening scenarios Jessie was running through her scared brain.

Upstairs, Josh had held the door open while Sam's face colored and while Alin blushed and shuffled her feet. "We'll behave, I swear," Alin promised Jessie, and leaned forward for a gentle hug. "Your children are in good hands, they're safe with us. Go. Have a good time."

"What's the fun in that?" Jessie teased. "Behaving, I mean!" With a laugh, she let the door close behind her, and took Josh's good fingers lightly in hers for the walk down the hall to the elevator. Dan was stationed outside the suite. Keeping an eye on his bosses, he walked twenty feet behind Josh and Jessie as they aimed for the elevator. As the door slid shut, Jessie waved at Dan but Josh did not. Instead, he stared at the floor.

"Josh," Jessie sighed, exasperated. "This night is important to Kayla. Either tell me what's going through that adorable head of yours, or lighten up. At least for the evening." She was half afraid he'd reach for a drink—or three.

Josh waved at the elevator door. "We just left our two youngest of the security team, who are horny as hell, with our kids. And you joked about it."

Sobering, Jessie leaned back against the elevator wall. "Dan's outside," she told him, a little hurt. "Sam and Alin might be in love, but they're not going to put aside their professional obligations and let anything happen to our children, Josh."

"We need to encourage Alin to go back to pursuing her R.C.M.P. dreams. That'll sort the two of them out."

"God, you sound like the Grinch that stole true love. I wish you'd talk to me, Josh. About what's bugging you, I mean. Getting jumped really threw you. You said it was just a random thing. You told the police that."

"Not tonight," he grimaced. "I don't want to talk about that tonight." Shoving his good hand in his pocket, Josh left the elevator the second the door opened. Arnie was waiting outside. His curious eyes met Jessie's floating ones as Josh strode into the dance alone.

"Come on," Arnie said. "You owe me a slow song."

"Yes. Likely many, Arnie." Forcing a smile, Jessie took the elbow Arnie extended, and they moved into the spacious room together.

Jessie was proud of herself by the time she and Jacob finally stole some quiet time together on the dance floor. "I've only checked on the kids three times," she said as he floated her around the elegant ballroom of the Fairmont Vancouver.

"And how many texts have you sent?" With a flourish, Jacob spun her under an arm. Jessie tried to appear happy, but even through Jacob's joy he could sense her false bravado. His eyes dimmed.

Jessie noticed. "Sorry, Jacob," she mumbled. "It's been a tough few days. And, in answer to your question, many. I've texted many times. And so has Matt, Deirdre, and I'm pretty sure even Arnie's driving Alin and Sam nuts."

"And Josh too, I'm sure."

She hesitated. "I don't know about that."

"Hmm?" Jacob was perplexed.

She cornered right. What was the point in worrying Jacob on his wedding day? This day was well earned. Jacob deserved bliss. Jessie just shrugged and said, "You know Josh. With him it's all work, work, work. His body's here but his heart and mind are already in Calgary working on *Sacred Peace*."

It was enough, for now. But Jacob, Kayla and all of their friends weren't fooled by Jessie's candid attempts to keep the evening light. Josh's presence was a dark cloud. And it was about to get darker.

But before it did, Jessie took his hand and nudged him into a dance. All evening, she'd shared slow songs with everyone else, but not him—his funk was disturbing. Despite his occasionally biting words about Matt, Josh mostly hung out with him, leaning against a wall as if the two of them were holding it up. Both men were sore and Matt should have really still been in bed, so taking posts in chairs and occasionally leaning against the wall rather than joining in on the fun on the dance floor seemed like the most viable options. Plus the wall gave Matt a good perimeter view. For Josh, sitting was painful. Standing was painful. He kept shifting his feet in some fruitless attempt to make his sore ribs comfortable.

When Jessie led him to the dance floor, he only spoke in grunts to anyone who approached, but nobody—not Charlie, Steve, Jacob, or anyone—pushed him. And all of them noticed where Josh's eyes were all night—on his wife. His brooding mood didn't seem to be a jealous thing. Heck, he was hanging out with Matt, who also had a slow tune spin or two with Jessie. It was clearly just the old darkness coming back to haunt him, having bullied its ugly way back into Josh's bloodstream courtesy of two ruthless thugs in a dark parkade.

Jessie wasn't going to let this night—such a momentous night for all of them, since in many ways it put a final stamp of approval on Jacob's and Jessie's abilities to move forward in a healthy way—end with Josh's dark mood. The song the two of them were dancing to was Bob Dylan's *I Believe In You*, an earnest, profound song of love that Jessie herself often played on stage. Taking her husband in her arms, she sighed into his warm neck and stayed there for the entire song. Time stood still; after all of their suffering and desperate attempts to hang on, the latest attack and renewed fears only served to create a numbness in their bodies. By this time, Josh and Jessie were seasoned warriors. Like any soldier fighting a constant war, they lived in a war zone that urged a constant state of PTSD, a biological 'fight or flight' heightened state of awareness, a knowing that their current reality was in all likelihood inescapable.

What this did for the two of them was put them back in their old bubble, the one where they, when life got too big and unmanageable, were reduced to their simplest state of being and the world was stripped away. Holding each other, wordless, they spoke through touch and the beautiful language of love. The rest of the room was detached—neither Josh nor Jessie saw, or wanted to see, any of their loved ones, even though they were close by. Partway through the song, Jessie wrapped her arms tighter around Josh's shoulders and pressed her lips to his neck. He was sore, but tonight they would find a way to make love without hurting him further. The move to Alberta was happening soon. Life would get crazy again, and the new fear stalking them would increase exponentially. Tonight Jessie was stealing from time; she was taking this night for what it was—a gift.

Breathing in her husband's essence, Jessie continued to lay tender kisses on his neck, behind his ear, under the layered hair she adored. Feeling her there almost mewling with love for him, Josh would have been moved to tears if he weren't so terrified. He knew he ought to tell Matt or Charles, or Arnie, maybe, about the threat made to his family a few short days ago, but what would be the point? Watching them work, Josh was well aware that his family was as secure as anyone could hope to make them. Three of the security team were watching the children at the moment, and there were more— some uniformed, some in plain clothes—with eyes on the wedding. No, Josh was slowly coming to an acceptance that, when he really stopped to think about it, frightened him. He'd had a good life. He was an Oscar winner, and the recipient of a lot of love that, at more than one low point in his life, he'd wondered if he would ever have.

If life got that bad again, he knew a way out. If life became untenable, if loss outweighed living, there was a way to numb the pain, and it went beyond the sedation of alcohol and drugs.

Now, with his wife hanging on to him as if she could read his mind, Josh pressed her body against him. His side protested, but other than a sharp wince to acknowledge the pain, Josh held on. His and Jessie's movements were slow and deliberate. Their friends and family were in their own bubbles, yet every one of them took note of Josh and Jessie. They were living proof that love was something to cherish, to never take for granted. Their love was a testament to all—of survival, forgiveness, and perseverance.

Matt's fling with the American producer hadn't amounted to more than a short term affair—his call, not hers. Now, he stood alone and watched Josh and Jessie cling to each other as if tonight was their last night together on earth. It was easy to watch them and not feel sorry for himself. They were meant to be together. Did Matt wish he had Jessie in his arms? Sure. But watching her with the man she loved was equally as absorbing, and equally as captivating as holding her himself. The only thing missing was the feel of her, the…taste of her. Memory served him well. Sometimes he accompanied it with a good bottle of scotch, sometimes with hefty craft beers from one of the many breweries that had sprung up everywhere over the last many years. But tonight he drank water to ease the nasty headache, and soaked up the couple he so desperately wanted to protect. Keeping them safe, keeping their love held safely intact was like constantly applying bandages around a wound that never quite seemed to heal. It was a long term challenge. It was necessary, because the world revolved more smoothly when Josh and Jessie were happy. The broken world needed that kind of love in it. It needed the long term joy and bliss of a couple in love. Hell, Matt needed it—to see it, to revel in it, to cherish it.

He caught a glimpse of Arnie. The Downtown Eastside savior was watching Josh and Jessie too, likely thinking the very same thing, Matt thought, minus maybe the ache to hold Jessie. No, Arnie wanted to see the Sawyers safe too, but Arnie and Matt were divided on how to make that happen. The future was not going to be an easy row to hoe.

Turning on his heel, Matt gave Josh and Jessie one last look—she was kissing her husband now, fully and completely on the lips, telegraphing not-so-secret promises of what awaited Josh upstairs in a big, comfortable bed.

Matt left the room.

Later, in Josh and Jessie's suite, giddy from wine and from the 'staycation' at the Fairmont in their home city, Jessie seesawed a toothbrush back and forth over her teeth, rinsed and spit, and dabbed her lips on a plush white towel before she left the hotel room's washroom in search of her husband. Josh was standing at the entrance to the room where Emily-Grace was sleeping, a mirror of the man who'd stood and watched his daughter slumber peacefully the morning before he flew back to finish his shoot. Now, though, Josh's shoulders were slumped. His good fingers were buried in a pants pocket, his dark dress shirt was untucked, and his chin was lowered.

Jessie approached from behind, but stopped five feet away and leaned against the wall. "What is it, Josh?" she asked him quietly, hopefully. Maybe he would talk now that they were alone under the blissful spell of their earlier waltz. Music…always it was music that spoke for them, for her. Always it was music that eased pain out of wounds the way the sun's hopeful rays dried the earth after a rain. "Tell me what it is."

He turned and faced her, the picture of dejection, his heavy burden weighing on his shoulders. Josh worked his mouth and tried to answer, but he couldn't. How could he tell his daughter's mother—his wife—what had crossed his mind that awful night? That a flicker of the child's image across his brain was enough to warrant a choosing? A choosing that, if he had voiced it, would have undoubtedly become an ending? A final judgment?

Jessie turned one ankle over and tried again. "I know you're mulling over something, Josh. Something's haunting you. I know you, babe."

He just watched her, his chocolate eyes liquid and pained. Josh's lips were numb. His heart was numb. He understood now, on a visceral level, what kept Jessie from speaking all those years ago when she first arrived on the wretched, lonely streets of the Downtown Eastside. Some truths were just too bitter to air.

"Josh, we can't do this, you and me. We're happy, babe. We're doing the best we can, living in the moment. Surviving. The key to our survival is communication. You know that. We've learned that the hard way."

"I'm just tired," he managed. Josh looked tired, all right. He looked about ready to slip to the floor. A slight shrug of one shoulder, and he echoed the thought. "So tired, Jessie."

Alarm shot through Jessie's brain. Like a flash of light, it almost blinded her.

"No," she proclaimed, immediately understanding the gravity of her husband's admission. He wasn't just talking about tonight. "We've come this far, Josh." Striding toward him, Jessie urged him away from the doorway. With nimble fingers, she started to unbutton his shirt, working her way from the top on down. Sliding her hands underneath the fabric so she could feel Josh's skin meld into hers, she laid a palm flat against his heart and raised her chin so she could meet his eyes. Jessie was sorry to see that he was struggling; Josh's gaze was about as troubled as she had ever seen it.

That was his truth here, today. Communicated to Jessie via the windows of his soul, Josh was telling her that there was trouble coming, deep trouble, and that he was powerless against its mighty grasp. All of them, the entire Keating-Sawyer team, may as well be tied up and shoved against a wall, for all the good they could do against the forces holding them captive.

"Are you going to tell me?" she begged. His heart was still beating; Jessie could feel its regular pulse underneath her fingers. How could this be? How could Josh be so physically vital, yet so emotionally helpless at the same time?

"Little one," he tried, "it's bad. What happened on *Sacred Peace*…which we now know really started back when Morgan and Nadia first decided to rip us apart…and which is still happening…it's bad. I don't know if we can get past it."

"Yeah, we can." A slow furor was working its way up Jessie's spine. "We have so far, and we will continue to work our way past it, Josh. You and me, we're warriors. Sawyer Strong," she declared, raising a fist high and giving it a mighty air pump. "We've got something Morgan can never take away. Something he can never destroy."

"Don't say 'each other,' Jessie. We've seen what he can do."

"Love, that's what. It gives us strength, babe. It gives me hope. Josh, you can't give up. I can't fight this war without you."

Josh took Jessie's hand and replaced it on his chest. He laid his own strong palm over top of it. Smiling was not an option; a flicker of love in his eyes was not an option. Instead, he sent her a look of pure knowing, that he understood what she was telling him—that they were connected beyond the limitless bounds of earth. But his stormy eyes were also communicating dread.

"Make love to me," Jessie pleaded. "No more bad stuff. Not tonight. Please, Josh."

Lifting her fingers, Josh brushed his lips against them. Angling his head, he pressed her palm against his rough cheek, and closed his eyes. After a long pause to soak her up, he walked her to their large, rented bedroom and buried himself in her body, in the only arms in the world he truly trusted…

…in the arms whose loss he feared the most.

Chapter Twenty-Two

It was a strange feeling, trundling up the lane to the Alberta ranch house in the silver Lexus. Before flying home to collect his family, Josh had been to the ranch with Ulysses, Charles and Matt. They'd hired a Calgary company to completely fence in the place; a ten foot high metal security fence was now the family's first line of defense against whatever nefarious forces stalked them in their seasonal home. Far enough back on the property that it wasn't noticeable at the house or in the clearing between outbuildings, the ugly fence was designed to protect without inhibiting the family's view of the nearby snow-tipped mountains and without being a constant reminder of what troubled them. But Jessie knew it was there, and its presence gave her the willies.

"Did y'all add razor wire to the top of the fence?" she numbly asked Josh as he gave the uniformed security at the gate a casual wave before driving through and cruising up the gravel lane to their *Sacred Peace* home. "You know, that coiled stuff they put on the tops of walls at prisons? And a machine gun turret every twenty or so feet?"

She spoke quietly enough so the children wouldn't hear. Bouncy and excited when they left home at six this morning, the kids were now as silent as Josh had been through most of the drive from Vancouver. It seemed all of them were recalling the scary night of the barn fire, which ousted Jessie and the kids from the ranch in a jarring and final way the previous year. As much as the memories of their time hanging out at the ranch were mostly good— picking wild raspberries, growing their own vegetables, spending time with Aunt Evelyn and her partner Gary, who planted the seeds of a love for nature in the three young Sawyer children—there was still a palpable worry associated with coming back. The high fence wasn't pretty. Like a wiry snake, it jutted out on both sides of the gate, incongruous in the natural setting, a stark and unwelcome reminder of the presence of darkness in the world.

Josh didn't like Jessie's comments. His low grunt and warning stare were expected, but still unsettling. The trip east had been a quiet one, from Jessie's point of view. They did the drive in one day—nine hours of highway driving and four stops for coffee, pee breaks and meals, making about twelve hours in total, most of it crammed into the Lexus, which was now littered with the refuse of a family road trip. Kids' toys, snack wrappers, a few Tupperware containers, and crumbs—lots of crumbs—were scattered over the back of the vehicle.

At least the kids were good travelers. They were well used to entertaining themselves on trips. The most difficult part was the silence emanating from the driver's seat.

In past years, there had been times when Jessie found Josh's silences unnerving, and vice versa, usually depending on what was happening in their often tumultuous lives. Since reconciling after the Langley kidnapping the silences were more acute, more frequent, but as Jessie opened up over time, Josh closed down. Always there would be a deep seated fear of loss built in to his psyche. Always there would be a wall he couldn't quite bring himself to scale. Since being jumped on his shoot, Josh's coping skills had regressed to an innermost layer. It didn't come as a surprise that he wasn't up for talking during the long drive. His brief but pointed revelation the night of Jacob and Kayla's wedding was enough to send silent communications the entire drive to the ranch, anyway.

Jessie had laid a hand over Josh's for much of the drive. He responded by twining his fingers in hers. Him staring at the road instead of meeting her eyes was okay with Jessie. Over the years, she'd learned what her husband needed from her. It was not usually spoken reassurance. Often, her touch was instantly calming for him, and it was generally accepted with a slow exhale and an immediate peaceful stillness.

He's being good with the kids, Jessie had considered as she listened to music on the satellite radio and admired the remarkable views as they cruised over the Rocky Mountains. *That's all that really matters.* In fact, Josh was being exceptionally patient with all of their children, even when their young voices hit the roof around three o'clock when Dylan lost his temper with his older brother. David, frustrated with Dylan's lack of coordination, had grabbed a video game from Dylan and finished it on his behalf. Calmly, Josh just pulled into a rest stop, turned to the boys, confiscated the game, handed it to Jessie, and removed David from the car. While Jessie consoled Dylan (with one nervous eye tuned into Josh and David) and while Emily-Grace looked up from her movie and held her breath, Josh walked his son to a picnic table, plopped him on the top, and eased his butt down next to him.

Dan and Sam were driving behind the Lexus, tailing Josh and Jessie in case…well, just in case. As the men got out and stretched their legs, Dan wandered over to Jessie's open door. Dylan was on her lap by then, getting extra hugs as his mother dried his tears.

"Everything okay?" Dan asked as, behind him, Sam scanned the area for vehicles. There were none. They were alone in this remote rest stop.

"Hope so," Jessie told Dan as she used a thumb to wipe a salty trail from Dylan's cheek. "Sibling rivalry." She shrugged, and Dan was pretty sure that the slight smile he detected on Jessie's lips extended to her eyes. He relaxed and smiled back. Sometimes it was nice to see this extraordinary family living through normal, everyday trials.

At the picnic table, Josh was saying more than he'd said all day, with the exception of ordering food and the occasional brief response to some running stream or cliff-side sight Jessie pointed at along the drive. When he eventually brought David back to Jessie's side of the car, the little boy was happy. He apologized to Dylan, whose gentle, loving nature was so quickly forgiving that he enveloped his older brother in a big hug.

Curious, Jessie studied Josh's face, and was saddened to see a cloud wash over him when he glanced behind her at Emily-Grace. Twisting around, Jessie sighed when she saw a tense frown line her daughter's petulant face.

"Can we puh-leeze go now?" the eight-year-old said in a spurt of impatient fury. "I want to see Stella." Charlie and Jane had settled into their quaint mountainside Canmore chalet weeks earlier, since Charlie had producer duties on the show.

"You just saw Stella at the wedding," Jessie reminded her. "What's so important that you can't let your brothers have a minute to make up?"

"Daddy didn't need to stop. He could have yelled at David while he was driving."

"Daddy didn't yell at David, Emily-Grace. They just had a talk."

If the word 'bullshit' was in her vocabulary, Jessie knew Emily-Grace would have spit it out.

Thoughtfully running a finger over her top and then her bottom lip, Jessie watched her daughter process what to fire back so she could further hurt her father. Instead, Jessie was surprised to see Emily-Grace just look up at her beloved but distant daddy. Something had changed between the two over the last while, something that Jessie couldn't put her finger on, but it had to do with the way Josh often watched his daughter, usually thinking, she supposed, that nobody noticed. To Jessie's knowledge, no harsh words had recently been spoken between them; in fact, Josh hardly spoke to his daughter at all. At bedtime, or mealtime, he focused on his boys, almost as if he was afraid Emily-Grace was somehow now out of his league and beyond his comprehension. The only real clue other than that was the way he'd so desperately held on to his daughter the day he came home from his shoot.

Jessie felt Dylan move in her lap. Turning back around, she saw Josh lift him out of her arms, careful to watch his own healing hand and to mind his sore rib as he scooped the little guy up.

"Back in your car seat, buddy," Josh mumbled. He wasn't looking at Dylan, though. His subdued eyes were still studying his daughter. When he felt Jessie's eyes on him, Josh inhaled for strength and took her in. She laid a hand over his, on Dylan's lower back as Josh settled him on his hip, and bit her lip, sending him a look that she hoped read *it's okay. Whatever it is, it'll be okay.*

Dan went back to his car, and the little caravan headed back out onto the highway.

Jessie checked her texts just as they started to drive. One got her attention and brought a big smile to her face.

"Josh," she said, tapping him lightly on the elbow. "It's a good day. Carter just texted. Ashley had her baby."

Josh didn't say anything, just compressed his lips together and glanced quickly over at her. Reaching down to his left, he touched a button and fiddled with the position of the driver's seat. The drive wasn't easy on his usual sore body parts. Moving the seat around from time to time put pressure on different points and eased the hurting spots.

"Don't you want to know if it's a boy or a girl?" Jessie laid her phone in her lap.

"I think Carter thought it was going to be a boy," Josh said finally, in a tired, raspy voice. He was staring straight ahead, focusing diligently on the road before them. "Or maybe he was just hoping."

"It's a girl, babe. They called her Ayasha. Josh," Jessie's eyes were glistening, "the name means Little One."

He looked over at her then, and a surprised, slow smile started on his lips. "Ayasha," he repeated. "That's really beautiful, Jessie."

"It is, isn't it? Ayasha."

Josh took her fingers in his. "Ayasha. It's a good name."

It was a bright spot in a long, gray day.

The day was gloomy to begin with; above them all day the sun had played peekaboo with the clouds as it tried to find a way to reach the Sawyers on the road below. The light was dull and pasty when the ranch house finally came into view, which Jessie didn't take as a good sign, but the rowdy welcome the road-weary family got when Josh pulled in and switched off the ignition was enough sunshine to compensate for the rebellious clouds.

Stella came running, jumping up and down with exuberant cries of, "Wait'll you see what's here, Emily-Grace! Wait'll you see!"

Charlie was right behind her. He'd had to grab her arm to keep her from jumping in front of the Lexus when it pulled in. "Daughter," he scolded, "give Emily-Grace the chance to get out of the car." Bending to whisper in her ear—something that appeared to be some kind of gentle, smiling warning—he caught Jessie's eye as Stella happily nodded.

"What are you up to, Charlie?" Jessie asked while she helped Dylan dismount the vehicle. "I know you. You're up to something."

Tossing his hands up in the air, Charlie chuckled. "I know nothing. It's your husband's doing." Approaching her, Charlie wrapped his arms generously around Jessie's shoulders. "Glad you guys are here," he said warmly.

"This place is not the same without you. Jane's got so many cookies made that we donated a bunch to the soup kitchen. She can't stop baking, but she only eats the gluten free ones, so me, Stella and Lucas are putting on the pounds."

"Liar. You look great, Charlie, as fit and handsome as ever." Holding him at arm's length, Jessie said half in jest, "You're only glad we're here so you can put my husband to work making you more millions. You have such a generous spirit, Charlie."

The comment was made tongue-in-cheek, but Charlie expected this from Jessie. There was a new divide between them; it appeared the day she first demanded he and Charles stop production on their series and, like a snowball, gained speed on the downhill slope. Charlie didn't have a chance to retort. A squeal from the girls, followed by high-pitched hollers from the small boys, alerted Jessie to the appearance of something unexpected in the barn.

Jane took her elbow and gave her a welcoming squeeze.

"What's going on?" Jessie asked as her eyes took in, for a long, lingering moment, the new barn that was built to replace the one destroyed by fire last year. Josh was greeting Charlie and Jane now. Jessie met his sober eyes as Jane's sparkling smile followed Charlie into the new structure.

Taking Josh's hand, Jessie stood in place. The two of them let their gazes drift over the coarse cedar shakes of the new barn. The wood was so freshly cut it had not yet turned a weathered gray. Built to fit comfortably into the aesthetic of the low level ranch, the barn was trying to exude the warmth of renewal. To both Jessie and Josh, though, its existence was too bright, too perfect.

It hadn't lived.

The building now before Josh and Jessie replaced a treasured barn that once lingered with a vitality and a life force that, a year ago, was cherished by the small family who spent time inside its cozy walls. The paint-faded walls of yore were rich with the chuffing and snorting of horses who lived in nicked and stained stalls long before Josh's horses were ever even dreamt of. Like the one that once held Blue—Josh's four-legged soul mate—in its loving sanctuary, the stalls were ripe with history.

This place had not yet earned that kind of love. The new barn was a falsity, a structure built on rubble and ruin, constructed to cover up pain the way a bandage hides an open wound but fails to be the actual thing that heals the skin.

Reflecting on that awful night when Alin bravely saved Josh's horses from certain death, Jessie had to avert her eyes. Josh's horses were here now; Toby and Misty had been shuttled up from Southlands earlier in the week by one of the Deacon grooms. They were cavorting in the nearby split rail fenced corral, seemingly as excited to see the approach of the Lexus as Josh was to have his horses a whinny away from where he would sleep from now until October.

Glancing at Josh before she planned to head into the barn to see what was getting the children so riled up, Jessie was sorry to almost see a vague orange hue in the chocolate eyes she loved. The fire was hardly a memory to both of them. It was a part of their souls every bit as much as the horses saved by Alin.

Ducking his head, Josh pawed the Alberta dirt with the heel of his boot before he shyly led his wife forward into the barn. He had to let her fingers go when, like a cannonball, Dylan's lithe, small body leapt into his arms.

"Huh." Stuffing her hands in her jeans' pockets, Jessie stood back by Jane and took in the happy sight of her husband, stubbornly pushing aside his sore body parts, tossing his youngest son up into the air. Josh was smiling widely.

Dylan was literally vibrating with joy. "We got a pony! We got a pony," he was crying over and over.

"Did we," Jessie muttered, loud enough for only Jane to hear.

"Easy," Jane cautioned with a happy upturn to her small lips. "It's a small one."

Josh brought Dylan down onto a hip. Grinning, he looked over at his wife. When their eyes met, a sweet light passed between them.

"Surprise, surprise," Jessie mouthed to him. "Omigod, I love that man," she whispered to Jane afterwards, unable to take her eyes off Josh as his boots clattered over the wide new boards beneath his feet so he could lift Dylan onto the pony's back. "But I'm gonna kill him for getting them a pony without at least discussing it with me."

"Ah, yes," Jane agreed, beaming. "Our thoughtless men. Charlie'd be dead ten times over if I actually followed through on those threats over the years."

Peacefully radiant, Jessie nodded in agreement while her eyes danced at the sight of her happy family. So joyful they were. All of the children—little Lucas, too, in Charlie's arms at the moment—were hovering around the pony. Even Emily-Grace was asking questions, tugging at Charlie's sleeve. *What does he eat? When do we get to feed him? What's his name?*

The light changed at the barn's open entry, and she forced her gaze away from the excitement and casually glanced over.

Matt was there. Wide-stanced in the open doorway, leaning on a sliding door similar to the one in the old barn, he was watching intently in a detached sort of way. Josh had his back to the door. Jessie gave Jane one last small smile and wandered over to her buddy.

"Missed you," she said as she snuggled under a raised arm.

"How was the drive?" Dipping his nose into her hair, Matt closed his eyes and inhaled. *Lavender. Mmm.*

A quiet sigh preceded the slight shrug Matt felt rather than saw. "Mostly silent. Not counting the kids."

"He has a lot on his mind."

Peeking up at him, Jessie pressed her lips to Matt's cheek and wriggled in closer. His free arm wrapped around her and enclosed her a little tighter. She felt the tension leave his body; a slow exhale took it away on a whisper and a dream.

"I gathered that," Jessie answered quietly. "Something about bad stuff. I'm plugging my ears from now on in. From now on I don't want to know. If it's okay with the rest of you," she looked up at him with a wistful, pleading hope, "I'm just going to pretend everything is okay. I'll go crazy with worry, Matt, if I think too much about all this."

"You do what you need to do, Jessie," he told her. "Just take care of your family. Let me do the worrying, okay?"

"You?" Jessie's body diminished itself in his arms. Matt sensed the change and held on tighter. "You're not sleeping, honey. I know you're still reeling from the effects of that concussion, and you smell like booze. I hate that smell." Wrinkling her nose, she buried her face in his chest, in the manly security she found there. Lately, with Josh, the security was missing. *I'm always holding him together,* Jessie considered with a start as she let herself melt into Matt's warm body. *I'm always trying to keep him from falling apart.* That reality felt traitorous to acknowledge. Tensing, Jessie wriggled her nose deeper into Matt's chest. He let his eyes close over.

When Matt opened his eyes, Josh was watching him. Josh was on the other side of the pony now, lifting David up to set him behind his brother. Shrinking slightly, Matt nodded a hello to him, but he didn't let go of Jessie. Judging by the anger and anxiety brooding under Josh's surface since the mugging, and how quiet and distant he was over the days the men were at the ranch together preparing for the family's move back to Alberta, Josh likely was, as Jessie said, quiet on the long drive east. *You don't do yourself any favors by pulling away from her,* Matt telegraphed across the pony's back to him. *All you're doing is making her desperate for connection. Any connection.*

Josh's eyes flicked behind Matt and Jessie. He glanced down at his daughter.

Stella started hopping up and down again. Her quick movements startled the pony, and Josh had to grab David at the waist to keep him from falling off. Dylan was no trouble—the youngest Sawyer had a good grip on the pony's rough mane and a grin the size of the hole dug behind the ranch house that would soon accommodate the family's new swimming pool.

Matt knew what was coming behind him. Kissing the top of Jessie's head, he said tenderly, "Don't be too hard on him tonight, okay? Josh means well. In his mixed-up way, you know he's just trying to make things better."

Jessie's head popped up off Matt's chest. Her eyes narrowed. "Make things better? Hard on him?"

A tiny whine got her attention just as a shadowy new body approached. Evelyn was walking toward the barn. She stopped about ten feet away. Stella brushed by Jessie and Matt, and started hollering at Emily-Grace. The little girl's dark hair bounced up and down in time with her wired and excited small frame.

"What?" Jessie probed. "Um, Matt? Is that what I think it is?" Her eyes locked onto a shivering white bundle, barely big enough to fill Evelyn's palm, that Evelyn was holding carefully against her chest.

Matt touched Jessie's chin. "Remember what I said. He means well. There are plenty of people at your beck and call to help you take care of a puppy."

"A puppy. We agreed not to get our kids a puppy. Please don't tell me there's a big screen television inside the house as well. No TV in Alberta. We agreed."

Matt was no longer listening. He was looking into the barn past Jessie, a look of almost boyhood wonder crossing over his face, settling in there like the calm after a storm. Forcing her frustration aside, Jessie turned to see what had caught his attention.

It wasn't a what. It was a who. Two whos—Emily-Grace and her father.

"Oh, Jesus, he breaks my heart," Jessie breathed as she, too, turned more fully toward Josh, who was still standing behind the pony, one hand clutching David's shirt and one arm sheltering Dylan, ready to grab him if necessary. Josh's eyes were guarded, afraid, flickering with an uncertain anticipation, on his daughter.

Emily-Grace had spotted the puppy. That was clear, in the way she was standing with her feet apart, knees slightly buckled, and both hands covering her face. Josh and Jessie's daughter was wearing pink leggings, a little baggy after the long drive. Overtop was a long-sleeved pink shirt covered generously with tiny blue butterflies. It, too, was wrinkled and tired. Her hair was messy, having long ago half escaped from the ponytail Jessie had started her daughter's day off with. Her face? Pink cheeked. She was rumpled and tired. But her eyes were glistening. Big fat tears were trailing delicately down her cheeks.

She caught her mother's eye. "Is it for me?" she asked Jessie from behind her palms. "Is that a puppy? Is it mine? Did you get me a puppy?" An innocence, a Disneyesque wonder, encircled Emily-Grace like a halo.

The barn had gone silent. Even Stella stopped announcing her interminable child-sized exuberance to the family and friends gathered back in this place where, the last time they stood here, the ground was covered with ugly black soot and the detritus of a much loved barn.

Jessie had to work hard to find her voice. "I think it is a puppy, Emily-Grace," she said softly. "But sweetheart…it's not from me." Lifting her eyes to Josh, who was half hiding behind his boys as if he was terribly afraid of how this might go, Jessie smiled.

Emily-Grace let her eyes linger on the little bundle of fluffy white fur held so dearly, like a fragile egg, in Evelyn's hand. The child had yet to move toward the wiggly little fella, and kindly Evelyn knew to stay back and wait for her to come forward.

Slowly turning around, moving first one foot and then the other, her hands still over her mouth and the tears still loosely streaming, knees still slightly bent as if she might crumble, Emily-Grace faced her daddy. The small shoulders were shaking. Every adult in the space was trembling. Even the young boys seemed to recognize the sacredness of this moment. The only sounds were the occasional pawing of the pony's hard hooves against the floor, shuffling fresh straw around its spacious stall.

With a strength and wisdom far beyond her years, Emily-Grace let down her hands. They hung at her sides, forgotten. "Daddy," she whispered, "did you get me a puppy?"

It was a few seconds before Josh could answer. He had to lick his lips three times and wipe his eyes on the sleeve of his denim jacket before he could make his vocal chords coherently respond. Looking at Jessie was not an option. Josh felt very alone then, despite the wealth of friends and family who surrounded him. He knew he'd catch hell from Jessie later for getting the kids animals they had decided together against buying. Now, seeing his wife bury herself in Matt's arms—seeking solace after the lonely drive, and rightly so, Josh thought—he decided he'd done the right thing. Jessie's disappointment in him would be worth it.

He looked down at his quaking daughter. "It's your puppy," Josh managed. "It's all yours, sweetheart."

Charlie couldn't help himself. He touched Emily-Grace's shoulder and bent forward to give her a half hug. At the same time, he gave her a gentle push toward her father. She didn't need any more encouragement. Charlie followed her so he could monitor the boys on the pony's back—he added Lucas in front of Dylan, and encompassed all three boys in his arms, while Josh knelt and accepted a big, genuine hug from his distant, and often bitter, little girl.

"Let's go meet the little monster," Josh murmured. Standing, with a wince courtesy of his rib, he carried Emily-Grace out of the stall, glancing at Charlie first to make sure he had a handle on the boys. David was wriggling to go meet the puppy too. Jane stepped forward and lifted him off the pony.

Josh shifted his daughter to his left hip. When he passed by Jessie and Matt, he didn't look at either of them. He couldn't; he had a feeling his jelly legs would turn to mush and he'd collapse into a puddle, and need Matt's strength around him, too.

Jessie moved a little aside so he could pass. Lifting an arm, she let her hand float onto the hand Josh had securely placed on their daughter's hip. It wafted away from the two of them the way a gauzy curtain is lifted and suspended in a light summer breeze before it settles back into place.

"Matt?" she asked tenderly after Josh set Emily-Grace on the ground, took the quivering bundle from Evelyn, and placed it in his little girl's trembling hands, "Can I say something and not hurt your feelings?"

A low chuckle vibrated against her cheek. "Can I have some bourbon after?"

She swatted him. "You've been spending too much time with Charlie."

"It's okay," Matt said. "Shoot."

Jessie turned to him. She was, quite literally, glowing.

Matt sighed and touched his fingers to her cheek. "Sweetheart," he murmured, "the thing about loving you," he swallowed past the lump of cotton that formed in his throat, "is that it fills my heart to see you happy. You and Josh…" Unable to continue, he shook his head and just gave her a happy-sad half-there smile.

"Thank you," she said, with a sincerity that rooted both of them to the here and now, to the honest truths that his admission decreed. With a small smile, Jessie bit her bottom lip, paused, and then leaned forward to press her lips against his. It was brief, and she didn't give a shit who saw—if Josh saw, even, because more than anyone, Josh understood Matt's place of honor in Jessie's life, in their lives. "I was going to say how much I love that man," she said. "And I knew you would understand."

Matt swallowed, gulped, and nodded.

Jessie leaned in for a hug. Burying her face in the warm hollow where Matt's shoulder and neck met, her warm lips tickled him with the words, "You even taste like booze."

He laughed. Swiping a loose strand of hair away from her cheek, he said, "Go." He gave her waist a little twist. "Go be with your family."

Giggling, Jessie let go of him, and moved outside under the deepening twilight, but she stayed back a step from the new puppy, which seemed to be absolutely already head over heels in love with its new young mistress, and she watched her husband and daughter radiate joy.

"A puppy and a pony," Jessie said to Josh a few hours later. Standing at the entrance to the ensuite bathroom, patting her face with a hand towel, she stopped and tossed the towel at Josh. He was lying peacefully on the bed, on his back, eyes closed, ankles crossed, hands folded across his stomach. The towel landed on his belly. He opened one eye and watched his wife flick off the bathroom light and come into the darkened room.

She crawled up onto the bed, tossed the towel aside, and straddled him. Jessie was alight.

"Fluffy," she said, feigning irritation. "She's trying to decide between Fluffy and Snow."

Josh's eyes lit up with remembrance. "Fluffy...it's from that minion movie. Despicable Me." Raising his hands, he employed a high-pitched falsetto to mimic the famous line from the movie. "It's so flufffyyyy!"

Wide-eyed, Jessie let her fingers graze Josh's chest. He was still fully dressed. Letting her fingers slide down his hard stomach, she slid one set underneath the wide belt at his waist. Both of his eyes flickered playfully open, and he placed his hands on her hips.

"Seriously?" He brightened. "I thought I'd be in shit."

"You should've asked. We should've talked about it." Jessie undid his belt. "You're not mad?"

"According to Evelyn, Precious, that scraggly orange barn cat, is expecting kittens, Josh. We're going to be overrun with animals around here. Babies."

"Animals are a good thing, Jessie. Unconditional love."

She melted. *For you, or for the kids?* Sometimes it was so easy to spot the ten-year-old version of this strong, kind man.

Gathering up some backbone, Jessie pointed at him. "You husband. Me wife. We parents." The hand flitted back and forth between them. Then it went back to his jeans, and pulled his zipper down. "We need to talk about those kinds of things." She winked, and pulled his jeans and boxers down over his hips. He had to raise his hips to accommodate her.

Josh moaned as she bent over him. "I should have gotten her a puppy a long time ago."

Jessie laughed again, looked up at him, smiled wickedly, and went back to pleasing her man. She would have told him she loved him in words, but she knew her husband well. Sometimes Josh just communicated through action.

And sometimes Jessie communicated the same way back.

Chapter Twenty-Three

"So, she went with Snow in the end, but to me the little mop rag will always be Fluffy."

Jessie was poised in front of the fridge in the open concept one-story rancher, wiping one of the shelves clean. Dylan, the family's rambunctious overzealous action junkie, always on fast forward, had spilled a half carton of milk when he went to put it back after pouring some on his cereal.

Sliding sideways to rinse the dishrag she was using to clean the spill, Jessie continued her puppy update. "Of course, I have yet to determine whether the name Snow is in reference to a certain Disney princess." She turned to Carlotta, who was alongside her lining the dishwasher with breakfast dishes. "A Disney princess who, I am sorry to say, is under the thumb of a mother who forces her to do boring old chores around the house. Well, stepmother actually, not mother, but if Emily-Grace is trying to send me a message, it's been received." Faking a grumble, Jessie fought against smiling but her lips quivered mischievously anyway. "Note that you, Carlotta, are the one putting the Sawyer family breakfast dishes in the dishwasher. Not my daughter. And you didn't even have breakfast here."

"Momma," Emily-Grace countered, sliding up beside her mother and peeking up at her from beneath beautiful long golden-tipped lashes, "Snow White was cast out of the kingdom for being the fairest in all the land. Fairer even than her mother."

"Stepmother." Jessie playfully tousled her daughter's hair before she went back to mopping up the spill. "Fairer, huh? Glad to see you still know your Disney princesses, little girl of mine who is growing up way too fast."

"Nuh-uh, I don't know them. I only know the newer ones."

"Hmmm?" Jessie wrinkled her nose. Beside and behind her, Deirdre and Carlotta exchanged amused knowing glances.

"Jacob. He reminded me about Snow White." Emily-Grace was giggling. Her cherubic smile could have lit candles, it was so radiant. She did a casual pirouette on the floor and skipped away.

Carlotta put in her two cents. "Jacob's been telling her she will one day outshine her mother on the stage. You better prepare yourself, Jessie."

"Jacob? That traitor!" From behind the refrigerator door, Jessie snuck a peek at her daughter, who was back out in the living area bending down to study the puppy, who was asleep in a small pile of baby blankets Emily-Grace had mussed up into a comfy bed. "Sweetheart, you don't want to sing on stage, right? You're just playing guitar for fun?"

"Duh, I want to be a dancer, Momma. Like Auntie Kayla."

"Dancer," Jessie repeated to Carlotta, using the rag to punctuate the point. "As my darling daughter has maintained since she could talk." Triumphant, she went back to giving the fridge a good wipe.

Deirdre walked over to her granddaughter to take a closer look at Snow. "Emily-Grace could already dance in your shows, Jessie. She's talented."

"Of course she is, she's my kid! We have a lotta home based dance parties, especially when Kayla's around, but Dee, no! Please don't plant that idea in my eight-year-old's head. A child that age goes to bed around the time my shows start, and let's not forget that little girls put on the stage too early learn things they shouldn't have to know until they're twenty, um, I mean fifty. Yeesh. The nerve."

Jessie's thwarted childhood slid across the women's brains. The house grew uncomfortably quiet for a few extended minutes, until the screen door slammed and Dylan ran in to grab a glass of water. Watching him streak back across the floor to the door in rubber boots, Jessie cringed. "I need a bigger rag." Dylan's footsteps tracked good ole Alberta mud all the way to the kitchen, and all the way back out.

Charles and Dee had cruised up the lane twenty minutes ago, with Carlotta and Ulysses in tow, Ulysses behind the wheel, and the women in the back of Charles' leased luxury sedan. The men were outside with Josh, talking horse talk, Jessie hoped, and avoiding anything more critical than doing a few repairs to the split rail fence around the corral. Gary and Evelyn were on the grounds too, measuring out the new season's herb and vegetable gardens, although Gary had started the day helping Josh replace fence bits, which Josh had been at since sunrise. Jessie stifled a wide yawn. Between the puppy being up three times in the night, and the jarring of the early morning hammering, she was short on sleep and even shorter on nerves.

Carlotta took a look in the tired eyes, closed the dishwasher door for the final time, and expertly whipped up a cappuccino. Gratefully, Jessie accepted a pottery mug from her outstretched hand—Jessie's third espresso this morning. She was vibrating but didn't have the heart to tell her trusted friend that she was at her java limit for the time being. Instead, she winked up at Dee and shook some cinnamon from a nearby sprinkler onto the soft milk foam. "Better make our meeting quick, Dee," she said. "Despite all my java, I still might doze off on you."

Emily-Grace laid down on her belly on the living room floor facing Snow, who was awake now, lying on her back nibbling at a chew toy held up in the little girl's fingers. "Momma, she has really sharp teeth," Emily-Grace called out. She, too, yawned, but her sheer delight at the seemingly magical appearance of this incredible puppy in her life easily negated her fatigue hangover.

"Mm hmmm," Jessie acknowledged. She pointed her mug at Dee. "Dylan can corroborate that. Nobody in the Sawyer household slept last night. Josh got up at three and found all the kids in Emily-Grace's room playing with the puppy. They had her out of the crate and on the bed. The bedding's been through the wash twice already."

"Did Dylan get bit?" Deirdre wandered back into the kitchen area. Accepting a teacup from Carlotta, she said appreciatively, "Thank you."

"Did Dylan get bit. Ha! Every finger on that child's hands is bandaged. Sometimes I think he takes after Josh more than he takes after his own father. Apparently Josh's mother stopped taking him to emerge for stitches unless he needed at least twenty."

Deirdre cleared her throat. The topic of Dylan's biological parentage still threw her a little. It got awkward sometimes, to say the least. Jacob…bringing him to mind was enough cause to move into a more formal meeting with Jessie. "Let's sit," she said. Taking her teacup with her, she crossed the small kitchen area and landed at a large repurposed harvest table Evelyn had found at an auction and picked up for the ranch house. Thankfully, some of the eclectic wooden chairs surrounding it had cushions. Deirdre chose one with a sunny bright floral chintz.

Following, Jessie rolled her eyes at Carlotta. "Watch my summer disappear," she sulked.

"Look at it this way, honey," Carlotta replied, as she started digging through cupboards to assemble ingredients for wholesome banana chocolate chip muffins. "You'll likely get a whole night's sleep at all those fancy hotels."

The thought alone was enough to stop Jessie in her tracks. She, and Carlotta too, knew quite well that Jessie would prefer no sleep at home with her family than being alone in some ritzy, foreign digs. A grateful smile was her reward to Carlotta for the reminder. A warm fuzzy made its way into her heart, and she cheered up at the sight of Emily-Grace playing with Snow before she set her mug down on the thick pine table.

"All right, Dee," she said, focusing her attention on the task at hand. "Let's get the business over with before the boys get bored of man talk and destroy our lovely quiet time."

A folder of papers was already waiting on the table. Deirdre reached for it and thumbed through to a printed calendar. Jessie found Dee's old fashioned ways utterly charming, but she pulled out her iPhone and grinned happily—and a little diabolically—at her.

Thankfully, the gracious Deirdre missed the pointed smirk and dug in.

Reading through the glasses riding on the edge of her nose, she started with, "Shall we talk about the Grammy protesters now or save the bad stuff for the end?"

"How about we skip the bad stuff all together?" Leaning back in her chair, Jessie watched Deirdre try to navigate waters that wearied and discouraged them both.

"Okay, then. The only shows you want to do over the summer months are the ones with Jacob. I'm agreed. It's just easier to coordinate the two of you when you travel and work together."

"And Kayla. She'll always be travelling with us now." Josh's bouncy sister was a sunbeam in the clouds. The girl was so in love, so happy these days, that her presence often dispelled the worry constantly dogging the Sawyers.

"Yes." Without looking up, Dee raised a finger and drew it, with a deliberate practiced ease, over the schedule. "Most of the big European shows will piggyback on the American ones. You can puddle jump between them, and take breaks here at the ranch. Once the kids are out of school for the summer, they can travel with you so Josh can work unencumbered on *Sacred Peace*."

A silent respect for Josh passed between them. Both ladies knew Josh would prefer to work 'encumbered,' meaning coming home to his family in the evenings.

"Josh and I will talk about which shows it makes sense to bring the kids to," Jessie said with an air of solemnity. "He may want to keep the boys around a few of the times that I'll be away. I don't know."

Dee finally looked up. "Charles and Charlie promised to try to schedule him off a few days in a row when they can, so he can fly out and join you here and there."

"S'good." Raising a hand to her brow, Jessie rubbed a few fingertips deeply into her skin. At the same time, she let out a little breath and tossed her hair before looking out of the big window beyond the sun porch below them. She could see the men out there, hunched around parts of the fence replacing rotten bits with fresh, new wood. Josh was to the left of the group, which didn't surprise her. Always, it seemed of late, he edged away from situations where he'd be expected to share in conversation.

Oddly, Matt was working with him, holding pieces of wood for Josh to hammer in. Sam and Alin were on hand to watch the kids. They were entertaining Dylan and David at the basketball net at the moment. Matt could've had the day off, but he was as much a part of the family now as any of them. When he could, he chose to be with the Sawyers.

We're practically a cult, Jessie thought as she watched Josh reach up to his mouth to pull a large nail out from in between his lips. He placed it against the wood and hammered it in. When he bent over his work, that piece of hair Jessie loved to tuck behind his ear fell over his cheek. She almost gasped at the look of him, tanned and rugged, his hair growing longer again to keep the *Sacred Peace* production team happy, and Josh's fans even happier. Matt had his back to Jessie, but he must have said something funny, because Josh looked at him as he straightened, and even from across the clearing Jessie could see his face light up. He laughed too, a rare sight these days.

The puppy and the pony, and just being back here at the ranch, were working their magical enchantment on Josh. He needed this—days outdoors in the fresh air surrounded by nature's warm and welcome fragrances, where unseen woodland creatures whispered in the wind from their lush earthy hollows; where Josh could hear horses whinnying and watch them run from the perfect vantage point, which was either propped up on a fence rail, or while he sipped coffee from the bright and vibrant sun porch.

Deirdre had to call Jessie back from her wandering thoughts. "Who would have ever thought Charles and Ulysses would be out there hammering away at fence posts?"

Jessie turned away from the menfolk and peeked shyly up at Dee. "And Matt," she admitted. "Vancouver's most GQ yuppie ever."

"He might want to watch that fancy aviator jacket around those big nails your husband is pounding into the fence."

"Ha. Matt and Josh. They've made their peace, Dee."

"Have they?" The question was a pointed one.

Jessie frowned and turned the cappuccino mug around between her fingers. "There's some kind of silent communication frittering between them. I guess they've got a brotherhood thing going on, after what happened on Josh's shoot. I admit, though, Dee, it's not all good."

Pushing her glasses back on her nose, Deirdre took that as a cue to bring up some of the tougher parts of the morning's discussion. "I know, honey," she said, looking over at Emily-Grace to be sure the child wasn't within earshot. She wasn't—she was lost in her new puppy. At the moment, she was bent over Snow on the floor, tenderly wrapping a soft blanket around the puppy's tiny, vibrating body. Dee was pretty sure she was singing. A twang touched her heart at the thought of Jessie as a child the same age, singing with the same innocent joy.

She waded in. "I want Matt to travel with you for the busy season coming up, Jessie. Is that going to be okay?"

Jessie stiffened. The nervous movement with her mug stopped. She stared at the endearing pink Prince Edward Island lupin hand painted on its side. "Truth? I want him with me." She looked up, raised her chin, and started fingering a new ringlet in her hair. "Is the film happening in October? Because if it is, I want him there too."

"Yes, it's confirmed. You'll be shooting in Montreal."

"And if Matt doesn't want to come?"

"Ultimately it's his choice, Jessie. And Josh's. You have to give both of those men the choice."

"To trust me, you mean." *I'll always be a whore.* Unable to hide the self-loathing and disgust that flitted across her pretty pink cheeks, on this morning when she was tired and struggling to keep herself from being temperamental and short-tempered, Jessie held Dee's gaze. In her expression was a resigned but proud stance that shouted *I know what you ultimately think of me.* If she hadn't been so weary, Jessie would have stuffed the disturbing thoughts deep into her body where they could hide in the shadow of her liver, or perhaps underneath a kidney, but as it was she was too damn beat today to muster up any self-respect. All she could muster up was a little fight.

Even kindhearted Carlotta cringed at what she said next.

"I guess we'll just have to trust Matt. I hope the man has balls of steel, because the old road gets lonely sometimes."

"Oh, Jessie," Deirdre chided. "Honey, why do you always have to be so defensive? All of us understand why what happened with Matt happened when it did. And we know how devoted you are to Josh, how committed the two of you are to your marriage. I'm not worried about you and Matt."

"I am. I'm desperately in love with that man. Matt, I mean. He's everything to me, Dee. But Josh…" Jessie shook her head and spoke with an almost awestruck adoration, with the reverence her often lonely husband deserved. "Josh…" She sighed. "No words, no song, no music, can speak for how much I love him, Dee."

Emily-Grace crept up behind her mother. Snow was cradled in her arms, wrapped up in the downy blanket, its pure, clear wet eyes almost the only part of the dog that was visible. "I love Daddy too, Momma," Emily-Grace said. The way she voiced the simple statement—as if the puppy in her arms finally gave her a reason to say out loud that she loved her father—made Jessie's heart do a flip-flop.

Gently, she reached out and touched the puppy's soft face. It looked at her the way she thought a new baby might, all trusting and loving, wrapped up in the blanket like that. "I know you do, sweetheart." Jessie leaned over and brushed her lips across her daughter's cheek. "Even when you don't say it, I know how much you love Daddy. Now go put that puppy in its crate and let it sleep. It's a baby, honey, it needs some quiet time to sleep. Make sure you have a clean pee pad nearby for it. Then wash your hands and help Carlotta with the muffins."

"Um, Momma?"

"Yes, honey?"

"Um, if it's okay with Carlotta, I'd kinda like to go outside with Daddy. I can help him with the fence."

"Oh." Startled, Jessie considered the request. Unsure, she looked over at Deirdre before she said, "Wear your boots and a hat. It's cold out there." Raising her arms as question marks as her daughter scrambled off to put Snow in her crate, which was tucked into a corner of Emily-Grace's room, she added, "Josh'll be buying her a bunny next."

Deirdre lightly touched Jessie's wrist. "It's not about buying her things. She just needed a gap to open up for her, that's all."

They had more to discuss, but all of the women in the house were quiet and watchful when Emily-Grace approached her father and Matt outside a few minutes later. Josh seemed equally taken aback. When he handed her nails to hold for him, he looked over toward the house. He couldn't see Jessie, but he knew she'd be watching. The look on his face…on the outside he was as strong as an ox, but it broke Jessie's heart to see how much this simple gesture on the part of their daughter meant to him, as if he might crack into a gazillion bits of dust and fade into the earth with relief and joy.

"The Oscars," Dee finally said, breaking into Jessie's distracted dreaming once again. She started to rhyme off dinners and appearances, but Jessie raised her hand, palm out.

"I don't care what the media chooses to say about me, Dee. I don't need to spend the next two weeks on the road. I want to be here." Seeing Emily-Grace with Josh cemented that choice. "Please don't make me go. Not after…" She gulped.

She and Jacob had appeared together at the Grammys in January. Protesters lined the streets, which floored her. Nobody was violent, it was a peaceful protest, but it drove reality home all the same.

"You have to do some, honey." Dee reached up. In one elegant movement, she lifted her glasses off her nose. "We've got Jacob scheduled to do more educational talks. He's smoothing things over."

The protesters were women's advocacy groups. What Jacob did in Florida was unconscionable. Most of the hype and media stir had died down, but a few small groups were still boycotting his shows. This was a furor that, in the days before the threats purportedly coming from Morgan in prison, would have been more cause for worry than Jessie allotted them these days. She simply was 'over' the Florida violence, but it seemed the rest of the world was not.

Dee broached a thought. "I've had some calls from Shawna Coupland. I want you and Jacob to do her show."

"When?"

"She wants to fit you in right away."

"To do what, to talk about old stuff that no longer matters?"

"It matters to your fans, honey. They need to see that you and Jacob are really okay, that you've truly made your peace and aren't sworn mortal enemies, which I think most of them think you should be. They don't understand why you so readily forgave him."

"They'll never understand why we've made our peace. It won't matter what I say."

"We're talking about a violent sexual assault, Jessie. I have to say that I'm not even sure I completely understand what happened or how you've managed to forgive Jacob. The way you've approached it has groups up in arms."

"If I go on that show, Dee, it's the last time I'm talking publicly about what happened between Jacob and me. He and I have moved on. He's with Kayla now, and he's blissfully happy. He's not a threat to me or to any other woman. You know that."

"I do, honey. I trust Jacob. But that doesn't mean I've forgiven him any more than some of his old fans have."

"You go to church, Dee. Is forgiveness not preached to you every Sunday?"

Deirdre hemmed and hawed. "I know in my heart that Jacob is a good man. But what he did was very, very wrong."

"And I know that you are still being kind to Jacob. But Dee, if you're hanging on to any resentment toward him, let it go. It'll just eat you up inside." Emphatic, Jessie lifted her hands to help express her thoughts more clearly. She waved them gracefully in front of her chest as she spoke. "We've talked about this. I accept my part in what happened. It was so, so stupid of me to go down there knowing what kind of state he was in. But Dee," she lowered her voice and gripped Deirdre's wrist, "I would do it again. I was really worried about him. I just wouldn't," she glanced outside at her daughter, "give in to him the way I did. It's so easy for me, you know?"

Restlessly tapping a finger on the table, Jessie hedged a little. "I'm glad that people—including all of you—seem to have forgotten where I came from, and what I did in order to survive. I pray to God none of my children ever have to live that kind of life. But Dee, I did what I had to do. It wasn't all bad. And I'm not all sorry. Unfortunately, my history makes sex easy for me. You want the truth? I should have just slept with Jacob that day. It was super shitty of me to get him going and then try to shut him down."

"What happened was in no way your fault, Jessie. What Jacob did was wrong."

"I appreciate that, Dee, I really do. And he knows that, too. Jacob is truly sorry for what happened. Stop going to church if you can't live what you're taught. Forgiveness, I mean. Cuz then what's the point?"

Shocked and more than a little upset by Jessie's emotional reminder of a past that she once spent far too much time pondering and wondering about, Dee just shook her head. "I still can't believe you ever lived that kind of life, honey. I wish…I wish…"

"What, that you and Charles had come along sooner? And rescued me the day I first landed on East Hastings?"

There were spots of light in Deirdre's eyes, little dewy drops of moisture. She glanced toward the window and smiled sadly over at Emily-Grace. "Oh, if I could have had you in my life when you were her age, Jessie. When you were a child. I would give anything to have raised you."

Sagging a little under the weight of the heavy conversation, Jessie bit her lip and tipped her head a little. She couldn't bring herself to smile at the woman who had become her manager, friend, and on many levels, mother. When she spoke, her voice was raspy and thick. "Just think how incredibly spoiled I would be, Dee. I'd be intolerable."

"You'd have been safe."

That was the end of the hard stuff. *Safe.* What a word.

What a fucking, big, hopeless goddamn word.

Jessie went back to playing with the ringlet in her hair, wondering *is a person ever really safe? Really?* More so, she also caught herself thinking *being a teen runaway made me strong. My life on the Downtown Eastside made me strong. I can handle the tough stuff.*

And...*I can let the small stuff go.*

Jacob. She loved him in Edinburgh, she loved him in New York. He was her best, best friend once upon a time. In all that time, he was never the bad guy he became for one brief day in Florida, when untenable circumstances derailed him and turned him into a monster. Jessie couldn't see the point of hanging on to an anger and hatred that would serve only to fester and create tension between them and those they loved. She couldn't see the point of hanging on to pain if she didn't need to.

There were more scheduling details to ponder with Deirdre, but Jessie grew quiet and reticent to talk. Mostly she just nodded and went along with Dee's plans for her, only piping up once in a while when she needed to. The protesters at the Grammys had been an awakening. Sexual assault—rape— was truly an unacceptable violence, despite the part Jessie felt she played in pushing Jacob that dark day. Maybe there was more that needed to be said publicly, not to lessen what Jacob did, but to urge awareness and prevention...and to use it as a platform to talk about forgiveness.

She agreed to do Shawna Coupland's show.

The first chance she got, Jessie screeched back her chair and threw on boots and her thick black North Face jacket. She let the screen door slam loudly behind her when she left the cozy warmth of the ranch house. Carlotta had the muffins just about ready to come out of the oven by then, but bringing up the violence of Jessie's past on this already exhausting day was draining.

It wasn't just what happened with Jacob that Jessie was finding disturbing—it was her collective past. A predator stepfather, a perverse South Carolina businessman, Downtown Eastside videos made for Caryn and Eric, Charlie's casual sex with others when he was in a relationship with Jessie, Nadia and Morgan's nasty maneuvering…it was everything. There was no escaping the bad things that happened to Jessie any more than there was solid assurance that her life would be magical and filled with love in the future.

The only way she knew to mitigate the sick feelings Deirdre's well-meaning plans dredged up was to replace the darkness with light. As she strode purposefully toward the corral, she stuffed her hands in her jacket pockets and brought Jacob to mind, not the dark Jacob who hurt her in Florida, but the sweet, loving man she knew him to be. He was with Kayla now, married and expecting a baby. All was well in his family life. The assault would never disappear, it would be a black mark on his career forevermore, but he was, in his heart, truly sorry, and not in any way a repeat offender. God, in the Bible, believed in forgiveness when it was truly felt and asked for. As far as Jessie was concerned, there was a well-earned peace between her and Jacob. The others? From her collective past? She tried to forgive them, as best she could.

The hardest person to forgive, she'd learned over time, was herself.

The darkness…the only thing that could take it away was light. To her right, Dylan and David were all joy and happiness as they played with Sam and Alin who, to Jessie's absolute thrill, were also evoking love everywhere they went. In front of Jessie, only a few steps away now, were a few of the men she and some of the women in her life loved. She tried to smile at Charles, but couldn't quite muster it, partly because she was saddened at how fatigued he looked. *Sacred Peace* was taking its toll on him. He was in his mid 70's now, a heart attack survivor, and in great shape, but he still looked tired, to her. She frowned, and turned toward Matt and Josh.

Laying a hand on Emily-Grace's shoulder, she brightened a little, but both Josh and Matt instantly noted the deep sorrow hovering beneath the surface of her damp eyes as she stopped and studied the new wood the guys were so carefully placing around the corral. Jessie couldn't meet their eyes just yet. She wasn't quite ready to let go of the old sadness that crept up on her when Dee brought up the conflicted emotions that sex brought to Jessie's life.

Josh paused in his work. His daughter was out here with him, quietly holding the nails and thanking him, with her small pale Jessie-eyes, for trying so hard. Now Jessie was here, unable to meet his eyes and almost overflowing with the awful old gloom that, when it snuck up on her, still had the power to render her mute. He looked over at Matt, and saw that he, too, was aware that something was suddenly haunting their girl again.

Jessie took in a breath and looked up at Josh then. Meeting those well loved, understanding eyes was like finding a lighthouse in a storm. As quiet and mysterious as he was being these days over the unspoken worries that hovered over him like volcanic ash, clinging to him like shadows, Josh was still stardust to her, perfect and strong and loving and real. Matt, too, was loved and trusted, but even though he was at Jessie's side now, he was no match for the man who captivated her from the second she knelt before him in Charlie's garbage pile all those years ago.

Josh was light; his eyes now, watching, concerned, were liquid, but despite all, they had a strength that vaulted across the crisp spring air to Jessie and landed in her heart and mind with a silent, unspoken, and deeply cherished love.

They didn't need to speak to each other, they just needed to be in each other's presence. With all the new separations coming up this year, they craved each other's company as often as was physically possible.

Humbled, Matt, who was on the other side of the fence, took a step back and reverently watched the silent communications pass between them. Josh smiled then, just the tiniest little bit and, with Emily-Grace standing humbly between him and Jessie, he bent forward and touched his cool lips to his wife's warm mouth.

"Little one," he said. "Needed some fresh mountain air, did you?"

"Nope," she responded, savoring the closeness, the bubble, of simply being this near to the man she loved. "I needed light."

He hesitated, then touched a cool finger to the back of his daughter's rosy cheek. "You came to the right place," he said. "Us Sawyers are all about light."

When Josh finally looked away from two of the people in the world he loved the most, he met Matt's wise, kind eyes. Matt's eyes were clear; the mountain air was healing for all of them on this invigorating day. Awaiting them inside at lunch would be hot soup, warm muffins and fresh biscuits, as well as laughter and love from a trusted group of family, and from a security team that may as well be family. There would be a new little puppy to gush over and, in the barn, a pony too, and a crisp outdoorsy scent that would cling to their bodies until the fire Josh would start that evening in the big indoor fireplace would replace it with the hearty scent of woodsy smoke.

Beyond them, erected where they could not see it, was a thick, high metal fence. It enclosed the family in its daunting, safe embrace and, for a while, let them have peace.

Chapter Twenty-four

"Congratulations on the two new Oscars, Jessie," Shawna was saying as Jessie took her seat on the popular talk show. "*If I Needed You* broke my heart."

"Thank you," Jessie responded warmly as she adjusted her butt on a soft yellow leather sofa. "It broke mine too."

The loneliness, the ache for Josh and the pain over Matt back when she shot the film assaulted Jessie. She swiped a finger behind her ear, purportedly to move a loose waft of hair, but at the same time she nervously licked her lips.

She'd been sick to her stomach before the show, vomiting in the green room washroom. It was her secret. Her entourage, with the exception of Matt, had been huddled around Kayla's phone to help her choose the best wedding pictures. Matt, Jessie's constant shadow, had raised his eyebrows when Jessie emerged from the bathroom groaning.

Universe, let me get through this live show without needing to puke, Jessie pleaded as she sent an anxious smile over to Shawna.

In Calgary, at the large condo he shared with Charlie for late night and early morning shooting, Josh held his breath and chewed on a knuckle. Charlie was with him, in a nearby wing chair, sipping bourbon with Charles, who sat at the opposite end of the couch Josh was seated on.

Off camera on the soundstage near Jessie and the powerful Shawna Coupland were Matt and Deirdre, with Jacob and Kayla by their sides. Matt winced at Jessie's 'broke mine too' comment.

The elegant Asian host crossed her legs. "Tell me what's happening in your life these days, Jessie. It's been a while since we sat and had the chance to really talk."

Oh, Jesus, can't we just skip all the inconsequential shit and pull out the big guns, Jessie steamed, but she steeled up her nerves, sat taller, and spent the next few minutes discoursing about children and ranch life and *Sacred Peace* and the upcoming festivals where she would be sharing the stage with Jacob.

The mention of Jacob proved a good bridge for the aforementioned big guns.

The sophisticated talk show queen jumped right in. "You still play with Jacob. The two of you record together, you're doing a number of shows this summer. A lot of people are still finding that unconscionable."

Ohhh, here we go…"I'm not excusing what happened," Jessie replied calmly. "But what happened with us is our story, and ours alone. I would not expect anyone else to understand."

"A lot of people think you just swept the assault under the rug. They find it insulting." The indomitable woman's eyes were kind, but the shark in her shone through. "They don't think you're in their corner."

Jessie flinched and tightened a fist into a ball on her lap. "I take some responsibility for what happened between Jacob and me."

"Some victims of assault can't let go. They make excuses so they can justify what happened, and they hang on."

"I'm not making excuses. I simply believe in forgiveness."

"You want him in your life."

"Yes," Jessie agreed. "What Jacob did was wrong, but as I said, our situation is ours alone. I would never try to analyze what happened to another woman, or tell her that she should forgive someone who hurt her. That's her call to make, and hers alone."

"What about your husband? Has he forgiven Jacob?" Shawna leaned forward when she spoke. Her posturing held Jessie almost captive; if not her, at least the lights and cameras did. "Your husband's an angry man."

Jessie bristled. In the condo in Calgary, Josh was listening, drawing blood on his knuckles as Shawna also drew blood, from Jessie.

"No," Jessie whispered, her eyes wide and damp. "My husband…is a sad man."

Her honesty drew a stunned, absolute silence in the assembled studio audience, although a quiet murmur started after a few hollow seconds. In the Calgary condo, all that could be heard was the ticking of the refrigerator although all three men were quite certain each of the others could hear the loud pounding of their hearts.

Josh was immobile. Frozen. *That's what she thinks of me?* He slumped deeper into the sofa and exhaled a low, quiet *pffft*. Nearby, Charles stopped breathing. Charlie forced his eyes away from the television and let his eyes land on his good friend. No one said a word.

Shifting uncomfortably, Jessie drew them back to her. "Look, I understand why people are still upset over what Jacob did. But I want them to know that, for me in my life, I look at things, at why they happen, and I seek out ways to forgive. I've lived my whole life that way. It works for me. If I carried grudges, I'd be living alone. If Josh carried grudges, his sister wouldn't be in his life right now. If Jacob carried grudges, his son wouldn't be in his."

Another small *pfffttt* in Calgary. Charles humphed.

Jessie continued. "Once you can let go of anger, it gets replaced with light. I've learned to reframe my thinking. Gratitude for what Jacob brings to my life is a part of that—we make incredible music together—and I know from the bottom of my heart that he is not a threat to myself or to any other woman."

"What about the man who destroyed your family, Jessie? Have you forgiven him?"

Jesus. We're going there? Dee, you are in such big shit right now. Jessie dug a set of nails into the back of the opposite hand and gulped out, "I'm trying. Some days I think I have. Sometimes it's a little gray."

"I expect sometimes it's very gray."

"Look, we're here to talk about Jacob."

Shawna cut her off. "You're trying to set him free—his reputation. You may as well be on a soapbox with 'Free Jacob' scrawled across the front."

Fidgeting, Jessie was fuming. Everyone in her close circle tensed as they watched her. From the sidelines, Matt whispered, "Easy, girl."

"Jacob did his time. Morgan's doing his. They both have to live with everything they've done—everything they're doing..." A collective gasp emerged from the lips of the Keating team who were aware of Morgan's seemingly current, ongoing campaign to hurt Josh and Jessie. Jessie tossed off the shock she felt energetically oozing toward her from them, and said, "I mean, living their lives now. Their everydays. They're not on the same end of the spectrum as a man who willingly hurts a woman, who beats her violently, who continues to use his strength and power to hurt women." Deuce McCall came to mind. "Or men who use their power to abuse children." Her stepfather infiltrated her thoughts.

Everyone lowered his or her eyes. Deirdre crumbled. This was her idea. Jessie would retreat after this. She'd want no contact with anyone. She'd close herself off and sleep until she could muster the strength to face the world again.

Trying to stay in control, Jessie recrossed her legs and went on with, "I just want to say that, well, the only thing people really need to know about Jacob is that he is a good man. He made a mistake, and he doesn't need to be judged for that for the rest of his life, even though I know he will be. And there's one last thing."

Shawna waited. "Yes?" she finally asked.

Jessie swallowed. "Stop, please stop, putting me on some kind of pedestal as Jacob's victim."

Off stage, Jacob turned in a circle and shoved a fingernail in his mouth. Kayla grabbed his hand while, next to them, Matt crossed his arms and wished to hell he could walk out there on the soundstage and hold Jessie close before she completely gave in to this woman's power and to her own personal demons. Dee was next to him. He could feel her sigh and lean against the wall but he was angry at her for encouraging Jessie—and Jacob—to do the show. He didn't touch her in reassurance, as he normally would.

Jessie was talking in a very low voice now. In Calgary, the men could see a wetness form across her eyes; they sparkled in the soundstage lights like summer's early morning dew glistening on flower petals. "In a lot of ways, Jacob was my victim. I loved him—I—love—him. I always will. We share a child together. He rescued me when I friggin' needed it. I was worried, so I went to Florida to try to help him, but maybe I should have stayed away and let him have his space. Our connection was too strong, and I started Jacob down a path I wasn't willing to finish. Stop being so angry at him, and accept that I'm equally to blame."

"He raped you, Jessie. No means no."

Jessie shrugged, but her eyes caught fire. Combined with the threatening tears, they gave the effect of mirrored disaster. "I'm not excusing him for the violence. I'm just trying to make sense of where it came from. Why it happened in the first place."

"Have you done the same with your old security? With Morgan and his wife?"

"They just wanted a family. They wanted what I had. That's all. Grief does crazy things to people."

"Grief."

"Yes." Jessie tried to relax. Maybe the worst was over. She was sweating now and ready to puke again. She wanted to run, but Jacob was going to be next to her on this small sofa soon, taking the heat too, and they would wrap up this yucky visit with a song. Time seemed to have stopped. The dizzy nausea in her belly was threatening to erupt. Jessie laid a hand over her abdomen and said a silent prayer that she could get through the rest of this awful interview.

"And grief can be a root cause of anger. As proven by Jacob."

Jessie hesitated. *Where is this woman going with this?* "Yes."

"No wonder your husband is an angry man," she said again.

Jessie blinked. *You fucking bitch.* Her final words, before Jacob joined them and went under the firing squad too, were uttered in a sort of dumbfounded confusion. "No. My husband…is a sad man."

In Calgary, Josh forced his troubled spirit up off the couch, padded across the living space to his bedroom, and slammed the door.

※ ※ ※

Later, Deirdre's instincts proved right. When the torture was over, Jessie yanked off her mic, stormed off the soundstage and refused to speak to anyone except Matt, with whom she had a quiet tete-a-tete before she locked herself in her hotel suite and tucked herself under the covers of a lonely, giant king-sized bed. Even Josh and the children didn't get to hear her voice, although Matt called Josh and told him she was fine, that she just needed to sleep it off.

The way a drunk sleeps off a hangover, Josh thought. He let her be, and was almost glad that she didn't call—those comments about his sadness were tough enough to bear without having to acknowledge them via voice anytime soon. By tomorrow, enough time would have passed between when they were spoken aloud and when he and Jessie talked that Josh hoped they could be ignored altogether.

Matt had taken Jessie's elbow before she disappeared behind her door.

"Okay?" he asked.

"As if," she bit off, wound up so tight she looked as if she were about to spontaneously combust.

"Need anything?"

"Yep. Keep the illustrious Deirdre Keating away from me until I calm down. I can't be held responsible for what I might say to her right now."

"She's feeling badly enough."

"Matt?"

"Um hmn?"

"I leave trails of sadness in the men I love. Don't I. Y'all would be a helluva lot better off if you'd all just never met me."

He didn't have a chance to answer. The door was closed quietly in his face.

Matt's silence that evening disturbed Deirdre more than Jessie's absence from the dinner the small group shared in Jacob and Kayla's suite. As for Jacob, whom Dee was really trying to help in the first place with her little escapade to New York City, he was so lost in his new role as husband and father-to-be that all the bad stuff swept off him like rain from a downspout.

There was another man feeling the fallout from Deirdre's effort to settle the lingering aversion around Jacob's violence. In Brody River Penitentiary, Morgan watched the show from the small television he kept on a shelf at the foot of his upper bunk. When Shawna Coupland said her goodbyes, the word forgiveness kept bouncing around his brain. Morgan was so lost in thought that at dinner he accidentally bumped into Caulfield when he was walking from the food line to his usual table. Grabbing his tea to keep it from spilling over when his tray jiggled, he took a step backward.

Caulfield leaned in and forced a pink-pepperminty breath at him. "You see it?" the older guy asked. "Out of sight, out of mind. That's what she thinks."

Did we watch the same show? Morgan asked himself silently as he tried to move past Caulfield. The correctional officer wasn't budging. He was standing in front of Morgan with his feet apart and a hand tapping his baton.

"I've got our next move figured out," Caulfield stated as matter-of-factly as if he was planning a night out at the movies. "We'll talk at the gym."

"I need to eat," Morgan muttered, unable to meet the demanding eyes of the man who, he thought, had entirely too much stake in his life—in a life Morgan just wanted to let slide past him the way water runs over the cool, polished stones of a river. "S'yoga night."

Caulfield nudged over just enough to let Morgan by. "Tomorrow then," he said, his voice thick with annoyance at the glib way Morgan was brushing him off. Morgan moved by him, but Caulfield's eyes bore a hole deep into his back as he walked.

Exhaling in relief, but quickly replacing that with alarm as he wondered what Caulfield had planned for the Sawyers, Morgan dropped his tray on a table and started to spoon great mouthfuls of rice into his body. A voice beside him caught him unaware.

"You remember your old buddy Arnie?" The voice was low, and deep. It was gruff, but not unkind. Instead, it was rather efficient and businesslike.

Morgan looked sideways. Vaughn. A muscled black man, he had an intelligence in his eyes that, Morgan knew, was responsible for elevating his position in Brody Pen as a respected inmate liaison to the warden. The guy was as powerful as Caulfield, only, Morgan thought, in a more genial way. He was in jail for cutting up women—killing at least two that Morgan knew of, although it was only talked about in hushed whispers around the perimeter of the yard, and only then when Vaughn did something on behalf of the prison population that warranted an equal—and less sinister—respect.

"What about Arnie?" Morgan, curious, kept spooning food into his mouth although his heart rate quickened. Any outside news—contact— was welcome. Especially from the Keating camp. Vaughn's presence at his side was not an accident.

"He wants to know what the hell, Morgan."

Ahhh. Of course. Josh and Matt…the post wrap party threats…

Caulfield had settled against a nearby wall. Morgan could see him standing there tapping his baton against a thigh now, watching and wondering. Caulfield was well aware that Vaughn considered himself on a higher prison plane than Morgan, despite the fact that Morgan was a celebrity inmate under Caulfield's protection.

Some dull place in Morgan's brain started to thump quietly, like a tribal drum. He wanted to communicate with Vaughn, because in his heart Morgan felt the big guy could be trusted. At least Arnie could be trusted, and there was—astoundingly—a connection between them. But Caulfield…the guy's eyes were fucking creepy. Even at this distance, his power was indisputably clear.

Vaughn seemed unaware of Caulfield, or of how Morgan was discreetly eyeballing his misguided guardian angel.

"I dunno," Morgan said, staring at his food, which now tasted dry and stale. He shoved the tray away and wiped sweaty palms on his jeans. "I dunno what the hell."

"Arnie has a lotta fuckin' power, Morgan." Vaughn was eating so calmly— he never had to be afraid. His actions and his words carried a lot of weight in the prison.

"Tell him I said hello." Mumbling, Morgan wanted to stand, but his knees were trembling so hard he didn't trust his legs to hold his weight. In his mind, Vaughn was the guy with a lot of power. Enough power to get a guy knifed in the yard, in fact. Arnie was too damn far away to warrant concern. Morgan's life was here, within the perimeter of one of the most dangerous prisons on North American soil.

"Lay off the Sawyers."

There it was. The warning Morgan knew was coming. He wanted to yell *you're talking to the wrong man,* but the man who needed the talking to was also capable of getting a guy knifed. But then…death wouldn't be so unwelcome now, would it? Morgan could think of worse things. This hopeless, caged-in existence was a worse thing.

The world started to spin.

Vaughn confidently finished his meal. He saw the white-assed lily livered guy next to him start to tremble. Rising, Vaughn grabbed the chocolate pudding—tonight's dessert—from Morgan's tray. He ate it while he sauntered away. As far as he was concerned, the message from Arnie was delivered. He put it out of his mind and chose to remember, instead, a delicious evening with a very young and quiet Jessie Wheeler back on the Downtown Eastside, the night Arnie—who James Vaughn would have been an ass not to respect—rescued her from his cutting games.

Morgan looked up and met Caulfield's stony eyes. Caulfield grinned and sidled aimlessly away.

Chapter Twenty-five

One thing about the new closeness with Emily-Grace was Josh's inability to let her out of his sight. It was as if the dried-up earth was now fresh and fertile again; she was at his side as much as Dylan these days, at least when he was home. They didn't talk much, but they didn't need to. Josh helped care for the puppy, and taught Emily-Grace things about puppies that made Jessie feel completely inadequate as a pet owner. Josh's childhood was filled with animals—horses, dogs, cats, you name it. His family even had goats on their ranch back in the day. Jessie's childhood experience with animals was relegated to the mice population in the potato field behind her family's small Bedeque, Prince Edward Island house, and to the occasional stray cat that wandered up to the Wheeler doorway seeking a handout.

Josh and Emily-Grace became inseparable. The move to the ranch was now a few weeks old. Josh and Jessie had promised the kids some time to get used to the change before they would start school in nearby Canmore. School was a necessary thing—the kids needed some continuity and socialization with other children. Dylan, even, would attend pre-school. He needed the stimulation even more than his older siblings, since he was the most rambunctious of the lot.

On the day they planned to start their children back at school, Josh and Jessie traveled with them in the Lexus. Dylan's preschool was in the same building where David and Emily-Grace were going to school. Security was in place. All systems were a go.

Until Josh opened Emily-Grace's car door, looked into her sad blue eyes, and caved. He closed the door and walked back around the SUV to the driver's seat.

"Get back in, Jessie," he demanded, unable to look over at Matt and Dan, behind them.

Jessie froze. She was standing outside the vehicle, staring wide-eyed at her husband as he moved around the car. Shifting her weight, she threw up her arms in confusion at Matt, who strode quickly over.

"What's up?" Matt asked.

"Ask him," Jessie said, pointing at Josh.

The old sick fear crept up Matt's legs and left him weak. Glancing over at Dan, who was waiting for the children to leave the car, he scanned the school grounds. Everyone was watching the famous family, it seemed. Sam and Alin were both close by, stationed at the doors of the school where the kids would enter the low building. Video cameras were in place, inside the school and out; local police were on alert that the Sawyer kids would complete their studies in Canmore for the last few months of the year. Yet, because of the continuous threat surrounding the family, the place felt completely insecure.

Matt half jogged around to Josh, who was pacing in a small circle by the driver's door. "You don't have to say a word," Matt said in a hushed tone, as he placed both hands on his hips so that his blue blazer flared open.

Josh spied the holster Matt occasionally wore, nestled into a strap crossing the man's chest.

So. Matt knew exactly what worries were running through Josh's mind, and he was thinking the same damn thing.

"Just get back in the car," Matt ordered. "I'll help you deal with Jessie."

"I'll bet you will," Josh muttered, but he didn't say it with a mean edge. Secretly he was relieved, as he had been many times in the past when Matt's simple understanding made things go easier for the family.

Laying a calming hand on Josh's bicep, which Jessie took note of with a stuttered inward *wh-what the hell*, Matt gave Josh a businesslike nod before he swung around on one heel and signaled to a bewildered Jessie to get back in the car. At the same time, he covered the distance to Dan in a few quick steps, and issued orders.

The Sawyer kids would not be going to public school.

The whole thing would have erupted the second the kids got gleefully home except for the fact that Jessie was too pissed at Josh's continued unilateral parenting to risk speaking to him. She was shaking by the time he pulled the big silver Lexus back up the lane and swung it to a quick stop outside the barn in its usual place. Wisely, he avoided meeting her eyes until Matt and Dan safely retrieved the kids from the vehicle. Sam and Alin weren't far behind. The younger folks met the children in the clearing, ran them inside to change them into play clothes, and took them into the barn to saddle up the pony. By then Jessie was losing it, but she knew her husband well enough to discern that something she didn't fully understand was at play in his mind and heart. He was dropping clues like breadcrumbs.

After sliding out of the driver's seat, Josh edged his way over to the split rail fence. He leaned against the top rail, jutted both elbows out to the sides, and rested his chin on his hands. In the corral were his two horses, Toby and Misty, who, oblivious to the new drama unfolding at the ranch, were calmly munching on new spring grass. Matt had settled quietly between Josh and the car, nearer the corral's gate, his back to it so he could watch Jessie and Josh at the same time, and respond to whatever cues they sent him.

It was a warm late March day, hot enough to discard jackets, the kind of day filled with the promise of summer and all its newness, so Matt ripped off his blazer and hung it on a corral post while he waited, wordless, as Jessie paced, ran long fingers through her hair, and averted her eyes from his gun.

Once the kids were in the barn with Sam and Alin, she pounced, but not on her husband. Moving quickly toward Matt, she gave him a shove and said, in a tense voice that wavered with a lack of control, "I need a run. I need a fucking run. Now, goddammit!"

Nearby, Josh switched from one foot to another on the bottom rung, turned his head away from his upset wife, and picked at a splinter in the top fence rail.

Matt didn't hesitate. "Meet you out here in five," he said brusquely and headed toward the house, to a room near the back, on the kids' side, that was used regularly by whichever of the security team needed it.

"I don't want company!" Jessie hollered after him, near tears with frustration.

Matt didn't stop. "Suck it up, princess. You're getting it." The words were tossed over his left shoulder just before he opened the screen door and let it slam shut behind his retreating body. Inside, he waited. He wouldn't put it past her to take off running in her jeans, in which case he'd go after her.

Jessie whipped around to Josh. Picking away at the rail, ripping little pieces of wood off of it and letting them drift toward the ground, he was still avoiding looking at her.

"Fuck, you frustrate me!" she cried. "Goddammit, Josh! They're going to school tomorrow. They need to be around other kids so they can have some chance at normal lives!"

At that Josh finally turned, slowly, his mind racing as he tried to figure out what he could say to his wife that wouldn't scare the shit out of her but that would have enough power to calm her down. In the end it wasn't his words that scared her so much as the defiant acceptance in his eyes, an acceptance that translated to *it doesn't matter what you think or how angry you are. This is the way it's going to be.* The unspoken assertion was solid proof that he was harboring some great secret.

But so was Jessie.

Josh went with the simplest thing possible. "Normal lives? Really, Jessie?"

She was red faced and gasping. "It's what I want. It's what I've always wanted! It's what I want for them!"

"We're way beyond normal. You know that. We're so fucking far beyond normal that we could be paraded next to the tigers in a three ring circus. With elephants on the other side."

"You know what your problem is, Sawyer? From day one, I'll tell you what your problem has been. You give up way too easy! That's your fucking problem!"

"Do I."

He was still way too calm. That disturbed Jessie even more. Rallying, she decided to throw in a test about her own secret, one she'd been concealing since Oscar week, when a familiar nausea started in her belly. "Like with having another kid," she growled. "I'm not getting any younger here. You did an about face on that one without talking to me, too. You won't discuss it anymore. You're running scared."

Straightening, Josh assessed his wife. This conversation wasn't going to end pretty, no matter what he said. "This is not a good time for us to have a baby, Jessie. You don't need to be sick all summer, for one. Dee's got you running all over creation."

"We said we'd have more after Dylan. More of," she gulped, and pushed Jacob to the back of her brain where he belonged, "our own. You and me."

"Jesus Christ, Jessie," Josh retorted angrily. In his mind, Dylan was his son. Not Jacob's. "Get a grip. Go for your fucking run and exorcise some demons before you come back, okay?" With that heartless remark, which was spouted partly to deflect the tension back at his unhappy wife, Josh stormed off toward the barn.

Matt pushed open the screen door. "You planning to run in jeans and boots, kid?"

With a mighty *roar* that had the youngsters inside the barn pause in wonder, Jessie skidded past him to her bedroom, whipped open a drawer, and retrieved her favorite Lululemons. She was stretching against the kitchen island three minutes later when Matt appeared in gray running shorts and a chest hugging green T-shirt. Appraising him, letting the fuming sparks in her eyes settle on the well-developed muscles in his thighs, and on the oh-so-touchable forearms she rarely saw since Matt so often wore long-sleeved shirts, Jessie fought the urge to fire off a teasing compliment. Those days were gone. Grabbing the earbuds that went with the iPod strapped to her bicep, and taking a final drink of water from a glass resting on the countertop, she pushed the earbuds into her ears and headed out the door.

"Try and keep up, loser," she challenged, and took off.

Matt ran without music. He'd gotten used to it in Prince Edward Island, after Catherine asked him not to. Now, he eased into a fast pace and let the forest sounds entertain him. Ahead of him, Jessie preferred not to think at all, but even the elevated volume of her running playlist did nothing to quiet the tumultuous voices in her head and calm her down. There was a new gate over the ATV trail they were running on; it, like the rest of the fence, was metal. Ugly and foreboding, it served only to enrage Jessie further. She stopped at the gate, gave it an angry kick, spun around to Matt, and cursed again.

Reaching past her, he undid the interior latch and pushed it open.

They ran as far as the creek bed before Jessie finally slowed and recklessly yanked the earbuds out. Wheeling around to him, she put her hands on her hips and stared him down.

"I'm pregnant," she spat. "Once again, Matt Kelly is the first to know. Aren't you the luckiest sunuvabitch on the planet."

"I wondered," he admitted. Licking his lips, he walked to the creek's edge and stared out over the soothing, trickling water.

Deflating, Jessie stepped over stones and stood by his side. "I don't know whether to say 'how'd you figure it out,' or 'stop spying on me.'"

"Your body," he said without looking at her. Across the creek, a pair of yellow eyes peeked out from the brush. Matt laid a hand on the mace he'd tucked into the back pocket of his shorts. It was there if he needed it. "You're filling out."

"My boobs, you mean," she said with a wry grimace. "Good of you to notice, casanova."

Silent for a while, they let their breathing start to slow to a more normal pace after the vigorous jog. They were avid watchers and listeners of the glittering creek water, which Jessie usually found uplifting but which today just added to her angst, since it seemed to be unstoppable, running quickly to some far off place beyond her control. Swiping a hand over her face, she focused on trying to relax after the slightly uphill run, and then took Matt's hand in hers.

In a deliberate, nervous motion, he pivoted around to face her. The crestfallen look on his face landed somewhere between longing and sorrow.

"Matt, someone's got to be happy about this baby," Jessie tried. "This poor kid hasn't got a chance if someone besides me doesn't welcome it."

"Josh will be fine when you tell him, Jessie," Matt said. "He's a great dad. He's just got things on his mind, that's all. The night we got jumped…he got a scare, kid."

"I know that, but…" Knitting her eyebrows together, Jessie tilted her head and searched out Matt's gentle eyes. "There's something he's not telling me. Is there something you're not telling me? All Josh said is that it's bad, Matt. That's all. It's gotta be bad if…today…the school…"

Matt's unhappy gaze wandered back over across the creek. The watchful, curious yellow eyes were gone. All that remained in their place was a mysterious darkness.

"Hey. You." Jessie took his elbow and turned him back toward her. This time Matt's eyes were as misty and wet as the river.

"It's a lot, that's all," he said. His voice was thick—dark and dreary, like motor oil in winter. "Another child…a new baby…"

"Jesus, Matt." Dropping his arm, Jessie backed away. "Why do I suddenly feel like running away again? I'm so tired of all this worry, this…constant worry, and the inability to live my life the way I fucking well please!"

"That's not all, Jessie." The quiet in his voice gave Jessie reason to pause. Freezing, she wondered what else he needed to say to her. It hit her hard when she clued in, because suddenly the man in front of her was the same man she'd made love to when Josh was so distant last year. For all intents and purposes, Matt had given up his life for her—his marriage, his home, his pride, even. And what did she give him in return? Heartache. Fucking heartache.

"Oh, Matt. Really?" Raising a thumb and finger to her mouth, Jessie pinched her lips together and fretted over what to say. She spoke quietly, reverently. "You and me," she said, letting her hand fall back to her side, "that's what's bugging you. We talked about what we would have called a baby if our little fantasy dream night and day had led to more. If…if Josh and I didn't reconcile. Remember?"

"I remember." The hurt in Matt's eyes verified the memory. It gave it a credence that Jessie wished to hell did not, now that all was said and done, exist. He didn't look away.

Moving to him was not an option. Like the teasing she wanted to lay on him earlier, there were new boundaries that had to be respected. Climbing onto Matt's lap in Charles' office that day had been too much—the kiss they shared that day was unacceptable. Brushing her lips against his in the barn the night she and Josh arrived back at the ranch…it only served to keep him hooked when, really, Jessie needed to let the man go.

"I suck," Jessie whispered. "I hurt people."

"Do you remember what we said? What we agreed would be a good name for a baby?"

She hesitated. "Micah."

"We didn't name a girl. We got sidetracked."

"Yeah. We did, didn't we."

He shuffled his feet on the stones beneath him. "I'm happy for you. Really." The stones clinked their approval as he moved.

Jessie didn't answer. The smile she'd awoken with that morning had turned permanently upside down the second she saw Josh walk back around the Lexus at the school in Canmore. Her lips were trembling.

Matt considered the boundaries he knew they needed to establish, but the way Jessie was looking at him now, like she was desperate to hold him but afraid to make the first move for fear of where it would land them, erased the wall between them the way he wished he could erase the ugly metal fence— and the fear it represented—surrounding the ranch. He crossed the few feet between them, and pulled her into his arms.

The move elicited a relieved moan from Jessie, who wrapped her sweaty arms around his shoulders. "I'm sorry you always end up getting hurt, Matt. I don't even know why you came back to us. You could be with Catherine now, that nice woman you met in P.E.I. You could be having babies with her."

Nuzzling his lips into her hair, pressing his mouth to her neck, to her bare shoulder, Matt's voice came out muffled so that Jessie had to ask him to repeat what he said. Lifting his face from that coveted hollow he loved to kiss during their one magical weekend, he paused, gave her just one sweet, tiny kiss on those favorite pink lips, and murmured, "You know why I came back. I came back to watch over you. Over you and your family."

"You've already given up so much for us, baby. You need a life of your own."

"I have a life."

"Sleeping with the producer on Josh's movie doesn't count unless it goes somewhere."

"It went somewhere. It had a beginning, a middle, and an end. It was plenty."

A light chuckle escaped from between Jessie's lips. Sighing, she leaned a cheek on his shoulder and said, "Just so you know, if you meet someone and need to go, I understand. I want that for you." Raising her head, she took his close shaven cheeks in her hands and added resolutely, "I want you to be happy, Matt."

"You'll be the first to know," he said, a tiny twinkle coming back into the light hazel-gray eyes Jessie adored. "I'll bring her to the ranch and make sweet love to her all night. You'll hear us."

"Too much information," Jessie laughed. "That room's on the kids' side. It's the kids that'll hear you. Charles'll fire your stupid ass."

Arm in arm, they started walking back toward the trail. A thought struck Jessie. "Do you think Sam and Alin have been making love in that room?"

"Nope. They know better."

"Phew. That would just be weird."

"They sneak out to the barn."

"What? The barn?" Stopping, Jessie stared at Matt. Turning to her, he laughed. She clued in. "Matt, you nerd. You had me going there for a second." Her footsteps were light on the trail. Jessie pushed one earbud back in and smiled at her good friend. For a moment, she held his gaze, and his fingers, too. Lifting the strong hand to her lips, she kissed the backs of his fingers as tenderly as she could muster on this difficult day. "I'll love you forever, sweet Matt," she said, and winked. "Even if you beat me back to the house."

He couldn't answer. Protecting her was hard enough. Loving her from a distance was deadly.

"Micah," Jessie whispered. Her eyes lit up. "I like the sound of that. It's Biblical, right? Do you know what it means?"

"It's a Hebrew name that means 'who is like God.' Or, 'gift from God.' My brother Michael pretty much has the same name. Michael is Micah in English terms. Micah is an old family name."

"I like the God part. And that it's an old Kelly family name."

"You feeling okay?" Matt cornered. It hurt too much to stand here with Jessie and dream—pretend—that the name they once talked about for a baby was still in play. "Do you have the secret weapon? Those crackers?"

"I've got a stash. Thanks for asking."

"Don't keep this one to yourself for too long, Jessie. This isn't the kind of secret I like to harbor."

"Nope." She sighed. "You prefer the kind of secret my husband's keeping."

A nearby rustle alerted Matt to the fact that they had lingered long enough at the creek. "Let's go," he said, and purposefully gave her a gentle push.

"It doesn't matter to me anyway, Matt," Jessie admitted as she replaced the second earbud and started her tunes up for the downhill run. "Cause the thing is? Whatever the hell he's hiding—that you and he are hiding—it's dark. And I don't wanna know what it is, Matt, I just don't wanna know. This baby—it's light. It's the light in all of this darkness that seems to stick to us like glue. And I gotta tell you. It's the light in me that keeps me going on days like these when all hell breaks loose in the Sawyer household once again."

Matt smiled, warmly this time, the old sadness replaced with the certainty, the knowledge, that he would be a part of this new child's life. Not the father, no, not the man Jessie loved and wanted by her side for eternity, as Josh was, but Matt was, and always would be, Jessie's close confidante and very, very best friend.

Her protector. Her angel.

In one swift movement, Jessie leaned forward and brushed her lips against his. He laughed when her words vibrated against his mouth.

"Race your stupid ass back!" She took off running.

Licking his lips, Matt tasted sweat. Her sweat. Her warmth. His eyes brightened, and he shook his head in wonder at Jessie's ability to raise his spirits just by virtue of being, well—her.

A new little Sawyer, he thought as he started down the trail after her. A new worry started to form in his heart, compounding into a large, round ball in his gut by the time he followed a happy, jubilant Jessie back into the clearing by the ranch. She was raising her arms, and calling, "I win," hopping up and down as, nearby, the children cheered her on with cries of, "Momma won! Momma won!"

Behind Jessie, Josh had Toby's lead clipped onto a hook on the corral fence so he could groom the large animal. Next to him, balanced on a low stool, dwarfed in the jacket Matt had left on the post earlier, Dylan was running a large brush through the horse's mane. Josh stood still when Jessie and Matt returned from their run. Watching them tease each other, he settled back on one heel and wondered what had changed during the run that made his wife so happy all of a sudden. She was the complete counterpoint of the woman who left the safety and security of the ranch less than an hour earlier.

As if she could read his mind, Jessie turned and faced him. Twenty feet away, she raised her arms and started backing toward the door to the house.

"All gone, Sawyer," she said. "Those demons you asked me to exorcise. Only I think it was 'fucking exorcise,' you said. All it took was a long, sweet run with Matt here." She licked her lips for emphasis. "Long…and sweet," she repeated, holding his gaze.

Matt was behind her. The wind was instantly knocked out of his sails. He stood still, afraid to look at Josh. Jessie was between them, moving with care toward the house, and Matt could easily picture the look on her face, the heartless expression she chose for Josh, the father of this new baby Jessie was so protective of. Translated into words, the look—her most haughty— would simply say *fuck you and the horse that brung you.* Or, Matt supposed rightly, it would say *Matt and I know something you don't. Something you don't deserve to know.*

Josh, dumbstruck by her ability to hurt him, couldn't help but wonder if Jessie had gotten up to something with Matt again. Hell, she'd just come back from doing the Shawna Coupland show with Matt by her side. They could get up to 'something' any damn time they wanted to, really.

Glancing behind Jessie at Matt, Josh was sorry to see that his wife's little game was hurting Matt too; Matt who, just a few short moments before, was as jubilant and happy as she was, but who now was just another pawn in one of Jessie's hurtful little games.

Jessie seemed to realize what she'd done. Josh swallowed bitterly and turned his attention back to Dylan. Jessie wheeled warily around to Matt, who was standing close by, ashen and sorry; defeated because even after all these years, Jessie still had the ability to shock him, and remorseful for the way she so often hurt the people she loved by firing nasty slings and arrows.

Jessie brought her hands together in front of her stomach and fidgeted, the long guitar-callused fingers so beloved by the world now just a mess of anxiety and confusion. *With a healthy toss of self-loathing tossed in,* Matt considered as he watched her. Jessie's eyes were wide and sorrowful. "I'm sorry, Matt," she whispered. "That was low."

Instead of answering in words, Matt sent her a message he hoped she read loud and clear. It was delivered by virtue of hurt, cross eyes, mixed with an equal measure of indignance and recovered pride.

Shame on you, it said, and it was received loud and clear.

Matt strode over to the barn and did post-run calf stretches by leaning his arms, outstretched, over his head on the rough, new cedar shakes. Jessie didn't join him. She hurried up to the house, let the screen door slam with a *crack* behind her, stripped off in the shower, hugged her barely swelling belly, and sobbed into the heat and steam.

The subject of sending the kids to school was not brought up again. The next morning when Josh trundled out to the kitchen for a late breakfast and a morning coffee—his set call was for noon—Jessie was on the phone to Alin's brother. Patin was a teacher who was patching money together with substitute teaching jobs while he tried to get hired by the board full time.

He said yes to tutoring the children of the celebrities Alin raved about, and was hired on the spot.

Chapter Twenty-six

A few weeks later, a peaceful silence wafted its way through the cozy rancher. Carried on the wings of the kind of calm only to be found during the inky solitude of the midnight hour when laughing, rambunctious children were nestled in sleep, and tired parents were snuggled up together, it was so perfect it was almost touchable. Living at the ranch was like staking a claim on another planet. It was an insular, protected sphere that boded no real danger, apart from scratched knees and bruised elbows. Rarely did Josh or Jessie leave their perfect bubble. Work was the only thing that called either forth. The satisfying exhaustion of a hard day's acting or of an adrenaline-fueled music set was always found to be missing some essential element, because it was time away from the ranch with the children and the assorted friends, family, security, and the new tutor who came and went with the casual air such easy companionships warranted. Even the sinister undercurrent of dread stayed away, the way oil separates from water, as if once the main gate parted and closed, sanctuary was assured for those on the inside.

But then one day the entire Sawyer family left their seasonal paradise to take a day trip outside of their perfect bubble. The large gate clanged shut behind them, and the offended, seemingly-sanctified milieu the family was living in reared up its resentment at their leaving with ruthless, reckless abandon, conquering the Sawyers and their close circle of trusted loved ones with catastrophic timing and callous detachment.

It was a Sunday, a day meant to be tranquil and relaxing, a day meant for slowing down, for spending lazy time around the ranch as a family. The pool was in; already in the unseasonably warm spring its heated water had been joyfully christened with shivering brave, small bodies who left colorful towels on the deck for Jessie to throw in the wash. An expectant serenity was suspended above the pool. Its mirrored surface practically begged to be broken with the splashes of arms and hands. Its water was refreshing, a welcome refuge for children whose main entertainments were each other. The kids were counting the days until hotter summer weather would make the pool a daily staple in their young lives.

Jessie was expected back in Vancouver on Monday morning. She planned to fly out at dawn with Matt and Charles by her side. The children would stay at the ranch with Deirdre and Carlotta so Josh could work during the day and so the kids could have some continuity and discipline in their schoolwork. Jacob and Kayla were to meet Jessie at the Keating building on Robson. Sometimes, by the pool at the ranch, or by a sputtering fire in the large hearth indoors after dark, Jessie worked out new tunes—tunes she and Jacob finetuned over Skype, or in person if he happened to be around. Now it was time to gather a team and record the songs—they would be the featured musical backdrop for *Sacred Peace's* second season. The song promised to Vaughn was not one of these.

Loathe to go, to leave Josh and the children in this magical, enchanted haven without her, Jessie had a tough time drifting off to sleep on Saturday night. The Sundays she was at the ranch were treasured gifts. They were too few and far between, and the way Deirdre had scheduled the summer they were going to be rare.

It was late April now. Jessie'd missed Josh's and Charles' birthdays early in the month. As a result, a well-meaning social coordinator on the *Sacred Peace* crew had decided there ought to be a get together to celebrate all of the spring birthdays. This gathering, in nearby Bragg Creek, would be a chance for everyone to bond, to put aside the stress of molding light and cutting shadows and tweaking camera angles and, for the actors, of knowing lines and having to be 'on' every time the unforgiving camera rolled.

The kids would love it. Jessie, not so much. She wasn't averse to the children socializing with the offspring of the crew and other cast. The production had even rented a small roller coaster as well as inflated bouncy castles to jump in and slide on, but it would be the kind of exhausting day that meant the wrong kinds of foods, and keeping an eye on her busy three while they all went in different directions, and really, truly, Jessie just wanted her family to herself for one final day before she had to leave for two weeks.

Josh, she could tell, was edgy about her Vancouver trip too. He was jittery at dinner on Saturday evening, and stuck close to Jessie and the kids all day instead of doing repairs around the ranch like he usually did. When he and Jessie finally tucked in for the night, he pressed his body against hers and sighed deeply. Her recourse was to wrinkle her eyebrows in curiosity before switching off the bedside lamp and taking his mind off his worries by focusing it on his pleasure.

After making love, Jessie curled up in the welcome, safe curve of Josh's body as he spooned her. Lying awake in the stillness until well past midnight, she reveled in the quiet exhales of his warm breath and the even rise and fall of his chest. His muscled arm around her relaxed when he finally drifted off to sleep, and she prayed his dreams were all light and peace. It wasn't until well after midnight that Jessie, too, floated off, but her dreams were short-lived. Some time just after three, small feet tiptoed anxiously into their bedroom.

Jessie was about to raise her head from her pillow when her oldest child's hand found Josh's strong paw in the dusky moonlight, and gently rubbed it.

"Daddy, Daddy," Emily-Grace whispered. "Precious had her kittens. Wake up, Daddy."

Stilling her body, Jessie didn't say a word nor did she let on that she was awake. Emily-Grace was doing so well with Josh these days and he, in turn, was focused on connecting with her, on doing things with her. He was engaged and interested in her, like he was those first sacred years after her birth, before their shared world was so violently spun off its axis.

A low grunt and a light rustle announced that Josh was stirring.

Emily-Grace's voice was more hopeful when she spoke again. She leaned in so close to Jessie that her curls waterfalled over Jessie's forehead, but the little girl wanted—and needed—her daddy. Josh was the go-to guy when it came to the animals in their midst. He would know what to do about these new little creatures that Emily-Grace had worried and fretted over since hearing that her favorite barn cat was going to become a mother for the first time. "Daddy, are you awake? Precious had her babies, Daddy. Alin told me. I don't know what to do."

Standing back, Emily-Grace started wringing her fingers. Jessie dared opening one tired eye. She could see her exuberant, worried daughter clearly in the whitish-blue moonlight, wound tight as a spring and near tears with exhilaration and concern. Jessie felt Josh move behind her. He lifted himself up on one elbow.

"Kittens?" he echoed, his voice husky with sleep.

"Yep. Alin said."

"Okay."

Jessie had to discreetly bury her nose in her pillow when Josh spoke. She could hear the easy acceptance in his voice. *You woulda made a good farmer,* she thought. *Always ready to heed the call when it comes to your beloved animals.*

Josh started to ease his body off the bed behind Jessie, on the wall side. "Let's be quiet so we don't wake Momma," he said.

Jessie saw Emily-Grace nod. She watched the little girl's eyes follow her daddy as Josh moved to a corner chair to grab the faded jeans and light blue three-button Henley he tossed there when he came to bed last night. The small eyes watched as Josh ambled around the foot of the bed, zipping up the jeans and fastening the faded wide brown leather belt that was still looped around them.

He reached for his daughter's fingers. "Shhhh," he whispered, his voice playful and happy now, although still dusky and a little raw. "We're hunting wabbits. Let's tiptoe so we don't wake Momma."

"Wabbits? Silly Daddy. Precious is a cat," Emily-Grace scolded. She was skipping alongside her father. Tiptoeing was no longer necessary.

"It's from an old cartoon I used to watch when I was a kid," Josh explained as, her nose to the pillow, Jessie giggled.

She heard him greet Alin just outside the door; rather, Alin stopped him in his tracks. It was Alin's night to patrol the property. Evidently it was she who discovered the new little kitty family.

"I'm so sorry, Josh," the young woman was saying. "Emily-Grace got up to pee and came looking for me in the yard. She's been coming outside every night, wondering about that cat. I told her about the kittens, but I didn't think she'd wake you."

"It's okay, Alin," Josh said. To his daughter he added, "You've been going outside every night?"

Inside the bedroom, Jessie frowned. Alin had told her about Emily-Grace's nightly wanderings in search of Precious, but Jessie didn't want to worry Josh. She'd shared that tidbit of info with Matt, instead, and was assured by him that Alin knew Emily-Grace's pattern—she usually woke sometime around the three a.m. hour—and that Alin always watched for the little girl and got her settled back in her bed each night without any lingering issues.

"I just always wanted to check on Precious, Daddy. I never knew if she could have those babies all by herself."

The voices faded then, and Jessie heard the screen door squeak its way open and closed. Rolling over onto her back, she gazed up at the ceiling and wondered what to do.

In the end, she pulled on some pajama pants and a tank top, grabbed a fuzzy cardigan, stuck her feet in boots, and tiptoed out of the house to spy on Josh and his often sullen and rebellious daughter.

A golden light was spilling out of the barn's wide doorway. The sliding door had been pulled open. As if carried on the magical dust motes floating gleefully in the beam of light, soothing voices drifted into the mystical, starlit clearing. Stopping to listen, Jessie dipped her head and absently toed the dry earth with a boot. Her heart filled with gladness.

The rustling of straw accompanied the voices. "We'll give Precious some time to feed and nurture her babies, and then tomorrow before we go to the party you and me will get her settled into a nice soft box. How about that, Emily-Grace?"

"What about now, Daddy? Why can't we get a box now?"

Jessie could picture her daughter standing by Josh, or bending over the treasured pet, maybe, her bony knees protruding through the thin fabric of her pink nightgown. Jessie hoped Josh had grabbed a jacket for himself and for their little girl on the way out. Likely Emily-Grace'd be wearing her barn boots. She practically lived in the dirty old things, and she'd be doing that thing she always did when her hair was loose and not tied up—pushing back the wispy wild ends, swiping at them again and again because they never stayed behind her ear the way she wanted them to.

Like father, like daughter. Jessie smiled and eased closer to the barn. Leaning a hand on the edge of the sliding door, she stayed behind it, but she peeked around the corner so she could clearly see Josh, Alin and Emily-Grace.

Josh's back was to her. Although he had grabbed a coat from a wooden peg by the ranch house door for his daughter, he hadn't bothered to put on a jacket himself, and the sight of his broad, muscled shoulders in the Henley left her breathless as he stooped over the nervous orange cat and her new little brood. Alin, in black clothing, her hair pulled into a tight bun on her head, was standing a little apart from them, unable to hide her admiration for this man and his patience and kindness toward both her and his young daughter in this, the darkest, most mysterious part of the night. She, like Jessie, seemed rather awed by this moment, which in many ways had a spiritual glow—a Christmas Eve enchantment—about it.

Josh's strong arm was cradled around his daughter. "We'll get a box out of the recycling tomorrow. I'll bet you have an old baby blanket from one of your dolls you can donate to Precious, huh Emily-Grace?"

"I do, Daddy. I have a yellow one."

They were both staring at the cat and her little family. Jessie could see Precious staring proudly back.

"Do we take them to the vet like we did with Snow?"

"Yep, you bet," Josh answered, shifting his weight from one foot to the other.

Covering her mouth so she wouldn't laugh, or cry, Jessie winced as her husband's knees cracked. His sore leg was always troublesome too, from the steel rod inside that was holding it together. He was rubbing his leg lightly, and he made a little grunting sound when he moved it.

"As soon as they're a little bigger, you and I can take them," Josh told his child as Jessie, unseen, spied on them. She could see the deep love in his eyes when he turned his head to gently talk to Emily-Grace. His layered hair fell over one ear. Underneath that, one cheek was all holy shadows and crags, carved by the mystical light of a single bulb. The effect from Jessie's point of view was gut wrenching. The tenderness in Josh's eyes as he shared this beautiful moment with his often reticent daughter was spellbinding, humbling, and absolutely, perfectly, divine.

"Thank you, God," prayed Jessie as her eyes moistened. "Thank you so much for this."

A quiet crunch came across the light gravel behind her. Flipping casually around, Jessie watched Matt approach. In playful warning, she put a finger to her lips. He stopped just behind her, and gently floated an arm around her waist.

"Heard the screen door," he murmured by way of explanation.

"You don't sleep well, do you Matt?" Jessie shot him a worried half-smile. "You're always on the alert."

Coloring just a little, he mumbled, "S'my job," and followed it with a more earnest, "the kittens come?"

Nodding, Jessie blinked back damp teardrops of joy and laid a cheek against the rough new wood of the barn's sliding door. Inside, Josh was helping Emily-Grace count the new babies.

"Six," the little girl said, and then, with an ecstatic dance-hop, she pointed at a spot near Precious' front legs. "Is that a whole 'nuther one, Daddy? Kind of under that one?"

"Ah," Josh answered wisely. "I think there might be seven. It's a little hard to tell, isn't it, honey?"

"How come their eyes are closed, Daddy?"

"It takes a few days for their eyes to open, sweetheart. They'll open up, you'll see."

Taking a few steps backward, Jessie turned and reached for Matt's hand to pull him toward her. "She'll be too excited to sleep. Let's put some chamomile tea on for us grownups, and some warm chocolate milk on for her. Josh is gonna be frozen."

They dug into their middle-of-the-night snack with everyone hunkered around the kitchen island lost in his or her own separate but unified knowing that the night was, on every level, going to go down in the collective Sawyer family memory bank as sacred and rare. Emily-Grace snuggled into her father's lap and fell asleep there, curled up in a ball with a sweet, happy smile lighting up her cherubic pink cheeks, one of which was pressed against her daddy's broad, trusted chest.

The sun was peeking over the horizon by the time everyone got back to bed. Nobody really cared, and Jessie managed to push the angst over heading back to Vancouver away when the morning's usual breakfast chaos, and getting ready for the Bragg Creek party, which was about a half hour away down a quiet rural road, took precedence over her fretting.

In their bedroom just before they were about to leave for the party, she took Josh's fingers in hers. "You're really something, you know that?" she breathed. The awed respect in her eyes, which hovered gratefully like milky moons just beneath the surface, was reflected in her movements. Crooking a finger of her free hand, Jessie seductively bit a lip, tipped her head to one side, and pulled her almost shy, embarrassed husband into their bathroom. With a foot, she gave the door a light kick. It closed behind Josh with a casual *thwack*. "You were so good with her last night, Josh," Jessie praised, running the tip of her tongue along his curious lips. He tasted like home; like the blueberries and maple syrup he put on the morning pancakes he made for the kids. "So freaking beautiful."

Josh didn't answer. Their children, along with the usual assorted security, were already gathering outside in the clearing between the house and the barn. The kids were about as wired as they got—they had new kittens to love, a party to go to, friends to play with, and a ninety person cast and crew to fawn over them. They were in heaven.

A sly grin lit up Josh's eyes. Shoving his hands in his wife's hair, raking his fingers through the large curls at the ends, he pressed his lips fully to hers and passionately tasted the sweet mouth he loved. Again and again he tasted her, probing the inside of her mouth with his tongue until she enveloped him fully in her arms and begged for more. A roguish demand flecked with deep seated anticipation settled into his eyes. Lifting his wife, Josh carried Jessie into the shower and flipped it on so it could muffle the ecstasy of their lovemaking. They didn't need anyone listening to them cherish and love each other this way. There was a peace to this day, to this time, and it was perfection.

There was a seductive deceit to the playful, beguiling morning, though.

Josh and Jessie had no way of knowing just how cruelly time was planning to steal back what it gave them last night—that magical, flawless peace— but somehow their souls seemed to be intuitive. Their souls were aware, and they transferred a deep, heavy need to Josh's and Jessie's bodies, in many ways gifting them the blessing of deep, shared love to help fortify them for the hard road ahead.

The rest of the day would not be recorded in the Sawyer family memory banks as cherished and picture perfect. The next hour would be remembered only with pain, and a grievous, aching hurt.

Chapter Twenty-seven

Things started to go downhill a few short minutes after Josh emerged from the house, the screen door twanging as usual against the home as he exited as if to add a final jarring exclamation mark to the transcendent night. Jessie would be a few minutes behind him, red-faced and slightly embarrassed in a girly high school kind of way. When she joined the others they would already be running late, and not one of the adults—especially not Matt—would be unaware that her hair was wet for the second time that day, that she was wearing different clothes, and that her radiant, fresh scrubbed husband was smiling like an unrepentant schoolboy.

Josh was halfway across the clearing before he noticed a squiggly white ball of fur cradled in Emily-Grace's loving arms. His earlier exuberance and simple joy scratched harshly across a record and turned upside down. Halting a few feet away from his little girl, he rocked back on one booted foot. "Honey," he started, unsure.

The sweet child from last night shrank from him. "I can't leave Snow here alone, Daddy. She's too little. She'll be scared."

The thing that Josh hated most about his life was its transparency. Everybody—the Sawyer family entourage, their family and friends, their security—was always witness to his attempts to succeed as a person, as an actor, as a friend, as a husband, and as a father. It sucked to always be on display this way.

Fidgeting with the keys that were dangling from his fingers, Josh stole a look over at Matt, but quickly averted his eyes from the man's cool stare. It didn't take a brainiac to know that Matt would have figured out why he and Jessie were running late, and why they both had wet hair. Ankles and arms crossed, Matt was leaning coolly back against the silver Lexus, rather dashing in jeans, leather desert boots, a white linen shirt, his favorite khaki green aviator jacket, and sunglasses, which he pushed back on his nose with a slow, controlled, much too patient finger. Josh was a macho guy who loved women, but even he was not immune to at least part of the reason why his wife occasionally got lost in Matt's aura. Even after sex with Jessie just now—hot shower sex that was mutually satisfying and a little bit wild and carefree in its spontaneity—Josh was unnerved by Matt, and he didn't need him watching and judging how he chose to parent the now obstinate little girl before him.

Josh took a deep breath and let it out in a confused little whistle. Raising a hand, he used a thumb and forefinger to uneasily scratch an earlobe. "Honey," he tried cautiously, "Snow's just a baby. She needs to sleep. Puppies like a little quiet time."

"Daddy, I told Stella I would bring Snow. The other kids are gonna want to see her too."

Eyeing Matt from his peripheral vision, Josh growled under his breath at the man's hard silence. Hell, as far as Josh was concerned, Matt should have dealt with this puppy issue while they were all waiting. He figured the guy chose not to out of spite. It pissed him off. Cocking his head at Emily-Grace, Josh stood in front of her, but his words were aimed at Dan. "Dan, can you get the boys in their seats? We're already running late."

From his side he heard a muttered *mmpphhff.* Too casually, Matt turned his head away and recrossed his ankles.

Josh balled his free hand into a fist and glared at him. "Get a grip, will you, Matt?"

Easing his body away from the Lexus, Matt fired *fuck you* eyes at Josh and started over to help Dan load the boys. "I'm not the one who's running late," he steamed.

"It's a goddamned field party. In all reality, nobody really gives a shit what time we get there." Josh bit the side of his lip and watched Matt scoop Dylan up in his arms.

Dylan started kicking. "I want to go in the truck!" he cried. "With Dan and Arnie!"

"Not happening, Dylan," Josh stated, in a voice he hoped sounded firm.

"We're travelling as a family to the party because Momma has to go away tomorrow." They were taking numerous vehicles. Josh would go on to Calgary with Arnie after the party. He planned to drive with Jessie and the kids in the Lexus on the way to Bragg Creek, followed by Matt in the Audi, and Arnie and Dan in the truck. Alin was sleeping for the day, after doing the all-nighter. It wasn't a surprise that Dylan wanted to ride in the truck—the newest King Ranch was a monster vehicle, way cooler to a high-spirited youngster like Dylan than a family car. Just as Josh was about to lose it with his stubborn kids, Jessie made her entrance.

"What's up?" she asked, galloping happily over to the glum looking group.

Dylan's cowboy boot caught Matt in the shin, and Matt yelped and set him down. Dylan ran to the truck and jumped up on the running board, only to be haplessly caught by Dan, who grabbed him around the waist with a hearty, "Whoa there, cowboy."

Jessie knew her kid. She caught on, and shrugged. "It's fine, Josh," she said. "Dylan can go with the big boys." She winked at Arnie, who choked back an unspoken *shit's gonna hit the fan now.*

He wasn't wrong. Josh's eyes sparked. "I already told him no." It was a warning. *Don't even think about challenging me on this.*

Swallowing, Jessie met his exasperated stare. She rubbed a fingertip over her lips as she pondered what to do. Then she spotted the puppy in Emily-Grace's arms and the pout on the child's face. Dylan was screaming now, writhing in Dan's big, capable arms, and Dan was waiting for direction.

"Awww, hell," Jessie groaned. She caught Matt's eye.

He was pissed, as evidenced by the invisible bullets he was firing at her. He was leaning belly first against the truck now, on the opposite side away from her, hands clasped high over the back bed rail. "If you two had been here when the rest of us were ready to go," he fumed, "the original arrangements would have been fine. Snow was inside the house, asleep in her crate, and Dylan was snoring in his car seat."

Piss off, Jessie fired back to him, in her best stormy glare. Sucking up her courage, she spoke to Emily-Grace. "I thought we agreed to let the puppy stay here. Alin's going to check on her when she wakes up, remember?" Kneeling in front of her daughter, Jessie grasped the scrawny elbows and peered into the wistful baby blues. "Snow's still a baby. There are going to be a lot of people at the party. All of the confusion might be too much for her."

Emily-Grace stomped a foot. Every man present raised an eyebrow—the child was the picture of her stubborn mother. "No, Momma. I'll take care of her. Me and Stella. She'll be fine."

With a guarded even move, watched by everyone, Jessie stood. *No, I'll be holding her while you play,* ran across her mind. Snow's soft blue travel carrier was still in the back of the Lexus next to Emily-Grace's booster seat, where it was left after the puppy's most recent checkup with the vet in Canmore. Striding forward, Jessie opened the side door. Leaning into the vehicle, she grabbed the carrier and set it on the front passenger seat. "Put her in. But she rides in the carrier, not in your arms, honey."

Exuberant, Emily-Grace marched past her fuming daddy and placed the puppy in its temporary home. All wide-eyed sweetness, she blinked innocently up at her mother. "I need to get her some food."

"You need to learn to listen." Josh, who quickly deduced that the fairy tale glitter that passed over them last night was now toast, angrily bit off the words. "And so does your mother." Parenting, from his point of view, especially with this sensitive child, was a constant series of waves. Some crashed on the beach, and some were calm little rivulets that trickled happily ashore. This one was brewing into a storm surge.

Flicking her hair, Jessie bit hard on her lip and looked over at him. He was steaming. She could practically see hot little waves of moisture evaporating into the air above his head. Gone was the sweet man who made desperate, crazy love to her only a few short minutes ago. "Josh," she warned, in a low, almost singsong voice. "Not sure that was called for, babe."

Marching forward, Josh shot daggers at her before he reached into the carrier and scooped the puppy out. "She stays here," he proclaimed to his two obstinate women. Wheeling around, he headed back toward the house, head down and the hems of his jeans dragging in the Alberta dirt.

It only took one stunned hiccupy breath before a shocked banshee wail followed him. A few seconds later, delicate hands furiously gripped the bottom of Josh's jean jacket, and small heels dug deeply into the ground.

"No, Daddy!" Emily-Grace screamed as she was hauled along by her father. "Momma said she could come!"

"Oh, for fuck's sake," Jessie muttered under her breath. Sighing, she fixed her gaze on David, who was watching the family feud with a practiced calm as he stood on the running board of the truck and looped his arms over the bed rail next to Matt. "Sweetheart," she said with an apologetic smile, as Dylan hollered bloody murder and as Emily-Grace sobbed, "would you care to join in? We could start a family band with these vocals." To her delight, David grinned widely. Lighting up, Jessie smiled effusively back. Then she pivoted around and followed her husband and daughter to the screen door while, behind her, Dan, Matt and Arnie exchanged knowing looks.

Jogging the last bit so that she reached the door before Josh and their daughter did, Jessie whipped around, blocked the entry, and held a palm up and out to Josh. "Some battles are not worth fighting," she reminded him. "Parenting 101. Let the puppy come."

"She'll never learn if we always give in to her, Jessie." Josh, to his credit, stopped moving, but the telltale nerve on his cheek was vibrating much too quickly for Jessie's liking.

"I know that, I'll talk to her in the car, okay? You take the boys in the truck and me and Emily-Grace will have a heart-to-heart in the Lexus."

"And what does that solve?" Balancing the growing puppy's belly fully on one palm, Josh reached his other arm behind him and forcibly removed one of his daughter's hands from his jacket.

"Jesus, Josh. You got her the goddamned puppy in the first place." The accusation was spoken in a subdued tone, but Emily-Grace quieted. She heard every word, including the two she'd soon be reminding her mother meant dropping money in the Sawyer family swear jar. Her parents were pitted against each other yet again, and she was emerging the victor. Holding her breath, she released her second hand from her daddy's jacket and waited, tense but expectant, her small fists curled up in child-sized frustration.

Furious, Josh knew he was beaten. He was one flat second away from storming away from the whole great crowd of them—his wife, his daughter, his sons, his staff, and especially Matt, whose accusing eyes derailed all of the sweet-won loving Josh had been awarded from his wife just a short time ago. A horseback ride in the woods, even one with a gnarly cougar at the end of it, suddenly seemed better than this unholy charade. "You fucking kill me, Jessie," he steamed, thrusting Snow into her arms and swinging around to march back across the clearing in humiliation and defeat.

Jessie, cuddling the puppy close, felt sick as she watched him go, his jean jacket swinging in time to his angry footsteps. Josh whipped open the doors on the truck and grabbed the screaming Dylan from Dan's arms before she even dared move.

Glancing down at her belligerent daughter, she ordered, "Go get Snow's food and dish. I'll message Alin so when she wakes she'll know we took the little furball with us." Sucking up her pride, Jessie walked to the Lexus and put Snow back in the carrier.

Arnie stepped forward and helped Jessie juggle some car seats so Emily-Grace could sit in the middle row of the SUV, behind the front passenger seat. They belted the puppy's soft blue carrier into the seat next to her, behind Jessie.

Daring a sideways look, Jessie watched Josh forcibly settle the writhing Dylan into his seat. When he was done, as Dylan started to calm now that he also was a Sawyer child who got what he wanted, Josh slammed the door and cursed his way into the barn to regain his shattered self-esteem, mumbling something about checking on the horses and the kittens as he moved.

"Matt," Jessie said, catching his eye and withering from his *you-messed-up* frown, "make sure he calms down before he drives, okay? Precious cargo."

"I'm following you," Matt rebutted angrily. "Arnie's your childish husband's babysitter today."

"You're crossing a line," Jessie stammered, curling her fists the same way her daughter just had, which would have amused Matt had he not been so damned pissed. She would have added, *you arrogant prick*, but the hard edge in Matt's usually gentle eyes scuttled the nasty rebuttal real quick.

Matt swallowed back his planned response when Emily-Grace emerged from the house, sauntering toward them like a proud princess, her head held high and her arms full of puppy food, a dish, and at least three toys for Snow to chew on. Growling, Matt signaled Dan, and together they headed toward the Audi since the truck would now be full with Arnie, Josh and the two boys.

Jessie pulled out first, quaking from the hard emotions of the last few minutes. Matt was right behind her, with Dan alongside him in the sedan's passenger seat. Josh, in the truck, left a few short minutes later—he'd only kicked a vacant stall's door five times. When he passed through the main gate to head for the highway, he silently rehearsed just how he planned to tell Jessie what he thought of her actions that day, and he wished to hell he could read the infuriating minds of women, and interpret the confusing, selfish brains of little girls.

⌒⌒

"Today?" Morgan asked Caulfield as, on his back on a bench, he did a dozen chest press reps. He'd almost dropped the whole damn barbell when the steely-eyed corrections officer leaned over and said he had a coupla guys on duty to even the score with the Sawyers for him.

Morgan replaced the barbell in its holder and sat up. "Today?" he repeated.

Caulfield was grinning, chewing spearmint gum this time instead of peppermints as he watched Morgan take in the news. "Sure thing," he said. "They're going to some kind of party for that TV show Sawyer is working on. They're sitting ducks. It'll be all over the news by dinnertime."

"Call it off." Morgan couldn't look at Caulfield. His voice was a whisper.

Caulfield frowned. "You deserve this, Mor-gie. You deserve retribution for what they did to you."

"They didn't do anything wrong. Don't hurt those kids. Please." Morgan was staring at a scratch on his knee. *This isn't my life,* he thought. *How is this my life?*

"Too late, son. Word is that the family is on the road. Josh is gonna get his. You wanna watch a man suffer?"

"Been there, done that." The gruff sorrow in those four simple words was as close as Morgan could get to telling Caulfield how much this hurt, all of it—the past few years, the regret and remorse and confusion and grief that he suffered, that Nadia suffered, that Jessie, Josh, and the kids and everyone around them suffered… "Please," he pleaded again. "Don't hurt those kids."

Caulfield bent closer to Morgan. In his ear he said, "You remember burying your son, Morgan? That must have really sucked. You never got the chance to bury your wife, right? Well, you can relax now. Oren C's looking out for you. You'll feel so much better tonight." Sauntering away, he was as proud as a peacock, shoulders thrown back and his lips forming a perfect 'O' as he whistled peacefully.

Morgan hung his head, and then stood. With a mighty cry, he punched his right fist three times into the nearby brick wall. He was in the prison infirmary twenty minutes later, awaiting removal to the hospital in Edmonton for surgery to repair the damage when all hell broke loose on highway 66 just past Bragg Creek.

Chapter Twenty-eight

Jessie was doing all right with Emily-Grace, feeling like she was getting somewhere as she talked and drove, sucking intermittently on a water bottle between sentences and wishing she could have spoken to Josh to settle things between them before she spun out of the gravel lane and onto the road near their ranch.

Occasionally she looked into the rearview mirror, or into the side mirror to spy Matt's Audi cruising along behind her. She knew he was concerned about the sheer number of people that would be around the outdoor party on this sunny day, hence the presence of him, Dan and Arnie, but she was also aware that he and Charles had easily convinced Charlie and Jonathon to agree to hire extra uniformed security for the event. Most of the cast and crew would have already arrived at the party by the time Josh and Jessie got enough gumption to actually go, and it was too early for the tourist season, so apart from the occasional pickup truck—some hauling horse trailers in this ranch-thick area of Alberta—there wasn't much traffic. So it was a complete surprise when a nondescript blue pickup came charging out of a side road just behind the Audi and passed it.

Matt and Dan had barely spoken during the short drive from the Sawyer ranch. When the truck appeared out of nowhere and flew by them, they perked up instantly. Matt cursed and floored the gas pedal.

Jessie only saw the truck at the last second. She heard it, first. It came careening out of nowhere and got between her and Matt. "Somebody's in a hurry," she said to her daughter, interrupting Emily-Grace's rather annoying syrupy sweet, "She's sleeping now, Momma. She just needed to be able to see me."

Ahead was a slight curve in the road. Ahead of that was a bridge. In between the curve and the bridge, on the right, was a low, graded embankment. Just after the curve, the pickup truck pulled out to ostensibly pass the Lexus. At the last second, its driver yanked its steering wheel to the right.

Jessie screamed and cried out for Emily-Grace to hang on. The Lexus wobbled violently as she struggled to keep it on a forward course. The pickup veered toward Jessie one more time. Sensing that it might try again, she braced for the hit, but she overcorrected and hit dense gravel on the shoulder. The Lexus flew over the embankment, rolled, and landed right side up in the spring swollen Elbow River. Instantly its nose, carrying the heavy engine, started to sink.

Jessie might've had a chance to get the window down before the electrical system gave up the ghost if the air bags hadn't deployed and rendered her momentarily senseless. What brought her back to awareness in the end was her daughter's high-pitched voice, Emily-Grace's second banshee wail of the morning, this time fraught with sheer terror.

"Oh, Jesus!" Jessie gasped when she realized the immediate peril of their situation. The heavy SUV was sinking quickly; icy water was gushing in around her toes, clawing at her ankles with determination and a hungry, violent appetite for dominance. Immediately, Jessie whipped off her seatbelt and turned around to her terrified child. It took a few tries, but the clasp on Emily-Grace's seatbelt finally gave. Hauling her forward, Jessie plunked her into the front passenger seat and twisted back around to the driver's door. Emily-Grace started clawing at her and screaming something nonsensical about the puppy.

"Are you hurt?" Jessie cried back at her. A quick assessment didn't tell her much. Emily-Grace was holding one arm close to her chest, but overall she seemed okay, physically, at least.

This time of year the river was murky and fast, but this close to the road it was only about twenty feet deep. The current had enough strength to move the Lexus but once the heavy vehicle sank fully and its nose stuck into the river's stony, muddy bottom, it hung suspended, ass up, and fought to stay there. It was dark and cold, and quickly filling with an eerie iciness. Like a racehorse on speed, adrenaline ripped through Jessie's body, and with it came a weird calm.

She grabbed Emily-Grace's bony shoulders and shook her, hard. "You listen to me," she demanded, "you know how Precious is taking care of her babies? Well, your mother takes care of hers. I will get you out of this car, Emily-Grace, but you have to listen to me. Stop screaming and listen! Promise me?"

The screaming subsided. In its place came a low, timorous series of moans. "Snow, Momma. Don't forget Snow."

An image of the puppy, belted in just behind them, slid across Jessie's frazzled brain. She could hear the puppy whimpering and its tiny claws scratching at the sides of its soft carrier. Closing her eyes, she sent a hasty prayer up to the gods and sucked in a breath.

"I'll get the puppy, Emily-Grace," she promised. "But you're going out first. You hear me? Are you listening?"

Emily-Grace kept twisting her head around to stare at the carrier. She reached for it, but Jessie grabbed her and begged her to focus. The water was up past Jessie's knees now. Emily-Grace scrambled up into a little ball on the seat and sobbed.

"Be brave, sweet girl," Jessie begged her, and turned to the window.

Matt and Dan saw the car roll horrifyingly into the river, and quickly sink beneath the surface. They were out of the Audi in seconds flat.

Scrambling down the embankment, Matt shouted back at Dan, "Call 911! Call 911!" He didn't recognize the sound of his own voice. It didn't seem to match his body, the body that was now running into the river, the disembodied limbs that shed his aviator jacket and desert boots as he went. Dan ran back to the Audi and grabbed his phone from where he'd laid it on the center console. He was on the phone with emergency services by the time Matt dove beneath the surface.

Kicking, pulling at the water with cupped hands so he could quickly propel himself to the SUV, Matt's eyes darted left and right until he spotted the Lexus. Ghostly and vague, it was bobbing uncertainly, tearing at invisible chains in a desperate attempt to be set free. This far under the dense, roiling river, it was terrifying to behold.

Pulling at the door was useless, but Matt tried anyway the second he got to the car. He could see Jessie inside; she had a firm grip on her daughter's bicep, but was turned toward the driver's door.

Agonized, Matt laid a hand against the window. Taking in a juddery breath, Jessie reached out an arm and placed her palm against his, on her side of the glass. She let her gaze drift up to see Matt's grief-stricken eyes latch onto hers. The terror each spied in the other's eyes was enough for Jessie to almost lose her cool and start to panic. It sickened her to have to do so, but she let her hand fall from Matt's. A scared moan accompanied it.

Jessie had a choice. She regained her focus. A determined anger replaced the terror. Matt knew the second she clicked into her reserves of strength— her eyes blinked once, and narrowed into furious slits.

Matt saw her turn back around to her daughter, but he couldn't hear what she said. He wouldn't have, anyway—he had to leave his girls in the darkness below so he could frantically kick back up to the light at the surface and suck in a few desperate breaths.

Jessie had Emily-Grace's shivering chin in her hands now. "Emily-Grace, you listen to me now. Do what I tell you. I'm going to kick open that window, but when I do, water is going to come rushing in. It's going to throw us back against your door but I'm going to push you out. You know how to swim; Matt will be there to help you. Are you ready?"

"I'm sc-scared, Momma. I'm so scared!"

"No time for that right now, honey. You're a Sawyer. And us Sawyers are strong, dammit! You ready? Take a deep breath, honey, the second that window gives. Take a real deep breath!"

Matt was at the window again, frantic, losing his mind. Jessie whipped back around and took a good, long look at him before she raised a foot and started kicking the window. Again and again she kicked at it with the heel of her favorite old brown cowboy boots, the ones she could have replaced twenty times over but was now eternally grateful for. The whole time she was kicking, her eyes stayed locked on Matt's. The panicked horror in his expression was surreal, a bad dream, a nightmare, but beneath the usually soft, tender eyes was love, and faith—faith in her, Jessie determined rightly, as she sobbed and kicked at the same time.

On the fifth kick, the safety glass shattered.

Jessie was right—water came rushing in, so icy cold it took her breath away. Her right hand had a viselike grip on her daughter's bicep. Closing her eyes against the force of the water, and her ears against the eerie creaking of the car, praying the SUV wouldn't suddenly pull loose from the muddy bottom and surge downriver, Jessie hauled Emily-Grace forward past her body and, screaming against the force of the water against her, shoved her out of the window toward Matt.

They were gone in an instant; Matt leveraged a foot against the outside roof of the SUV to gain an extra push, hauled the little girl to the surface, and deposited her into the arms of Dan, who had tossed his phone on the ground and swum out to them.

Matt sucked in the deepest breath he could. His lungs were bursting, on fire. Diving back under, he cursed Jessie under his breath when she shoved the puppy's blue carrier at him. Dangling it from his left fingers, he groped for her inside the Lexus, which was filled with the river's glacial water now, but something was going wrong. She stopped helping him. Her body went limp and was pressed now up against the passenger side door.

Struggling with the carrier, Matt had no choice but to let it go. It started to drift downwards as he propelled his way half inside the shattered window and grasped a handful of Jessie's plaid shirt. Closing his eyes, desperate for a breath of his own, his lungs a mess of heat and searing pain, he braced his sock feet on the window frame and thrust his body back and upward, hauling Jessie's prone figure through the window as he moved.

He got her to the surface about the same time the King Ranch cruised around the curve.

There were two other vehicles there by then—both were Bragg Creek locals out for Sunday drives. The older couple in one was grabbing picnic blankets out of their sedan's trunk when Josh spied Matt's Audi parked crookedly on the side of the road, both front doors flung open. Screeching to a halt, he tasted bile in his throat as a numb scream started in the pit of his stomach. Jessie's SUV was nowhere in sight. A hand clenched his bicep— Arnie was saying something to him that Josh, in a bizarre panicked stupor, could not make out. Yanking his arm away from Arnie, he hollered at the boys, "Stay in the truck! Stay in the truck!" Leaping out, he skidded down the embankment toward Dan, who was cradling Emily-Grace in his arms, trying to calm her, to warm her up.

Arnie was out of the truck too, but he had the sense to grab the blankets from the frightened older couple and issue a hasty demand as he pointed behind him. "There're kids in the back," he cried, "watch those kids!"

Josh slid to a stop by his daughter. Grabbing her out of Dan's arms, he sobbed as he kissed her, as he ran his eyes and hands over her to be sure she was breathing, that she was, at least on some level, okay. Then he thrust her back into Dan's big, safe arms and ran out into the river where Arnie, who bypassed him, was now struggling through the frigid water. Josh saw Arnie retrieve Jessie from Matt's frozen, exhausted grip.

Unable to make sense of the fact that his wife was limp and nonresponsive, when he got close enough Josh hauled Jessie out of Arnie's arms and waded back to the embankment. Arnie dropped down on his knees beside him and used his muscular boxer's body to forcibly shove Josh aside. Taking control, he glanced quickly up at the dripping, shivering, half-limping Matt before he bent his cheek to Jessie's mouth in hope beyond hope that he would feel her breath on his skin. Straightening, he bellowed orders at Matt.

"She's not breathing! Starting compressions," he asserted. Placing his hands over Jessie's chest, he started to administer CPR. "Start mouth-to-mouth! Now!"

Behind him, Dan was struggling with Emily-Grace, who was writhing and screaming, "Snow! Snow! Snow!"

In a surreal slo-mo haze, Josh turned to her, then focused his eyes back on his wife's still body.

Something gave in his soul.

The way a soldier snaps to attention, old memories of loss and a sickening horror gutted him, and he lost it. Dan thrust Emily-Grace into the arms of the second onlooker, a young skinny local in his twenties, and grabbed Josh's biceps from behind. He yanked him backward, keeping him immobile. Later, Dan would quietly explain to Josh that he did that because Josh was screaming and kicking and getting in Arnie's and Matt's ways. Josh didn't quiet until he heard Matt cry out to Arnie. And when Josh quieted then, he stopped kicking also, and focused a strange, hurt gaze on Matt's ashen, quaking, dripping face.

"Easy with those compressions, Arnie!" Matt was crying. "She's pregnant! She's pregnant, okay?"

When they finally got a staggered few breaths out of Jessie, and rolled her over onto her side toward Matt so she could vomit out the murky river water she'd swallowed, Matt stored up some courage and forced himself to meet Josh's wide, frightened eyes. Josh was lying half on his back and half on his side, no longer struggling against Dan, although Dan had an unrelenting hold around his throat, around his arms. Behind Josh and Dan, Emily-Grace was still in shock, screaming, "Daddy, get my puppy! Go get my puppy!" In front of Josh, Matt was telegraphing an anguished look that landed somewhere between *I'm sorry, I'm so, so sorry that I knew before you,* and *Now do you see what I mean to her? She told me before she told you…*

Reality started to come back to Josh. The world started slowly spinning, and he gathered his wits enough to realize that his daughter was alive, and that his wife would survive. It occurred to him that Morgan did not win this round, but that there would be other battles in this old-new war, and now there was apparently a new child to consider, one that Matt, for some reason, knew about, while Josh did not.

He wanted to disappear. Josh wanted to sink into the river and go away forever. A grown man, an international star, he was running out of steam. *Maybe Jessie's right,* he thought. *I do give up too soon.* But he felt like it. He sure as hell felt like giving up.

Something—no, someone—started clutching at him. It was a small body, pushing at him; it was a small voice, begging him to go into the river to get that puppy. Josh pulled his arms out of Dan's strong grasp, sat up straighter, and grabbed his daughter with both hands. Pressing her to his body, he held her as she screamed her pain to whatever gods would listen, and Josh buried his face in the wet ringlets that hung despondently around the little girl's face.

Staring at the mute darkness behind his eyelids made so much more sense than having to look into those desperate eyes, into those pale, small Jessie-eyes that were frantically begging him to save a beloved new puppy that was, by now, surely long gone, forever relegated to being a snowy white spirit floating in the hereafter.

By God, there was not a set of eyes present that Josh wanted to look into right now; there was no courage left here today, and no faith in a whole lot of anything or anybody. Dan's big hand was on his back, assessing him, offering warmth and hope, but Josh just held his daughter close and let her cry. He ignored the big blond man and was quite thankful when he heard Arnie demand that Dan head back up the embankment to check on Dylan and David.

Josh finally opened his eyes and looked up from the tangled mess of his daughter's hair when he heard Jessie struggling to breathe, coughing and vomiting. There was a blanket over her now, and someone had curled one around Emily-Grace as well. Matt was no longer watching Josh. He was bent over Jessie, stroking her hair away from her face, offering tender words of faith and love, Josh supposed, as he rocked Emily-Grace and prayed for her hopeless cries to stop.

There was a shuffle nearby, and Arnie turned around to him. Josh adjusted his body so he was on his knees, handed Emily-Grace over to Arnie, touched the back of a finger to Jessie's cheek, and stood and faced the heartless river that almost claimed his wife and daughter. Bending, he grabbed a stone and pitched it, with a mighty cry, out into the current just as sirens could be heard wailing in the distance.

In his mind was playing an old movie, one that featured Nadia's sensuous body and Morgan's silent, watchful eyes. In his heart was a stone, round and smooth, impermeable, just like the one he threw into the river, and in his ears was the sound of endlessly running water.

He looked up, raised his arms out to the sides, and closed his eyes. In a small voice Josh murmured, "You win, Nadia. But you win my way. You hear me? You win MY way."

When he turned back around, he saw Jessie lying on her side, still struggling to breathe without choking. Her eyes were open—she was watching him. Matt was still with her, his white linen shirt soaked and clinging to his chest; his hard body shaking and shivering in the cold. He was spooning her now, trying to somehow transfer whatever body heat he had left into her cold body. Moments later, an ambulance careened to a halt, just behind the first of the police cars to make it to the accident scene. EMTs struggled down the embankment, slipping and sliding in their big boots while trying to hang onto armloads of gear.

Josh swiped the back of a wrist across his mouth, leaned over, hauled off his boots, and waded into the river.

Chapter Twenty-nine

"I thought, you know, if I could find Emily-Grace's puppy we could give it a proper burial. Maybe that would give Emily-Grace some closure." Head in his hands, staring hopelessly at his bare feet, Josh was telling Charlie why it seemed like a good idea to go back into the water at the accident site. Facing each other, the guys were sitting in a tiny enclosed, glassed-in room at the trauma center used to give families and friends of emergency patients some much coveted privacy. Outside, in the hallway, Charles and Dee were talking to Matt and Arnie. They were waiting to be called in to see Jessie and Emily-Grace, who had been transported to the trauma center of Foothills Medical Center in Calgary for assessment and observation.

Josh looked up. "All I saw was the Lexus, like some kind of ghost, moving slightly in the current like a dark flower in the wind, looming there like a tomb." Standing, Josh paced the twelve-foot deep space twice before landing back on the small sofa where Charlie had found him five minutes earlier. "No puppy. Just images of my wife and daughter inside that car, like fish trapped in a goddamned fishbowl." Meeting Charlie's frightened eyes, Josh added, "I can't imagine what it must have been like for her."

"Or for Matt." Charlie's statement was almost devoid of emotion. He'd been replaying what it must have been like for Matt to find Jessie and Emily-Grace stuck inside their watery prison, all the while trying to hold his breath and figure out how to set them free. The terror must have been unreal.

"Matt." Curling up a lip in distaste, Josh glanced absently to the side. Some earlier family had obviously been in the space before he and Charlie. A child's action figure was sticking out behind the garbage can, its limbs crooked and distorted. Oddly, Josh wondered if it was Spiderman, or maybe Superman; its red and blue plastic legs were all he could see of it, but that was enough. Recoiling, he hoped that whoever the child was at the hospital to see was recovering. Relieved that Jessie and Emily-Grace were okay, physically at least, he forced himself to peer back over at Charlie. "Thank God for Matt. Really. But…Charlie…" He sighed, leaned back, and rifled the fingers of his right hand through his messy hair. "D'you know she's pregnant?"

"What? No." Trying to put two and two together, Charlie stammered out a, "That's great news, Josh. Congrats. Number four. Wow."

"Matt knew. I didn't."

"What? Josh, this isn't the time to be pissed at Matt for having Jessie's ear. Unless that's not why…you don't think…"

"I don't know what the hell to think, Charlie. Those two are so close they're practically the same person."

"Ask him." Someone was pulling open the glass door to the space. It was Matt. Charlie heaved out a weary sigh and rose, placing his hands on his thighs for leverage. His body suddenly felt super heavy. "Look, I'm gonna run back to the condo and grab some dry clothes for you fellas." Waving a hand toward Josh's and Matt's now bare feet, he said, "Hippie days are over, guys." The joke fell flat. He met Matt's solemn eyes. "You've got stuff at Arnie's place, right? Or should I grab you one of his old gray sweatshirts and a pair of runners?"

"I've got stuff there. Yeah. Thanks, Charlie." Matt didn't even attempt to crack a joke about Arnie's tough guy fashion sense. Or lack thereof.

Before he moved to leave, Charlie laid a hand on Josh's shoulder. "Take it easy, Josh," he said. It came out exactly as the careful demand he meant it to be, slightly terse but overflowing with friendship. "I'll be back in a bit." Clapping Matt's shoulder on the way by, Charlie brushed through the door and stood outside to talk to Charles and Deirdre before he took off. Shanda had driven up from the party grounds at Bragg Creek with him; she was poised by Charles, a coffee cup in her hand, her brow furrowed in worry and her eyes locked on a very despondent Josh.

Inside the glassed-in space, Matt dropped into Charlie's vacated seat and faced Josh, who Matt could tell was having a hard time finding the nerve to even look over at him.

"Josh," Matt started, "they're going to be okay. Emily-Grace was sedated before they traveled her. Jessie's with her now. They're together. We'll be able to see them soon."

"They're together. Good. All," Josh cleared his throat, "all three of them, you mean."

Matt read his meaning, and sat back. "I take it there's something you want to ask me." Gripping his thighs, he tried to stave off the increased shaking that started the second the shock of how close a call this was sank in to his adrenaline fueled brain.

Josh noticed the state he was in, but chose to ignore it. "I don't think I want to know," he said.

"Yeah," Matt corrected him. "You do."

Josh blinked and stared at the half dead action figure on the floor. "Tell me then…get it over with…"

"Ask me."

"Fuck, Matt. Seriously."

Matt ran a set of fingers over and over his tense jaw before lowering them once again to his thigh. "Is there a chance the baby could be mine? That's what you want to know."

Unable to answer, Josh just kept blinking back the unthinkable, but he moved his eyes up to Matt. There was a grief, a misery in Matt's eyes that made Josh sorry for thinking what he was thinking, and before Matt even answered his own tough question, Josh regretted ever entertaining it in the first place.

"We had our time, Josh. Jessie and me." Matt spoke quietly, and eased his grip on his strong legs. He reminded Josh of a priest from childhood—wise and sensible and kind. "Our relationship isn't like that anymore. The only babies that beautiful girl wants are yours."

Wiping his nose with a tissue he grabbed from a low table next to the sofa, Josh said harshly, "The fact that I'm even thinking it is pissing me off. Jessie pisses me off. She'll be pissing Dee off too, when the shock wears off and reality sets in."

"Not today, Josh. Jessie doesn't deserve that today."

Nor do you, Josh thought. *Not today.* Out loud he added numbly, "Jessie's supposed to be doing a film in Montreal in October. Might be a little hard to shoot out the pregnancy at that point, wouldn't you say?"

Matt just raked a hand through his hair and watched him. Josh was all over the place. It was like he had no clue where to let his scattered thoughts land.

Shoving back a need to yell, or to cry, or to leave this awful place and bury himself in a bar somewhere, Josh stared hard at his friend. "I don't wanna know," he said for the second time, but this time he was referring to what happened during those horrible moments while his wife and daughter were trapped inside their submerged vehicle, a vehicle that Josh knew would haunt him, because he was stupid enough—and desperate enough—to dive down to look for the puppy, and to let the drowned SUV sear its loathsome phantom self on his consciousness.

Matt faced Josh with a resolve dusted with pride. "She was so brave, Josh," he murmured carefully. "You should be proud of her."

Watching him, Josh settled into a quiet calm. He stopped twitching, stopped swiping at his nose, stopped breathing, almost. "Tell me, then," he demanded, matching Matt's respectful tone.

A finger came up to the corner of Matt's left eye. "Her eyes," he said. "She was determined. She only panicked for a second. When I got there," he choked back the panic, the memory, "Jessie had Emily-Grace in the front seat. I could see that she was issuing instructions, calming her. She started kicking at the window. Those boots," he chuckled darkly. "Deirdre's been after her to stop wearing them. Jessie's had them resoled and stitched up so many times…" He drifted off, then added, "Dee'll frame the damn things now."

"She kicked the window out." The realization wasn't a surprise. The shattered window, spooky and jagged in the foggy depths of the Elbow River, was burned on Josh's retinas. "Jessie and Emily-Grace must be cut. You… must be cut."

"Those windows are made of safety glass. They're designed not to cut if they shatter. Josh…just be proud of her, okay? Your girl's a fighter. I've…" Matt sighed, but it was a proud sigh. "I've never known a woman like her."

"Our girl," Josh corrected him. "I've long ago realized that Jessie doesn't belong to me. She belongs to everybody. I'm sorry I thought…"

Extending an arm, leaning forward, Matt laid a hand on Josh's shoulder. "You had every right to think what you did. I'd take her off your hands in a second, Josh."

Panic streaked across Josh's face. He swallowed, and waited for Matt to complete his thought.

"I think about it sometimes…what it would be like…and then I remember the only times I've ever really seen her give up. They were times when she was afraid of losing you." Matt smiled, but it came out crooked. "You might think you share her with the world, Josh, but when all is said and done, that girl is yours, and yours alone."

Standing, Matt rested a hand on the door handle. He wished to hell he could stop trembling. Glancing up, he saw, through the glass doorway, Shanda watching them. He'd only just gotten to know her. To him, the *Sacred Peace* female lead was 'Marilyn Monroe beautiful' in a simplistic, more pixie-like kind of way. Her eyes were moist and she looked poised to vault past Matt and enter the small room. Her gaze flicked over to Matt alone, and then past him to land on Josh.

Twisting at the waist to look behind him, Matt saw what she was seeing. Josh was struggling not to break down.

Josh grabbed Matt's forearm. In a gruff voice he said, "Matt, what did you hear that night, the night we were jumped…?" He gulped.

Frowning, Matt tensed. He turned his back fully to Shanda and let his hand slip off of the door handle. "All I know is that it was some kind of threat. What are you saying, Josh?" He took a jagged breath. "Today was no real surprise to you. Was it?"

"They asked me to—to choose. Which of my kids…" In desperation, Josh gripped Matt's arm so tight it left an ugly bruise for Matt to helplessly study in the days to come. "I didn't, I—I couldn't," Josh said as Matt sucked in another breath and instantly went white. "But Matt, she went across my brain then. Emily-Grace. Why? Why did I see her in my mind when I was threatened like that?"

The despondency in Josh's eyes, in his shrunken shoulders and limp, bare toes peeking out from under still damp denims, was too much. Matt could feel the pressure building up in himself, from his own cold, drying clothing;

from some deep well inside his body that now, the hardest part of the day over, was threatening to overflow. He couldn't bring himself to say a word other than a shocked, "What?"

"It could have been her. Today. How is a man supposed to live with that?" Josh was crumpling.

Matt held him steady, although he was, in truth, holding himself upright too, by clinging to his friend. "This isn't going to help you, Josh. But whoever ran your wife off the road today likely thought you and your entire family was in that vehicle."

"Jesus, Matt. We would never have all got—"

"The only thing you'll accomplish by allowing yourself to consider what might have happened is to torture yourself, Josh. There's no doubt that the driver was hired, likely by Morgan's minion, that Caulfield fellow. Asking you to choose was likely just designed to torment you. Don't let it. By letting Morgan get to you, you let him win."

"But Jesus Christ, Matt. I thought of her. I can't fucking—even—" Raising his hands to his head, elbows jutting out, Josh spun away from Matt and paced back toward the wall. When he turned back around, he may as well have been a prisoner asking for the grace not to be shot, or a repentant, anguished sinner begging for forgiveness. "I can't think right now." He sniffled, and swiped at his nose with his sleeve. "I can't fucking live with my thoughts. Any of them."

Matt covered the few steps between himself and the husband of the woman he'd watched over for much of his adult life. Gripping Josh's biceps, he forced him to listen. "Don't cling to some fleeting image of your daughter crossing your mind when you were under that kind of duress, Josh. Emily-Grace is your firstborn, and she's had a goddamned tough time of it in her young life. She lashes out at you—that's the only reason she came to the surface that night. There's no question in my mind, in hers, or in Jessie's, of how much you love her. And I've got news for you. She needs her father now more than ever. Don't you give up on her. Ever. Or on Jessie."

"I just can't deal right now, Matt. Another baby…another life…"

"We've made it this far. We'll beat Morgan at this vicious game of his. But your family needs you, Josh. Look, I'll get Arnie to take you to an A.A.

meeting, okay? With a half dozen armed security at your disposal if need be, okay?"

Josh's gaze flickered behind Matt. Charlie and Shanda were both watching him break down. Reaching deep for a modicum of pride, he stood a little taller and let his eyes settle on Arnie.

Arnie.

The Downtown Eastside angel. Procurer of guns, and friend—if anyone on the Downtown Eastside could actually be trusted enough to be considered a friend—to some of the shadier personalities who inhabited Vancouver's troubled streets.

An idea planted itself in Josh's mind. He licked his lips nervously.

I have a plan, he thought. *I know how to save them.*

From the corner of his eye, Josh saw a doctor approach the cluster of family and friends outside the private room. Brushing by Matt, he shoved the door open. Matt's panicked voice stopped him, but only for a second. The glass door stood half open, suspended between agony and defeat, and hope and a future.

Matt was responding to the beleaguered, slightly expectant look that flickered, as brief as a falling star, across Josh's somber eyes. "Josh…I saw that look. Don't do anything stupid. You're not alone. We're in this together."

With an aching intensity, Josh repositioned his body to fully face the man responsible for his family's security. "I've got news for you, Matt," Josh said, determination and purpose settling across his face. "They're my goddamned family. Not yours. This fight's between fucking Morgan—and Nadia's ghost—and me. I'll do whatever I need to do to set Jessie and my children free. You've already done far, far more than any of us could ever ask of you. But from now on let me be the goddamned hero, okay?"

There was a long, frozen pause between the whoosh of the door opening further, and Matt's bare feet carrying his heavy body back to where he'd been sitting just a few minutes ago.

Images of Jessie started to roll around and around in his brain, in his heart…Jessie, Josh's wife, not his, furiously kicking at the Lexus' window, one balled fist communicating a fierce need to smash it to bits, the other hand desperately clutching her daughter's arm…only a few precious moments later, Jessie's listless body in Matt's arms…then her eyes, fluttering open, unable to focus at first, her body heaving as she vomited out the icy river water that almost claimed her…

These and more vibrant, colorful images danced across Matt's heavy mind, happier ones of Jessie creating starry-eyed musical magic on stage, alone or with Jacob, and then…then…that incredible time when she finally gave into the bond she shared with Matt, on that dreamlike night when she pressed her lips to his, fully and completely, outside La Casa, and let him run the backs of his fingers over her breast… the drive to his condo, made interminable from sweet anticipation…making love in his condo, her on her knees at first, taking him in her mouth with a tender, loving confidence, in his home, in a place she'd never before visited…loss and longing for Josh, so much of that, too much of that…the cut lip, the bruise on her face after Jacob's rage in Florida…so much love and hope and belief in goodness there, in those light blue eyes…so much forgiveness, despite all the bad…

He wanted to go see her. By the footsteps in the hallway outside, it seemed the group was trudging off behind the doctor. At least, Josh and Charles and Dee were. Charlie and Shanda were still standing there, watching him through the glass, it seemed. Arnie and Dan were nowhere to be seen.

Matt exhaled and tried to catch his breath. He dropped his forehead into his hands and gasped. Outside the small space, Shanda laid her elegant fingers on Charlie's arm, handed him her coffee cup, and softly said, "Give me a minute."

Inside, she slipped into Josh's vacated seat on the sofa and wrapped Matt's cold, trembling fingers in her caring, warm hands. "I wonder," she breathed, "if anybody is ever really truly aware of the price you pay to watch over that family."

The fingers holding his were tenderly rubbing Matt's knuckles, his nails, his palms, the strong backs, trying to inject some warmth and life back into them, to stop the pain that was cutting Matt in two. Shanda brushed her thumbs over his skin, squeezed Matt's fingers again and again; too, she brought his hands to her lips and kissed them.

"I know what she means to you, Matt," she acknowledged. "I can't imagine what it must have been like for you today. You saved her life. You saved Emily-Grace's life."

He was gasping, trying to even out his breaths. "They shouldn't have…been run off the road in the first place…I was too…I was too slow…"

Adamant, Shanda cut in. "No, Matt, honey, nobody could have predicted what happened. You were exactly where you were supposed to be."

"I was dreaming—I was thinking about them, about her and Josh. They disagreed about bringing the dog. They mess so much up. I was replaying old shit. Putting myself in there and changing the outcomes."

"It's always perfect when we put ourselves in their places, huh? Cause we know all the answers."

"That's the thing, Shanda," Matt choked. "I used to think I did. But these days I've come to realize I don't know any of the answers." Josh floated through his mind—desperate for some kind of release from the horrible split-second thought he had when he was asked to choose which child Morgan could have as redemption. His shoulders shook more as Matt removed first one hand and then the other from Shanda's grip, and buried his face in his palms.

Outside looking in, Charlie turned away so the man could set his grief loose in peace.

Swinging over to the sofa Matt was sitting on, Shanda wrapped her arms around him and held him while he cried. When he was done, and pride and embarrassment took over, he pulled away from her.

"I'm sorry," he said without looking at her. "It's just a lot right now."

Shanda was easy on him. Her voice was a gentle flower in a summer storm. "You're a good man, Matt," she murmured. "I know we don't know each other all that well, but it's easy to see what a good man you are. Jessie and Josh are so, so lucky to have you."

"Some days I'm not so sure." Matt was thinking about the new baby, feeling sorry that he couldn't avoid wishing the baby was his. On the positive side, he mixed those feelings up with gratitude—gratitude that Jessie was happy, that her children ranked first in her life, way beyond fame and success. That she was with the man she loved beyond all others.

"Your jeans are damp." Shanda smiled at him, and Matt, surprised at the sweet way she said the words, and at the light hand she laid across his thigh, looked up to see tranquility in the quiet way she was studying him, and that she had dimples, small ones, that lit up her porcelain skin. A quiet calm eclipsed the fear and uncertainty that haunted him. A tiny light flickered in his eyes. "Charlie and I are off to get some dry clothes for you guys," she was saying. "How about I grab you a coffee on the way back? What do you like?"

The graceful hand was still resting on his thigh. Taking in a slow, quiet breath, Matt wrapped his fingers around hers. "Chai tea would be fine," he requested gruffly, not quite completely in control yet. She handed him a tissue so he could swipe at his misty eyes. "I'm more of a tea guy, usually," he rambled on, suddenly nervous in the presence of this beautiful actress. "Except when Jessie really pisses me off. Then I go for the hard stuff."

Tilting her head back a little, Shanda laughed. To Matt, her easy delight could have been Peace Tower bells pealing over Ottawa. "Chai tea it is," she answered as happily as she could manage, given the weird, frightening day. "Although I would've figured you for more of a green tea kind of man."

"I guess you don't really know me."

Pausing, Shanda bit her lip. "I guess I don't." She tilted her head to one side as her face lit up. "But I'm kind of thinking that I'd like to. Know you." Rising, she leaned on his thigh for leverage as she unfolded her slim body. Shanda smiled warmly down at Matt before she slipped her hand out of his and left the room.

Watching her go, Matt leaned back against the sofa and caught himself thinking, *I wonder if she's a casual kinda coffee girl, or does she need it administered intravenously the way Jessie does…*

He jumped up, grabbed a Kleenex so he could blow his nose, and moved to toss the used tissue in the garbage. Peeking out from behind the garbage can was the action figure Josh had spotted earlier. Matt bent and picked it up. He set it on the low table against the Kleenex box, and rearranged the legs and arms so that the figure appeared confident and strong.

When he pulled the glass door open to go off in search of Jessie and Emily-Grace, his eyes were still damp, but he was smiling.

Chapter Thirty

Josh was with Jessie when Matt found them. Charles and Dee said their goodbyes and left with Dan, since Ulysses was off for the day. They wanted to meet Sam and Alin at the ranch so they could watch over the small boys and offer what comfort they could on this scary day. The boys were old enough to know something bad had happened at the river; they, like Matt, were not entirely overlooked, but they came second to the primary victims. They would need comfort, and Grammie and Grampie wanted to offer it.

Matt paused outside the large window where, inside a hospital room, he watched Josh pull a chair up to the bed where Jessie lay spooning her sleeping daughter. From where Matt was standing, he could hear him talking to her. They were talking about the pregnancy, although it seemed Jessie was struggling just to form the words. Exhaustion, most likely. Matt hoped the doctors hadn't sedated her, although if they did he hoped the EMTs remembered to tell them she was expecting so they would choose something that wouldn't harm the baby. The injuries she sustained in the rollover weren't severe, but Matt was certain Jessie likely felt like she'd been run over by a Mack truck. Both her and Emily-Grace would be sore for a while.

"You got…a puppy and a pony…without telling me," Jessie was slurring. "I was just…waiting til…you seemed more…open. To…the idea, I mean."

Josh didn't answer. He started running his fingers through his daughter's hair, wondering how the hell he could protect another child, and at the same time, why the hell he would ever resist the idea of creating another life with this beautiful, caring woman he so desperately loved.

"We said…more…like maybe five…we said five…Josh…you'll love this baby, right? You want this baby?"

His chin tipped up, and Josh fixed his glistening eyes on his wife. She was sleepy, all right. He never loved her more, lying there cradling their oldest child after saving her from what could have been a final, frightening fate. "Of course I do," he murmured lovingly. "More than anything." Something mysterious flickered in his eyes, but Jessie was too beat to notice it or to comment on it. "I'm so proud of you, Jessie," he said. "Matt told me what you did."

She didn't respond. Instead, Jessie just mustered up a tiny smile for him, and let her eyes close. Josh stayed put for a few minutes, but when a nurse tiptoed in to check on her patients, Josh asked her to put the rail down behind Jessie, and he climbed up behind her and wrapped his arms around his wife and child.

Matt turned away.

It was much later in the day before he had a chance to see Jessie alone. Charlie and Shanda had dragged Josh off to the cafeteria to practically force feed him. Tiptoeing into Jessie's room, Matt settled in the chair. Emily-Grace was awake now, silent, playing with her mom's fingers. Carefully, she sat up. With Matt's help she climbed into his welcoming, trusted arms, and curled up into a little ball. A large tear rolled down one cheek. Matt kissed it away, and whispered, "I love you."

Jessie watched the tender interaction. She couldn't speak. Raising a hand so her palm faced outward, she held it up and waited for Matt to raise a hand as well. When he clued in to what she was doing, he mimicked her movement and pressed his palm gently against hers. Slow tears were trailing down Jessie's cheeks. Smiling through the pain and terror of a day that was supposed to be fun, she wrapped her fingers tightly around his. Burying her sea-pearl eyes in his much-loved gaze, she brought his hand to her chest and pressed it against her heart.

"Thank you," she whispered. "Thank you."

A slow, sad smile spread across his face. "I'm so proud of you," he managed. "So, so proud of you, girl. You did good. You did so damn good."

Trying to smile back up at him was tough. Jessie glanced down at her daughter in Matt's arms, and back up to him. Her worry was telegraphed loud and clear.

Matt shook his head. He knew she was asking about the puppy. "Couldn't," he choked. "I couldn't let you…" He shook his head.

Jessie swallowed back the pain that devastated her at the idea of Matt choosing her over the puppy, and she nodded. But in her heart was a knowing, a sure and certain knowing, that she was not worth more on this day, to her daughter, than that beautiful white ball of fur.

Matt saw self-loathing flicker across Jessie's face, and he bent forward. "I love you," he told her, her eyelashes like butterfly kisses against his cheek, and Emily-Grace's small body pressed close to his chest. "And don't you ever forget it."

Jessie's fingers let go of his hand at her chest, and buried themselves in Matt's messy spiked hair. Pressing her smooth cheek against his close-shaved one, she nodded. When she finally sighed and let him go, she caught herself absently wondering whether the wetness on her pillow was from her tears, or his.

～ ～

Morgan saw the accident on the local news. He had known he would hear about it, he just didn't expect to see it. What he saw was a crane at the accident site, leaning its viselike arm out over the embankment, hauling Jessie's dripping SUV out of the Elbow River. He shuddered and braced himself for the news.

When the announcer said that Jessie and her daughter survived and were resting comfortably, but that the child's puppy had succumbed, Morgan flipped off the television, lay down on his bunk, turned his body to the cinderblock wall, and shook with relief.

The next day at lunch, Vaughn came to his side again. Caulfield was nowhere in sight. Oren C was not on the schedule; even enforcers like him were occasionally awarded a day off. In Caulfield's usual place against the wall was a stunning black woman. Effusive blue eye shadow that sparkled when it caught the light was bright enough to go so far as to highlight her high cheekbones and gave her slate gray corrections uniform some life. The serious way she was studying Morgan while he studied her back was unsettling.

Her name was Murphy; Morgan never had cause to call her that, but as far as her ID went, that was her, which seemed incongruous to him. Nothing against the name Murphy—he just figured this particular goddess as more of the Dauphina or Latifah or even Beyonce type—she was a corrections officer but she carried an aura of glamour that wasn't fitting in these dungeon-like parts. He had no clue what her first name was. Nobody did. Maybe she had some ritzy, stylish first name that balanced out the more mundane Murphy.

Maybe we oughtta get Caulfield laid, Morgan thought as he pushed peas around his plate with his good left hand. *I bet she'd be willing. Maybe all he needs is a good lay.* The air next to him stirred briskly when Vaughn sat down, as if it was now electric and alive—sizzling, snakelike—where before it was stale and musty.

"We gotta miscommunication, Morgan," Vaughn declared. "You ever listen to Jessie Wheeler's music?"

Morgan scooped up a pea and let it roll off his fork. When it hit the plate, he expected it to land with an eager *whooop,* but it just fell flat. It rolled to a stop and lay lifeless.

Vaughn continued, "My favorite is that Sting cover she does. Fields of Gold." Tapping Morgan on the sleeve, so hard that half of the peas slid off the edge of the plate Morgan was gripping with his white-knuckled left hand, he added, "I listen to it over and over. It's real pretty. My woman loves it."

Glancing up, Morgan saw Murphy curl her lips down. When she narrowed her eyes at him, the blue shadow sparkled like diamonds. Morgan looked back down at his tray and started scooping up spilled peas with fingers so big they crushed the petite vegetables so that when they landed on his plate they lay there all mushy and deadlike.

He was thinking about Caulfield getting laid. He couldn't help but wonder what woman would be brave enough to hook up with the likes of him, or with a terrifying enforcer like Vaughn.

Vaughn cut into his thoughts. "Retribution don't solve shit, kid. Ya won't get no peace that way. Ya hear me? Call Caulfield off the Sawyers. They've had enough."

I can't, Morgan wanted to scream. *I tried.* He wanted to tell Vaughn that Caulfield controlled the numbers in this vicious equation. That Caulfield saw this equalization, as he called it, the pièce de résistance of his entire career. That the man was obsessed with making things as right as he felt they could be in Morgan's fucked up world.

Under the table, Vaughn pulled a small tool out of his pocket. It was a handmade knife, crudely constructed out of some kind of plastic, made by melting something—a dinner tray, maybe, Morgan thought—from which a blade was molded. Sensing the movement, looking down at it, Morgan wasn't sure what it was made from. Didn't really matter. He cringed. The thing looked deadly.

Vaughn played with it under the table, tossing and turning it in his fingers before pressing it against Morgan's thigh and pushing so hard that he cut Morgan's jeans and drew blood.

"Nothing else happens to the Sawyers," he demanded. "If it does, you'll be lying in the morgue next to them. Ya hearin' me?"

Morgan found his voice. "I'm not scared to die," he said. Nadia and his child were long gone from a world Morgan only knew in these current years as sinister and unforgiving. He looked at the peas, and didn't wince when Vaughn pressed the knife against his leg again. In his bandaged right hand, his fingers tensed.

"You should be," Vaughn told him, slicing roughly to the left before bringing his big tree trunk legs up and over the small seat attached to the lunch table. "At the hands of a cutter, ya oughtta be real afraid to die." Vaughn bent down and whispered in Morgan's ear. "I know how to make a guy bleed real slow."

I'm numb, Morgan thought. *I won't feel a thing.* Pressing a good thumb against his leg, he lifted it, and stared at the blood smudged against the tip. He pressed the thumb to his food tray, on top of one last lone pea, lifted it and shoved the thumb in his mouth, the squashed pea clinging to his skin.

Standing, he whipped the tray to the left so the whole thing went flying, and strode away.

Vaughn had moved to the wall and was leaning next to Murphy. Neither of them said a thing, but Vaughn touched the corrections officer's fingers before he lumbered away.

Chapter Thirty-one

Josh couldn't sleep. It was two days after the Lexus was run off the road, and he was wired. Jessie had lain down with Emily-Grace, although to Josh's knowledge, she wasn't sleeping either. Kicking a leftover puppy toy so that it skittered across the floor like a frightened mouse, Josh whipped around and faced Arnie, who was nursing a cup of java at the kitchen island. Matt was half-sitting, half-leaning on the window ledge behind him. Charles and Dee, with Carlotta in tow, had just left for Calgary with Ulysses. The little boys were asleep.

"I need a drink," Josh pleaded. He was burning a hole in the floor with his steady back and forth pacing. "One fucking drink, Arnie."

Matt straightened.

Josh picked up a coloring book and viciously threw it across the room. He voiced his demand again, louder. "I need a fucking drink! I can't—I can't stand my head right now! The things flying around in there—I don't want to see, I don't want to hear, I don't want to even fucking hear the sound of my own breath!"

Arnie pushed his mug aside. His eyes drifted left and landed on a place behind Josh. Jessie was there now. She leaned a shoulder against the door frame and stared back at Arnie, and then her eyes flicked behind him to Matt, before she shifted over to Josh, who turned to face her.

"I can't settle," Josh told her. "I can't stay here and think and think and think, and listen to everybody pretend that my family is not a target. And… and watch Carlotta make cookies after muffins, and muffins after cookies, and listen to the boys fight about their toy cars, and listen to yours and

Emily-Grace's interminable, fucking silences, and not lose my goddamned mind!"

Jessie put her hands in the back pockets of her jeans and walked toward him. Removing one hand, she placed a palm against his cheek and said, "I know how hard this is on you. But you and I—we have a little girl who needs us, who just lost the one creature on this planet she trusted the most, and we have to keep it together, Josh."

"I can't! I can't," he repeated. "We've gotta go back to work. You need to go to Vancouver. I need to go back to *Sacred Peace*. But I can't even see straight right now. One night," he begged. "Let me have one goddamned night."

Behind Josh, Arnie fidgeted on his stool. Interrupting Josh and Jessie was not an option. In the end, Jessie spoke to him first.

"Take him," she ordered. A scared flush rose on her pale cheeks. "Take him and let him drink. At your place, Arnie, supervised, with Charlie nearby." Her eyes swifted back over to her husband. "One night, Josh. Promise me. Get rid of some demons. I'll get Trudy down here, or—or— I'll get her to send you down a prescription for something safe you can take that'll help with the anxiety. But for tonight—just one night. You have to promise me."

The room was eerily silent. Only the crackling of the fire in the hearth, and the occasional hoot of an owl or whisper of wind in the leaves blowing in from outside had anything to offer.

Josh did an inventory of his wife. He started at the bottom of her toes and worked his way up the sweet body he loved beyond all measure. If any-one understood his need to be free of the chains that bonded him to this place—to his life, to his soul tonight—it was her. Jessie was a graduate of Vancouver's notorious Downtown Eastside. She understood the laws of the streets, of what drove people out of their senses and into addictions. She knew what had the power to calm her husband, and she knew what would bring him home.

She punctuated her assent with that. "You are loved, Josh Sawyer," she said, leaning in to press her lips against his. "By me. By your children. Listen to Arnie. Do what he says. And please come home."

"I will." Breathless, humbled by her faith in him, Josh let his hands rise to Jessie's hips. There was one brief moment, one sweet pause, in which he thought he might stay, and in which Jessie prayed he would.

But then Josh lifted a hand, placed it behind her neck, kissed her hard, with a desperation and longing that frightened both of them, and he left, grabbing his truck keys and avoiding Matt's judging eyes on the way.

Jessie's heart picked up its pace. Scared now, she called out to Arnie as he spun around on the high chair and grabbed his jacket from the back. "Text me, Arnie," she demanded. "And for God's sake keep him in the condo."

Arnie fired her a rare withering, heated look that Jessie shrank away from. His jacket dangling from his fingers, he stopped at the door and turned back to her. "He's a grown man, Jessie. Ultimately what he does is up to him. You know this better than anyone—you can't save a man who's drowning unless he wants to be saved." A few seconds later, the screen door slammed shut behind him with its usual gunshot crack. The truck fired to life, flinging gravel every which way when Josh threw it into gear and stomped on the gas. It was rumbling furiously down the lane when Jessie let her sorrowful eyes drift over to Matt.

Exhaling with a low *pfffft*, he heaved his body away from the window ledge and wandered over to her. "He's been losing it all day, Jessie. For the last few days, in fact. I'm not surprised."

"Me either." She held out a hand. "Please," she begged. "Come lie down with me and Emily-Grace. I don't want to be alone right now."

Matt only hesitated for a second. Taking her outstretched hand, he followed Jessie into the master bedroom, where she and Josh often made love, where their daughter was asleep on the big bed, one small arm curled around her beloved singer-dolly, an old worn bunny blanket under one pale pink cheek.

Jessie curled around her daughter and felt Matt's body sigh into hers when he lay behind her. Tucking a hand into his, she closed her eyes.

"My dad…maybe we made things even," she murmured. "He drowned. We survived. Maybe we evened things out between us, with the universe, I mean."

A sickening twist seized Matt's belly. Squeezing his eyes tightly shut, he tried not to think about evening things out. He tried not to think about

Morgan's vicious game, and vengeance and redemption and how all this crap could possibly ever come to some kind of reasonable, safe fruition that would give this beautiful scared family peace, once and for all.

With her back to Matt, with the even coming and going of his breath giving a gentle rise and fall to his chest, Jessie let her statement about her dad go unanswered. The warmth and comfort of Matt's beloved body soothed her, and the love in his spirit gave her rest.

Charlie took off running down the hall to Arnie's condo after the building's superintendent rapped sharply at his door.

"You better come," the gray haired man said. He was so keyed up that Charlie half expected him to take flight. "Sounds like your security man's come to blows with someone."

"Great," Charlie grumbled under his breath as he jogged quickly down the dimly lit hallway. It was midnight, and he'd been at paperwork all day, some of it funding related, and some of it juggling scenes to accommodate Josh's absence from set. "I'll handle it," he said to the super.

The guy, Stan, was hovering like a nervous bumblebee at Charlie's side. This was an elite building—not the kind of place where your average Joe could afford a condo. Stan didn't need physical altercations happening in the building he was hired to oversee. Stan especially didn't need guys like Arnie, reputed to have connections in sketchy places, upsetting his neighbors in the middle of the night by fist fighting and hollering and throwing things around.

Charlie whirled around. "I said I'd handle it!" he yelled. Quieting, pushing his palms downwards in a calming motion, he apologized. "I'm sorry, Stan," he said. "Don't call the police, buddy. Please. I know Arnie, I'll sort this out." What Charlie didn't tell Stan, who Charlie was relieved to see turn around and start walking back toward the elevator, scowling in a stuck-up aristocratic way with one corner of his lip turned down and thick gray eyebrows angled toward the floor, was that Josh Sawyer was likely the guy Arnie was fighting with. Arnie had drummed on Charlie's door when they first landed from the ranch—*to warn me*, Charlie supposed. Hell, if the paperwork hadn't demanded his attention, Charlie would have been in there too, downing glass after glass of booze with his buddies.

Outside Arnie's condo, Charlie raised a hand and hammered on the door. The loud voices within stopped immediately. When Arnie yanked the door open and left it hanging for Charlie to grab before it closed in his face, Charlie's eyes widened in astonishment. The dining table lay on an end, rosewood legs stuck out like toothpicks; magazines were scattered across the floor; a pizza box, tented upside down, had dominion in the middle of the main room, its single forgotten slice bleeding tomato sauce like water.

Worse, the nerve on Josh's cheek was vibrating. He was red-faced and furious, but there was something else at play in the way he was pacing and circling the room like a boxer—a desperate kind of worry. And layered deeply underneath his torment, a certain indefinable calm that Charlie, for all intents and purposes, could not put his finger on.

Arnie was shaking. One of his fists had landed on Josh's shoulder, according to the way Josh was angrily rubbing it.

Charlie stormed further into the condo. Speechless, he watched the men lock eyes at a distance of ten feet. Josh stopped his anxious pacing and anchored his heels into Arnie's floor. Disgust and torment colored Arnie's usual unruffled countenance; a kind of warning—*not to say anything?*—sparked across Josh's fiery eyes.

Empties littered the counter. Beer cans. Alongside them was a bottle of Jessie's old standby, Jim Beam. An abandoned half full crystal tumbler sat ignored, its power crippled without trembling knuckles gripping it, willing it to medicate, eradicate, destroy.

Jabbing a finger somewhere in the air between the two guys, Charlie fumed, "You know, there are some people in this building who believe in the promise and renewal of a good night's sleep. Especially on a weeknight, boys."

No answer. Neither Josh nor Arnie looked away from each other. Lightning flashed between them, so concentrated that Charlie later swore he saw flaming blue heat.

Charlie tried again. "You mind tellin' me what the hell you two assholes been fighting about?"

Josh backed up. He grabbed the deserted crystal tumbler and, linking his eyes back into Arnie's, tipped it back and emptied it in one good swallow. "I'm outta here." A smoldering rage flashed in his eyes. "I'm so fucking sick of this shit." Spinning around, he grabbed his jean jacket from where he'd tossed it on the nearby couch and started toward the door, hauling the jacket on as he moved.

Charlie grabbed his arm and swung him around. "No way, Sawyer," he protested. "You're not leaving." Scrunching Josh's jacket up where he was clutching it, panic infused Charlie's voice. He tried hauling a fired-up Josh back into the room, while at the same time trying hopelessly to rally Arnie into action. "Arnie, little help here?"

Arnie stood rooted to the spot. "Get your own damn help," he spat. "I'm done."

Josh stopped trying to fight Charlie off. In his mind, a single bullet left his brain, gob smacked Arnie's usually gentle eyes, then reverberated its way back to Josh. It was a deliberate and final last spike on the hostility dividing them that night, and it ended the impasse.

The nerve on Josh's cheek slowed to a more reasonable pace. "Then I guess we're on the same page," he muttered. Shaking Charlie off, he stormed out of the door and down the hallway toward the elevators.

Stunned, Charlie took in Arnie's stiff posture—the big hands in his coat pockets, the steadfast way he had difficulty swallowing before fixing Charlie in his sight.

"What the hell just happened here?!" Charlie was torn between tearing after Josh and trying to reason with Arnie, who they—all of them—so desperately needed during these insane, unpredictable days.

Charlie didn't wait to find out. Jessie flew into his mind. The kids. Cursing at Arnie, he took after Josh and swung into the elevator with him just before the sliding door shut him out completely. Josh wouldn't look at him. It didn't matter. The condo building was downtown. They were mere blocks from bars. Charlie strode alongside Josh until they found one that looked tenable, and he went inside and got roaring drunk.

Chapter Thirty-Two

$\mathcal{A}$rnie didn't bother texting Charles or Matt, or calling Jessie to tell her he'd quit. He shoved jeans, shirts and his shaving kit into his duffle bag and hailed a cab for the airport. By dawn he was back in Vancouver making love to his wife, Lucie, and wondering why the hell he ever agreed to work security for the Keatings in the first place.

Matt checked his phone when he rose in the morning. Astounded, he faced Jessie with grim eyes and thin, pressed lips. They were at the island, Matt on a high chair and Jessie about to rustle them up some coffee. Alin had just driven up from Calgary with Deirdre and Carlotta. They were helping the boys get dressed so they could send them outside with Gary to ride the pony. A glum Emily-Grace was lingering by her mother's side, her favorite pink bunny blanket wound around her fingers, and singer-dolly clutched to her chest. She wasn't dressed yet. At the troubled look crisscrossing Matt's face, Jessie blinked and bent to her daughter just as Deirdre approached from across the open concept space.

"Honey, go with Grammie to find something to wear. Momma needs to make Matt some coffee this morning. He looks like he needs a cup. Or three."

Emily-Grace let out a small whine and snuggled her face into her mother's side. Jessie stooped down so she could face her straight on. "Sweetheart, please. I really need a few minutes with Matt." Her heart was starting to race. Could things get any worse?

"You had all night with him," Emily-Grace announced, her face pinking up in confusion. "He slept with us!"

Carlotta didn't overhear, she was in the master bedroom tidying up the bed and gathering laundry, but both Alin and Deirdre paused at the child's declaration. Neither had the bad taste to say anything directly addressing the topic, although Deirdre did manage to toss in a quiet, "Where's Josh this morning, Jessie? I didn't see his truck. Did he go to set?"

Sulking, Jessie threw her a look that was meant to mean *I wish* but which bordered on frustration. "No," she replied. "He's not at work. I don't think." Casting a hopeful glance at Matt, she frowned, stood, and leaned both elbows on the kitchen island when the angst in Matt's eyes clearly read *No way.* "Emily-Grace," Jessie refocused, looking sideways at her daughter, "go get dressed and go out to the barn to see the kittens. I bet Precious and her babies are missing you."

"No. I don't wanna see the kittens, Momma. I hate Precious."

Jessie groaned and laid her forehead on the island. "Oh, Lordy. Dee? Help?"

Grammie Dee came to the rescue. "We don't need to go see Precious just yet. We can pick some wild strawberries and make us all strawberry short-cake for lunch." It was a warm day. The new pool was heated, and should have been welcome. Its watery depths however, made it not in the least desirable. Deirdre pushed the idea of swimming aside and lovingly took Emily-Grace's hand in hers. Before going to the little girl's bedroom in search of daytime clothes to replace the nightgown, she said to Jessie, "When you're ready, we need to talk about the film in Montreal."

"Not yet," Jessie croaked. "I'm not ready to talk about that yet."

Deirdre wrapped her fingers tighter around Emily-Grace's. "It's a good thing," she said, gesturing toward Jessie's abdomen. "I'm just not sure about the film, honey. They'll likely want to recast. They'll have to."

"Don't say—" Jessie gulped. She gave Emily-Grace a look. The kids, as yet, didn't know about the new baby.

"We'll talk later." With Emily-Grace walking quietly beside her, big eyes luminous and afraid, Deirdre walked away.

When they were out of earshot, Jessie forced her eyes away from their backs, crooked a hand on a hip and sullenly faced Matt. "What now?"

Matt held up his phone. "A text from Charlie. He and Josh are both taking the day off work today. They're sleeping off their wild night at the bars."

"They went out? Charlie went with him? I'm gonna kill Arnie!" Clenching her hands into fists, Jessie tried to stay calm. All night she had mulled over the disappointed glint in Arnie's eyes when she asked him—well, told him, really—to let her alcoholic husband drink.

"You can't."

"What?" Jessie would have hit the panic button except that Matt didn't look upset in that kind of way; he just seemed overwhelmed, overall. "I can't kill Arnie? You're scaring me, Matt."

Tossing his phone on the island, Matt raised the opposite palm. "Whoa there, girl. Not what I meant. Arnie's not around to kill. That's what I meant. According to Charlie, Arnie's taking a break. Charlie thinks he's gone back to Vancouver."

"What?" Astounded, Jessie took a step back. "What the hell? What did Josh do?"

"Pissed him off, I guess. Let me try calling Charlie." Sliding off his chair, Matt picked up his phone and moved off toward the sun porch. Jessie had the coffee made by the time he came back. "All Charlie knows is they had a fight," Matt reported. "A, well, a physical fight, apparently. But Josh isn't talking. And it would seem Arnie isn't either."

"Surprise, surprise," Jessie grumbled. "Who do I kill first, then? Charlie or my husband?"

"Nobody," Matt determined as he accepted a mug of coffee from Jessie. "But be prepared. Dan's off today, his wife's in Calgary for a few days, and Sam's on the night shift here tonight. Ulysses is with Charles, trying to step up security for your Vancouver trip. I might have to run into Calgary later."

Jessie's voice softened. She warmed her hands on her coffee mug before she spoke to Matt again. "We can't let him drink again. Right, Matt? You'll go get Josh and bring him back here with us, where he'll see us and know we love him and where he won't be tempted to drink again. He'll be so damned sick today that he'll never want to anyway, right?"

Matt stirred cream into his coffee. It floated there like melting snow, hopeful and pure until it lost its substance and disappeared. "Right," he said, unable to look at her. Lifting his mug a few seconds later, he took a sip, set the mug down with a thud, and grimaced. "I don't know how you people can drink this stuff," he complained, "and enjoy it. Pure jet fuel. It'll rot the guts right out of a man."

"I know how," Jessie answered honestly. "You place it between your lips, suck it back, and swallow."

At that, she took a sip of her own dark drug, recoiled when she took too big of a sip and burnt her tongue, and sent a silent prayer to her husband.

A cellphone ring jarred Charlie awake at three in the afternoon. His bedroom in the Calgary condo was dark; the day had begun with the promise of sunshine, but over the last few hours, clouds moved in and stole the light. Outside was gray and rainy now, the kind of spring day ducks like the best. The lack of sun made Charlie's room dim and lifeless. Everything was a dreary, creepy shadow—even the jeans he tossed on the floor at some point during the night were a scrunched-up mystery. Charlie had no recollection of pushing them down over his hips and taking them off.

The way he saw it last night, if Josh was getting drunk, well he sure as hell felt like numbing the pain too. Jane was in Canmore with their children. Charlie had called her on the way to the first bar. Rarely did Jane stand in the way of helping their friends—her heart was golden. Her sincere love and affection for Jessie and Josh ran nearly as deep as Charlie's. But last night on the phone, she was nervous. And she had a right to be, because Charlie's voice was a hollow ring instead of his usual frustrated determination and confidence. Still, Jane came through for him, and didn't pile on the guilt like Charlie half expected her to.

Now, rolling over onto his back and groaning loudly, he wished to hell she'd given him shit. Maybe he would have listened, and not tried to match Josh drink for drink. But hell, sometimes a guy just needed to throw in the towel and let go. None of the usual Keating-Sawyer security was with him and Josh last night. Today Josh would be bruised and sore. Vaguely, Charlie recalled harsh words being spat at them in some redneck cowboy club. Soon after, there were fists and curses, a lot of curses. Thankfully, some *Sacred Peace* fans were there. Someone knew someone on the crew—a grip, Charlie thought. It wasn't more than fifteen minutes before half a dozen *Sacred Peace* grips and electrics showed up at the club, and thank God too, because the guys Josh was mouthing off to were determined to teach his rogue ass a lesson.

The cell's irritating cry, a classic phone ring, was still cutting into Charlie's brain, splitting it in two. For a second or two the punitive noise eased, thankfully, so Charlie could lie back and moan pitifully, but then it started again, urgent and demanding.

"The things I do for my friends," he griped, swinging his legs over the side of his bed and cursing from the way the simple motion made his head pound and his gut cringe. Nearby was a deep charcoal gray designer chair. Charlie's quilted black Columbia jacket was lying limply over the back of it. It seemed so far away—his scramble was more of a bent over hunchback crawl, but he managed to grab it, collapse back on the bed, and start fishing in the pockets for his phone.

Jessie, blazed the caller ID.

With a wry twist of his lips, Charlie punched the green 'answer' icon. "Why you messin' up my beauty sleep?" he rasped into it, skipping the courtesy of prefacing his comments with a hello. "Wake your hunky husband up instead."

"Duh, Charlie, it's three o'clock in the afternoon. Musta been some party."

The worry in her voice cut Charlie's next sharp comment off before he loosed it from his weary voice box. Sitting back against the headboard, physically lifting his legs up onto the bed with his free hand, he gave an exaggerated moan instead. "Ohhh, my aching head. Josh better be feeling just as bad."

"He is, Charlie. Trust me. Or he wouldn't have gone drinking in the first place."

Charlie sighed and mumbled an apology. "Sorry, Jess." He dug three fingers and a thumb into his forehead and rubbed, hard. The self-applied massage didn't do a damn thing to quash his suffocating headache. "You should be prepared, when you see him," he warned. "I seem to recall some hulking bastard in a black cowboy hat coming at us with fists cocked and guns blazing."

"Great. We'll make a good pair."

"You feelin' any better, sunshine?"

"Nope. Supposedly my ribs are bruised from the airbag and the seatbelt, but I can't feel 'em. They're all mushed up with the agony in the rest of my body. And don't waste your breath asking about Emily-Grace. She's every bit as sore. And then some. She's one mad, scared little girl."

Jessie was standing in the sun porch, watching Gary walk the boys around the clearing on the pony while Alin and Matt watched. These days, Dylan spent every minute he could on horseback. David's boredom with other activities dictated his participation. Dylan could already ride without an escort, but David was timid. Emily-Grace was watching them, her bunny blanket and singer-dolly clutched in one hand, and the second hand tucked securely into Matt's warm fingers. Carlotta and Deirdre were outside too, chatting with Evelyn about a peculiar infestation of striped beetles in the cucumbers. Evelyn had a container of cayenne pepper in one hand; her cure-all for garden pests. Jessie found herself wishing she could manifest a huge man-sized container in which she could soundly and completely bury Morgan.

Behind Jessie, back in the kitchen, was the detritus of a late lunch. She'd get to the dishes in a minute. Waiting to hear from Josh was no longer viable. She'd promised herself to let him sleep it off til at least noon, and prided herself on not jumping on him until now. But there was a problem.

Charlie was starting to mumble something about hoping his girls were feeling better, when Jessie cut in. "He's not answering his phone, Charlie. He's with you, right?"

"Huh? Yeah. We stumbled home sometime after two. Alone, in case you're wondering, not by lack of many invitations, by the way, which I lost count of after your husband's invites quadrupled mine. Man, that guy pisses me off—"

"Charlie! Dammit!"

"Okay, okay. Awright, lemme think. We got pizza, I think, or was it some kind of Mediterranean thing? That was after the curbside sausages, his was German and mine was spiced up with Italian magic, or maybe it just tasted funny because of the booze…"

"Can you just—"

"I'm on it. Easy, girl-child. He's likely just deep in slumber, lost in some sweet dream about the beautiful girl he stole from me. Gimme a sec." Padding out into the hallway in his boxers, Charlie yawned and scratched his stomach while he walked. Josh's bedroom door was halfway open. Charlie gave it a push. "Sawyer. Your woman's on the phone." He peeked in. It took a few seconds for his eyes to adjust. Josh's room looked the same as Charlie's in the eerie gray light. A few bits and pieces were tossed here and there—clothes Josh hastily shed when he got home in the middle of the night. Jeans, a T-shirt, a hoodie.

Charlie stepped into the room and tried to focus on the bed. It was unmade, a rumpled mussed up mess. At first it was hard to tell if there was a body in it, then Charlie's brain sorted out what he was seeing. Scratching his nose, he sauntered further into the room and took a good look around.

Over the phone came Jessie's voice, too calm. "Give him a boot in the arse, Charlie. Wake up his goddamned ass."

"Hmmpph," Charlie returned.

"And how the Jesus am I supposed to interpret that?" Outside at the ranch, Matt was lifting Emily-Grace onto the pony. Jessie saw him try to take her singer-dolly and blanket from her, but she was holding fast to them. Gary led her around the yard as, from the corral, Toby and Misty watched from underneath large horsey eyelashes, totally unconcerned.

Matt pivoted around and scanned the sun porch for Jessie. She leaned her forehead against the window and emitted a long, slow *grrrrr*. Her buddy was walking toward the house when Jessie heard Charlie finally say, from a confused spot in the center of his living room, "He's not here, Jess. I'm gonna hazard a guess that he went out to round us up some coffee."

"Are you. That's what you're guessing, is it Charlie? Jesus Christ. Jesus H fucking Christ."

Matt was inside now, standing at the entry to the sun porch, watching Jessie struggle with the tough emotions engendered by dealing with a troubled husband suffering from a constant battle with addictions, and from the acute anxiety of a slow burning terror they barely understood, which had sent Josh spiraling back to the desperate need to be numb in the first place.

"Jessie?" he asked quietly.

Ignoring him, into the phone Jessie said, "Just call me if he comes back, okay? Or if you hear from him?"

"What the hell'd you want me to do, Jessie? Snuggle up with him? Chain him to the bed?" Hungover and disgusted with himself, Charlie dropped down onto the couch and bent over.

"Yeah, Charlie, that's exactly what I expected."

"You know what, kid? I'm not Josh's security. I'm not his babysitter. He's a big boy."

"You suck, Charlie. Thanks for your understanding."

"I've been a goddamned saint for you, Jessie. Don't patronize me. I've got a headache the size of Calcutta and a stomach about to—"

"Oh, poor Charlie," Jessie soundly—sarcastically—cut him off. "Poor, poor Charlie. My heart's breaking for you." A quiet choke followed by a sniffle zipped through the line.

"Awww, dammit. Jessie…"

"Look, I gotta go. I'll be on your doorstep by suppertime." She paused. "Charlie, I'm sorry you always get dragged into our problems. I'm real sorry *Sacred Peace's* shooting schedule is all fucked up this week. You've been great. Really. You're always great."

Charlie started to add, "I'm sorry too, I suck," but the line beeped its three little exit blips and Jessie was gone.

In Calgary, curled over himself on the couch, picking out a dust ball on the floor, Charlie let his eyes go out of focus and contemplated going back to bed. In the end he decided against it in favor of hearing the voice and reason of his greatest fan instead. Staring down the condo's small hallway to the open door of Josh's empty bedroom, he speed dialed his wife.

At the ranch, Jessie stirred up her courage and faced another man who would do anything to help her, but whom Jessie felt was, far too often, dragged under a truck by hers and Josh's issues. Shoulders caving in, she said to Matt, who was idly watching her with an air of almost detached, unconcerned acceptance, "All right. I'm going to Calgary. I need to see my husband."

"You need to rest. Your body needs to heal."

"Josh took off, Matt. Surprise fucking surprise." Leaning her forehead against the window again, relishing the coolness of the glass against her aching head, Jessie closed her eyes. A small voice made its way to Matt's ears. "Did you have any luck figuring out what Josh and Arnie were fighting about?"

"Arnie won't take my calls. He won't take anyone's calls."

Letting her eyes flit open, still leaning against the cool glass, Jessie angled her head around to look at him. "Musta been some fight."

"If you go to Calgary, I'm going with you."

Jessie considered that, but ended up shaking her head. "Maybe not this time, honey. Maybe I'll just put on my old gray hoodie and go incognito, okay?"

"Not an option, Jessie."

"I need to borrow your car. It's a little wet and cold out there for the old Mustang."

"You can borrow my car, with me at the wheel."

"Matt…you've done so much. All of you guys, you bend over backward to help us. Maybe this time Josh and I need to sort out some shit on our own."

"What kind of shit? The 'how the hell do I get Morgan to back down' shit? That's not something you and your rebel husband can do on your own, Jessie."

"Maybe it is. I think—I think Josh has a plan. I think that's why he was fighting with Arnie."

"He was likely fighting with Arnie over wanting to go out to the bars."

"Arnie wouldn't leave because of that. He's a tough guy."

"Not that tough, Jessie. None of us are so tough these days."

Straightening, Jessie eyed Matt carefully. Sure enough, there were cracks in his façade. His clothes were practically still leaking water from that horrible day when she went into the river, when he had no choice but to dive down and stare helplessly at her and her daughter from the outside of a completely submerged vehicle.

"Babe," she said softly. "You think that's why Arnie's gone AWOL? He's running scared?" She shook her head again. "You don't know Arnie. He's seen and heard it all. There's nothing left that can frighten him."

"Yes, there is. Loving your family—trying to protect you when you're under siege like this—it scares him. Especially when the head of your family is falling apart. Arnie feels helpless."

"Maybe he just wanted to see Lucie. He misses her. She's quiet, but she's his rock. And just for the record, Josh isn't falling apart. He promised me. He just needed a break from the sadness. That's all. One night." Abruptly, Jessie started out of the sun porch. She had to brush by Matt to leave the room.

He grabbed her arm as she attempted to pass. "Jessie…"

"No," she snapped, with more of an edge to her voice than she intended. "Some things are between Josh and me, Matt. I'll call you from Calgary. If you need a ride somewhere, take Dan's car."

"What are you afraid of? What I might see? What I might hear?"

"What you will see, sweet Matt, is me trolling the streets looking for my tragic husband. What you might hear is me begging him to come back to the ranch with me, to grow some balls and help me figure this out instead of continuing to withdraw, to run away."

"Fear does hard time on a man, Jessie. Fear takes a man and fritters away at his balls. You take a man like Josh—"

"I know all about Josh, Matt! I know everything there is to know about him." Jessie tried to shake off Matt's arm but he tightened his grip. "Look. I took a chance on him when the whole world said he was worthless, and he's had to prove his worth to that dark world again and again. But you know something? He's never had to prove it to me. I know what he's worth. I look into those eyes and I see the most beautiful soul on earth. I look into those eyes and I see love, that's what I see. He can drown himself in booze for all I care, if it takes the pain away. But I want him doing it under my watch, where I can hold him while he pukes. Where I can make sure he's safe."

Frustrated, Matt let go of her arm. "You've got kids, Jessie. Scared little kids who don't need to see that kind of breakdown in a marriage."

She guffawed loudly. "You call that a breakdown? A husband in need of his wife? I call that love, Matt. Not abandoning Josh when he needs me the most, is love."

"He abandoned *you*." Matt said the words so quietly that Jessie had to hold her breath and process the movement of his lips.

"Not this time, honey," she replied, raising her chin and looking down at him through glistening eyelashes. "No, this time he just needed a little break from the pain. That's all. And I need a fucking drive."

Matt was leaning against the driver's door of the Audi ten minutes later when Jessie left the house in an old gray hoodie, ratty sneakers and jeans. A knapsack slung over her shoulder, she was leaving with hugs and worried blessings from Carlotta, Dee and Evelyn, and from the kids and Alin. Sam was just trundling up the lane.

Jessie stopped twenty feet back from Matt. "Are we gonna fight about this?"

He held his arms out to the sides. "Try to get past me."

"I'll kick you in the goddamn balls." He didn't budge. Jessie switched tactics. "I need some privacy, Matt," she begged. "I need music. The loud kind."

"I've already got that Metallica ballad playlist you like plugged in and ready to go." Leaning into the car, Matt withdrew a thermos and held it up to her. "Coffee. With an extra dose of Baileys." Leaning in again, he replaced the coffee in a cup holder and pulled out a fluffy blanket and pillow. Biting his lip, he sent her his best hopeful puppy dog look.

That did it. Jessie broke. Rolling her eyes, she slipped around the car and tossed the knapsack in the back seat. "You must think you know me," she protested, but a gossamer mist lit up her eyes in the gray day. Turning, she called out to her children, "Who wants more hugs?" Kneeling in the dirt, Jessie winced in pain as she held Dylan and David, together, close to her body. Emily-Grace was next. Jessie stood to hold her, and they hugged cautiously, careful not to ruffle any sore spots.

Emily-Grace spied Matt sliding in behind the driver's seat. Her eyes started to swim. "You're both going? In the same car? Will Daddy be home soon?"

Oh, Jesus. "Sweetheart," Jessie said in her best *I'm sorry* voice, "Matt's a good driver. He will do his best to get us safely to Calgary, and home again. Remember what Momma says about worrying?"

"That it doesn't do anyone any good."

"That's right. We are Sawyers, and we are strong. Now one last hug and a kiss too." She brushed her lips against her daughter's soft cheek. "I will be home real soon." As she was getting in the car, Jessie looked back at her daughter, all small and sad, standing by the barn. "I think you and me need some music, sweetheart," she said. "What is it I always say about music?" Her dad's words to her, when she was just a tad younger than Emily-Grace, came to mind.

"Music has the power to heal." Emily-Grace spoke in a timorous childlike singsong voice, with a serious understanding glint in her small eyes that said she'd gotten that memo before, and that she respected it. She was holding singer-dolly and her bunny blanket close to her chest. "We'll play some music when you get back home?"

"I can do you one better than that, honey. How about you come to Vancouver with me this trip? We'll leave the boys with Daddy." Behind the car, Matt blanched at that lovely idea. It seemed Josh was once again barely capable of taking care of himself. "Jacob will be there," Jessie added, "and we'll drop by the workshop space to do some dancing with Kayla and her crew. Grammie's coming back to La Casa too, and Carlotta."

A small smile worked its way across Emily-Grace's worried face. "Thanks, Momma," she said. "I'll come with you."

When Matt pulled out and pointed the Audi's nose down the lane, Jessie visibly relaxed. Snuggling the pillow Matt so thoughtfully brought for her in close to her body, she let out a breath and said, "It's one bloody day at a time in the Sawyer camp, isn't it, Matt? One bloody second at a time." But, like her daughter, she was smiling too. Reaching down, she took Matt's fingers in hers and brushed a thumb over them. "But this particular second? It's okay. For the most part, it's okay. At least…it'll be okay. I can feel it."

They turned left at the end of the laneway, and right at the end of the gravel road. An hour later, Matt cruised into the underground parking lot of the condo where much of the *Sacred Peace* gang stayed when late nights and early mornings demanded the out of town people get a little extra shut-eye. Half an hour later, with a slinking, tired, hungover Charlie in tow, they went looking for Josh.

Chapter Thirty-three

Matt laid eyes on Josh first, but not until shortly before midnight, and not until they were all completely soaked by a cool, unforgiving rain. They'd tried the clubs first, and heard of a few sightings, but it wasn't until the three started wandering down sketchy alleys graffitied with dragons and big, bold lettering announcing everything from the beauty of the world to its utter downfall, that Josh came into view.

Matt didn't holler for Jessie and Charlie until he knelt by Josh first and took a quick body scan. Josh, slumped back against the exterior brick of a restaurant, was breathing, but he was barely responsive. Slapping him on the cheek, trying to revive him so he could get a better feel for what they were dealing with, Matt spoke loudly. "Wake up, buddy. Time to go now. Party's over."

Josh's eyes fluttered open but he had a hard time keeping them that way. His face was wet from the rain, and the droplets sticking to his skin—some trickling down his cheeks like tears—unnerved Matt, given Jessie's watery struggle a few short days earlier. "Aw, Jesus, Matt," Josh slurred. "Puhleeze… tell me…Jezzie's not here."

"Damn straight she's here, Josh. She's worried sick."

"I donnn need her…seein' me….like this…"

"Sure you do," Matt grumbled, trying to keep hostility from coloring his thoughts but unable to refrain from thinking how much better he could be for Jessie and the kids than this man who, in all likelihood, would be struggling with addictions his entire life. A reminder of what Josh had told him at the hospital, about being asked to choose which of his children should—well, die—and the ensuing guilt Josh was carrying about having Emily-Grace float across his mind at that moment, snuck up on Matt. He softened, and added in a much kinder tone, "You know your girl, Josh. Jessie only wants you close to her. She will never judge you."

"She's too…damn good…for me. Too…damn good."

"She's a goddamned hero, in my books. Let's get you up, buddy. Let's get you home." Hooking his arm under Josh's bicep, Matt started to help Josh rise. At the same time, he called out, "Charlie! Jessie! I've got him. Here."

They came running.

Standing back, slowing as she approached, Jessie let her eyes drift over her husband as Charlie vaulted forward to help Matt hoist Josh to an upward position. Even in the rain, it was clear that he had pissed himself. The stench of urine in the alley was much stronger where Josh hung back against the brick, suspended against the wall by his friends like a longhaired, sorrowful Jesus. Vomit had dribbled down his chin and left a filthy trail on his jean jacket and on his white T-shirt and jeans. Swallowing, Jessie thought of their children as she stepped forward. She prayed they would never have to see their father this way, so…vulnerable. So hurt.

Standing in front of her husband, she lifted her left hand and placed it against his bristly cheek. The vomit didn't concern her. It stunk, he stunk; but she hardly cared. Josh was here, alive, and so damn sad and scared of something she still didn't quite understand, that all she cared to do was hold him and tell him he was loved. She did that—lifting her right hand, Jessie stroked back Josh's damp hair and bent forward to press her cold lips against his.

His eyes had closed, partly from fatigue and a bone deep weariness, but mostly from self-loathing and bitter, repulsive shame. Now, feeling his wife's essence, her aura, her body, so close to him; feeling those beautiful, sweet, loving lips press against his—tasting of the cherry lip balm Jessie'd nervously applied over and over again all evening—on this, one of the lowest points of Josh's life, was a remarkable testament to the capacity Jessie had for loving, and for forgiving, him.

Josh's eyes opened and melted into hers. The things that hurt him were not things he had any control over. The way he responded to those hurts was beyond his earthly power of control.

"So in love with you," Jessie murmured to him, and laid a damp cheek against Josh's cool face when his knees buckled and his eyes squeezed shut with remorse and sorrow.

Behind Jessie's back, Matt and Charlie glanced at each other, but only for a second. They had both long been witness to the deep love these two shared. Both had a respect for Josh that was earned over time, partly for his love for Jessie, and partly for who he was as a person, most days. Many women would have given up on him before they even got started. But not Jessie. Jessie had lifted Josh right from the start, from the very first night she followed him out to Charlie's garbage. Jessie had a lot of love in her heart; she shared it widely, with everyone. But when it came to Josh, the beauty in her soul radiated an effervescent, transcendent energy that went way beyond the bonds of earth. Watching her with Josh now, her body almost glowed, from the inside out.

Back at the condo, Jessie led the guys toward the large bathroom. From the time they found Josh, she hadn't spoken to either Charlie or Matt. The men were also quiet, subdued and humbled by Jessie's unconditional acceptance of Josh's sad state of disrepair on this wet, cold, Calgary night. Now, she directed Matt and Charlie to steer her stumbling husband toward the shower. Together, they braced him face first against the tiled wall. Josh helped as much as he could. He was not the fighter Charlie had on his hands last night. Tonight he was weakened, weary, and wholly trusting of the way his wife was ministering to his needs.

He was wholly trusting of her.

Jessie started peeling off Josh's soiled jean jacket. Charlie took hold of a cuff and helped her pull it down over Josh's hand.

"Toss his clothes in the wash," Jessie demanded soberly without looking at Charlie. "Matt, hang on to him so he doesn't fall over. Please."

Josh was standing as tall as he could in the shower, trying to appear strong. His eyes were closed and he was leaning against the tile, braced on his forearms, which he held above his bowed head once the jacket was off as if they could tent him from the remorse and regret of this hopeless night, from the degrading humiliation he knew he would see in the eyes of Matt and Charlie if he dared open his own eyes long enough to look.

"Charlie, look in the pockets first," he heard Jessie say. "Jacket and jeans.

Might need to run a few extra cycles. The wash, I mean. To get the stains out." *Stains,* thought Josh dully. *What stains?* It occurred to his muggy, fuzzy brain that he had, somewhere along the line, pissed himself.

Slim arms were around his waist now, from behind, undoing his wide leather belt, messing with the engraved silver buckle Jessie picked up in Texas and gave him one Christmas. Josh had a collection of those now.

His fly. Now the small hands were unzipping his fly, taking the smidgen of pride Josh had left down, down, down with the small zipper. Before Jessie pulled on his jeans to bring them down over his hips, she grasped the bottom hem of his T-shirt and carefully lifted it over his head.

Matt had to help her maneuver Josh's heavy, uncooperative arms.

The T-shirt landed in a grungy clump on the shower floor. Josh stared at it, unsure and weaving as he tried to stay upright, when all he really wanted to do was slide to the ground, to the drain, so he could slink his lonely way inside its dank, dark hole.

"May as well turn the shower on," Jessie said to Charlie, who had the best access to the faucet at the time. "Be sure it's not too cold. Or too hot."

Josh felt her hands at his waist again. Leaning closer to the tile, he laid his forehead against it, and wondered why Jessie was wincing in pain as she moved his jeans, together with his boxers, down over his legs. She encouraged him to lift his foot—the right one, and then the left. Naked now, his jeans shoved aside with Jessie's careful hand, Josh stooped lower, bowing to the warm shower Charlie started for him. It was everything he could do to continue to draw breaths here in this excruciating moment, with Matt and Charlie witness to his defeat, in the knowing that Jessie, after all she'd just been through, did not deserve this—did not deserve his weakness, like blood, on her hands. She had saved their daughter, for God's sake. Calmed her, comforted her, talked her through exiting a dark, drowning car. Emily-Grace, who Josh…

No, I will not allow myself to remember the darkness surrounding my daughter's light, pretty face. Of the terror that accompanied her image when she appeared in my brain that night when Matt and I were jumped.

Fully dressed minus the hoodie, Jessie stood behind Josh in the shower as the soothing water calmed and restored him as best it could. *Funny how water can be so unthreatening,* she thought. *Even healing.* She could feel the tension leave Josh's body as he stood there propped against the tile, his eyes closed, droplets falling from his eyelashes like tears. With one arm wrapped tightly around his middle, Jessie used the other to draw a bar of soap over his broad back and toned stomach. She ran a finger lightly over the new bruises on his body. One was from Arnie. A few were courtesy of some fired-up rogue cowboys.

"Shampoo," she whispered to Charlie, who sprang to attention and dumped a splotch of coconut shampoo in Jessie's upturned palm. Lathering it into her husband's hair, Jessie was glad for the water pouring over them all, because it meant Matt and Charlie wouldn't know she was crying.

They did anyway, because Jessie's shoulders were shaking and her pretty lips were turned down while she worked the shampoo through the vomit that somehow got its way into her husband's layered hair.

Soon it was time to rinse out the soapy suds and with that gentle, repetitive ministration, Josh was temporarily cleansed.

Chapter Thirty-four

They were all soaked by the time they got Josh into bed. Jessie drew the covers over his naked body and kissed him again. "Sleep, sweet man," she murmured, and stood and watched beams from the emerging moon in the clearing skies come into the room and bathe his body in light.

She left the bedroom, leaving the door partly open, and soundlessly joined Charlie and Matt in the nearby living room.

Charlie was sitting on the rectangular coffee table, facing Matt. It appeared they'd been having a heart to heart. He held out a bundle of clothes. "Here. Put something dry on."

It was a strange feeling, being handed some of Charlie's clothes—a T-shirt and a pair of sweats—after all these years away from sharing such intimacies with him. Reaching out a timid hand, Jessie blushed and took the clothes. "Thanks, Charlie," she said honestly, and went into the bathroom to change.

She emerged a few minutes later with the sweats rolled up around her ankles. "I'm not wearing a bra," she announced as she hunkered down on the sofa under Matt's raised left arm. "Do either of you care?"

After what Matt and Charlie had just witnessed—a pure kind of love that Jesus preached but which most people were utterly incapable of—the guys could only shake their heads. Nobody was in the mood to joke around.

Matt pulled Jessie to him and kissed the top of her head. "You constantly amaze me," he said. She was too torn up to bother asking why.

Charlie hauled his heavy body upright. Someone was knocking at the door. Opening it, he wasn't surprised to see Shanda in the hallway, fidgeting with her fingers, a worried cast to her attractive face. As she strolled into the room, Matt straightened noticeably. Jessie wrinkled her eyebrows and clutched his right hand in both of hers. She was sitting tucked up against him, gleaning what strength she could from his warm body.

"Did you find him?" Shanda was asking. "I just heard."

"Come. Sit. Anybody hungry?" Charlie led her to a chair kitty corner to Jessie and Matt. "We found him. He'll be okay. He's sleeping it off."

Nobody was hungry, but Charlie ordered a pizza anyway. For a while, they talked almost aimlessly about odds and ends—*Sacred Peace*, when Jessie would go to Vancouver on a rescheduled trip, her plans for the summer… everything disheartened her. The idea of leaving Josh and the kids, after these latest trials, was simply terrifying.

After a while, Jessie got up to go to the washroom. When she started back around the corner, Shanda's and Matt's heads were bent together in conversation.

Charlie was in the kitchen wrapping up the leftover pizza. His gaze followed hers as he popped the plate with the pizza on it into the fridge. Wiping his palms on his jeans, he studied Jessie. "Want to get some sleep?"

"Yeah," she said, but she didn't move.

In the living room, Matt stood and reached for Shanda's hand. He helped her rise, and they started toward the door, Shanda shyly, Matt gently holding her hand like a nervous schoolboy.

Looking over toward the kitchen, Matt met Jessie's confused eyes. He held up his phone. "Call me if you need anything," he said. "I won't be far away."

"Oh," Jessie responded hotly, eyes now wide and accusing. She crossed her arms in utter bewilderment. "Shall I call you when you're climaxing, or would you prefer I wait for the afterglow?"

Stunned, Shanda froze, one hand resting delicately on the door handle. A wave of ice shot out to Jessie from Charlie's general direction, and it wasn't coming from the fridge.

Matt just shook his head in disbelief. "She's an actress, Jessie," he said, oblivious to the way Shanda's ears perked up at his words. "I'm not really in her league. I'm sure it's just a one night fuck. Get over it."

Nobody said a word for a few long-assed minutes after that. Jessie couldn't bring herself to look away from him. Matt deserved this, hell, darling Shanda deserved to be with someone as sweet and wonderful as him. But to let him go when she, Jessie, so badly needed him?

"This why you wanted to come with me?" she tossed out to the room, avoiding his gaze until his prolonged silence garnered her attention. "So you could hook up with Shanda?"

"Go get some sleep, Jessie," Matt commanded. He raised an arm to settle gently around Shanda's waist. "If Josh is too much for you tonight…the puking and all…there's always the couch."

He slipped through the door behind Shanda. He let it slam behind them. Their footsteps echoed down the hall, and disappeared.

Sucking on her bottom lip, Jessie dipped her chin and stared at the floor.

From behind her came Charlie's thoughts on what he'd just overheard. "Ouch. Damn, Jessie."

Maneuvering her drained body around to face him, Jessie sighed and leaned her butt back against the cabinet. "God, I can be a bitch. What part of me thinks that Matt does not deserve a good lay? Seriously. Sometimes I can't stand myself, Charlie. Really."

She looked so remorseful and dejected that Charlie couldn't help but smile. Pulling her close, he wrapped his arms around her and sighed. "The man just saved your life. Again. You two are so wound up in each other that I'm honestly always surprised when I see one without the other. I suppose you were hoping to snuggle up with him, were you?"

"Not for sex," Jessie whispered. "Just because. That's all. Just to be close to him. To feel safe. Hey," she added, suddenly cornering right to shake off the heat. Placing her hands on Charlie's hips, she peeked up at him from underneath lashes that were so tired they drooped. "Did you hear the latest? Josh and me are having a new baby."

"I heard. That's good." Charlie wiped a strand of hair away from her face. "I guess me and Jane better get at it again so your new little one will have a playmate."

"Not much you can do from here," Jessie giggled in her girly thirteen-year-old voice. "Unless you know something I don't." Sobering, she shrugged and said, "You do work an awful lot, Charlie."

"Some of us have to."

Jessie got the hint. "Let's see what tomorrow brings. Today, I mean. Um… morning. Give us a day. We'll catch our breath and get back to work sending your little TV show back up into the stratosphere. Josh with the acting, and me and Jacob with the music."

"Jess…I hate to ask this, but do you think he'll be okay?" Charlie's serious tone was upsetting. He gestured toward Josh's bedroom. "He's an alcoholic, kid. This was a big fall off a pretty high wagon."

"He'll be okay."

"How do you know?"

"Because," Jessie announced as she trooped bravely toward Josh's room, "he promised me. G'nite, Charlie. And…" She paused at the door and smiled sadly back at him, "Thank you. Thank you so, so much."

"S'okay," Charlie responded, swallowing past the catch in his throat. "I didn't look, by the way. I wasn't comparing or anything."

"What?" A second passed before Jessie clued in. "You might not want to bring that up to Josh, that you helped undress and shower him. I'm seriously hoping he won't remember. He'll have a hard enough time finding some self-respect after this night, Charlie."

"Shit. That was stupid of me. I'm sorry, I was just—"

"I know what you were doing. You're adorable, Charlie. I love you. Good night, honey." Slapping the door frame lightly, Jessie stepped inside and lightly closed the door behind her.

In the kitchen, Charlie hung onto the fridge handle for strength and released a long, slow pent-up breath.

In the bedroom, Jessie climbed in behind her husband, and buried her face in his still damp hair. Josh stirred, but didn't wake. Curving her body around him, Jessie pressed her lips to the back of his head and drifted off to sleep.

Down the hall in Shanda's condo, Shanda shook her head slowly at Matt. "We won't get far with that attitude, Matt," she warned. "The whole 'one night stand thing.' And I've got news for you. I want a family. I'm a romantic. I'm hoping for the best, here."

He hesitated. "I'm too old for you," he answered. "I'm all done in, Shanda."

"You're in better shape than David freaking Beckham," she laughed. "There might be a few years between us, Matt, but…" Standing back, Shanda appraised the body she was about to unclothe. "I've been wondering what's under those clothes. And I can't wait to feel my skin on—"

She didn't get to finish that thought. Since the hospital, Matt had entertained a few sweet fantasies of his own. Pressing his hands around the small of Shanda's slim back, he drew her close, almost melted when she moaned at the feel of his body against hers, and pressed his lips to her sweet mouth.

Chapter Thirty-five

"This is outta control. I haven't been in your bed in years, Charlie."

Jessie had half bounced, half limped into Charlie's room a few minutes earlier and carefully, with only minor wincing, copped a squat up against the headboard. Arranging a pillow behind her, she laughed when he threw another one in her face and groaned.

"Lemme sleep," he demanded, trying to pull the covers up over his head but growling in annoyance when they got stuck under Jessie's butt. "And just for the record, you're not in my bed. You're on it."

Still wearing the T-shirt and sweats he loaned her late the night before, Jessie bent over and rerolled up the cuffs of the pants. Stretching out, she crossed her ankles and did a visual scan of Charlie's bedroom.

"This is just a crash pad, huh?" she noted. The room was mostly bare, with the exception of basic furniture like a dresser and nightstand, and a chair similar to the one in Josh's room. "I hope it's not, like, a honey nest or something."

"As if." Charlie's irritated rejoinder was muffled. His head was buried fully under a pillow.

Jessie lifted the corner of it and awarded him a caustic warning smirk. "I'd kick your ass if you ever stepped out on Jane. You made a lousy boyfriend but you seem to be a damn fine husband. And I don't ever want to hear otherwise."

"I'd kick my own ass." Giving up, Charlie slid the pillow off his head and hauled himself up to sit beside Jessie.

Smiling, she rumpled his hair. "You're absolutely adorable in the mornings. I'd forgotten."

"I'm adorable all the time. Ask Jane."

Throwing her head back, Jessie laughed wholeheartedly. "I'm glad. Really, I am." Tucking an arm into his, she wriggled her body close and laid a head on his shoulder.

Charlie sighed and soaked her up. If it were up to him, he'd freeze this moment forever, if just so he could keep her safely under his care in perpetuity.

"I'm sorry I blamed you and Charles for what was happening to Josh last season, Charlie," she said with regret. "As we've come to learn, *Sacred Peace* was just a foil. What was happening to Josh was just a foil, I guess." Poking absently at a fingernail as she talked, she felt compelled to add, "It would appear Morgan just wants Sawyer blood on his hands, as retribution. Doesn't seem to matter whose."

Considering that, Charlie decided there wasn't a whole lot he could offer in terms of hard facts. Instead, he went for Jessie's old standby—hope. "Just don't give up. There's gotta be a way around this monster."

"I think I know a way." Her blue eyes were shining when Jessie caught Charlie's gaze. "I've said this before. I need to get in to see Morgan."

A low mumble slipped between Charlie's pursed lips. "Charles and I talked about this. He thought about it, but now…he won't allow it, kid."

"Fine. He doesn't have to know about it. But personally, Charlie, I don't see why he's against it. I don't know what he thinks he's accomplishing by not letting me in to see Morgan. Charles is not protecting me by not giving me the opportunity to look that guy in the eyes and reach for some human part left in him."

Charlie *pffffted* his disagreement. "Morgan's been in prison, Jessie. For a while now. He was a shell when you knew him—imagine what he's like now, in there with all those hard core cons."

"I know that, Charlie," she countered, "but he loved us, me and the kids. He was with us on tour. Morgan was quiet, yes, but he never stepped out of line. There was nothing evil about him. Just a lingering sadness. That's all. And I've got the scoop on sadness."

Charlie reached his right arm across his chest to Jessie and slipped his fingers into her hair. Pressing his cheek to her head, he closed his eyes.

Ducking out from under him, Jessie sat back a bit. "Charlie, I'm just saying he's got to still be reachable. That's all."

A cool darkness deepened Charlie's already serious countenance. "Jessie, kid, that man did terrible things to you, to your family…he…raped you…" He could barely say the contemptible word.

Jessie blinked. In a tiny voice she said, "Whatever. I barely remember." But Charlie couldn't help but notice that she started digging the nails of a thumb and forefinger into the loose skin around the thumb of the opposite hand. Without looking directly at her hands, he pulled them apart and held the offending hand.

"Well, let me remind you. He set the house on fire, Jessie. With you in it. You can pretend you don't remember all you like, girl. But I fucking remember."

"Morgan killed his wife, Charlie. His own wife. He killed the woman he loved before she had the chance to fire again and kill me. Or Matt." The thought of Matt…with Shanda now…her Matt…Jessie had to look down, away from Charlie. There were so many people on Morgan's hit list now, she figured. "I need to try, Charlie. I need to look into his eyes and beg him, if I have to, to let us be. Once and for all."

"Sweetheart…"

"Charlie, please listen. You know Charles better than anyone. You need to find out who he talked to, to get in there that time that he and Matt went, inside Brody's hallowed walls. You can't get in otherwise without being on a list approved by the inmate, and let's face it, I wouldn't be on Morgan's list."

Charlie scowled. "Would anybody?"

A long pause was Jessie's answer. Charlie had to look at her to see why she wasn't talking. Her eyes were wide and hurting. "God, the guy must be lonely."

"And only you would care," Charlie reflected. "I'd tell you you're too soft, girl, but…you wouldn't be you any other way."

Rallying, Jessie tapped him on the arm. "Charlie, listen. I need a private visit with Morgan in some quiet room where nobody will bother us. Well, except for a guard, maybe. They likely won't let me see him without a guard."

Pitching a pillow against the wall in frustration, Charlie said, "You want to get inside Brody? Ask Matt to get you in. You've got a lot of shows this summer. I don't want to be responsible for you checking out on us again and going silent."

"Yeah, well, I'd like to be alive to do those shows! I'd like to be able to travel knowing that my husband and kids are safe. I need this, Charlie! You have to do this for me."

Pushing her aside, Charlie swung his legs over the edge of the bed and sat hunched over, with his back to Jessie. "I don't have to do this. There's got to be another way."

"There isn't. I've been over and over and over it, Charlie. I can't see any other way. I just can't." Crawling on her knees over to him, Jessie encircled her arms around his shoulders and turned her face into his neck. Charlie lifted a hand and rubbed her arm.

"Matt'll do anything for you," he said again, with a hard edge—almost jealously, Jessie thought. "Ask him."

"Matt won't do this. You guys—you all think you can protect me by building this big wall around me. But you know now, Charlie, that your wall has holes in it. It's crumbling. Last I looked, it was leaking water like Niagara fucking Falls. Please. Please, Charlie. Arrange this for me. Get Charles' contact list and make it happen. Don't tell him what you're up to, or I'm done. He'll put the kibosh on me on the Brody end of things."

Burying her face deeper in his neck, she inhaled. This man sitting in front of her in his boxers and wrinkled T-shirt was the old Charlie Jessie had once thought she'd be spending her life with. Breathing him in, she was relieved— and somewhat saddened—to see that he still smelled the same, of some musky male soap and the same old Charlie sweat. Surprised at the wave of nostalgia that spread over her, Jessie exerted a little pressure, jumped a little at the sharp pain in her ribs that was left over from the SUV rollover, and fought back the urge to crawl into his arms.

If anyone would help her get in to see Morgan, Charlie would. Period.

"Josh…" she entreated wistfully, "he's up to something, Charlie, and it's scaring me. Arnie wouldn't have walked out on him over something so simple as Josh wanting to go to the bars. I need to do something first. I need to try to save our family before he does something stupid."

Grumbling, Charlie did what Jessie didn't have the courage to do. He gave her arm a little pull to encourage her into his lap. She moved quietly, gratefully, into the arms of a man she trusted with her life. Into the arms of a man who could have chosen to exit her life all those painful years ago, but who, now, kept her and her family close because he needed them as much as they needed him. Josh included.

"Can I take this as a yes?" she whispered into the small hollow at the top of his chest, at the base of his neck. Closing her eyes, she laid a palm flat over his heart.

"Harrumph," he said. Charlie's throat was closing over. There was a soft light coming into the room from outside now, backlighting them. A muted shadow formed on the pale wall where Charlie was focusing his gaze. He may as well have been holding a child in his arms, according to the image he studied as he held his old fiancée and considered what to do. Yet there was something about this woman that Charlie was quite certain, based on years of experience living in her close circle, had not in all reality been child-like since the day her father drowned in a submerged car. The way she and her daughter had almost drowned too—being run off the road by someone hoping to prove a point...or, perhaps to kill...

She acted like a child, at times. Jessie sometimes resorted to silly childish giggles, to childish behaviors. But she was as seasoned and aged and as wise as someone who'd lived a thousand lives. Yes, sometimes she needed to retreat, to gas up for the next step, to renew her energy by withdrawing from a world that, far too often, was bitter and cruel to her. But she always came back. She was a fighter. And that, Charlie reasoned, was part of the reason she was so deeply respected and loved, by all of them, despite how much she frustrated and infuriated them at the same time.

"I'll do it."

Jessie squealed, her relief tickling Charlie's neck because she didn't want to be loud enough to chance waking Josh, next door. "Thank you, Charlie," she exhaled gratefully. "Thank you, thank you, thank you!"

"You realize Matt's gonna have to be in on this."

She stiffened. "No."

Pushing her away so he could look into the ice-blue eyes he adored,

Charlie tried to hold firm. "He'll know, regardless. He knows every step you take. And don't go getting all sulky about Shanda. They'd be sweet together."

"She only wants him because she can't have my husband." Jessie frowned. The petulant child was back.

Charlie's lips curled up, just the tiniest bit. Jessie was such a quandary, sometimes. "That's not at all fair to Matt," he said. "I've seen the way women look at him. He's a friggin' GQ model. I've heard you say it."

"Regardless. Charlie, if we involve Matt in a trip to Brody, he'll tell Charles. And that'll be the end of it."

"Why don't you try trusting Matt?"

"I trust you. You and I are going to do this." For effect, she poked a finger in Charlie's ribs. "You. And me."

"Me. In a prison."

"No one'll touch you. I won't let them, you big baby. Look, when you contact this person Charles used to get special access, make sure he—or she, I suppose—provides security for us. I mean, I'm sure they do anyway. But we won't be bringing anyone from our own team."

"Bullshit. Choose someone. And not Alin. No offence to her, but she's small."

"Scaredy cat."

"Dan's the best option. He puts his head down and does his work. Can he be trusted?"

"Yeah, but what if Charles finds out? He'll fire his ass, and we don't want that. Charlie, let's just you and me do this on our own and trust that the warden will give us backup security. We'll drive up together. We can do it in a day if we plan to leave at five."

"What is this hang-up you have about never letting me sleep, Jess? Bags under my eyes look like shit on camera."

"Doofus." A rustle next door alerted them to the fact that Josh was stirring. Nervous, Jessie shot a look in the direction of his bedroom. She slid off Charlie's lap. "My tragic rebel awakens. Make this happen soon, Charlie. Call me."

"Yeah, yeah," he grumbled, and watched Jessie slink out of his bedroom. Sighing, he stood wearily and rubbed a tired hand over his eyes. Slumping out into the hallway, he wandered into the john for a piss and then over to the open doorway of Josh's room. Josh was lying on his back with one arm crooked behind his head. Jessie was prone now, too, half sprawled over him, an arm around his chest and a leg over his, although she was on top of the covers, and he was, at least partially, underneath. She looked so peaceful, lying there holding her husband's broken parts together this way.

Leaning sideways against the door frame, Charlie was saddened to know her new peace was because Jessie was placing a faith in this visit to Morgan—in him, to make it happen—that she believed might change the tide of reprisal against her family for the losses Morgan suffered a few short years ago.

"Coffee," Charlie muttered, saluting these two favorite people who, he was always glad to see, were at their utmost joy when in each other's company. Even when they were arguing, there was a sacred connection at play between them. Always, always, always, when lost in each other's eyes, a hallowed bond encompassed them like silk ribbon wrapped around a gift. "Down the road. I be back."

"Thanks, Charlie." Jessie rubbed a hand over Josh's chest. Still looking at Charlie, she winked. "Give us at least ten minutes, okay hon?"

"Jesus," he stammered. "You want my soul too, Jessie?"

Josh, finding that comment curious, knit his brow together as, beside him, Jessie fired Charlie a warning look. Charlie left them alone, threw on some jeans and a jacket, shoved his feet into boots, and clicked the door quietly behind him.

Chapter Thirty-six

When Charlie sauntered back fifteen minutes later, Jessie was standing at the large living room window looking out, hair wet and arms crossed. She took the tray of coffee from him and they went over to the kitchen island to sit and to sip their hot beverages.

He had a white paper bag in his hands. Tossing it on the counter, Charlie sat across from Jessie and pushed it toward her.

"Yum. Breakfast wraps and pastries. You really are something, Charlie."

"Don't you ever forget it." Grabbing a chocolate croissant, Charlie took a hefty bite and licked his fingers. "How's Josh seem this morning?" he asked with his mouth full.

She shrugged. "Quiet. Sick. I was only jokin' about the lovin.' My man's gonna need a day, Charlie."

"Take it. He's not on the call sheet today."

She was going to say something further, but Josh appeared at the door to the washroom, rubbing a towel through his hair, jeans on but unbuttoned, bare toes peeking out from underneath. Meeting his eyes, Jessie used the backs of her fingers to carefully push a takeout cup in his direction. At the same time, a quiet knock came at the main condo door. Croissant in hand, Charlie walked around the kitchen island to go answer it.

Josh let his towel fall to the floor. He slouched across the room to half sit on the stool facing his wife. Accepting the coffee, he pulled a small plastic plug out of the hole in the lid, and took a cautious sip.

"You okay?" Watching him, Jessie offered a small smile in his direction. At the same time, she laid a tender hand on his knee.

Angling his face away from her, away from everyone in the condo—Matt and Shanda included, who were following Charlie into the living room area, sending Josh and Jessie surreptitious glances as they walked—Josh rifled his fingers through his wet, mussed up hair and said nothing.

"Hey," Jessie said, rubbing his thigh, "let's take a day, Josh. We'll go back to the ranch and just be with the kids. You and me. Nobody else. We'll send them all away."

That got his attention. Josh lifted his cup and took another sip. He swallowed, and nodded. Jessie tore off the paper around a breakfast wrap for him, but he pushed it away. "Not ready for that yet," he declared between gritted teeth. His stomach was swirling his innards in impossible directions. The smell of the wrap alone was enough to warrant a concerned glimpse into the washroom.

From the living room they heard Charlie ask Shanda what time her call was today.

"In an hour," she replied. "Are you coming in today, Charlie?"

"Yep. I need a shower. Heading out soon."

Shanda was looking past Charlie at Josh, letting her eyes graze over his bare chest and tousled hair. Jessie twisted around and caught her eye, forced her fingers not to rise into a solemn 'fuck you,' and drifted further around to silently communicate that message to Matt with narrowed eyes instead. Rotating back around to face Josh, she moved her hand from his leg to his stomach, and made sure she leaned against the counter so Shanda and Matt could watch her brush the backs of her fingers up and down his oh-so-touchable skin. "Shanda's eyes are popping out of her head," she murmured coquettishly to Josh, blinking solemnly up at him.

Josh's eyes flickered over to his *Sacred Peace* costar. Jessie suddenly regretted calling his attention to Shanda. She had neglected to remember just how close Josh and Shanda were. Hanging her head, with a stiff, silent, self-lecture she chided herself about acting like a jealous sixteen year old. Dropping her fingers to the top undone button on her husband's jeans, Jessie let her fingers rest. Her back was to Matt, Shanda and Charlie, but their stares so hotly fused into her skin that she swore she could feel the sizzle.

"Josh," Shanda finally said, wandering over to him, "are you coming in today? We need to run some lines."

"He's not," Jessie said for him, her eyes not leaving Josh's, although his were aimed at Shanda, but flicking between her and Matt, who was standing about ten feet behind Jessie with his hands thrust into his jeans' pockets. "We're going to the ranch." Letting go of Josh, she flipped around to Matt. "Stay here. And call off the rest of the minions." Everyone cringed. Matt bristled. "We're taking a day."

Josh had yet to speak to the group. He leaned one elbow on the counter and tensely licked his lips as he and Matt wordlessly connected.

Matt stepped forward. "I'll ride ahead of you."

"Ha! What the hell's the point, Matt? Ahead or behind? Who fucking cares?"

"Jessie," Charlie warned.

"Seriously. Get a grip, Charlie." To Matt, Jessie said, "I appreciate your service, " she accentuated the word *service*, "but Matt, if someone wants us, they are damn well gonna get us. They can shoot us. Pick us off like pigeons. And you being in a car in front or behind us is not gonna make one damn bit of difference."

"Cool it, Jessie. This man just saved your life. Again."

"Charlie…I mean, really." Swinging back around to face him—he was standing just behind Shanda now—Jessie fired another shot. "You think I don't know that? You think I've forgotten?"

Sliding off the stool, she half jogged over to Matt and grabbed his hand. Holding it up and positioning it against hers so that their palms lay flat against each other, she buried herself in Matt's cool gaze and bit off, "I cannot tell you how incredible it is to feel this man's skin on mine. Without a goddamned aquarium window in between us."

Thoughtfully, Shanda put a finger to her lips and chewed on the nail. Josh reached down and took her hand in his. They shared a tender look that Charlie was privy to.

When Jessie wheeled back around with Matt's hand in hers, she noticed. "Go to set, Charlie," she demanded. "The few of us left here could probably have a real sweet little foursome."

"And that's my cue. Jesus, you're something else, Jessie." Marching off with an appalled shake of his head, Charlie disappeared into his bedroom and started rooting around for clothes to take into the shower.

Jessie's bottom lip was trembling.

As humiliated and embarrassed as Josh was for everything he was sluggishly starting to recall about the last few days, he recognized that she was not the rock everyone thought she was. She was just hiding behind frightening feelings—leftovers from the rollover into the river, and from the overhanging, nauseous dread that was clinging to all of them—that she had no clue how to process. He sensed a complete meltdown coming on.

Giving Shanda's fingers a squeeze, he let go and put his wife's mind to rest. "The ranch would be good, Jessie. Let's go." Taking his coffee with him, he eased himself painfully off the stool and said to Shanda as he passed her on his way back to his bedroom, "I'll come in tomorrow, Shanda. Will that work for you?"

"Yes," Shanda answered, trying desperately not to reach out to touch his bare skin as he passed by her, and trying even more desperately—and failing miserably—at not letting Jessie and Matt notice.

"Oh, for Pete's sake," Jessie growled as Shanda's eyes fluttered back in her direction. She started toward Josh's room but stopped by Shanda and spat at her, practically under her breath so Josh hopefully wouldn't hear, "Don't worry Shanda, ain't nobody getting a taste of Josh today. He'll spend the day sick as a dog, while his kids tiptoe around trying not to bother him."

Matt hadn't moved. Jessie fixed him in a hard stare. "But Mr. Sexy over here…" With a stony half smile, she appraised his body from toes to spiky hair tips, "Now there's a man who can make it happen. *It* being magic. Many times over, in fact."

Disgusted, Matt looked away.

Jessie winked at Shanda. "When all is said and done, honey, you likely got the better man." She went to move past Shanda but stopped suddenly. Josh was at the bedroom door, a clean T-shirt retrieved from the storage room dryer hanging from his hand, pure confusion and loss dancing across his subdued eyes. He slinked back into his bedroom, and slammed the door behind him.

"Aw, hell," Jessie stammered. "How freaking bad do I suck right about now."

From behind her, Matt called out to Shanda. "How about I buy you breakfast? Anywhere you want. You and I," he wandered forward and reached past Jessie for Shanda's delicate fingers, "can go anywhere the hell in this city we want." Glaring at Jessie he said, "And nobody will bother us. Apart from a few curious autograph seekers and selfie takers, I mean."

"You two…" Shanda offered wisely as she walked to the door with Matt at her side, but glancing back at Jessie to make sure she was listening, "you're like…" Stopping, she gazed between the two of them.

Barely breathing, they were lost in each other, in the grief that being separated after life-altering, life-stopping, life-saving trust for years, had granted them. To both, it felt like a physical tearing apart, as if they were each other's Band-Aids—over oozing, open wounds—being ripped off.

Shanda finished her sentence. She said it with a dainty hand waving in the air like she was pushing invisible air around. Like she was manipulating tiny bits of crackling electrons—the missing sparks from Matt's and Jessie's spirits—that needed to be put back into place to restore amity between them. "You're like…you're so lost in each other's souls that I can't tell where one of you starts and the other begins."

"Jessie's like that," Matt said, going to the door and reaching for the handle. "She has a way of getting under a person's skin. She sticks her claws in and twists, and hangs there like a tick. The only way to get rid of her is to light a match and burn her off."

"Nope," Jessie choked. "Apparently that doesn't work, Matt. It's been tried. Morgan, remember?" Near tears now, shoulders hunched over, she wrapped her arms around her belly and squeezed. Anything to keep the pain of loss inside. "You can't get rid of me that easily."

Thank God for that, Matt whispered inwardly, clenching his teeth, his eyes latched firmly on Jessie's. He pulled open the door and lifted a hand to set around Shanda's waist as she walked through.

He said it a second time, out loud, directed at Jessie herself. "Thank God for that." He paused for a second, smiled sadly at her, and waited for her to smile back.

Tossing her curls, Jessie ducked her head and swallowed bitterly. Then she let her gaze drift back to Matt. Her eyes softened, and glistened in the new white light of the morning's fresh, pure essence. She lifted her fingers to her mouth. Pressing her lips against the fingers, she closed her eyes, turned the hand outward, and formed an O with her mouth. Blowing gently, she sent a kiss to Matt. When she opened her eyes, she chewed on a corner of her lip and rocked back on one heel.

Her smile was a few lingering seconds in coming. But it did come, eventually. It was a sincere wish for Matt to enjoy some well-earned time off.

He took it as it was meant, sent her a quiet, "Call me if you need me, Jessie," and left her standing there alone.

Chapter Thirty-seven

"Take a walk with me," Jessie said to Jacob.

"What?" he asked, pulling his guitar off of his body and laying it upright in a cushioned stand. "Now? Where? You've already had lemongrass tea, a mocha, and oh let's not forget the chocolate monkey smoothie Deirdre and Emily-Grace dropped off earlier. Large, I might add. Plus water."

"Wondered why I've had to pee so much today. I was just blaming it on baby Sawyer."

"Too much coffee's not good for the baby, if that's what you've got in mind."

"Policing Kayla pretty good, are you, Jacob?"

"Missed out the first time, Mizz Wheeler. Making up for what I lost."

"Oh, you made up for what you lost, Ryan. Trust me."

Jacob adjusted his weight to one leg and leaned on a nearby keyboard. Thankfully, its power wasn't on, so no weird sounds emerged, but Jacob knew that if he could hear the notes he played, they'd be as messed up as the sudden tightening in his gut. "I know," he said to Jessie. "I don't deserve Kayla. And I don't know how you can stand having me in your life."

"Easy. It's called music, doofus face. We are a team, you and me. And seeing you happy makes me happy." Her voice softened. "That day? You weren't the Jacob I know and love."

"Thanks, Jess. Really."

Jessie lit up. "So, since Josh isn't around this week, I suppose you're gonna start policing me too, huh?" She didn't see the point of admitting that Josh seemed to have little or no interest in their new little Sawyer. It saddened her, but Jessie didn't feel up to going there in conversation with Jacob. These days he was so focused on his sweet new wife and baby-to-be that she was surprised he noticed her at all. *As it should be,* she smiled to herself.

"Damn straight I'm policing you." Jacob wagged a finger at his singing buddy. "No more coffee."

Jessie hunkered up her shoulders. "Mochas are mostly chocolate."

"No more refined sugar, then."

"You trying to take all the joy out of my life, Ryan?"

Jacob would have laughed if they hadn't just hit on some of his life's lowest points. He put on his best sad puppy dog face and hooked his thumbs over his jeans' pockets.

"Come on, sulky baby," Jessie teased, allowing a small smile to make its way to him. "I need a walk." Standing in front of Jacob, she ran a finger over her top lip and tipped her foot over on its side and back again as she waited for him to decide what he wanted to do. "I can't focus."

"Apparently. All right."

Matt was with Jessie on the trip. A quiet observer on the jet a few days earlier, a silent watcher every day since, he had checked in on Jessie and Jacob—and Charles—at the Robson studio earlier in the day, and had just gone down to the building's gym, trusting the superstars in his care to stay put and hunker into the daily grind of writing and recording music for the *Sacred Peace* season two soundtrack.

Unbeknownst to him, Jessie had other plans.

Outside on Robson, she kept up a good pace heading east. Jacob had to almost jog to keep up. She didn't slow down until after he put forth a few thoughts and finally begged her to.

"Josh must be wired about the new baby."

Jessie tensed. "Not ecstatic."

"You feeling okay overall? Kayla's soaring through her pregnancy."

"Her brother's been doing all the puking for her. It's a, whaddaya call it? A sympathetic thing."

"Thought that was only between twins," Jacob huffed. "Slow down, woman!" Considering what Jessie said and the sullen way she wasn't responding, although she did grump and slow her pace, Jacob tossed in, "Oh. I guess you mean that he's been drinking. I heard. Kayla's worried."

"She needn't be. He's okay. He's back at work. Shanda and Charlie are taking him to A.A. meetings." Stopping at the corner of Robson and Burrard, Jessie waited for the light to change. Grateful for the chance to catch his breath, Jacob waited alongside her. Nearby, two teen girls giggled and pointed them out. Jessie ignored them, but Jacob straightened and held his breath. She looked sideways at him. "Take it easy, Jacob. Not everyone got the memo on your diabolical deed."

"Guess I can't be calling Josh down anymore, can I?" He gave her an appraising smile. "You're either a glutton for punishment, or you really do more than just preach forgiveness, you know that, Jess?"

The light changed, and Jessie started across the busy intersection. The loud screech of car tires skidding across the pavement startled her. Staggering back a step, her hand shot out and she grabbed Jacob's wrist.

"Easy," he cautioned, throwing a look to a white Beamer. "Prob'ly just some stupid girl texting while she was driving."

"Fuucckk," Jessie gasped. "Scared the bejeesus outta me." Her heart was doing triple time.

Swallowing nervously, Jacob took her hand and led her to the opposite curb. "I hate that you're always so scared. It kills me."

"Well, let's just hope it doesn't kill me." *Or any of my kids,* Jessie considered, in a morose attempt to not alert Jacob to just how scared she was, for all of them.

His son included.

Fifteen minutes later, Jessie strode past Jack Deacon's Downtown Eastside workshop space on East Hastings. Jacob stopped outside the door. "We're not going in? I figured this was where you were headed."

"Nope. Get with the program, Jacob." Jessie didn't bother slowing down or turning around.

Jogging, Jacob caught up with her. "You want to fill me in, Mizz Wheeler? Sawyer? Wheeler-Sawyer?"

"You'll see." They passed a grizzled old guy hunched over a shopping cart filled with blue bags that bulged in odd places. "Hey, Edgar. How are ya, buddy?" Skidding to a stop, Jessie took a quick look around. When she was sure nobody was watching, she pulled a fifty dollar bill out of a pocket and pressed it into the old man's hand. "Get a good dinner, Edgar," she said. "Steak, maybe."

Edgar's eyes were voluminous and milky. They filled with light when he realized who had just handed him the cash. A wide, toothless gap appeared between dry, cracked lips as he silently grinned and thanked his old pal. Jessie laid a healing hand on his shoulder and smiled. "Be well, my friend," she said, and moved on.

"Nice Jesus move there." The admiration in Jacob's voice was genuine, but Jessie tilted her head away from him as he huffed along half behind her.

"Wish I could do more."

"You can't save them all, Jessie."

Oh yeah? Watch me. A quick look back to Jacob and Jessie saw gears of apprehension whirring and swirling under his pretty boy curls.

"Matt's gonna kill you when he finds out you took off."

"That'd be we," she corrected him. "Us. Plural."

"Hey, I'm just trippin' along behind your stupid ass. I'm an innocent bystander."

"Are you." Jessie ground their brisk walk to a halt outside a seedy gray brick building marked with a faded sign—GYM. "Tell the protesters that at our next concert."

"And you weren't there grinding up against me—"

"Oh, for God's sake, Jacob. Let's not play that old record again. We've done that today already. I've got a whole new list of stupid deeds to be sorry for. You and me and our crappy shit ranks somewhere below minus ten and the kind of dry ice that shatters when you look at it. Come on."

Glancing around, Jacob scrunched his shoulders up into his crested nylon bomber jacket. His gaze landed on a young white guy hunched over on the cold sidewalk, his back against the decaying brick. The kid, a determined long-haired teen maybe fifteen years old, was messing about with a syringe, shooting poison into his veins—heroin, no doubt—less than a dozen feet away, right there in plain view for drivers cruising down East Hastings to see.

"Shit," Jacob breathed.

Slinking into the gym behind Jessie, he recoiled at the pungent, heady sweat that instantly accosted his nostrils and stayed there like shit stuck to a dog's ass. It blew his mind to see how comfortable Jessie was in this whole sketchy environment. Watching her weave through weights and benches to make her way deeper into the dark space, an image of her at their last show popped into his head. Jessie in the latest haute couture gown and sparkling diamonds was an entirely different person than his old girl here today. Considering what she'd said earlier about how he wasn't the Jacob she knew and loved back when things got way out of hand in Florida, he wondered which Jessie was the one he preferred—this street-hardened woman who seemed to fear nothing here in this rough neighborhood or the elegant, sophisticated songstress who often played for politicians and celebrities and who'd won four Oscars and a multitude of Grammies?

Both, Jacob decided. Jessie was a deeply layered soul. Like an onion, you could peel her away in bits and pieces, and all you would find at the center would be a purity made up of the same core stuff. Loving Jessie meant loving the good and the bad—the childish bits, the damaged bits, the angry bits, the Godly bits, the mother, the wife, the friend, the singer, the pseudo daughter. The homeless teen, the erotic star from years of yore, the—Jacob gulped—sexual assault victim. The victim of rape.

The gutsy survivor. He wanted to hug her for never giving up. *Especially,* Jacob humbly considered, *on me.*

A stocky, clean-cut man holding a clipboard approached. "Jessie? It's been a while." He didn't seem at all surprised to see her. Extending a hand, he shook Jessie's before nodding at Jacob. "Better keep a low profile, son," he warned. "There are some in here who haven't forgotten what you did to our girl."

"Jesus, the whole damn world owns you," Jacob muttered inwardly as they followed the guy to an indoor boxing ring, from where a series of low grunts and loud thwacks were announcing either a practice or an actual fight. A few fellas with tattoos inked on bulging biceps were leaning into the ring, not cheering but watching intently, their bodies reacting to the punches thrown in the ring with physical, zealous recoil.

The man who greeted them hopped lightly up onto the side of the ring before ducking and climbing between two thick ropes in order to gain a footing on the ring's flat surface. "Arnie," he called, his voice formal and demanding, "someone here to see you."

One of the boxers stopped moving. His opponent jogged backward, dancing a little as he moved.

Arnie spotted Jessie right away. He turned to his friend. "Take ten." Pulling off a protective face mask, Arnie dropped it to the ring floor before crawling through the ropes and hopping down. Brushing by Jessie without a greeting, which surprised Jacob, Arnie led the way to the back, to a dimly lit interior office where a bare bulb was the only light source illuminating a messy paper strewn desk. He gestured to some scraped up thick wooden chairs by the wall.

"I'll stand," Jessie announced, placing her feet wide apart as if she needed the extra bracing against the bare cement floor. Without looking at Jacob, she said, "Wait outside."

"What the hell? You drag me down here and then—"

"Now, Jacob. Arnie and I got things to say to each other."

"Fine. I'll…" Letting his eyes drift over the gym, Jacob was a little freaked out at some of the big guys lining the space, punching bags and skipping ropes and working out. Their bulging arms alone were practically the size of his torso. And they were all eyeing him with ill concealed distaste. "Oh, shit," he mumbled, sending Jessie a silent prayer to hurry up, and at the same time wondering what the hell she was up to. His phone buzzed. Retrieving it from a back pocket, he eyeballed the screen. Matt was calling. "Damn." Jacob shoved the phone back to where it came from, stood quietly in one place with his shoulder against the exterior wall of the small office, and started to quietly whistle what he hoped was a happy tune.

A door slammed hard beside him. He jumped, and cocked an ear in the hopes that he'd hear what was being discussed inside.

Inside the office, Jessie had raised a foot and tersely kicked the door shut.

Arnie banana'd behind the desk. Like a rooted, rigid tree stump, it stood between them. He raised a chin, and waited.

"Talk." The demand was issued from between Jessie's gritted teeth, so that when the words were spoken, they smoldered their way into the muggy space like wood smoke from a campfire. Jessie's hands were stuffed into the pockets of her aviator jacket, curled into sweaty little balls.

"You know the streets, Jessie. You know the code. We don't share."

"Josh is my husband. You work for me. You share."

"I work for nobody."

"Bullshit. You can't walk away that easily. You got those big new digs to pay for."

Arnie leaned a set of bruised knuckles on the desk and sent Jessie a fierce stare that made her cringe. The stare didn't last. He buckled and moved his eyes to an empty yogurt container sprawled listlessly on the ratty desk.

She dove in. "Tell me what pissed you off enough to send you flying back to Vancouver a few days after my daughter and I were almost killed. I know you weren't scared. You're too goddamned tough to be scared. Big guy like you." Looking him over, Jessie wasn't surprised to see just how fit Arnie was. The guy was a boxer. In the past, she'd taken lessons from him, first for self-defense and then for roles she took on as an actor. What did surprise her now was the way he was having a hard time looking her in the eye, and the way a moist wetness was settling into those gentle eyes she'd trusted from the first moment she met him.

She angled her head at him and squinted in the semidarkness. "You're scaring me, Arnie. What the hell is this?" A slow, sick nausea crept down her throat. Jessie tried to swallow past it.

Arnie turned away from her and grabbed a small ragged towel from a nearby bookcase. His back still to her, he started rubbing it over the beads of slick, greasy sweat that lined his face like teardrops.

"Arnie, what—" Changing her stance, Jessie lowered her voice. "He asked you to get him something. A gun."

Arnie paused, then started moving the towel over his arms. He was wearing a sleeveless shirt, some old gray T-shirt he'd cut the sleeves off of. Below that were black shorts, loose fitting enough to reveal the tense, tight abs Jessie relied on to help protect her, should she or her family need his fit body and quick mind on some diabolical occasion.

She shuddered. "Does Josh think he's gonna get into the prison or something? Carry out that murder you alluded to at your place that day?" Jessie laughed—a high, weird, scared laugh. "Arnie, please. You gotta tell me what's going through Josh's mind. I know it's bad, because you wouldn't have bailed the way you did if it wasn't. Besides, you wanted to go there, to that kind of darkness, so if that's Josh's plan, I dunno why you all of a sudden turned tail and ran…it doesn't add up."

When Arnie swung back around to Jessie, his eyes were sharp and pointed. He glared at her and shook the towel in her general direction. Moisture flicked off into the far, dusky corners of the tiny, cluttered office. "We got a code. We don't talk. You wanna know? Ask your husband."

"Arnie," Jessie pleaded, leaning slightly forward. Removing one hand from a pocket, she gestured back and forth between them. "You and me, we go back. We go back a long way. We have a history, Arnie, you and me, long before I ever dove headfirst into this crazy world that's got me and my family by the balls right now. You talk. I listen. We have a trust. It's a trust that was born of mutual experiences, and of mutual understanding. Of going hungry, of selling sex, of procuring guns when I needed them. You hardly blinked an eye when I asked you for a weapon. What's so damn different about whatever the hell Josh has planned that has you running scared? Huh?"

Arnie's eyes were locked on Jessie now. But they were still damp. He tossed the used towel on the desk and stood, teetering, for a few seconds before he spoke again. His words emerged soft and bitter. "I can't protect you. Matt…can't protect you. None of you. Josh thinks he can, but he can't, Jessie. Not the way he's planning. There is no good ending here."

Staggering backward, Jessie took that in. "What's—what's he planning, Arnie?" The musty air around her congealed into a dense, thick fog. "Please—I can't breathe." Gasping, she bent forward, desperate to suck in some useable oxygen.

Arnie ignored her plight. His last words to her were uttered as she wheezed before him—as she tried in vain to digest his incomprehensible demand.

"You need to leave, Jessie," Arnie said. He, too, was choking on the stark reality before them. "Please. Just go."

This was not the dependable tough Arnie Jessie knew. If Arnie was giving up on them, then truly there must be no way out of this untenable tunnel of terror.

Darkness was closing around Jessie's eyes, leaving her alone in this new horror. In the terror that made her realize that Arnie knew about something ominous in Josh's world that she did not. That she could only guess at. And what she was guessing was unfathomable.

She took the high road. Mustering up that strong, indomitable Sawyer courage, Jessie reanchored her body and fired bullets back at him. Her vision cleared and her lungs sucked in revitalizing oxygen while she gave him hell. "You men, you think you are all so damn tough. But inside, you're all just stuffing, like in my kids' teddy bears! No guts, just useless, goddamned stuffing! Well, Arnie," she steeled up her shoulders and spat at him, "I've got news for you. I—am tougher—than all of you assholes put together. I know how to win this, and I will win this. I will not let Josh go down."

Circling slightly, her pulse racing, Jessie wiped at a dribble of spittle that formed on her lips as she cried foul at her old friend. "He is my husband. I love him. We have children together. We are under attack, but everything that's happened so far?" She waved a hand uselessly in the air and pressed her lips together. At the same time, fireworks poured from Jessie's eyes, their Technicolor brilliance testimony to a lifetime of learning how to fight. "Everything that's happened so far, Arnie," Jessie repeated, "is just a goddamned battle. Battles. Many. One after the other. How many has Morgan won, huh? Really, truly won? None! That's how many! And that means that we, us Sawyers, are gonna win the war. You'll see. All of you—you'll see."

There was a long pause before Jessie threw her last knife into the fight. "And you? You suck for walking out just when Josh needs you the most. When I need you the most." Wheeling fully around, Jessie stormed from the room, from the stinky gym, and from the defeat and loss and worry she saw in Arnie's usually kind eyes.

Jacob, with a scared and confused look to Arnie first, followed. He found Jessie crouched over on the sidewalk outside, puking into the gutter. "Jessie, what the hell?" Bending over her, Jacob held back her hair. When she was done, he helped her stand. "All I've got's a sleeve," he said, holding out his arm. "Use it. What's mine is yours."

His attempt at lightening the mood fell flat. Tear trails on Jessie's cheeks were wiped with her own sleeve first, and then she dabbed at her chin. "The thing is, Jacob," she said. "You always said Josh was a loose wire, a gun waiting for a spark. I think you were always right about him. He's always been unpredictable. He's always been just barely hanging on. Even in the good times, I find myself watching him for clues of when he's gonna lose it again. And I know, I know…" She was sobbing now, so hard that her body was shaking. "I know that I caused a lot of those shaky foundations under his feet to give way, to fail. I'm the cause. Me. But I also know that he can hang on if I throw him a rope. Nobody else is gonna throw Josh a rope, Jacob. Nobody. Just me. I'm the only one who can save him."

"You can't save someone who doesn't want to be saved, Jessie."

Astounded, Jessie stopped fidgeting and stared at him. "Is that what you think? Did Matt tell you that? That Josh is giving up?"

"No, Jess, I'm generalizing here. I'm just…" Jacob glanced behind Jessie to the kid who was shooting shit up his veins when they first got to the gym. "Addictions," he explained carefully. "That's all I meant. Josh just went off on a binge, right? He left you a few days after you almost died, and he went off and drank himself into a coma. The way all of us expect he always will when life gets too big for him."

"The way all of you always expect he will," Jessie parroted slowly. "Even Kayla? Is Josh's sister in that group of sweet, loving souls?"

"Jessie, come on. Please. Stop torturing yourself. Let's just walk back before Matt finds out we're gone." Jacob didn't bother telling her that Matt had called him three times since they'd arrived at Arnie's gym.

"So that just leaves me," Jessie said. She rooted her feet to the ground. "To believe in Josh. To help him stay in the fight. He will, you know." She started walking. "He'll stay in the fight because I'll help him stay in the goddamned fight." Charlie flitted through her mind. He had yet to call her with plans for their visit to Brody Pen, and she was getting anxious. It would seem, according to the frightening visit to Arnie, that time was running out.

Like a small puppy, Jacob trotted along behind Jessie. "Don't be stupid, Jessie. Don't do anything rash. You've got this new baby to consider…"

Interjecting hotly, Jessie retorted with, "Our new baby needs a father. A mother. A sister and brothers. He—or she—needs a safe life that can be lived in peace. I feel like I'm in a fucking war zone." Passing the junkie, she stopped abruptly and took a few steps backward. Glazed, lost eyes tried to focus on her. Jessie knelt down and took the teen's hands in hers. She peered into his eyes and tried to find a bit of soul there, a little spark of light somewhere, that said the kid still had fight left in him, but all she could see was darkness.

In his unfocused way, the teen blinked sleepily back at her, but he wasn't looking at Jessie, not really. The lost eyes were vacant, their gaze picking out some nonexistent spot behind Jessie, some random piece of sky above and beyond busy East Hastings Street.

"You can do this," she tried, a tear leaking from the corner of one endlessly sorrowful eye. "End this thing, I mean. The drugs." She was echoing what she said to Josh all those years ago. But this time, when she stood and paced off down the sidewalk next to Jacob, Jessie had zero faith that this boy, alone on one of the sketchiest streets in Canada, had even heard.

Behind her, though, the kid was half smiling. Seemed that whatever dreamy place he was seeing beyond his actual reality was, without a doubt, a much, much better place than the one he was enduring.

Chapter Thirty-eight

Jacob was right. Matt was incensed at their unwarranted and unexplained disappearance, but to his credit he didn't say a word. He knew and understood his superstar charge well enough to discern that today was not turning out to be one of Jessie's more stellar days, although he didn't know why. Jacob, loyal to a fault, crunched quietly on a lip when they were at La Casa for dinner later, and didn't say a word about where he and Jessie scooted off to earlier in the day, or how upset Jessie was after their visit with Arnie. That part was obvious, anyway. She was a morose, silent dinner table companion.

As the days went on, things settled into a regular routine of hard work at the studio. Unfortunately, for Jessie that included withdrawal from almost everything and everyone social as she focused almost entirely on songwriting and recording. Calls to Josh's cell were answered; Charlie, too, was responsive and communicative, but conversation with both guys was stilted, for the most part.

At least, Jessie caught herself thinking, *Josh is at work and is doing okay, Charlie says. So for now I know he's safe.* She was looking forward to having him and the boys—who were spending their days at the soundstage with their father, in tutoring with Patin or playing with the childcare provider the production had hired for the children of cast and crew—arrive Friday evening to spend the weekend in Vancouver where, Jessie believed, they could all be together, safe and sound and enclosed in their own little family circle.

Josh's Harley was still in Vancouver. It wouldn't be moved to Alberta for another few weeks. Josh was hankering for a drive before the jet even went 'wheels down' in Van. Anxious to feel the warm west coast breeze on his face and the rumble of the powerful bike between his legs, he was planning to go for a cruise on Saturday afternoon while Jessie was tidying up a music track at the Robson Street studio, and while the kids were snuggling up with their grandmother in North Van.

The entire family was staying at La Casa for the weekend. Jessie stayed there the entire two weeks she was working in Vancouver, partly for safety and partly because it made sense in terms of continuity for Emily-Grace since her momma was working long days on Robson. The boys treated La Casa like a second home and were happy to be spoiled by Carlotta and Grammie Dee for the weekend. There were always people around, though, and sometimes it got to be a bit much. Saturday morning Jessie begged for a few hours of freedom by creating reasons to drop up to the UBC house. Taking her husband by the hand, she dropped into the driver's seat of their rented SUV and headed south to their UBC home for a cuddle and some serious, sweet loving.

The scary conversation with Arnie didn't come up. Their lovemaking was about reconnecting and hope. So soon after the river incident, Jessie was loathe to dampen any of their fragile spirits with anything remotely despicable. Giving voice to her worries during their brief time together would only reignite the darkness.

Matt was due to pick Jessie up from the UBC house to escort her down to Robson, so Josh would have access to the rental after he put away the big bike later in the day. A few minutes after Matt texted to say he was on his way, Jessie pulled Josh to her and zipped up his thick leather motorcycle jacket for him. Her lips were angled down into a sad droop as she bent forward and pressed them to a corner of her husband's warm mouth. "Please be careful," she begged. "You know I worry about you on that thing."

"You worry about worrying, little one," he replied, reverting to his usual response when she was like this. "I'll be fine. I'll see you at La Casa for dinner."

"How about we don't go to North Van for dinner? How about you and me go to the downtown condo and snuggle up outside, on the terrace? We can watch the seaplanes land before, during, and after we make love."

That brought a smile. The instant flush on Josh's cheeks lit up his eyes. "I'll get us some takeout," he promised, but the usual layer of worry was still at play under the soulful chocolate eyes.

"Noodle Box?" Jessie pleaded hopefully. "Cuz we're such classy people."

"Noodle Box it is." Josh planted a few soft kisses on his wife's cheek, landing one especially treasured moist one up by the corner of her eye. Sighing, he took a step backward, lingered until her fingers fell away from his, pivoted on the heel of one thick black motorcycle boot, and was gone.

Matt was in the driveway waiting when Jessie appeared at the top of the flagstone walk. They still, for all intents and purposes, weren't really talking beyond the usual formalities. There just didn't seem to be anything to say after the whole life saving *slash* you can't protect us *slash* you-screwed-Shanda thing.

After a quiet drive downtown, Matt pulled up to the curb outside the Keating building, handed Jessie over to building security, and drove off to park the car in the underground parking. Jessie leaned against the elevator's back wall, closed her eyes, and wished she was on the back of the Harley rolling up Cypress behind her husband, with her arms around his waist, and hope in her spirit.

Only Josh wasn't cruising up Cypress. The big bike eased to a stop outside a quiet mall in downtown Vancouver, two dozen blocks east of where Jessie was about to go to work. A few minutes later, Josh was standing at a fast food counter, an Indian place. A small white woman came to take his order, but paused and didn't say anything for a full minute when she realized who was standing across from her.

"Hello, Lucie," Josh said deliberately, respectfully, his arm crooked and his Harley half helmet cozied up underneath it. "Got a long-assed minute?"

He selected a toothpick from a nearby dish, stuck it between his top front teeth, and tried not to radiate a sense of hopeless desperation.

They chose a table in a far corner of the food court, despite the fact that the place was mostly deserted anyway. The place wasn't a busy mall to begin with. On a landing above them were movie theaters, but some of the films had already started and although there was another scheduled to start soon, it was some obscure foreign film, so only a few folks were trickling toward the escalator that would carry them up to the theaters.

Josh started them down a shady path as soon the woman he came to see slipped into the seat across from him. Needing to keep his trembling fingers busy, he unzipped his leather jacket as he talked. The *zzzzippp* was jarring in the open, echoey space, and unnerving to both of them. "So," he said, over the sound of the zipper going down, which seemed far too ordinary for the day, and which exposed his body in a way he wasn't sure he wanted it to be exposed, to her, "he tell you?"

"Tell me what?" Lucie asked. "Why he came home? Nope. Arnie just sat in his chair by the big window, stared at the street below, and smoked himself into oblivion."

"He drink?"

"Booze? Hell, no. Arnie's been off that shit for years. You know that, Josh." Sudden awareness crossed Lucie's strong cheekbones and left them highlighted a nervous, dusty pink. "You?"

"Yep." Josh was studying the tabletop.

"A lot?"

"Into oblivion. For a time."

"So."

"So."

Josh peeked up at Arnie's wife. They'd met at La Casa a number of times, but had never, in all their time breathing the same air, just talked one on one. Arnie was generally a quiet man. Josh doubted Arnie's woman knew a whole heck of a lot about him, but he didn't really care. He came here to get something from her, and he intended to walk away a victor.

He sat back. He'd set his helmet down on the chair next to him. Picking it up, Josh turned it over and over in his hands, just for something to do, for somewhere to focus the over-the-top energy that was making him want to reach for another beer, or maybe some good ole Jim Beam, to numb his frazzled senses.

"What is it you need from me, Josh?" Lucie was attractive in a hardcore kind of way. A loose, messy bun swept her hair up from high cheekbones; her small dark eyes watched Josh with a cautious, pronounced disinterest.

She was accustomed to protecting herself, Josh could see, and he wondered what darkness Arnie had rescued her from.

"That guy that Arnie knows in Brody Pen," he finally said. "I need to get a message to him. An uncensored one. In code or whatever. Not by a regular phone call or a letter that might be monitored."

"Arnie won't help you out with that. He wants nothing to do with you. I'm not even allowed to say your name."

"Does he do that thing where, when you say my name, he pretends to throw it on the floor and spit on it?" Josh chuckled darkly.

"Then he crushes it with his foot. Something like that. What the hell'd you do to him? Should I be pissed at you too?"

Josh chewed on a nail and focused on his helmet while he thought about what to tell her. Could Lucie be trusted? In all honesty, he wasn't sure. But she was his last hope for his family's freedom. Wriggling himself into a more comfortable sitting position, he sat up straighter and said, "I asked him for something he wasn't willing to give me."

"Why wasn't he willing?" This was news to Lucie. "Arnie has always bent over backward for Jessie. He'd do anything for her."

The bitter way she said that made Josh crook his head and stare almost down at her, curious. "Not that your husband ever gives much away, Lucie, but I never thought you had a problem with that."

"I don't. Not really," Lucie admitted. "It just irks me sometimes, the way everyone jumps at her every beck and call. So she sings. Whatever. I sing in the shower. I don't need to make millions at it."

"She pays a tough price for her singing, Lucie."

"I know. All the power to her. She can have the big time. Hell, there's a homeless guy lives in a wheelchair on East Hastings who spits out opera like he's saying the alphabet. He could sing circles around Jessie."

"And he's likely a helluva lot happier." Josh deflated as he recalled Jessie's constant nagging to just 'live a normal life.' It wasn't her who put the pressure on herself to succeed in the big time. It was everyone else around her. Including him. "Look, Lucie," he said, recovering, bringing himself back to the present. "What I asked Arnie for—it might hurt Jessie. It—it will. It'll hurt her. But the thing is—he doesn't see the big picture. You're right about

Jessie. She clouds peoples' judgment. All they see is her. All they want is for her to be happy."

"And obviously you don't."

"'Course I do. More than anything. She'll get there."

"Why do I feel like there's a 'without you' in there?"

"You see me, Lucie? I can't sit still, here. I'm so desperate for a drink that I haven't stopped thinking about sneaking out for one since the last hangover started to fade into the realm of hazy, fuzzy memory. Ask yourself how good I am for her."

"The way Arnie tells it, she's lost without you."

"Look, the thing is…it's not just about her anymore."

"Your kids."

"They outnumber her."

"Three to one. I see."

Josh held up four fingers. "There's a new baby on the way." He wiggled the fingers. "I can pay, Lucie, if you can get to Arnie's guy for me. You can quit this job."

"I can already quit. Charles pays Arnie very well."

Looking around, Josh was surprised that anyone would want to stay here, working in a food court slinging sub-par Indian food to a few stragglers.

Lucie read the curiosity creasing his brow. "I like it. I need a place to be. I like people."

"Well, good. That's good, then. Spend the money on something else. Furniture. A new car."

"I like the bus. I got a couch last year. Josh, I don't need or want your money. But…"

He perked up.

"I'll hook you up with a person who might take you up on that. The money. Not Arnie. Like I said, he's done with you."

"All right. So long, old Arnie." It hurt to say that, to admit that the guy would no longer be Josh's trusted security. Absently Josh wondered why Jessie had yet to bring it up to him. "When?" he asked Lucie. "And can I ask who? And what they can do for me?"

Lucie took in a deep breath. "The person you need to talk to in the prison is called Vaughn. He's a mean bastard, a cutter. He's in the clink for cutting up two girls. He woulda been charged with cutting Jessie, too, if she hadn't begged Arnie to leave it be."

"What?" Josh chilled.

"She figured she survived Vaughn's knife, the other women didn't. That was enough for her." Lucie leaned forward and rested her forearms on the table. "Arnie heard that Jessie was with Vaughn one night—for cash, you get what I'm sayin', Josh? And so Arnie went looking for her. Vaughn respects Arnie, always has. Those people out there who love your wife's music would be some mighty glad Arnie found her that night, if they knew."

Swallowing three times in quick succession so he wouldn't puke, and reeling with this new darkness about his wife's shady, obscure history, Josh half mirrored Lucie's movement and leaned his elbows on the table. He dropped his forehead into shaking hands. "Funny," he said in a weird voice, "there are days when I feel like I don't know my wife at all."

Lucie paused. "Maybe you don't want to know her."

"The hell I don't."

"All of her, I mean. Her past. It's easy to skid past the bad stuff and go straight to the designer clothes and the luxury lifestyle, Josh. Isn't it?"

Looking up, Josh considered that. Momentarily speechless, he just shook his head. "Sometimes, Lucie?" he said. "You see that side of her, the homeless, scared side. But you know what? It's not always when you think you'll see it. It's when she's singing, with her hair all fancy, after some highly paid technician's glued tiny crystal diamonds onto her fingernails. Those are the only times she really lets go of the demons that haunt her. It's like she's safe there, in the music. It protects her while she lets the pain go. And that's how I know she'll be okay. After…" He let the sentence fade off into the ether.

Thoughtful, Lucie studied him for a moment before she glanced over at the small takeout counter where she was supposed to be working. Her boss, a sixtyish graying East Indian man, was giving her the hairy eyeball. "I gotta get back to work," she said. "Look, Josh, come to my place tomorrow. Same time. Arnie won't be there, he'll be at the gym. Can you do that? I'll introduce you to a friend of mine. She has a direct line to Vaughn."

Josh perked up. "Uncensored? An uncensored line?"

"Uncensored." Lucie pointed at her lips and then to Josh's mouth. "Direct line."

"Who is she?"

As Lucie stood up to go, she said simply, "Her name is Murphy. She's a corrections officer."

"Seriously? She works at Brody?"

"Five days a week. But lucky for you, she's in Vancouver a lot. Must be serendipity. Flies home most weekends to sit with Vaughn's ninety-year-old grandmother. Murphy has Vaughn's ear." Rather uncouthly, Lucie gestured to her crotch. "And his dick. And she'll do anything for a buck. The warden at Brody would shit a front end loader if he knew the truth about her."

"Can she be trusted?"

"Can anyone be trusted, Josh?" As she started to move away, Lucie said, "Stay there. I'll bring you a plate. You like butter chicken?"

"Not hungry," Josh muttered. But by the time he finally pointed his Harley up the winding road to the lookout on Cypress, his belly was full and his heart, deathly afraid.

～ ～

The next day, Josh begged off a family trip to Science World with the excuse that he wanted to do some spring cleanup around the UBC house. They were at the house so the kids could have some playtime at home, and pick out some toys to take down to La Casa later. Nobody wanted to admit it out loud, but Charles and Dee needed a little break from all the action too.

Taken aback when he told her he wasn't coming with them to Science World, Jessie felt serious doubt creep into her consciousness. "B-but Steve and Sophie are coming with us. We haven't seen them in ages!"

"Don't start, Jessie, I just need some time alone, okay?" Josh wasn't in the mood for games. "Bring them back here later. We'll have a rip-roaring old fashioned good time."

"Duh, you and the kids are flying out at six."

"Me and the boys, you mean. Let's not forget that our daughter has chosen to stay here with her beloved Grammie and her perfectly sane mother."

"That's low. Geez."

"Jessie, don't read more into this than is necessary. I won't take off to a bar. I won't buy booze. I swear."

"Since we're on that topic—"

"What?" Josh cut her off. "You want to talk about my problems? Now? Your beloved Matt will be here any second with his growing army of baby-sitters, uh, I mean security."

"Matt and I are hardly speaking, Josh. He's hardly on my beloved list these days."

"Amazes me that you even talk to Jacob. Seems like when your old lovers hook up with someone new, you write them off for a bit, eh? Too hard on the old ego?"

"Oh. My. God. You are being so insane right now! What the hell, Josh?"

He slid open the back door by the pool. "I'll be outside. Have a good time at Science World. Learn lots."

"What I need to learn," Jessie fumed, stomping out to the deck behind him, almost tripping over toys as she moved, despite the fact that all three children were currently upstairs fawning over toys in their playroom they hadn't seen in a while, "is what you demanded of Arnie that sent him running scared."

Josh stilled, but he was disarmed only for a few seconds. An Oscar winning actor, by the time he turned back to her, his face was a carefully constructed mask of normalcy. "I wanted to go to the bars. He didn't think that was such a good idea."

"Bullshit." She crossed her arms and tapped a set of toes up and down, up and down.

Quietly, Josh held her gaze as he stepped one of his own feet lightly on top of Jessie's anxiously moving foot. The low taps against the deck were like some kind of bizarre clock ticking, a countdown. The nerve on his cheek twitched. "D'you ever consider, Jessie, that not everybody is interested in babysitting us all of the time? That maybe Arnie just got sick and tired of my ugly face? Of my propensity to go running for something to numb the pain every time shit goes haywire?"

"He wouldn't bail on you."

"No," he cut her off, "what you mean to say is that he wouldn't bail on you. He doesn't give a sweet goddamn about me."

"Yeah, he does. Of course he does! God, you're being a selfish asshole today, Josh! I'm just trying to understand here! I want to help you!"

"If you want to help me, take the kids and go to Science World so I can work in peace. I just need some peace and quiet." At that, Josh marched across the deck to the back corner where he whipped open the door of their storage shed and rummaged around for an old broom he always used to sweep the deck.

Astounded, Jessie rocked back on her heel and watched him until David came running and begged her to referee a fight between him and Dylan over some old toy.

It killed Josh not to spend the afternoon with Jessie, the kids and their friends. But he had no choice. He landed at Arnie's new condo precisely five minutes before he was expected. One look at Murphy's glossy blue eye shadow and the hungry, determined eyes underneath long, feminine lashes, and he knew he would get what he wanted.

"Money talks," he grumbled as he strode darkly toward her and Lucie. Within five minutes, the deal was done.

Chapter Thirty-nine

Vaughn approached Morgan in the small community room where Morgan's range of Brody Pen inmates were allowed to hang out for an hour or two during specified times each day, if their behavior during the day warranted the privilege. Usually only a half dozen inmates were there at any one time, and usually the television was blaring. Since the room wasn't in his home range, Vaughn got in on a special pass; it was Murphy that secured it for him. Didn't hurt to have the kind of respect around Brody that enticed a woman like Murphy to be on your side. It also didn't hurt that there was a very big carrot dangling at the end of a stick, for Murphy. It behooved her to make adjustments for her lover, to clear a trail for Vaughn. It was not unusual for a long time inmate with a solid track record of good behavior, who was known to cooperate with the corrections officers and liaison with the warden on behalf of the other cons, to move almost freely around the pen.

Even more so, things were stirring up at Brody. Both sides of the equation had picked up on tension between Vaughn and Morgan, that worsened after Jessie Wheeler's SUV was run off the road. Little things, like Vaughn's rascally passel of worshipful disciples catcalling and making threats of violence against Morgan, and pulling out homemade knives to viciously hold in front of him as he moved nervously past, or ordering him off a bench during the afternoon air—these were the things that alerted everyone that trouble was brewing. It got so bad that the warden called Vaughn up to his office in some conciliatory attempt to settle things down, to get to the bottom of the issue at hand. He even offered coffee. The warden was a smart, intuitive man. It was always the little boiler-type things that escalated to all out explosions, and he didn't need the kind of blood on his hands that a full scale prison population riot would produce. His annual funding review was coming up. Alton wanted a squeaky clean penitentiary. Murphy's request for Vaughn to visit Morgan wasn't only given; it was expedited.

At a time when Caulfield was present.

That was the other thing. All sides at Brody were aware that Caulfield had to act on Morgan's behalf. Morgan could issue orders, but his hands were tied. No one, as yet, had put two and two together—no one had figured out that Oren Caulfield was pulling the strings that were pissing Vaughn off. The man was powerful, but he was known as a devoted officer who cared about the guys under his watch enough to right the wrongs they felt were done to them. They came to him. He was their enforcer. Nobody pegged him as a supreme commander who was, at least in Morgan's case, fully in control.

When Vaughn entered the small community room, he sidled in like an overgrown ape, swaggering from side to side with an agitated confidence. The officer at the door keeping an eye on things was the young redhead who, Morgan discovered over time, was amenable and friendly, at least as friendly as he could really be, given the circumstances. He'd been told to send the other half dozen guys in the space back to their cells when Vaughn made his big, burly entrance. Not a soul grumbled when they had to leave. The kind of respect a man like Vaughn had wasn't limited to keeping the prison politics and social order in hand. It was also interconnected with cycles of life and death.

Vaughn reached up to the television and poked a thick finger on the volume up arrow before he faced Morgan and Caulfield. Wouldn't do to let any of the minion officers watching the room via remote camera overhear what would be discussed in the next five minutes.

Unaware this meeting was happening, Morgan was seated when his nemesis strode into the room with a menacing air. At Vaughn's heavy footsteps and the quick retreat of the other inmates, Morgan vaulted up and faced Vaughn—a man he feared, a man who had made very clear violent threats against him. Morgan's eyes darted down to Vaughn's hands. The huge fists were clenched, but as far as Morgan could tell, they were empty. *Phew.*

Caulfield was standing by the door. He sauntered over. "What?" he asked, ignoring Morgan altogether.

Vaughn glanced at Morgan. The guy was as pale and defeated looking as ever. His eyes appeared almost blank. A curious grunt later, Vaughn fixed Caulfield's stony, rock hard eyes in his. "The Sawyers," he said. Time was limited. Getting to the point hard and fast was critical if they were to come to any kind of agreement. "I've asked you to lay off them. They've had enough."

"We will. When the debt is paid."

Vaughn put a booted foot up on a chair. "I'm here to renegotiate your payment."

"And why would I—we," Caulfield sent Morgan a conspiratorial, sleazy half grin, "want to consider that?"

Behind them, the magnified score of a sci-fi movie was blaring on the TV. Their voices were low. Vaughn dove in deeper. "Because I've got an offer you can't refuse."

Morgan stopped breathing. When Vaughn walked into the room, he'd half expected to be sliced and diced and left for mouse food. Now he couldn't help but wonder if this hell he was living in—the one orchestrated by Caulfield, seemingly an endless tyranny of power and destruction in a world Morgan thought he'd left behind, in the lives of people he still, all things considered, cared about—was coming to an end.

Vaughn raised a hand. He rubbed a meaty finger and thumb together. "Josh," he said, loud and clear, the single word making the hackles on the back of Morgan's neck rise in morbid interest.

"He think he can buy his family's safety? This has never been about money." Caulfield was infuriatingly cocky.

Vaughn wanted to slug him. But he was here to do a job. Murphy wanted a house in Vancouver so she could keep an eye on Vaughn's shrunken, ancient grandmother for him. Sweet, she was, Murphy…and the grandmother? She raised Vaughn after his father strangled their mother in front of him when he was four. The real estate market in Vancouver was the most expensive in Canada. Vaughn's eyes darted up to the clock. Time was ticking by. He had to wrap this up and get back to his own range before one of the less respectful of the 'guard mafia' got ornery and needed to be taught a lesson. No point in stirring up more pots than he had to tonight. Prison Break reruns were airing on the tube. Vaughn had a restful night on his bunk planned. "The money's just a bonus," he said.

Caulfield paused. Turning sideways, he spit into a nearby garbage can. "You got somethin' else to say on the matter? Or are we done here?"

Vaughn smiled, the slow, reckless widening of his mouth accented by a lowering of his shoulders that Caulfield, watching, found curious. Curious enough at least to gain his full attention.

Morgan was observing carefully too, with what he hoped was passing as detachment, but inside, his guts were roiling.

Vaughn made his offer. *Josh's* offer.

The first thing Morgan did when he got back to his cell later was clutch the sides of his cell's toilet bowl and puke into its open-mouthed glare.

Part of the reason he couldn't keep his mashed potatoes down was out of sheer relief.

The other part was due to the reappearance of his old enemy, the one that softened him and made him weak.

His old friend heartache was back.

For Jessie and for her children.

～ ⁓ ⁓

Josh got the good news via text from Lucie. He was just off set reclining in a cast chair, quietly listening to Shanda rattle on about her plans for the weekend, which involved driving up to scenic Jasper with Matt, when his screen lit up.

Thinking it was likely Jessie, and hoping Shanda wouldn't notice, Josh dared a discreet glance at the phone in his hands. After scanning the text once, then sitting up a little straighter and reading it again, Josh missed a good two minutes' worth of Shanda's monologue.

She called him back to her with a light tap on the bicep. "Sawyer. Am I boring you?"

Trying to refocus, Josh treated her to a subdued smile. He'd expected to feel revulsion and fright when this message came through.

But all that truly ran through Josh's veins at the concise text, which read *good to go,* was sweet, blissful, sheer relief.

He closed his eyes and thanked God for listening.

Chapter Forty

Two weeks later

$\mathcal{S}$ometimes there was magic in the air. Sometimes, all of the components came together—lights, sound, band, moods—and gave Jessie and Jacob's concerts lifts into the stratosphere. Sometimes their shows were exceptional. Sometimes they rocked.

This was not one of those times.

On the plus side, not a single protester was in the audience waving a placard expressing distaste for Jacob. It seemed his actions in Florida were finally being mitigated. Not negated, in the public's eye there was no real forgiveness for that kind of sexual violence. Just mitigated. To a point. Via the regular and constant appearances he was making at conferences and schools and forums, scheduled of course by the tired but determined Deirdre.

He sang at these events—he always sang, at least a song or two. Music was the key to getting Jacob through the tough days when the reminder of what darkness he was actually capable of floored him, telling him he was not the stand-up man he used to think he was. Standing in front of dozens, hundreds, and even sometimes thousands of women—and men—and admitting how low he sank the day he raped Jessie, a woman he loved beyond all measure, was the hardest thing he ever had to do in his life.

He did it for her. He did it for countless other victims of assault.

He did it for his new child. Jacob and Kayla would soon have a daughter. They planned to call her Lily, a name they read meant innocence, purity, and beauty. To Jacob and Kayla, the name Lily signified a new start.

The festival Jacob and Jessie were playing this weekend was just outside of Paris. Deirdre and the children were with them, back at the hotel at the moment. Kayla was along for the fun too, having stepped aside from the workshop tour in favor of spending time with her new husband.

Watching them together, Jessie couldn't help but feel a sad mixed-up kind of joy. Jacob's old warning about a life with Josh that would always be edged with uncertainty was running over and over in her mind these days. Not that she would ever let Josh go, no, that was not an option. Not now and not ever. But hanging on to a man she so deeply loved, but whom Jessie had to almost constantly monitor for signs of immersion back into the troubled booze-lined nest that Josh, when he was drinking, somehow interpreted as safe and secure—especially given his actions after her 'accident'—was absolutely, completely, emotionally exhausting.

Still, there was so much light in Jacob's eyes. *How can I not be happy for him?* On stage now, Jessie looked over at him. They had just played their most famous, well-loved ballad, the one they wrote together in New York just after Josh and Jessie separated. The one about Josh—about leaving, and healing. About trying to move on after loss. Usually this ballad was magical. Playing it live on stage with Jacob was always surreal. It united them. It gave the two singers a unique connection that was solely theirs. It raised and elevated them; it empowered them to rise above the many hurts of the difficult years, and it showed the world that two people can love each other, hurt each other, and somehow, in the fallout, find forgiveness.

Tonight the ballad did none of those things. For once, all that the melancholy tune served to do was make Jessie's heart hurt more. Jacob was oblivious. The song was as incredible as always, to him—its gentle rhythm and sincere, open lyrics were as extraordinary as ever. Standing back now, watching Jacob—on her left, as always—accept the raucous applause that seemed to go on forever and ever when they played the ballad, Jessie felt like a statue made of ice. The band, the audience, the watchers hiding in the wings at stage right—assorted crew, Matt, Kayla—suddenly didn't seem real. It was like they were living in an entirely different dimension, separate from Jessie. The eerie feeling was unsettling.

A wave of energy washed over Jessie. *Truth bumps.* They crawled up her legs and made her hair stand on edge. Stepping back from the microphone, she let the hand clutching it fall to her side. There was a gazillion pound weight on her chest now; it pressed against her lungs, suffocating her. She was trying to recall why it felt so familiar, then she remembered coming to her senses in the Lexus after it rolled, as it was starting to sink. That was it, the feeling. Like she was suffocating, like the air around her was being drained away like water from a pool.

A slow panic was rising in her stomach. It was putting pressure on her lungs, and reducing the cheers of the crowd to a distant and muted buzz. Jessie gasped and lifted a shaking hand to her throat. Jacob was off in his own sweet world of adulation and bliss. Turning away from him, Jessie sought out Matt in the rainbow twilight just off stage.

Matt had watched Jessie and Jacob sing the ballad. He stood there, as always, and soaked it up, even though he and Jessie were barely speaking these days. The funny thing was, in terms of physical closeness, their dialogue was as clear and communicative as ever. Jessie still touched his hand when she walked by him. She still let her fingers softly graze his, or twine themselves in his, even, in that childlike way she'd never fully been able to let go of. Usually this happened by the craft table back stage, or in the 'green room' trailer or tent she and Jacob were assigned to on these summer festival trips. Occasionally Jessie touched him when they were seated next to each other in whatever vehicle was driving them here, there and everywhere. She went so far as to lay a hand on his thigh, sometimes, not in a sexual or provocative way, just in her absent Jessie way, that was all. It was a casual thing, her touching him, and somehow the actions made up for the words neither could find the courage to say, for fear of what they might unleash.

Matt was not fully innocent—he accepted her touch. He never pushed her away. He relished the times she brushed against him, or leaned fully into him and wrapped droopy arms around his shoulders like she briefly did last night while waiting for the cue to take the stage for sound check, when she was super tired and Dee was back at the hotel with the kids. Matt let his arms slip around her waist, then, and his lips touch her neck; let his eyes close over so he could float there, his warm breath sending whatever renewed energy it could into Jessie's weary spirit.

Not sexual, he told himself. *Just…because.*

Lightning quick, he was jarred out of the wistful reverie when he saw Jessie, still awash in the bright stage lights, seek him out. Out of character, she was walking toward him now, or, more realistically, almost limping. Idly he wondered if she was still feeling some physical fallout from the roll-over, or if something about the show tonight was tiring her or hurting her more than usual.

"Something's wrong," she whimpered just offstage when Matt strode toward her and smoothed wispy hair back from her forehead so he could see her eyes more clearly. "Something bad's happening. I can feel it."

Matt went on alert. He took a quick scan around before asking, "What do you mean something bad? Here? Are you okay, Jessie?"

Her breaths were quickening. "I—I can't breathe, Matt. My heart…it feels like it's gonna jump out of my chest."

Placing his palms on both sides of her cheeks, Matt demanded that she look at him. "Anxiety, Jessie," he told her in his most authoritative voice. "That's all this is. Look at me. Slow down." His heart was suddenly racing too, but it wouldn't do to let his girl see that. What Jessie needed was for him to take control. The thing was, it was getting harder and harder to do that these days. Because, most days, Matt felt like crumpling up too. Some days he thought that curling up beside Jessie in bed, and hanging on for dear life, was the only way he could ever possibly help her feel safe.

Mustering up some courage came surprisingly easy to him now, though, in the heat of the moment. Talking Jessie through anxiety was almost more of an emotional muscle memory thing than an actual systematic process. "Easy, sweetheart," he said in the most firm but gentle tone he could man-age. In terms of the show, they were on the encore, at least…the ballad was the first encore song, but Jessie had a slow tune scheduled next, before she and Jacob were supposed to finish with a happy anthem that would send their fans home to their ordinary lives on a jubilant high.

On stage, Jacob clued in that something was wrong when he finally glanced over at Jessie's mic to find it empty. Nor was she at the piano, which was where she was supposed to be for her final solo tune. Peering past her mic, he spotted her with Matt, who was intently speaking to her about some-thing. She was nodding, but even from the far end of the stage Jacob could see her back moving in and out—her lungs expanding and contracting—as if she'd just sprinted from here to their hotel and back.

Raising an arm, he tried to quiet the crowd as he stepped back from his mic. Scanning the stage behind him, he signaled the band to hang on, to wait for his cue. Christian had already vacated the piano bench to make room for Jessie to do her song. Jacob caught his eye. Christian slid back in place and started playing a pretty instrumental piece that, to the fans at the huge outdoor show, was an acceptable bridge to the next song.

Jessie sensed Jacob approach before she felt his hand at the small of her back. Closing her eyes, she let Matt talk to him. At least her breathing was returning to normal.

"Anxiety attack," Matt told Jacob. To Jessie, he said, "Better now?"

"Yeah. Y-yeah," she stammered. Finally, she was able to draw full breaths again. "I'm coming, Jacob," she said as Kayla approached and, concerned, took Jacob's hand. "Going back out there." Sucking in one last big inhale, Jessie gave Matt a long, thoughtful look. "I felt something, Matt," she said softly. "Energetically, I mean. Something shifted somewhere. Something not good."

"You're in Paris, Jessie," he admonished, his voice equally subdued. "Last time you were here, something very sinister happened. You're getting that vibe."

"No, honey," she responded. A deep well of dread took root in her heart. Matt saw it appear in her eyes; it was like an ominous black cloud passing in front of the moon. Shaking her head slowly from side to side, Jessie said, "It's Josh. He and I—you know—we can feel each other." There was moisture just under the surface now, big bubbles of it aching for release.

Uncertain, Matt bent forward and pulled her body close. There was nothing else he could say or do that could offer comfort for words that big, for words that carried so much terrifying weight. Closing his eyes, he relaxed slightly when Jessie let her body sigh into his. They stayed that way for a few extended moments, until Jessie gleaned whatever strength she could from her good friend, turned, and made her way on shaky legs over to the grand piano, a plastered smile masking the worry on her pallid face.

Relieved, both Jacob and Christian found their rightful homes on stage—Christian on a secondary keyboard off to Jacob's right, just off center, and Jacob in his usual spot. When Jessie started to play, everyone collectively exhaled, and no one but their own little circle were any the wiser.

During her shows, Matt often had Jessie's cellphone in his pocket. Since he generally kept his own line free for emergencies—in case Deirdre needed him, for instance—he called Josh on it just after Jessie started to play the slow tune on the piano.

Josh answered on the first ring. "Show over, Jessie?" he asked. He sounded happy. He sounded calm. That was Matt's first clue that something in Josh Sawyer's world had, as Jessie suspected, likely changed.

"It's me, Josh." Matt locked his eyes on Jessie's back. Stretching out an arm, he held the phone toward the stage.

From Calgary, where he was at the soundstage's craft table waiting for a bagel to toast, Josh kept the phone at his ear and paused to listen. Jessie was playing a slow tune she wrote for him way back when they first met—it was one of her biggest hits. Her impassioned voice as she sang about her love for him was, to Josh, effervescent glitter bleeding from a weeping rainbow.

There was a canvas chair close by, shoved there by some zealous A.D. when the *Sacred Peace* gang was changing sets, likely. Emitting a ragged, low, frustrated *uhhhhh,* Josh sank into it and buried his face in his free hand.

Matt waited until the entire song drew to a close before he said another word. He didn't give a shit if Josh was about to be called to set. As far as Matt was concerned, the man needed to hear his wife playing, for thousands of adoring fans, a song she had written for him. Josh and Jessie had many love songs now, after years of loving and hurting and wondering and aching and healing, but this was one of the earliest shared between them, written when all Jessie had—in terms of wanting Josh—was hope.

When the last perfect note graced the keys, opening the door for Jacob and Jessie to start the show's rousing finale, Matt put the phone back against his ear. He spoke sharply and without prejudice, his voice gruff and his words meant to convey everything he'd been thinking over the last few weeks but was too uncertain and confused to say.

"Whatever it is you're up to, Josh, let it be. Stop it. It's not too late."

Speechless, Josh struggled. "I-I don't know what you're talking about, Matt," he finally spouted, wondering what the hell this call—and Jessie's song, played live for him from Paris—was really about.

Matt eyeballed Jessie to be sure she was okay before he stuck a finger in one ear and walked to the far edge of the wing so he could hear better. "Like hell you don't," he argued. "End it. Jessie got some kind of premonition or something about you tonight. Whatever you think you can do to stop this madness, or whatever you're planning to do to escape it, if that's what you're up to, don't. You hear me?"

A solemn voice made its way from Calgary to Paris. Around Josh were grips and electrics, the usual crude crew jokes being tossed around like balls on the beach as they hurried to paint, with light, the next set they'd be shooting. Josh was completely unaware of their presence. He was staring at the floor, watching an ant carry a crumb a gazillion times its weight from next to his boot to a crack in the crude wooden floor. "It's not your business, Matt. Not yet. But it will be, okay? Soon."

That was it. Matt almost collapsed. He had to bend over and grip a metal railing as he grasped the significance of the comment. On stage behind him, Jessie and Jacob, guitars in hand, were back at their usual mics, launching into the last tune. Matt would have to look Jessie in the eye when she walked off stage.

His voice was hoarse but thin when he said, "We'll talk when I get back, Josh. All right?"

"Yeah. Fine." But Josh's words rang hollow. False. As if the person who spoke them hardly knew he'd uttered them out loud.

Chapter Forty-one

"I can't get that song out of my head. Why, Matt?"

For the first time in a while, Matt was sitting next to Jessie on the jet. Everybody'd noticed that they'd held hands the entire flight, and now, after flying for a good chunk of the night, the group was almost home. Nobody batted an eye. Everybody understood that Matt and Jessie were each other's lifelines. Like electric cords joined together to form an extension, their clasped hands simply voiced their connection.

Jessie and Matt had only napped a little on the overnight flight. Their renewed amicability was far too precious to waste on sleep.

In response to Jessie's concern, Matt stayed quiet.

Jessie jumped in again. "The slow song I wrote for Josh. The one I played during the encore. That song." Hesitating, she took a reading on Matt's pensive expression and decided to corner right and take them in a different direction, since he didn't seem to quite know how to respond. He was staring at her hand, the one he was holding as gently as a fragile egg, watching his thumb move back and forth over her skin. "I called Charlie," Jessie stated rather matter of factly. "He said Josh has been quiet but he's okay. They took the quads out last evening after work. Since Blue…well, this season Josh hasn't been as keen on taking the horses out as he used to be. Thank God for small mercies."

Relieved just to be talking with Matt again, Jessie brightened. It was partially a false attempt at steering him away from what she would soon have to tell him, but part of it was sincere. Having Matt by her side as a trusted ally and friend—and savior, at times—was very, very welcome in these troubled times. She cocked an ear so she could hear Deirdre, on the small sofa behind them, read Dylan's favorite pony book to him. Unlike the older two kids, Dylan was wide awake. Adding the new baby to the inventory of her children, Jessie smiled and laid her free hand over her belly to feel its fluttery kicks.

"Um, so I talked to Deirdre finally," she said. "About the film in Montreal. They've recast."

"That's too bad."

"Not really. I won't miss it. I had to promise lion lady that I would do something else after the baby's born, though. She'll have me working by January, if I know her."

"The kids seem happy. About the baby, I mean."

"I guess so. They might change their minds if this new little one's anything like Dylan, stealing toys and attention." Jessie smiled, but it upended itself real quick when she mustered up the courage to take Matt down another road. She shifted her position in her seat as she started to speak. "Um, so Charlie and me, we're going for a drive today, Matt. We need some time to talk. I need his perspective on how my husband is doing, since Charlie's with Josh more than I am these days."

"Drive? Where?" Matt ached to lay his free hand over the hand he watched Jessie place on her belly. His eyes were stuck to it like glue. She kept moving her fingers, just a little here and there, sideways, and up and down. It was clear to him that the new Sawyer baby was making its tiny presence known.

"It's all so real now," Jessie whispered, trying to distract him from the drive in which she had no intention of including him. Reading Matt's mind, she smiled over at him and lifted their already joined hands onto her abdomen. "The baby, I mean. Feel this little guy give the world the old Sawyer F U."

"You think it's a boy?" Taking a chance, Matt used his left hand to pull the bottom hem of Jessie's top up. He felt her stiffen, but she didn't protest. "Need to feel your skin," he murmured without meeting her eyes.

"Mmmm. Okay." Swallowing, Jessie watched Matt's left hand move over her exposed belly. Wriggling down a little in her seat, she helped him navigate the baby's movements. "It's been a while since you felt a baby move like this, huh Matt?"

"I'm not too old to be a father again, according to Shanda, if that's what you're thinking."

"You could be a dad and a grandpa all at once if your daughter hooks up one of these days."

A bittersweet wave passed over Matt's face. Catching it, Jessie wondered what was bothering him, whether it was the mention of the daughter he rarely saw, or the life he left behind with Julie, or perhaps what he and she—Jessie—might have shared if life took a different twist more than a year ago.

Finally looking up, Matt caught her watching him. He was loathe to lift his hand from her belly but was honorable enough to do so after what seemed like an appropriate amount of time to linger there, sharing this miracle of life with her.

She sighed. "Matt, I was just thinking…"

"Uh oh. Should I be scared? You thinking—it worries me."

She swatted him.

His eyes twinkled, just a little. "You look rather serious there, Jessie."

"Relax, handsome. We can handle this, you and me."

He sat back and secured his right hand and her left back on his thigh again. This time, Jessie paid closer attention to the light brushing of his thumb against hers, and the way he accented the movement with barely disguised sadness that he communicated with downturned lips and frequent swallows. "Speak," he ordered, with a raspy 'lack of sleep' voice.

"I just wondered…do you ever think about what might have happened between us if Josh hadn't gotten hurt that night?"

The thumb stopped moving. It was a good few minutes before Matt found the courage to talk without giving away too many of the difficult feelings he usually tried to conceal from Jessie. "I think about it all the time," he finally admitted. "You?"

"Sometimes. When you were gone…hiding out in P.E.I…I thought I was gonna lose my mind."

"You and Josh…you have this thing…" Shaking his head, Matt said, "I don't even know what it is the two of you have. It's indefinable. The way you look at him, it's like he's not even real. He's an apparition."

"Jesus, Matt. Don't say that, please." Shivering, Jessie took her hand out of his, turned sideways, and curled into him, her back against his side. Soon her belly would be too big to do that, to draw her knees up that way. Reaching for his arm again, she laid it around her right shoulder, pressed his forearm to her chest, and clung to it. Sighing, she leaned her head back against him. With a toe, Jessie pushed up the blind over the jet's small window. A radiant dawn was forming over the gorgeous brilliance of the virginal snow-capped rocky mountains; she could barely see them in the distance, cotton candy pink in the nascent light, capably dividing the provinces of Alberta and British Columbia where she and her family spent most of their time. *Or guarding them*, she thought. *Like an insurmountable border. A wall. Huh. Easy to see where my mind is at.*

"It's true," Matt was saying. "Yet you fight like there's no tomorrow. You'd think by now, with everything you've been through, that you'd never fight."

"Our fights aren't the threatening kind, Matt. We've got each other figured out. Well, mostly," Jessie said, considering the gloomy feeling that Josh was hiding something from her.

"Then cherish each other, Jessie. Don't tell him he can go drinking when you know he can't handle it."

"It might not make sense to you, Matt, but that *was* me cherishing him." Her childlike self again, Jessie started playing with Matt's fingers, wringing them and massaging them. Watching over her shoulder, he soaked up the gentle ministrations. "Josh needed that. He needed a good binge after what happened to us."

"He's an alcoholic, sweetheart. He's a damn good guy when he's sober, but he's not a guy who should be drinking. Ever."

"I didn't know what else I could do for him, Matt. He was jumping out of his skin. Which, by the way, he isn't doing anymore. I don't know why he's so damn calm lately. He's too calm."

Behind her, Matt closed his eyes and emitted a tiny, "Jesus." Josh being calm meant that he'd found some peace. But there was no peace on the horizon, not while roughnecks were jumping him in underground parking garages demanding he choose which child to give up; not after his wife was intentionally run off the road into a river, with their daughter—whom Josh felt on some level he *did* choose—buckled into a booster seat next to a beloved pet.

"I'll talk to him."

"Heard that you already did. You let him hear my song."

A tired chuckle was Matt's answer. "He needed to hear it, sweetheart. From now on, you play music for that man you love. You don't send him out to the bars."

"I'll try, Matt. Thank you. For being you, I mean. And for being here."

The arm Jessie was hanging on to tightened around her. Arcing his head to the side, Matt buried his face in Jessie's hair.

Clearing her throat, which was suddenly full of rocks, Jessie teased him with, "So. Shanda, huh?"

"Jessie…let's not go there right now. Okay?"

"If she breaks your heart, I'll kick her from here to Timbuktu."

"If you take off with Charlie without me, I mean without me tailing the two of you at least, I'll kick your ass from here to Timbuktu."

"Where the hell's Timbuktu anyway?"

"Damned if I know. Don't change the subject."

"Damned if I know either."

Charlie would be waiting at the airport in Calgary. Panicked, Jessie had called him from backstage after the show, stealing off in a corner to do so, telling Matt she was calling Josh. She did call Josh, but snuck a quick call to Charlie in there as well. According to Victoria, they would be landing in twenty minutes. The Asian hostess knew her travelers well. She dropped fresh cappuccinos into the cup holders in Matt's and Jessie's comfy seats.

Jessie held hers up. "Just one," she told Matt. "The worst part of being pregnant is rationing my java. Kinda sucks. And no smoking. Ever. I miss the occasional smoke with Arnie. Come to think of it, I miss Arnie."

Matt chose to remain silent again.

Jessie rotated around and peered closely at him. "Maybe if you talked to him, he'd come back."

"Arnie and I…we haven't really seen eye to eye on some stuff lately, Jessie. I don't think talking to him is going to do any good."

"Try? Please?"

Biting back a nervous retort, Matt shrugged. "I don't know, kid. Maybe."

She squeezed his arm and sighed with relief.

Charles, too, would have a car waiting, a large SUV that could carry

Deirdre and the children. Josh would already be at the soundstage for an early call. The plan was for Charles to take the kids to see their father before Deirdre and Charles, with Alin in tow, headed to the ranch, where Dan was waiting.

Matt's Audi was already at the airport. When he stepped down the jet's few steps, he greeted Charlie with a wave and stopped by him to say hello. Charlie, arms and ankles crossed, was leaning back against his newest black Porsche. The men watched Jessie and Dee lead a stumbling, sleepy Emily-Grace and a yawning David to the waiting SUV.

Dylan ran by and gave Charlie a high five before he leapt into his waiting grandfather's arms.

"My kid is never gonna eat what that kid eats," Charlie grinned. "He sleep at all?"

"That's his problem. He's overtired." A crack in his jaw when he yawned made Matt rub a hand over the sore joint. "Ouch," he added.

"He's not the only one, I see. Go home. Rest." A hard thwack on Matt's back was Charlie's way of offering support. "I hope you're headed to the condo and not planning to drive all the way to the ranch."

"Neither. I hear we're taking a road trip."

Charlie stiffened. "That what you hear? You hear wrong, my friend. We," Charlie pointed to himself and then to Matt and back again, "are not taking a road trip. That girl," he pointed to Jessie, who was gently nudging Emily-Grace into a booster seat, "and I are taking a road trip. We need a day to get reacquainted, apparently. She called me from Paris."

"Getting reacquainted where, Charlie?" Matt's serious voice came into play.

Charlie raised an eyebrow and studied him to see just how pissed Matt would be if he knew where he, Charlie, was taking Jessie today. *Super pissed,* he decided when he saw Matt's eyes narrow and his arms cross. *Like, ghost pepper hot sauce pissed.* Charlie recrossed his ankles the opposite way. "Not for you to know, buddy," he said. The declaration came out a little bit squeaky.

"You want to be the hero this time, Charlie? Is that it?"

"Matt, settle. Geez. No, she swore me to secrecy. She'll have my balls if I tell because you'll get in the way and likely leak our little secret to Charles over there, who looks like he's all mushy and joyful when the kids are around, but who you and I both know wouldn't even bother to sharpen the knife to cut my balls off with if he knew where we were going today." Gesturing to his privates, Charlie's eyes grew wide in mock alarm.

"Uh huh. That's what I thought. How're you planning on getting her in?"

"I made a few calls. I was hoping to pilfer Charles' contact list but it's kinda hard to do that when the guy practically sits on it." Lowering his voice, because Jessie had turned around and was intently watching them, Charlie said, "That city counselor Shanda used to see. He's an MLA now. He knew someone who knew someone who knew someone…you know the drill."

"I'll be right behind you, Charlie."

"It's an eight hour drive, Matt. You won't make it to the burbs. What'd you do on the jet instead of sleep? Join the mile high club with Jessie?"

"Contrary to what everyone thinks, Charlie, Jessie and I aren't sneaking around behind Josh's back. We talked. I felt the baby kick. It was nice."

"You…felt the baby kick. I see."

"Shut it, Deacon."

Jessie was on her way over. "Y'all set, Charlie?" she asked. "You and I and the bright blue sky! Road trippin'. Let's git us some java first, shall we?" She was swinging her arms like a schoolgirl. A deep frown followed. "Damn. Had my pregnancy java quota for the day already." She wrinkled her nose before adding, with a questioning look, "Does a four thirty a.m. coffee even count?"

Charlie grinned and opened the passenger door for her. "Just like old times," he said to Matt as Jessie gave Matt's arm a squeeze and his fuzzy cheek a kiss before she hopped in. His back to Jessie after he closed the door, the jovial side of Charlie disappeared. "What the hell happened in Paris, Matt? She was out of her mind when she called me. Hence my frantic evening calls to people in the normal world whose work days normally end at five."

Quiet, catching Jessie's eye before he spoke, Matt chose not to answer and said simply, "If you lose sight of me in the rearview mirror for more than a few minutes, park your spoiled ass in a busy rest stop, go to the john, and text me where you are. I'll keep an eye on things on the road. I won't even try to go into the prison with you, but I'll be waiting to help you pick up the pieces when you come out. And Charlie? Keep her close. Don't let her go wandering around gas stations looking for road snacks. You do the buying."

"Sir," Charlie joked, raising a hand and saluting, which made Jessie laugh, although she couldn't hear what was being said. She planned to sleep while Charlie was driving. By the look of Matt, she figured he'd go to the condo he and Arnie used in Calgary, and doze off too.

"See ya, Matt," she called a few minutes later from a lowered window after Charlie put the stick in gear and hit the gas. "Thanks for this."

"Be safe, Jessie," she heard him say as they passed by. He was just sliding into the Audi.

"All is well," Jessie said to Charlie. "We're off."

Reaching across the stick shift to her lap, Charlie took Jessie's fingers in his and exerted a little pressure. "Sleep, little girl," he said. "It's a long drive." Glancing into the rearview mirror, he saw Matt pull out behind him.

"Thank God for Matt," Jessie said as she settled back with a pillow Charlie had thoughtfully grabbed for her. "I thought he'd never let us go."

"Yeah," Charlie agreed, eyeing Matt and praying the tired guy would have the sense to pull behind him in a drive-thru to grab a coffee, at least. "Thank God for Matt."

Chapter Forty-Two

An the parking lot outside Brody Pen, Jessie was far more tired than when they left the airport. Almost drunk tired. "Something about the adrenalin, likely," she told Charlie, but he knew better. Jessie'd hardly slept on the drive north. She was too busy mulling around the possibilities of what they might be faced with when they were brought to Morgan, although she didn't share a single one of those thoughts with Charlie. He could see the movie playing in her mind, though. Josh was the star. And she was the hopeful heroine.

Charlie yanked a duffel out of the trunk which, on the Porsche, was in the front where most cars' engines were, since the 911 was a rear engine car. Jessie tried to giggle, but it came out flat.

"I still think that's the weirdest thing," she said. "Having the engine in the back."

Charlie didn't answer. His nerves were getting the best of him. Zipping open the duffel, he frowned and retrieved a black baseball cap, which he held high so she could see it before he plunked it on her head.

"Seriously, Charlie," she groaned. "I've been flying all night. I look like shit. Nobody's gonna know me."

"Half of these men have your picture on their walls, Jessie. And the other half have likely—" He bit his tongue.

Crossing her arms, she rocked back onto her right foot and started tapping the left against the asphalt. "Really. So what you're trying to say is that the other half have gotten off to my old films instead. That's disgusting, Charlie."

"That's reality, Jess. These men don't have a lot of distractions. Their entertainment is likely mostly self-served."

"I think I'm gonna throw up."

"Who did you think would be watching your blue movies? Royalty?"

"Nah. Just city councilors, rich businessmen and snotty actors. The seedy types who hide behind three-piece suits and masks of charming insincerity."

"Harrumph. Get moving. At least you're the jeans and boots type." Giving her a push, Charlie flipped around at the last second to eye the parking lot. He relaxed when he saw Matt pull into a spot a few rows down. Not that there was anything Matt could do to help them when they were inside, but at least he'd be there, as he'd said, to offer comfort if need be when all was said and done. And to watch out for them on the long drive home. *Get some zzzzzs now, buddy,* Charlie silently ordered. *You've got at least an hour, I'd say. I'll wake you up with a text from the john on the way out.*

The penitentiary loomed before them like some great behemoth from a World War II film, although razor wire looped in circles around the top of the great fences surrounding the prison brought a World War I imagery to mind. Huge towers were staggered around the perimeter—*guard towers,* Charlie thought, wondering whether high power rifles were trained on them as they made their way to the main gate. The idea of it made him involuntarily shiver.

Jessie looked sideways at him. "You okay?"

"Fine," he mumbled, and shoved his hands in his pockets. "Peachy. The things I do for my ex."

"Your ex." Jessie smiled. "Isn't there a statute of limitations on calling someone your ex?"

"Not that I'm aware of. I wouldn't want there to be, in your case. The only reason I get any street cred now is because I was once engaged to you. You know that, right?"

"As if. It's that adorable charm your fans suck up like sponges."

They were trying, but their humor was falling flat. Both knew this was a make or break kind of visit. The kind that held lives in the balance. The sacred kind of lives.

Inside, they were greeted by a corrections officer who asked for their identification. It was likely a ploy to stall them and chat them up, they figured, but the guy was so serious and their visit so nerve wracking that neither Jessie nor Charlie felt like wisecracking with him. They talked about *Sacred Peace* and some of Jessie's films, and were starting to wonder when they would be moved into the prison when the warden himself came to get them.

Charlie shook his hand. Jessie did, too, but the man scowled at her. She didn't need to ask why. There were men in the prison for rape. This man would not agree with much of Jessie's colored past. He would be one of the few who would simply consider her lucky to have escaped a life of pain and years of prostitution on the Downtown Eastside. Jessie could see it in his eyes, in the way he stared darkly at her. Thankfully, he soon passed them off to a more amenable young fellow, a chatty redhead who walked them through a door that locked behind them, then another door that locked behind them, and alongside layers upon layers of walls and razor wire topped fences that led into the storied bowels of the notorious prison. They passed guns fitted into holes in the walls; at one point they walked by a yard where men in jeans and T-shirts were gathered in clumps chatting, or exercising. One man had a parrot or some other kind of colorful exotic bird on his shoulder.

The young escort explained that the prison was running a program for some of its more cooperative inmates in which pets could be brought in for a day, kind of like the therapy animals used in hospitals and in long term healthcare facilities. "It's to help the men learn to bond," the young fella told them. "Most people choose dogs, and some choose cats, but that guy used to live in Costa Rica. He says he misses the color."

"Imagine," Jessie whispered behind his back to Charlie. "Misses the color, does he?" Brody River Pen was gunmetal gray and beige. All of it. At least, the parts of the prison they were privy to seeing. Charlie was shaking in his boots. He didn't smile back.

When they reached the room they were told Morgan was waiting in, the guard gave them a heads-up.

"Look," he said. "Morgan's a quiet guy. He rarely shares what's on his mind. I'll be in the room with you, and his usual, uh, escort, Caulfield, will be there as well. When you're ready to go, just say the word." He glanced at Charlie, who was a sickly shade of green. "He's cuffed to the table, Mr. Deacon."

Jessie would have snickered at the formality if she weren't about to try to bargain for her family's survival. As it was, she met Charlie's eyes, pressed her lips together, and simply nodded.

He wrapped an arm around her shoulders, whispered a heartfelt, "Be strong," and the door was opened.

Morgan tried to stand when they came in, but he was, indeed, cuffed to the table, to the center of it, so he collapsed back down into his chair again. His arms lay useless, but it appeared instantly to both Jessie and Charlie that they were not normally so. He was so muscled it looked like his time in Brody was really just an all-inclusive pass to a gym.

Jessie made her legs move her to the side of the table opposite him, but she didn't sit. Charlie was too repulsed by everything Morgan stood for to even consider coming close. At first, he couldn't look at the guy. He couldn't meet the haunting eyes Charles and Matt called dead.

There was another man in the room besides Morgan, Charlie and the young redhead. Caulfield. They knew about him, that he was likely some kind of intermediary in Morgan's sick game. His links to exterior crimes were hearsay at best, never proven, and he was well protected by his mafia guard cronies as well as the prison population, but the sight of him offended Charlie. His very presence there offended Charlie. He caught Caulfield looking at him and chose to fix his pressure-cooker gaze elsewhere.

Jessie was facing Morgan now. With the ball cap on, almost hiding her eyes, she had to tilt her head up a bit to see out from underneath. She was in a position of power over Morgan in many ways, not the least of which because she was standing over him. A new numbness had worked its way into her body the second she saw him sitting there, crouched like a frightened child over his shackled arms as if he was waiting for her to lash out at him with a whip hidden underneath her leather jacket.

Glancing over at Caulfield, Jessie chewed on a lip and grabbed the back of the metal chair opposite her old security. Caulfield didn't appear menacing to her, he just seemed arrogant. Regardless, he gave her the willies. She shuddered, and he raised his chin proudly and rested a hand on the wooden baton at his hip.

"Fuuuccckkk," she said under her breath and wished to hell the creepy guy wasn't in the room.

Focusing her gaze on Morgan, Jessie pulled out the chair. *Scrreeechhh,* it cried as she dragged it out far enough so she could sit. Easing cautiously down, she kept Morgan squarely in sight.

Behind her, Charlie tensed and wished he could trade places with Matt. He was fairly certain Matt was feeling the same about now.

"Um," Jessie started, as Morgan resolutely stared at his hands. "Will you talk to me, Morgan? You and me…we used to be friends. We used to work out together."

He swallowed, and the sound bounced off the reflective space as if it was placed there by some film's post-production sound editor. It didn't seem real, and it didn't seem like it belonged. Morgan didn't seem real. He could have been a wax statue placed there for the sole purpose of training people on how to talk to inmates who badly hurt other peoples' families.

Jessie tried again. "Morgan…please. Can you just look at me?"

Angling his head away from her, he fixed his gaze on the window, on a long-legged spider crawling along the ledge in search of freedom.

"Okay," Jessie said, deciding to throw out some bones to see if he'd bite. "Morgan, we know the directive to attack Josh in the parkade came from you. We can surmise the guy who ran my daughter and I off the road was also acting on your orders. I don't know about all the stuff that happened to Josh last year, him getting pushed into the river, and the chowder incident, and all that. I guess maybe they were likely your doing too."

By the door, Caulfield grunted. Jessie and Charlie snapped their heads in his direction. The man was grinning. Charlie looked around for a garbage can. He was fairly certain puking would be on the agenda sometime in the next few minutes. Catching the eye of the redheaded guy, who seemed amiable enough, he settled. The kid was calm. He didn't seem concerned. He had kind eyes.

Jessie leapt back in. "I won't beat around the bush here, Morgan. I've come here to ask for mercy. To beg, if I have to. You see…you see, I get where you're coming from. I know how awful it is to lose somebody you love. I lost my dad. I lost my boyfriend, when I was just a teenager. He was killed, um, right there when I was, uh, in the room with him. He died in my arms."

Trembling, Charlie wanted to reach for her. Josh was gonna kill him if he ever found out about this secret visit. And it seemed he likely would…

apart from when she first came home from Edinburgh and cried out the morbid details of her troubled past at La Casa, Jessie had never really talked about Sandy, about witnessing his murder. When she released all that old anguish at La Casa that time, she went to bed for three days. This, today, was going to cost her. Josh would know something big was up—how could he not? Jessie might not go home and dive into booze or weed the way he did, but ducking under the bedcovers or even simply retreating was, at least on some level, equally as destructive to a family, to a marriage. It was just a different kind of drug.

Charlie tuned back in.

"I thought…Morgan, I thought I was gonna live my whole life with him. With Sandy. I know you thought the same about Nadia. With your boy, with Darin. The pain of losing him…like that…I'm just saying I know. I get it. I know how much it hurts. I know it hurt you to see us happy, our family. To lose Nadia…like that…because of us…But honey, I feel like I've paid for my sins. I've paid for them so many times over. So many, many, many times over. I'm here to ask you to let myself…and my family…live in peace. *Please.*"

The way she said the word *please*…Charlie would remember it for the rest of his life. It was up there in the memory books, now on par with the recollection of grabbing the doorknob and walking out of his and Jessie's engagement all those years ago after Terri's funeral in Ashland. The word was fraught with all of the agony Jessie had suffered in her lifetime. It was laced with sorrow, regret, longing, sadness, pain, misery, heartbreak and loss. All rolled into one thick simple soaking wet word.

Please.

Charlie half expected Jessie to start sobbing and add the preface *pretty, pretty* to the word *please*. But she didn't. She held on. *You were brave in the Lexus when it rolled,* he thought. *When it sank into your watery prison. Be brave now, little girl.*

She was feeling it, the same choking feeling that accosted her in the submerged vehicle, and at the concert, when? Last night? Or whenever, in Paris time. It felt like ages ago. This small room with its metal chairs and frightening men, and handcuffs on a workout partner Jessie used to trust, who had sex with her before he poured gas over the floors above her and lit a match, was every bit as nauseating and suffocating and terrifying as that awful, sunken car. Now if Matt were just here, to save her, to pull her out of this useless attempt at peace…but he wasn't. And he'd likely give her hell for coming here in the first place.

Morgan had yet to meet Jessie's desperate, pleading eyes.

She had one last thing to say. "Yoga," she whispered. "I hear you're doing yoga, Morgan. That's good. That's a good thing, right? Yoga is all about peace. About finding your center. It's about balance, the mind and body kind. You can have peace, Morgan, if you want it. You can choose to let us go."

He didn't waver, although, under his bent face, somewhere in the shadows, Jessie thought she saw him blink.

"Oh, fuck," she choked, shoved back the chair, and started to turn so she could stand. She was using one forearm for leverage. It was still on the table as she moved—she almost screamed when Morgan's great bulk of a hand gripped her wrist, hard. Spinning fully back around to him, Jessie gasped. He was looking at her now, staring at her, hard into her eyes, pleading right back at her, it seemed. Begging her to understand something.

Recognizing some part of the old Morgan in him, Jessie fell back into the chair. "What is it," she begged. "What is it, Morgan? What do you need me to do? I'll do anything. Fucking anything. Please."

"I'm—sorry." He said it with the same kind of passion and intent that Jessie had called forth for her desperate *please*.

"Wh-what?" she asked. "For the past, Morgan? For what's happening now? Or for—for the future?" A sob accompanied the final question. It would have been followed by more, except that Jessie didn't want to lose it here, now. She had more to learn, and in order to learn, she had to listen.

But there was no more. That was it. He appeared to have nothing more to say. Morgan was still gripping Jessie's wrist, hard enough that she would later find bruises there, which she would study with a detached, lonely curiosity in the days to come.

"I see light in you," she wept, her lips curving up just the tiniest bit in wistful hope. "I swear to God. I see light."

A great, hulking sob emerged from Morgan's chest. Large tears formed in his not-so-vacant-after-all eyes, and started to roll slowly down his cheeks.

He and Jessie were locked in a silent impasse, as if their souls were somehow, unbelievably, connected. Neither seemed to want to look away from the other—neither was capable of looking away, of losing the connection, the communion of extraordinary shared, raw, gaping losses.

After what seemed like an eternity, something in Jessie gave, and she broke. A scream started somewhere deep inside her soul, an agonizing, burning scream that had the capacity to sear her insides in two. Charlie vaulted forward and hauled her out of the chair, because she started wailing on Morgan, hitting him with the frustration and futility earned by the acute and final knowing that she was powerless. That she had no control over her family's destiny insofar as this man who had already so sorely wronged her was concerned.

It was a lonely, terrifying, disintegrating place to be.

At the door, where Charlie dragged her kicking and screaming, still begging for mercy, Jessie grabbed the door frame and hung on for dear life, afraid to let Morgan out of her sight without some kind of hope for peace.

Morgan sobbed as he watched her go, as he watched the only person who ever really truly seemed to believe in the goodness of him, be dragged away in mortal fear for her family. And she had a right to be, he knew, because although he wasn't the conductor of this deadly orchestra, Morgan was privy to its power and of how it was going to end.

He didn't want Jessie to go, to leave him in this godforsaken, soulless place. Between her and him now was Caulfield. The man had moved forward to get out of the way of Jessie's flailing arms and feet. The young redheaded guard was at the door in front of Charlie, paving the way for an undignified exit from the hopeless meeting.

Charlie mustered up some courage. He fixed Caulfield in his stare before blinking angrily over at Morgan. "How could you?!" he beseeched them, yelling over Jessie's wails. "How could you run a mother and her child off the road? How can you live with yourselves knowing what kind of agony you're putting this family through? How could your reign of terror possibly make anything better for you? Ever?!"

The room would've gone silent if Caulfield hadn't snickered. Charlie was still hanging onto Jessie, who felt like she was outside of her body looking down on herself kicking and screaming in Charlie's strong grip. Reaching deep, she tried to settle.

A word was breathed into the room, by her. Jessie stopped convulsing long enough to form it in her mouth. It came from her heart, from a place of goodness and faith in humanity; and maybe, just maybe, it came from the Divine.

"Namaste," she wept through the pain she'd already suffered, through the pain she was continuing to suffer, and through the pain she knew was yet to come. "Namaste, Morgan. The light in me…honors the light in you."

With a final look into her old security's despairing eyes, Jessie wrangled her body out of Charlie's grasp, and heaved her exhausted, bone weary soul out of the stifling room.

As he promised Charlie, Matt was waiting in the parking lot. Charlie would have growled at him for half sitting on the Porsche if the day were in any way a normal one. But as it was, he almost leapt into the man's arms, he was so grateful for his presence.

Not at all surprised to see him there, uninvited, Jessie stood back and proudly straightened up her shoulders at the sight of him, all wary and tired and scared and strong. It only took her a few seconds to make the decision to go to him, and when she did she fell into his arms with a mighty cry and a sorrowful truth.

"I can't—I can't—he won't…"

Matt was holding steady. He was fatigued beyond reason. Peering over Jessie's shoulder at Charlie, he was very, very sorry to see his friend shake his head.

"Let's go home, Jessie," he said. "Let's get you back to the ranch so you can be with Josh and the kids. All right?"

"You tell him, Matt? He know we were here?" Pulling back, Jessie swiped at her blotchy face and hiccupped away the tears the way her kids did when they cried.

"Josh? No." Matt shook his head. "He doesn't know, and he won't hear about it from me."

"He'll kill me if he finds out."

"Yep. He will."

"I need to know what he's up to, Matt." Jessie turned to Charlie. "One of you must know. Please tell me you know."

Both men melted into the pavement. Both shook their heads and muttered a quiet, despairing, "No."

"I can't stand it. I can't stand living like this."

Neither guy said it, but both were thinking the same thing. *Josh.* They were afraid he, also, had finally lost hope.

Charlie walked tentatively over and wrapped an arm around Jessie's shoulder. "Let's go home," he said. "We'll grab some greasy takeout that's terrible for nauseous, pregnant women and eat on the way."

Tossing her curls, frowning sadly, Jessie reached over to him and dug around in his coat pocket. She held up his car key. "You know," she said, her voice flat and dull. "I have a lot of regrets about the time when you and I were together. The main one is that you never let me drive your stupid-ass sports car."

Charlie's eyes widened just as Matt launched himself toward her, but Jessie, being a dancer, a runner, and an avid practitioner of yoga, was in the Porsche and had the doors locked before either man could reach her.

"I need a fucking drive!" she shouted at them from behind the window. "I just need music, and a goddamned fucking drive!"

Firing up the car wasn't a problem. Shifting it wasn't easy, the first time, but she got the hang of it. Her Mustang only had three gears.

"Jesus Christ," Charlie cursed, and paced in a tiny circle. Matt clutched him by the coat at the shoulder and hauled him toward the Audi. They heard the Porsche radio come to life on full blast.

"Not a problem," Matt steamed. "She'll stop for smokes."

"Then Josh'll really kill her. And us. She's pregnant, Matt, remember? Tell me she won't smoke."

"She'll smoke. One or two. Then she'll bury the pack under the front seat and you'll find it next spring when you trade up."

In the Audi, Charlie didn't even have his door closed before Matt was skidding his way across the pavement. It didn't matter. Jessie was in the sweet little sports car, the one that cornered like it was on rails and could go from zero to sixty in 3.6 seconds. She ditched her protectors before they got to the first light.

She zipped up the ranch lane ten hours later, a good hour before the men. It was one in the morning, and Josh, who Jessie hadn't texted but who Charlie had, was frantic.

By the look of her, and the fact that she had ridden up alone in Charlie's car, she was in dire straits. Josh opened his arms. When Jessie collapsed into them, she shut off her brain and went into retreat mode until three days later, when Deirdre urged her awake, and flew her off to Rio for an unexpected appearance at a summer festival. The entire Sawyer family went along, and the festival that should have been an annoying blip on the busy calendar, gave them all a little taste of Heaven.

Chapter Forty-three

When it came to gift giving, Charles and Deirdre were generous. But original, unique ideas were not always plentiful. After the concert in Rio, they outdid themselves. Their announcement after the Rio show was a genuine, welcome gift. It was made in the RV the clan was using as backstage quarters.

A few minutes earlier, Matt had tossed Jessie a towel to wipe the sweat off as she raised her arm high for one last wave to the crowd and left the outdoor festival stage. Jacob jogged along behind them and flanked her on the other side.

"Where're Josh and the kids?" was the first thing Jessie asked as she dabbed at her forehead and neck. The family had watched the performance from a small set of side bleachers reserved for family and friends, and for the members of other bands on the festival schedule.

"In the RV," Matt said, surreptitiously eyeing the assembled techs and other backstage folks while he guided his stars safely to their private quarters. "Josh and Dee are getting the kids' things packed up."

"Sweet. So we can leave right away."

"After you get your sweaty bod cleaned up," Jacob grinned, wrinkling his nose. "Can't see even your white knight wanting to sit next to you right now, Jess."

She coiled up the towel and gave him a playful swat.

"Children!" Matt scolded. "Behave."

"I think that was one of the hottest shows I've ever done," Jessie retorted, twisting around to give Matt a playful swat too. "Dee loves to punish us.

That's likely why she and Josh are hiding in the RV—air conditioning. You'd think they'd want to hear our full set, eh Jacob?"

"They could sing our full set." Laughing, Jacob stood back so Jessie could move ahead of him down a short flight of metal steps. "Although I challenge your cowboy to rip on a guitar."

"Emily-Grace'll be able to soon, if you keep spending time with her. She's gonna be quite the little rocker."

"That's my girl."

A happy smile lit up Jessie's flushed cheeks. The best times, in her opinion, were when everyone was getting along. These moments when Josh, Jacob and Matt were all close by, completed her circle. It was a cherished bonus to sit back and revel in the way the guys were dealing with their shared lives these days. The precious Sawyer children were being raised with love, growing up in the comfortable, easygoing bosom of more than just Josh and Jessie.

Sending a hushed prayer up to the gods above, Jessie thanked the universe, for the umpteenth time, for this perfect grace.

She hopped up the steps to their backstage RV, crossed the floor and immediately sank down into cool comfort in one of the wing chairs at the far end. "Bless the brilliant mind who invented air conditioning," she moaned, throwing her head back and dabbing at her neck with the towel. Dylan leapt into her lap. "Ouch! You little monkey!" Curving her arms around him, Jessie squeezed him as tight as she dared and sighed into his Jacob curls. Looking over his young head to spy Jacob watching her, she beamed. The joy on his face was worth every bit of the old pain.

Jacob walked over and kissed Dylan's curls. "You're gonna be a big brother," he said.

The little guy held up two fingers. "Two times," he answered.

"He won't be confused at all." Bending down again, to Jessie this time, Jacob brushed his lips against her forehead. "Great show tonight, girl," he said. "One of our best."

"Having everyone here helps," Jessie said, looking around at her happy family as they buzzed around doing their thing. "Life just feels right when we're all together."

Josh was watching her with Dylan and Jacob. He was in the small kitchen poking kids' books into a blue Paw Patrol knapsack. Everyone—Matt, Charles, Dee, Ulysses, Jacob, Jessie, the kids, Dan (Sam and Alin were taking a break), even Kayla tonight—was crowded into their backstage quarters. Emily-Grace and David were quarreling over some electronic toy; Kayla and Jacob were hugging now, and sharing tender little kisses; Charles and Dee were trying to talk Emily-Grace into helping David with his game instead of bossing him around; and Jessie was cuddling with Dylan, talking to him about the new baby, Josh figured, since he was rubbing her belly.

Taking a deep breath, Josh pivoted around on a heel and faced the door so his back was to the entire group. The only person who noticed was Matt. Josh's movement was small, and nobody else saw him do it, but to Matt the action screamed *Listen*. Something was definitely still very off in Josh's world. He looked back over at all of them at one point, and started rubbing his cheek, roughly, with one palm, and his eyes were wide and damp.

"It's perfect, Josh," Matt said, wandering closer so Josh could hear him over the din. "Look what you've got here."

Josh gave Matt a subdued *hummph*. "It's perfect for a minute," he returned abruptly.

Matt paused. "It's a good minute, though, right?"

Temporarily forgotten, the Paw Patrol knapsack was still dangling from Josh's fingers. Josh let it hang, and studied Matt.

To Matt's utter astonishment, after a brief pause Josh said, "I know you'll take care of them."

Jessie happened to look up at that moment. She couldn't hear what was said, but the way Matt stood stock still as the blood ran from his face said enough.

After a few long seconds, he turned and found himself the subject of her breathless scrutiny. There were no words to help dispel the alarm that shot up his spine and made his skin crawl at Josh's casually spoken statement. And this wasn't the time to talk about it.

Would I take this family on, if I could? Matt wondered. *Would I make them mine?* Matt was significantly older than Jessie. His daughter was a woman now, living independently, in need of very little care. Jessie had three young children and another on the way. Matt's knees hurt sometimes, his shoulder ached where the New York bullet had seared a sinister trail in his flesh. He tired more easily than he used to. He went to bed before ten, some nights. A lot of nights, unless he was on Sawyer duty.

But yeah. Hell, yeah. *I'd raise this family in a heartbeat,* he thought.

Shanda crossed his mind. And zipped right out again when he lost himself in Jessie's pale blue eyes.

Turning back to Josh, he found his voice. "Josh, we'll talk, okay?" he said. "As soon as we get a chance, as soon as we can be alone. We need to sort this out."

Josh nodded. "I just wanted you to know."

Know what, exactly? Matt wondered. *That you're planning to make some kind of exit?* Sickened, he avoided meeting Jessie's questioning eyes for the time being. Hurts this big had the capacity to destroy her, even if they were only suppositions buried in a faraway look.

Deirdre saved him. It was time to make the big announcement. David and Emily-Grace had sorted out their issues, and Jessie and Jacob needed showers after the steaming hot show. Now was the time. Clapping her hands together, she smiled gratefully at Jacob when he whistled to get everyone's attention for her.

"Jessie, Josh and kids," Deirdre said, her eyes sunny and bright, "I know you're all tired, but if you're up for it, Charles and I would like to let you know that we've freed up your schedules for the next week."

"What?" Josh asked, a little too quickly. Jessie narrowed her eyes and sent him a confused, querying look, which he ignored as Deirdre continued.

"*Sacred Peace* doesn't need you this week, Josh. They're scaling back for the week to shoot B-roll and to let the cast and crew take a breather, to work banker's hours. Jessie, you were supposed to do the Charleston show, but with that hurricane coming up the coast, the organizers aren't taking any chances. They've pushed the show to the following weekend, hoping to pick up whatever artists can be available. You've both got a free week."

"Dee! That's great! Thank you!"

At least Jessie is enthusiastic, Matt thought, watching.

"There's more," Charles spoke up and smiled at Jessie. Dylan was leaning back against her chest, yawning. They needed to get to the jet so the kids could sleep while they flew. "We booked you a quiet house on the water in Prince Edward Island. Your sister Sara will be next door."

At that, Jessie leapt up. With Dylan in her arms, she launched herself at Charles and then Dee, but couldn't speak for tears and joy. A week on her beloved gentle, healing island was just what her traumatized family needed. They could see her mother, and old George, who was ailing these past few months. They could build sandcastles on the beach, and roast spider dogs over outdoor campfires. Best of all, she and Sara could drink coolers by the ocean—non-alcoholic for her, she decided, rubbing her belly and eyeing Josh, who was awfully quiet—and talk about the ups and downs of raising kids.

Spinning around, she looked at Matt. She was almost afraid to ask. "You coming?" she finally said. Jacob and Kayla, and Charles and Dee, by virtue of Jessie's raised eyebrows, were also included in the question.

Deirdre answered for all of them. "This is the best part, honey. We might have to pull in some trailers and tents, but we've invited a whole crew of your friends for next weekend. We'll fly them in and see that they get cars, food, whatever they need. Steve and Charlie and their families are already a go; so are Jacob and Kayla, and Carter and Ashley and their new baby."

"Eeekkk!" More hugs. Kayla was glowing.

"We're waiting to hear from Sue-Lyn and Maggie. Shanda will join Matt in a nearby cottage for the entire week, and Charles and I—with Carlotta and Ulysses of course—will fly in midweek. Dan here's taking a well deserved week off to be with his wife, but Sam and Alin will be around to help keep things secure for the kids."

"Word has it that Gary and Evelyn are even coming down." That was from Charles.

"Sounds like a perfect reunion," Jessie exclaimed. "You guys are absolutely the best."

"We'll keep it on the down low as much as we can, but you have to promise us you'll abide by Matt's rules. Okay, Jessie?" That was the only sobering moment—Charles' gentle reminder that they were still under assault.

"You got it, Gramps." Ecstatic, Jessie handed Dylan over to Jacob. "Can we go right now?"

"Ranch first, to get packed for a week in P.E.I. We'll head east from there the second we're ready."

"All right. Okay. Thank you, you guys. Really. You're the best."

Leaping up the few stairs to the bedroom and shower at the far end, Jessie hollered back to Jacob, "I'll try to leave you some hot water, doofus. Gimme ten."

When the shower started up, the gang went into high gear, packing up and putting their things in the SUVs lined up outside to take them to the airport. Within the hour, they were airborne. In twenty-four short hours, they landed at the old Summerside air base they always used for its privacy and, when Jessie stepped down onto the tarmac, she dropped to the ground and pressed her lips to the warm sun-kissed asphalt of her sea-breezy island home.

The week was everything Jessie hoped it would be, with the exception of her husband's subdued, distant demeanor. The only time Josh really opened up and allowed himself any meaningful conversation with anyone the entire week was after most of their friends finally pulled out late on Sunday. Matt and Shanda had retired to their cottage, Charles and Dee were long asleep, and Josh and Jessie were alone. Sara, too, had already said her goodbyes for the evening. Tomorrow morning would be a sad but grateful final 'so long' until the families would be able to meet again.

Josh was reclining on a comfy beach lounger by the fire, poking at remaining glowing embers with a long stick when Jessie approached from behind. He gave a ghostly wood split a big shove. It rolled over and landed in a spray of sparks and ash.

"Kids are asleep," Jessie told him as she stepped over his leg and plopped herself down in between his thighs, facing the fire. Sighing, she leaned back against his chest and took his vacant hand in hers. "I didn't think they'd ever settle. What a week. I need a vacation to recover from my vacation."

"It was a good week," Josh said. Angling his head backward, he pointed his stick toward the sky. "Even at the ranch, the sky doesn't look quite like this. I've never seen so many stars all at once."

Following his gaze, Jessie looked up. Hugging his hand to her chest, she cried, "Look, there's a falling star! Did you see that, Josh? Over the Basin!"

Their little clump of cottages was situated on the north side of the small island, in Darnley, overlooking the Darnley Basin, in the same area where Matt had rented his summer place next to Catherine. The view was sublime. There were so many stars in the sky above them that it was hard to look away. The view was breathtaking.

A weird chuckle escaped Josh's lips. "A falling star," he echoed. "Imagine that."

"Make a wish," Jessie demanded, misinterpreting his meaning. "You're supposed to make a wish."

"A wish. Okay." Josh was silent. The only sounds were the spitting and spewing of the sparks on the fire.

"You make it?"

"Yep."

Jessie twisted around. "You gonna tell me?"

He smiled at her. In the glow of the embers, his eyes were calm, luminous pools of chocolate light. "What I wished for?" He shook his head. "Nope. But I bet it was the same thing you wished for."

She paused, and strained her leg so she could stretch up for a kiss. "I bet it was too." Closing her eyes, Jessie let herself feel and taste him, the full mouth she loved to tease with her tongue. He responded in kind, dropping the poker stick on the ground next to the lounger so he could envelop her securely—safely—in his arms. They stayed that way, dressed in light summer clothing with a fresh, salty breeze jubilantly wafting its fairy breath over and around them, until Jessie gave Josh one last, perfect kiss, and backed away so she could focus on him.

"God, that was sweet," she breathed. "We haven't kissed like that in a long time, Josh."

"Let's do more than kiss, Jessie. Let's go inside."

"Or not." She smiled, a wicked little grin on her lips as she flipped around and faced him. Taking his hands in hers, she cocked her head and winked. "Everybody's asleep. It's one in the morning. Which is only ten, Alberta time. It's early yet, all things considered, so we can stay up but nobody will see us. Or hear us." She giggled. "It's the best of both worlds."

Josh was ready to play. He wanted to. But there was something he wanted to ask her first. He sobered them up pretty quick when he brought it up. "Jessie…where'd you go that day with Charlie? When you came home in his car."

Sitting back, Jessie scowled. "Matt didn't spill the beans? Or Charlie?"

He was quiet, and looked away over the Basin, which mirrored the moon-lit sky as if it was a painting.

"Oh, I forgot," she whispered in her little girl voice. "You hardly talked to anyone this week. 'Cept about hamburgers and stuff. Like how much to cook your steak." Wriggling, she said, "Matt's wanted to talk to you for a while. You keep blowing him off. Charlie's tried. You may as well have just said F U."

"We came here to rest, Jessie. Not to dredge up the old drama."

"The current drama. And isn't that what you're doing right now, Josh? Asking me about our road trip that day?"

"You went to see Morgan, Jessie. Didn't you?"

"What makes you think that? Three days of burying my head under the covers?"

Poking her in the ribs, Josh said, "You get too skinny when you do that. You can't do that around the kids, little one. You gotta get out of this pattern of hiding when things get rough. They need you. They'll need you more and more as they grow up."

"They need you too."

It was the first time Jessie came close to voicing her thoughts over the intuitive worry that her husband might be planning something he was refusing to share. Josh read her mind. He chewed on a lip and studied her. Backlit by the remains of their fire, she was radiant, but she was also pale and tired. Truly, the week had been busy, and the weekend even more so. He touched her cheek. "You're beat, Jessie. I'm beat. Let's go to bed."

"It's never enough. With you, I mean. We don't have enough of these moments anymore, alone like this." Catching her breath as if a thought suddenly struck her, Jessie said, "Josh, do you remember the day we really, officially met for the first time? I knew who you were, but it wasn't until that day outside Charlie's club that I ever talked to you. I always wonder how much you remember about that night."

"I remember all of it." He was watching her intently now. Memorizing her.

"I didn't expect it. To bend down in front of you and look into your eyes and feel what I felt that night."

"Which was?" Not that he needed to ask. Josh knew. But he wanted—needed—to hear her say it.

"That *zzzzip* that ripped through my body. It was this crazy energy, this surreal feeling that I already knew you."

"Past life."

"You believe in those, babe?" She was squinting at him now, trying to sort him out. To offer the same kind of help that got his fire going again all those years ago. To pull up their auspicious, soulful beginning in the hope that it could somehow light the way forward, to mitigate the darkness Jessie intuitively felt was coming.

Brusque and unsure, Josh forced out an answer. "I don't know. Maybe. I'd like to. Because…"

She completed the thought for him. "Because it means future lives."

"Yeah. That."

"I'm not through with this one yet."

Josh paused. "Where you going with this, Jessie?" His hands were sweaty now. Pulling them away from her, he wiped them on his thighs, and swallowed.

The way she was looking at him—determined but scared—Josh felt the earth move underneath his feet. The deed was done, though. Things had already been set into motion. There was no coming back from the deal he cut with Morgan, via Murphy and Vaughn.

"You're not through with this one yet, either, Josh. This life. Hope, remember? There is always hope."

"I'm not gonna do anything stupid, if that's what you're thinking, Jessie. Like," he almost choked, "kill myself or something."

"Josh, I…I'm only gonna ask you this once, babe, but only because I know Matt never got that heart-to-heart with you. And because I'm worried. You've been so distant…even with Steve and Charlie."

"Ask away." He blinked, and tried to hold her gaze.

Jessie reached for his fingers again. "I know you've made some kind of decision. I can see it in your eyes. I've been feeling it. You and me, we're so…

connected. In tune. And I know it's not something you feel you can share with me, with anyone. But I want you to know, whatever it is…" Slowly, thoughtfully, she shook her head. "It's not too late to change your mind."

"It's fine, Jessie. It's okay. It's under control."

There were tears in her eyes now, little pinpricks of light that mimicked the stars above. She raised her chin. With a burning intensity, she locked her eyes in his. "So there is something."

"Look," Josh said. "I've thought a lot about what's been happening to us. The day you and Emily-Grace went into the river was…" He blinked back the hard emotions the horrible memories wrought, but held her worried gaze. "It was the last straw, little one. Something's gotta give."

"What, Josh? What's gotta give?"

"You went to see Morgan, didn't you?"

"Y-yeah," she confessed. "I did."

"And?"

Jessie didn't respond. She didn't have to say a word. Those three days in bed…the way she was swallowing over and over and working her mouth as if she was trying to conjure up something to say that would make things better…

The results of that visit were crystal clear.

Josh's next words were barely even a hushed whisper. They were accompanied by a thickness in his voice that he had zero control over. His throat burned when he spoke. "I have to save our family, Jessie. Our kids need to be able to grow up in peace."

"How?"

Josh exhaled, a long, low exhale that seemed to drain him of any remaining energy. He tilted his head back and peered up at the stars. "Look at that," he said softly. "There's just gotta be more, Jess, don't you think? How can the universe be so beautiful if there isn't more?"

Jessie panicked. His voice was so flat, so…completely done in. "We'll move here. We'll hide. Morgan's minions will never find us. We'll just be normal."

"We'll never be normal, little one." Touching her cheek again, Josh bit his lip. "I can't imagine not working. I can't imagine not acting, not watching you work your magic on stage anymore. That sounds like prison to me."

Flinging her arms out to the sides, Jessie swung around at the waist. "Look at this place, Josh! It's unreal! This is living, the way we lived all week—lying on the beach, hanging out with the kids…we can change our names. We'll get a place off the beaten track. Nobody will ever be the wiser, and Morgan will never find us."

"I guess you've had some practice, huh?" Josh was only half joking. "You're good at the disappearing act."

"And I was happy." Puffing up her chest, Jessie frowned. "We can be happy."

"Not me. Work is who I am."

"We," Jessie huffed, "are who you are, babe. Your family." Taking his hand, she placed it on her abdomen. "This is your baby."

He chuckled sadly. "For a while there I thought it might be Matt's."

She slumped. "I know you did. I'm sorry for what I did to make your thoughts go there."

"Matt would be an incredible dad. He already kind of is, to your kids."

Jessie blanched. "To *our* kids, Josh. They're our kids."

Yawning, Josh leaned back and stretched before he gave his wife one last, almost beatific smile. It scared her, the peace she saw there, within the windows of his soul. The liquid puddles his eyes were now, were as calm as the Darnley Basin, and equally as sublime.

"You promised me some lovin,'" he said.

"Please. Baby…please…don't pull a Jessie Wheeler. Don't freaking run away, if that's what you've got planned. That won't solve a blessed thing. You'll just be abandoning us."

"Past lives, remember? The mysticism of stars and all things universally transcendent?" Josh pressed his lips to Jessie's forehead. In a husky voice, he said, "I will always be with you, little one."

It offered no comfort whatsoever. But his mouth was on hers then—to shut her up, Jessie later thought—and then he was leaning back on the lounger, taking her with him. Crouching over Josh, then laying her body down on top of his, Jessie allowed the flow of his gentle hands to caress and touch her. She was right, there was nobody awake or around them to watch their lovemaking outdoors in the breathy air of this naturally beautiful retreat, but neither of them would have cared if there was.

They were out of words. There was nothing left to say. Only their bodies were left to come together, to unify Josh and Jessie in harmony and in a long sought after peace that, on this last night in Prince Edward Island, still seemed so damned out of reach.

Chapter Forty-four

She thought maybe she'd gotten through to Josh. Or to Morgan, even. Because the summer continued on its merry way as usual once the Sawyer family got back to the ranch. Josh went back to *Sacred Peace* to finish the season, and Jessie joined Jacob—often with the kids in tow—for the final stretch of summer festivals Deirdre had so carefully organized. A new script arrived, for a film Deirdre wanted Jessie to consider doing in late January or early February, as a replacement for the Montreal film she was supposed to shoot in October. Matt removed himself from the family here and there to spend time hanging out with and making love to Shanda, and hiking mountain trails that he was too afraid to dare taking Jessie or any of the Sawyer children on, for fear of what unknown danger might lie hidden in the verdant trees and rocky gullies. Long summer days and endless starry nights melded into hours of cherished family time as the children instead safely explored the Alberta landscape within the parameters of the ranch, where they were gated in. The way a child lays a blanket lovingly over a precious doll, a sleepy peace settled over them.

In early September, Josh gave Emily-Grace a new puppy. "It's a cousin of Snow's," he told her, kneeling in front of her so he could look into her eyes when he entrusted the puppy to her care.

"I don't know, Daddy," she said, her bottom lip trembling. "I didn't do so good the first time."

"You did wonderful," he told her, and extended a hand to scratch the tiny animal's fluffy white head. "What happened to Snow was not your fault."

Emily-Grace's Jessie-eyes peeked up at him from behind wet eyelashes. "How about I leave this puppy home when you tell me to next time, Daddy?"

"That'd be fine," he agreed in a hoarse voice, and had to stand and turn away from her so he could collect his wits.

The second week of September, just as Alberta was enjoying an Indian summer instead of expecting its first snowfall, which usually came around this time of year, *Sacred Peace* was scheduled to shoot outdoors for three days. Josh was jittery and off his game. He started spending time alone in his trailer, the same way he did when he first started on the show. On the third day of outdoor shooting, Jessie drove the kids to the Calgary condo for tutoring with Patin, and then retraced her drive and dropped out to the set. Matt was with her, only too glad to accompany her to the location twenty minutes outside of Calgary, since Shanda was also on set that day.

"Hopin' for a nooner, are ya Matt?" Jessie teased as she parked her new SUV in the designated crew parking, a gravel lot at the entrance to a series of wide trails down which the crew was set up with their cameras and gear.

"Aren't you?" Matt flippantly returned when he opened his door. "You and Josh can still do it, can't you?"

"From behind," Jessie said, a wry twist to her lips.

Matt's head whipped around and he gave her a look. "Too much information," he said, and skirted the front of the car.

"I wish," Jessie sighed, countering her earlier comment. "The truth is, I don't much feel like sex, and Josh is either getting it somewhere else or he isn't finding my growing belly attractive, because he doesn't seem to be too hot to jump me these days."

"He's being better about the baby, though, right?" Matt lifted an arm and Jessie scooted underneath. They started toward base camp, a little huddle of trailers and trucks east of the parking area.

"I wouldn't say so." Glum, Jessie pouted. "He used to be so adorable, buying all the kids stuffed animals and toys and stuff before any of them ever made an entrance into this crazy world. Even Jacob's kid," she added, which was a bit of a shock to say out loud, "but I suppose part of that was him making up for lost time."

"He's likely beat, Jessie," Matt considered. "*Sacred Peace* is nearing the end of a long run. He'll come around."

"He won't even touch my belly, or talk to this baby the way he used to. He's just not bonding." Glancing over at Matt, Jessie smiled sadly. "You need to come over and lie down with me again. You can talk to my baby for me, okay Matt?"

"It's so simple for you, isn't it Jessie?" Matt slowed, and turned her toward him. With a tentative inhale, he puffed up his cheeks and then blew the air out so it sounded a little whistly.

"What?" Jessie asked, curious.

"Lines," he said. "There aren't any for you."

Jessie huffed and frowned. "Why should there be? I love a lot of people, Matt. For a time, I had nobody to love. Pardon me if I see the world a little differently from most people." Her voice got soft. "I won't apologize for loving you. And I won't try to pretend I don't." Lifting a finger, she touched it to his shoulder where she knew the bullet scar lay hidden from view. "You and I are one, honey."

Matt grew contemplative. "I'm thinking of asking Shanda to marry me."

"Oh. Oh! Well." Jessie had to turn, to catch her breath.

Regarding her with a watchful eye, Matt waited. Shanda was turning out to be a beautiful, kind partner, and he was sinking deeper under her spell the more he distanced himself from Jessie. Still, now, watching Jessie reel under the impact of his words, he couldn't help but be thrown by her, by how childlike and innocent she appeared in a long, flowing red floral sleeveless maternity top, despite her womanly curves and swelling, rounding belly.

"Not right away," Matt proclaimed in the end as he reached for her hand to get her to relax. "At Christmas, maybe."

"Christmas…that would be nice. Josh proposed to me at Christmas. It was my favorite night. Ever." Jessie managed a small smile. "I'm happy for you, Matt. Shanda's amazing. But you better get used to how she looks at my husband, because she doesn't hide her feelings for him very well." Wrinkling her brow, she started walking beside him when they saw Charlie wave from base camp and start to make his way over. "That's kinda weird, actually. You and me still make googly eyes at each other, and I know Josh has some pretty deep feelings for Shanda."

"Maybe we should arrange a trade…"

Floored, Jessie stopped outright. "Matt Kelly! Did I just hear what I think I just heard?!"

"Kidding! Kidding," he laughed, and waved back to Charlie, who was at their side in a few seconds.

"What are you two on about?" Charlie asked. "The crew can hear you laughing down in the woods, and they're a quarter of a mile away."

"Matt wants to be a swinger." Jessie was giggling.

Charlie grinned. "Does he. You still got it, you old coot?"

"Duh," Jessie winked, "David Beckham over here can outsex any twenty-five year old. Of course he's still got it."

"Now *that's* too much information," Matt chided, as his cheeks flamed pink.

"Jessie'd know," Charlie muttered under his breath to Matt. "Wouldn't she? Still makes me sick to think about her past."

Quiet, reflecting on the strange turn in the conversation, the two of them stood together and watched Jessie walk toward Josh, who was striding toward her from base camp. He was in costume, in jeans and a sheriff's shirt, minus his usual cowboy hat.

Jessie couldn't take her eyes off of him. "God, you're some man," she breathed to herself as her eyes lit up. "And you're my man." Making a mental note to 'service' him later—*gotta keep him happy so he doesn't stray,* she thought inwardly—she took him in her arms and pressed him as close to her body as she could, with their growing baby in between. "Hey, beautiful man." She sighed, and closed her eyes.

Her lashes fluttered against his cheek. Josh laid his fingers against her face and kissed her, a long, sweet kiss that made her legs go weak. "I love you," he rasped. "Always and forever, little one."

Before she had a chance to ponder what that meant, why he was so serious and loving all of a sudden, a new giggle started in her belly.

Eyes alight, Jessie turned back around to Matt and took a few steps toward him. She was still loosely clinging to Josh's fingers, and gave him a little pull so he turned slightly. "I might get my nooner, after all," she joked.

A split second later all hell broke loose.

The sharp crack of a crisp, clean, single gunshot split the air in two. Fired from some unseen sniper's hole in the woods, it was followed by the rustled flurry of someone sprinting through trees, shoving thick brush aside as he—or she—ran like a bat outta hell. In those first few seconds, everybody thought the gunshot was production related—some member of the props team, perhaps, playing a joke on another crew member by firing off a blank.

Jessie's gaze was focused on Charlie and Matt. The world went into slow motion. Matt shoved Charlie to the ground and vaulted toward her. Weirdly, Jessie turned her head toward the woods, and wondered why the hell what she'd just heard sounded like a gunshot. She'd worked on enough films to recognize the wicked crack. Hell, she'd watched enough movies, or witnessed Josh firing at tin cans enough, to know the sound…and what it meant.

Josh's fingers drifted out of hers.

"Oh, fuck," she gasped, and spun around.

He was staggering backward, clutching his chest. A tiny pool of blood was forming there in the heart of the shirt that wasn't even his, that wasn't even him. Like a sinister snake, the blood started to trail downwards, stealing from Josh the life that Jessie loved.

Matt was on Jessie before Josh fell, forcing her to the ground as he had done so many years before when Nadia pulled the trigger on her. "Lie still!" he commanded in a loud cry, but Jessie didn't hear him. All she could hear was a heartbeat pounding in her ears—like a clock with a dying battery, sluggishly working its way to silence.

Writhing underneath Matt's body, half on the ground and half on her hands and knees because the mother in her knew instinctively to protect her unborn baby, Jessie started to scream. In the end, Matt let her go and spun around to scan the woods for any signs of the terrorist who'd just fired a gun at Josh Sawyer.

The perfect blue skies above them were wrong that day. They shouldn't have been there, hanging over them like hope. There should not have been birds in the sky gaily swooping over the tree tops. No way should water be trickling happily, merrily, in any of the nearby brooks that wound their way through the forest, fed from the glacial mountain rivers above. There should not have been *Sacred Peace* crew joking and laughing before the gunshot rang out; there should not have been squirrels leaping gaily from branch to branch, and a light breeze rustling gladly through leaves.

There should only have been darkness in the sky, black clouds and an absence of light. In the woods, only coyotes should have been peering out from underneath big branches, their yellow eyes ominous and haunting in the quiet day.

And there should only be a happy couple sneaking kisses in this gravelly parking lot. There should not be a well loved man lying on his back, bleeding from his chest, and gasping for air. There should not be a woman screaming for help, "Charlie!!! Charlie!!!" as she crawled to her husband's side and straddled him, knees on either sides of his legs, her scraped raw elbows and forearms flanking his body.

Shaking, wanting to vomit, Jessie ran quaking palms over Josh's chest. Drawing a hand upward, she couldn't make sense of the dark, sticky wetness on her fingers. Behind her, she heard footsteps thudding toward the trees— she later found out they belonged to Matt. Someone was crawling toward her—Charlie. He was on the phone begging someone to send the set's EMTs.

Jessie stopped screaming. The sudden silence was eerie, although others were running toward them now—Charles, and Jonathon, who heard the gunshot from the lunchroom tent. Matt came back. In a stupor, he knelt and watched Jessie tremble over her husband.

She let her gaze drift upward from the dark stain spreading across Josh's chest.

Gasping for air, any air, bringing up one knee and then letting it fall again, repeating the action, he was conscious and was watching her.

"What have you done?" she asked, in a voice much too calm for the evil outcome to this perfect blue-sky day. Louder, she said it again, although this time it was more of a desperate cry. "What have you done!"

His lips formed a sentence. A proclamation. It came out in a whispered hush. "I'm tired, Jessie. I'm so damn tired. Please…just let me go."

"No," she demanded. "NO!"

"Matt…"

"I don't want Matt! I don't want Matt. I want you! Don't you give up on me. Don't you give up on me!"

"You'll…be safe…now. The kids…the baby…Morgan…got what he wanted. We're…even now."

"What? Josh!"

Then Charlie was there, telling Josh to *Hang on, buddy, the ambulance is coming, just hang on.* The set medic was running through the woods, from where he'd set up his gear near the next shot's location.

Jessie buried her eyes in her husband's distant stare. "You want to go, Josh? You want to go? To leave me? To leave us, our children, this new baby you have yet to even meet? You search your heart, babe. If that's what you really want, then you go. You go and be with the stars and the spirits and the sky, if that's what you want. You go be with God. But Josh." She almost broke down, but she held on, and although Charlie was clawing at her, trying to let the medic at Josh, he loosed his grip and let Jessie have her say. "If, in your heart, you want to stay—with me, with us—then babe, you stay. You fucking stay. Because, my sweet, kind, beautiful man, you are loved. And you—are wanted."

He was blinking back at her, but other than the smallest, slightest movement—a nod, which Jessie later wondered whether she actually really saw—there was no real way of knowing whether Josh comprehended what she was telling him. A last flutter in his eyes, and, his hand in hers, the dimming light faded and he drifted away. Bending down to him, Jessie pressed her lips against his. His mouth was warm. "Come back to me," she begged. "Come back to me."

It took both Charlie and Matt to pull their girl off of her husband.

Jessie wrestled her body out of their arms, swiped her forearm across her mouth, and backed away. There was fire in her eyes, and anger in her heart.

Wheeling around, she strode toward the new SUV, shoved her bloodied hand against its sunshiny door for support, and collapsed onto her knees. When more emergency workers finally arrived, she was vomiting by the front tire. Charlie was crouched behind her trembling body, sobbing into her hair, and wondering why she wasn't crying.

When he helped Jessie up afterwards, they turned together and watched the EMTs load Josh into the ambulance. "You need to go," Charlie declared. "He needs you."

Jonathon was standing silently on the perimeter of the shocked crew, his face drawn and his eyes darting here, there and everywhere. Mostly, he was watching Jessie for cues.

"Tell Jon to go," she said way too calmly, to Charlie. "I've said my piece. This is Josh's call now."

"No," Charlie insisted, reaching for her hand. "He and his father barely speak. Josh needs you."

She turned to him. "Why?" Big tears were welling up in her eyes. "So I can watch him die?"

"No," Matt barked, striding up to them as Charlie stood and stared at her in speechless wonder. Matt grabbed her hand. "So you can help him live. Come on, Jessie. Sawyer Strong, remember? He might have given up, but I know you haven't. And I know you never will, when it comes to him. Get your ass in that ambulance and feed your light back into that man's spirit."

She didn't move, but the tears were starting now, in earnest. "You come with me, Matt. I can't...I can't do this without you."

Blinking back at her, Matt almost caved. He almost pulled her to him and held on, to keep her to himself, to keep her from going to the man she loved above all others. In the end, he simply nodded and said, "I'll ride in the front."

"Charlie..."

"Go, Jessie. I'll see that the kids are okay."

A kind EMT, a young black-haired woman with a wide girth and a worried but professional manner, helped Jessie into the back of the ambulance.

Settling beside Josh, Jessie took his hand. She couldn't see where his fingers stopped, and where hers began.

A gentle pressure alerted her to a closer study of their entwined fingers— was it real or imagined? Josh's head tipped in her direction, and his eyes fluttered open.

Jessie looked up from their joined hands, and smiled sadly at him. "Always and forever," she murmured, praying he could hear her. "Always...and forever."

The End.

Thank you!

If you liked this book, please take a few moments to leave a review on Amazon or Goodreads, and consider sharing your thoughts on social media. Self-published authors like myself count on your support to help us continue our writing journeys!

Have a wonderful day ☺

Susan

Join the *Drifters* family by signing up at **www.susanrodgersauthor.com**. As a welcome gift, I'll send you a free bonus/deleted chapter from book one, *A Song For Josh*. Happy reading!

www.susanrodgersauthor.com

Facebook: search **Susan Rodgers, Writer**

Twitter: **@srbluemountain**

Instagram: **SusanDrifters**

Pinterest: **Susan Rodgers**

email: **fatcat@pei.sympatico.ca**

About the Author

Susan Rodgers' first novel *A Certain Kind of Freedom* was a Finalist in the Writers' Federation of Nova Scotia Atlantic Writing Awards for unpublished manuscripts. Her short story from the novel of the same name, published in two anthologies, has received rave reviews, as have the Drifters novels, Susan's all-time favourite books to write.

Owner/Operator of Bluemountain Entertainment, Susan is a 'Diploma With Honours' graduate of Vancouver Film School. She produces mostly documentary style client films and short dramas with plans to one day shoot a Feature Drama based on the novel Atlantic Blue.

Formerly a Museum Curator, in winter Susan lives with her partner Steve and her striped cat Oliver (Lucy Maud Montgomery once said the only good cat is a striped cat) in Summerside, Prince Edward Island, Canada. In summer, she hides in a small trailer in Darnley, P.E.I., where she writes novels, paddles kayaks, and crafts sandcastles on the beach. She makes frequent trips to Vancouver to visit her son Christopher, where she enjoys life in the hippie city while listening to great music and sipping on good espresso.

Books by Susan Rodgers

Drifters series:
A Song For Josh
Promises
No Greater Love
Riptide
Whispers of Home
And Then There Was Silence
Let the Music Cry
If I Could Sing You Home
After the Rain
Into the Blue
A Sacred Peace
Watch Over Me
The Light In Me
When The West Wind Moves
Listen To The River

Feature Screenplays:
The Story of Jack & Emma
Still the Water
Beautiful Jane
They Were Dreamers (adapted)

Short Stories:
S12
A Certain Kind of Freedom
A Gentle Peace